MANSION OF MURDER

Grady, the guide in the Winchester Mystery House, had just started talking when the kid interrupted again.

"Oh, yuk, Mommy," he said in a voice Grady thought would pierce his own brain. "There's a ghost in that closet over there!" He pointed back toward the Morning Room. "It's a lady ghost. She's naked and she's flying right off the floor, but boy does she *stink*!"

Grady went rushing back. The velvet cordon rope was still swinging back and forth, evidence of Billy's illicit intrusion— and beyond, the closet door, standing open.

Grady could see something else, too, something his eyes almost refused to comprehend. Blond hair scattered with wilted flower petals. A neck too long to be real. A body tattooed all over in crusty black designs.

Grady had turned a deathly white. "Please, folks, stay back . . ."

Then, from somewhere behind him, a woman began to scream, a high, shrill, siren wail of horror.

Charter books by L. V. Sims

MURDER IS ONLY SKIN DEEP

DEATH IS A FAMILY AFFAIR

TO SLEEP, PERCHANCE TO KILL
(coming in April)

Death Is A Family Affair

L.V. SIMS

CHARTER BOOKS, NEW YORK

For Michelle and Phyllis
The Best of Teenagers

DEATH IS A FAMILY AFFAIR

A Charter Book/published by arrangement with
the author

PRINTING HISTORY
Charter edition/December 1987

ISBN: 0-441-14161-7

Charter Books are published by The Berkley Publishing Group,
200 Madison Avenue, New York, New York 10016.
The name "Charter" and the "C" logo are trademarks
belonging to Charter Communications, Inc.
PRINTED IN THE UNITED STATES OF AMERICA

10   9   8   7   6   5   4   3   2   1

Special thanks are due my research assistant, Denise Herberger, who helped me dig into some very dark corners, and to Gail Kurisu, Shozo Kagoshima and Keith Kittle for their patient assistance with my endless snooping and meandering through the Winchester Mystery House. A debt of gratitude is also owed Linda Hamamura, who will know why. Above all, loving thanks to my husband, Sergeant Bill Sims, SJPD.

PROLOGUE

THE WORLD WAS so silent. So still. Gretchen opened her eyes and tried to turn her head. She felt heavy, surrounded by warmth, protected. Womb safe. Her arms and legs felt rubbery and leaden.

What a trip!

She wanted to giggle, but she was too lazy. Too happy. Too perfectly, wonderfully satisfied. She was always satisfied, but this time had been so much better.

She could feel the soft warmth of her own flesh, the silk of her thighs pressed together, her ankles touching, her buttocks nestled into the plush of a fur rug.

If I was a kitten, I'd purr. . . .

She knew she was beautiful, with the flowers woven into her hair. Beautiful. A goddess. The scent of still other flowers hung on the air around her. Roses. Bloodred. Virgin white. Heavy and sweet. Warm and lazy.

From somewhere, music began to play, quietly at first and then a bit louder. The darkness seemed velvety soft.

We wanted to try, and we did. And it was true. Wonderfully, beautifully true! A good thing, a sacred thing, made so much better!

It was then that Gretchen realized she couldn't see anything. Nothing at all. Her eyes were open, but she could not see one single thing. She tried to turn her head again, only to gasp with pain. She was tied up. Her feet. And her hands, behind her back. Something, a rope or something, had been wound around her throat.

No! This isn't it . . . this is not the way it's supposed to be!

She was not wearing any clothes, and she was sweating. Her mouth was parched and dry, so dry that her tongue felt swollen. Her long hair clung to her forehead and back and shoulders. Her pulse raced faster with every breath. Her body twitched and quivered, vibrating with the beat of her heart. And with fear.

This isn't funny! If this is a joke, it just is not goddamn funny!

She wanted desperately to scream, but her throat felt constricted, like it was closing in upon itself, choking off her last breath. If only she could see. . . .

Calm down! This is a joke . . . only a dumb, stupid joke!

Gretchen ran her tongue over her lips, but it didn't help. She worked her jaw, trying to create enough saliva to swallow. If she could swallow, she could yell. Scream.

There was nothing funny about being tied up! Nothing!

The music grew louder. Someone was singing. The voice was strange and yet somehow familiar. She tried to make out the words, but all she could hear clearly was the pounding of her own heart. Without realizing that she did, Gretchen began to whimper.

Help! Oh, God, I know I went along with it. I know that I'm probably being silly now. I know you won't really punish me, but please! I know I'm chicken, but please let the joke be over!

Then came the other sound, a strange metallic clicking. For a minute she thought the sound came from inside her own head, an aftermath of their adventure, an adventure gone somehow terribly amiss. And then the light. Blinding. Shooting into her brain like bright needles of pain. The light dimmed slightly. Her eyes adjusted and then grew wide with surprise and horror.

"Hello." The voice caressed her, soft and deadly. She recognized that voice now—and the eyes she had hoped never to see again.

She opened her mouth, and this time she was able to cry out. A little. A low, rasping, terrified croak of a scream.

"What's the matter, Gretchen? Are you afraid of me?" Now there was laughter in the voice. "Are you scared to death?"

Oh, Mama, why didn't I listen? Help me, Mama! Oh, God . . . Oh, God . . . Oh, God . . .

The first thrust was poorly aimed. The blade bit into her shoulder and then ripped downward, leaving a gaping red slash from collarbone to left breast. For a split second she was only numb. But then the pain came. She screamed again, louder this time. A ragged animal cry of agony. When the blade raised again, gleaming red in the light, Gretchen closed her eyes. Her mouth opened wide.

"M-A-A-M-M-A-A-!"

CHAPTER 1

THE JUVENILE DIVISION squad room was quiet and dimly lit as Investigator Peter Willis sat reading the report. The day detectives were gone, the two assigned to swing shift out in the field. But Pete was not a Juvenile detective. He was bone tired and his eyes burned. For what felt like the millionth time, he scanned the lines again.

The report was straightforward. A seventeen-year-old was missing. She was a suspected runaway. Investigator Steven Bruner, the Juvenile dick in charge of the case, had been neat and precise, recording the facts as he saw them in small, crisp script.

Name: Gretchen Elizabeth Willis. Sex: Female. Date of Birth: August 2, 1970. Height: 5 ft. 2 in. Weight: 102 lbs. Hair: blond. Eyes: blue. Last seen at about 9 A.M. at her home (10 Loma Linda Drive).

The girl had been wearing a pair of white shorts and a yellow T-shirt. Investigator Bruner noted that she and her mother, a single parent, had argued. The mother, a Ms. Sally Nelson, believed that her daughter had run away to punish her. A case of teenage manipulation. But after twenty-four hours, Ms. Nelson decided that she had better call in a report.

She knew none of her daughter's friends and had no idea where the girl might be staying. She was concerned because the new school year was scheduled to start the following week. According to Ms. Nelson, her daughter was classified as a "gifted minor," a bright child who received perfect grades.

Except for the grade average, and the seeming lack of prior incidents, it seemed an ordinary report reflecting a far too common social problem.

But Pete knew this was *not* an ordinary report. He knew with everything in him that something was very, very wrong.

Pulling a colored school photograph from his wallet, he held it next to the black and white duplicate on the report. A pretty face smiled up at him. He felt like a knife was twisting in his guts. Gretchen would not run away from home, not if things with Sally had been *that* bad. Not without calling him first. She was too bright to do something so dangerous.

He flipped the photo over, reading the neat script on the back: *To Uncle Pete . . . the man I'll always love best . . . kisses from Gretchen, your Little Goddess.*

Pete rubbed eyes that felt sandblasted from lack of sleep. Someone came up behind him. He jumped as his shoulder was touched.

"There some reason you're sitting at my desk, Willis?"

He turned and, trying to smile, looked up at Steve Bruner. The effort failed. Slowly, he stood, still holding the report. "Sorry, Brew, nothing personal. I just wanted to go over this again."

For a moment the other detective looked irritated, but then he simply sighed. "No offense taken. I know you're worried. It's natural."

"What *isn't* natural is this report. Gretchen didn't run away, Brew. She isn't hiding somewhere just to punish her mom. That isn't her style."

Steve Bruner was sweating. He took off his jacket. "Damn, it's still hot as Hades in here. I hope the friggin' air-conditioning will be fixed by Monday."

"Did you hear what I said? Gretchen is not a runaway."

"Yeah, I heard you, but your former sister-in-law thinks otherwise."

He refused to meet Pete's eyes. He put a scuffed attaché

case on his desk, popped it open, and lifted out a thick stack of papers. "You see these, Willis? Kids. All reports on runaway kids. Ages nine to eighteen. I have a file cabinet over there chock full of more just like them. Hundreds of missing kids. Thousands."

"But Gretchen is different." Pete spoke in a near whisper.

Bruner turned toward him. "Look, Pete, I can tell the kid is special to you. I can empathize; I have kids of my own. In case you're wondering, I don't work this late for my health. I'm a day detective, remember? If you've come up with something I should know, tell me. Otherwise, I'm gone. My family expected me two hours ago."

Pete said no more. He walked slowly to the door and out into the corridor. The air was hot and still. The corridors were quiet. He stood staring at the floor for several moments, and then his shoulders straightened. With heavy, determined steps, he took the elevator down to the first floor and left the Police Administration Building.

It was nearly ten o'clock when he pulled to the curb in front of the small house on Loma Linda Drive. The drapes were closed, but he could see light shining through. He got out, looking up and down the street as he went to the door. It was a quiet neighborhood, a good place to raise children. He knocked three times, waited, then knocked again. Louder. He could hear movements from somewhere inside.

"Who's there?"

"It's me."

"Pete?"

"Yes. Come on, Sally, open up."

The porch light went on. A chain lock rattled. The dead bolt was shot, and the door finally opened.

Sally Nelson, his former sister-in-law, faced him through the screen. That, too, was locked, but she quickly unfastened it, swinging the door outward. She was wearing a blue terry-cloth robe and a worried expression.

"Come on in, Pete. Have they found her? Where is she staying?"

"How could we find her? There isn't a damn thing in the report you gave us." She closed the front door behind him.

"And why all the locks, for crying out loud? Gretchen couldn't get in if she wanted to."

"If I remember correctly, Pete, it was you who insisted that I install all those locks. Gretchen has keys to the back door."

Sally Nelson pulled her robe closer. "I thought you might have news."

Dishes were scattered on the coffee table, as if she had been eating in front of the television. She saw the direction of Pete's gaze, and went to clean up. Her face flushed slightly. There were two plates. Two sets of flatware. Two cups.

"Someone here?"

Her color deepened. "No, of course not. A neighbor came by earlier, but she's gone now. Do you . . . well, have you eaten?" She still had not asked him to sit.

"I'm not hungry, thanks." He knew his tone was half accusatory, but he was too tired to care.

She disappeared into the kitchen. He heard her put the dishes down and turn on the water. She called to him, "Make yourself comfortable."

He sat down in a small, feminine-sized recliner, but he was not comfortable. Not at all. He kept looking around the neat living room, straining his eyes toward the darkened hallway beyond, unable to shake the feeling that someone else was in the house.

It's none of my business, he reminded himself.

Sally had a perfect right to have any guest she wanted. A more than perfect right. Especially when Gretchen was not at home.

When Sally returned, she seemed more self-contained. She sat on the sofa, poised half on, half off the edge of a cushion. "I just can't believe Gretchen wants to hurt me so much."

"Gretchen doesn't pull shit like this, Sally, and you know it. *I* can't believe you really think she ran off just for spite. She isn't like other kids. Why would she do such a dumb thing?"

"I've already told you, just like I told the other policeman. We had an argument. Gretchen and I just haven't been getting along lately."

"Why?" Remembering the last moments he had spent with his niece, Pete felt a twinge of hypocrisy.

She looked at him and frowned. Her face flushed again, with irritation this time. She stood. "How in the hell am I supposed to know? I'm only her mother. She doesn't like the things I have to say, and I don't like her attitude. She doesn't always like the way I live, and vice versa. It's the same old story, an age-old complaint between the generations. And as much as I hate to admit it, she has taken off, gone off and hidden herself somewhere to get even with me. The only thing that makes me worry at all is that school starts in two days. But I'm sure she'll be home by then. One thing about our Gretchen, Peter—she would not want to miss school."

"But where is she now? Where would she go if she was angry and upset?"

Sally Nelson gave him a long, level look. "Frankly, *you* were my first and best bet. I didn't put that in the report, of course. You're a cop, and I didn't want to make you look bad, or even to involve you in our family problems. But, then, I guess I should have known you would involve yourself."

"You make that sound like an indictment. I am family. Gretchen is my niece. She's my only family, really. Drew's only child."

"Oh, yes, let's not forget good old brother Drew." Sally's lip curled downward. She ran splayed fingers through her short brown hair. "Go home, Pete. And if you can't do anything else, do what I'm doing—worry and wait, until Gretchen is through with her little game."

Suddenly there was the sound of breaking glass, as if something had shattered on a bathroom floor, or in the tub. Pete stood and took a step toward the darkened hallway.

Sally nearly ran to intercept him. She stepped in front of him, blocking his path. "Go home, Pete. Please, just go home."

"Who's back there?"

There was true anger and belligerence in her face now, and in her stance. "That's none of your goddamn business! Ever since that son of a bitching brother of yours ran off, my life is none of the Willises' business. I've got my own name, my own home, and Gretchen, lest you forget, is *my* daughter. If I didn't know how Drew treated you, how you feel about him, I wouldn't let you anywhere near Gretchen. And no matter what, you have no rights here, not legally, and certainly no right to question me about anything!''

Pete turned his back on her and moved toward the front door.

"Wait."

He heard her voice catch, and looked back.

A tear ran down her cheek. "Everyone needs to be loved, Pete." She looked tired and dejected. Her voice quavered. "Once in a blue moon everyone needs to be held and comforted—even mothers."

He held out his arms and she went to him, burying her face against his chest, weeping softly. The memories were still there, bonding them, pain remembered from years long past.

"I know," he spoke into her hair. "I know."

"Make her come home, Pete. Please, make Gretchen come home!"

To this he said nothing. He simply held her, rocking gently to and fro.

The home of Detective Sergeant Dixie T. Struthers was nestled high in the Santa Cruz Mountains. An elderly black woman and a white man with a thick head of silvery hair sat on the wide redwood deck which skirted the entire front of the big chalet-styled house. The surrounding forest sang with night sounds.

"I swear, I don't know why you allow her to do such things," Reversa Green said. She was sewing a button onto a woman's suit jacket. Bright yellow lights allowed her to see, and kept the insects away. Night had cooled things down, but there was no trace of chill in the air. Reversa wore a sleeveless cotton-print dress. Threads of gray showed in her dark hair.

"And just what would you be having me do? Dixie's too old for me to be bossing around."

"You're her grandpa, aren't you? Besides, I boss her plenty."

"You sure do. You boss everyone. Thing is, no one listens." Patrick Flannigan chewed at the cigar he held between his teeth. "You bark like the old she-dog you are, but Dixie went with her fella anyway, didn't she? And I don't doubt for a minute that they're having a high time."

Reversa scowled fiercely, but the merest hint of a smile played about her lips. She enjoyed nothing quite so much as an argument with Dixie's paternal grandfather. "Hummph!" she snorted. "High, indeed! Flyin' that rickety old plane up into the wild mountains! I've always known *he* has more gumption than brains, but Missy should show better sense!"

"I think that's just what she likes about Art Cochran. He hasn't got much use for *sense*, or all the burdensome things in the world. He just likes to have himself a good time."

They both stood up, Reversa gathering the sewing into her arms. But just as they turned to go inside, Poke, Dixie's Irish wolfhound, came to attention, growling deep in his throat. Within seconds they heard a car engine. Headlights bobbed along the drive leading to the house and then crossed the wooden bridge which spanned the creek.

Patrick looked at his watch. "My God, it's after midnight, but I think that's Pete Willis." He patted the huge animal and frowned. "Sure hope nothing is wrong."

Watching the young homicide investigator emerge from his car, Reversa also wore a worried expression. "Must be, him comin' all the way up here at this time of the night. That boy doesn't look good, not good at all."

Pete approached, then stood at the bottom of the deck stairs, looking up at them. The yellow lights turned his face sickly pale, the dark circles beneath his eyes stark and vivid. "Sorry to barge in on you like this, Mr. Flannigan—so late. I just needed to . . . I felt like I had to talk to someone who could . . . is Dixie home?"

Patrick motioned him up. "When are you going to start calling me Pop? Everyone else does. Come and sit, Pete."

The shadow of a smile crossed Pete's features. He mounted the stairs slowly and slumped into a deck chair.

"Dixie turn in already?" he asked.

"I don't know, son, she's not here. She and Art got a wild hair up their collective you-know-whats and took that biplane of his somewhere up into the Sierras."

Pete exhaled a long, slow breath. He was getting punchy, his vision blurring. The drive to Dixie's house, up out of the hot city air, had done little to clear his head and nothing at all for his weariness. But he had come anyway, driving almost like an automaton, seeking out the one person he knew would understand. He longed to see Dixie, hear her calm, sensible voice. If Dixie T. Struthers told him that everything would be fine . . .

Pete's head nodded. Patrick touched his shoulder, and he jerked awake.

"Come on, youngster. You're in no shape for conversation with anyone. It's too late for you to drive back. We have a nice extra bed, and I'm putting you in it. Dixie will be home sometime tomorrow—time enough then to talk."

With Patrick on his left and Reversa on the right, Pete felt himself half lifted and guided into the comfortable warmth of Dixie's home. He was only vaguely aware as they led him up the flight of stairs to the second floor. Still half dressed, he fell across a bed and closed his eyes.

But Pete Willis didn't sleep for long. Dreams came to him. Horrid, vivid nightmares. He kept seeing Gretchen's face, surrounded by the halo of soft, flaxen curls. She was looking up at him, tears running down both her cheeks. He saw her as she had been: a laughing, cherubic baby; then the young half woman, half girl she had become.

Suddenly Gretchen's face contorted. In his sleeping mind, Pete watched her expression waver, becoming a mask of fear and agonized pain. His ears were punctuated by her screams. He kept hearing her cry out, for him and for her mother. Over and over again.

Dawn was just seeping through the window as he got up and quietly let himself out of Dixie's house.

CHAPTER 2

THE SMALL, HIGH mountain lake was peaceful beyond belief. Mist rose from the water. Snow-bearded mountains threw jaggled, majestic reflections from every direction. A single, warbling bird call gave voice to a slow dawn.

Dixie pulled an Army surplus fatigue jacket up around her ears and blew into her hands. Fragments of her breath hung in the air.

"Cold?" Art's voice was half distracted, his eyes fixed intently on his fishing line.

"Only a little." She shifted her weight, causing the inflatable rubber dingy to rock gently.

In the near distance, parked just at the lake's edge, was a bright red Stearman, Art's biplane, the one he used for stunt flying. His pride and joy.

"Ha!" He was grinning from ear to ear as he pulled back on the line. A giant rainbow trout leapt clear of the water. "It's invited to breakfast you are, my beauty!"

The fish was fourteen inches at least, gleaming bright silvery green and iridescent pink in the dawn light.

"Grab the net," he told Dixie, giving the line slack, leaning back and then reeling in again.

Dixie took the net from the bottom of the dingy. She watched Art as he brought the fish in, and smiled at his boyish enthusiasm, his sandy cowlicked hair and startling blue eyes.

They had landed in the valley the morning before. The trip itself had, as usual, been taken on an impulse. A last-minute whim. That was one of the great things about dating Art Cochran—*escapades*. With a man like Art, a girl could never be bored. Frightened from time to time perhaps, but never, ever bored.

Dixie had suggested that they take her plane, a more sedate Beechcraft Bonanza, but Art insisted that the Stearman, his renovated World War I vintage spooker, would be more *fun*. He was right, of course; taking the Stearman had been more fun. More exhilarating. More hair-raising. And one hell of a lot colder. In the Sierras, even in late summer, the air was thin and often nippy.

They had not come unprepared. A tarpaulin and thick down sleeping bags had kept their night dry and cozy. And romantic. They had cooked over an open camp fire.

That first sight of the valley, with its stretch of meadow, pine trees, and sapphire-colored lake, had taken Dixie's breath away. And the fact that human beings had in all likelihood never before set foot there, made it all the more awesome. This was truly virgin land, untouched and unspoiled, glittering like a jewel beneath smog-free heavens.

"Get it! Get it!" Art pulled the last of his line in, lifting the thrashing fish for Dixie to scoop into the net. After putting his pole to one side, he took the trophy from her and held it up. The trout flapped noisily against itself. "Have you ever seen a prettier sight?"

She laughed. "Absolutely not, not since yesterday afternoon."

Art cocked his head to one side, clicking his tongue mournfully, and then addressed the fish. "Ah, the lady grows jaded already, but never you mind—we who are about to feast salute you!"

An hour later they had indeed feasted on the feckless trout, along with scrambled eggs, fried potatoes, and camp-fire biscuits. Except for two tin cups and a thermos full of hot black coffee, Art was stowing all their gear neatly into the Stearman's storage compartment. The sun was well up now, dazzling the rugged peaks, perfuming the air with the soft smells of impending autumn.

Dixie knelt on her haunches, sipping coffee, staring out over the calm surface of the lake. At times like this she wished that she could forever avoid a return to the scurry of city life, to a world where human beings lied to each other, cheated each other—*killed* each other. Looking at the lake, feeling the warmth of the sun on her face, it seemed impossible that anything on earth could be wrong.

A twig snapped and she turned, smiling up at Art as he came to stand next to her. "You about ready?" he asked.

"I suppose." Her soul drank in the serenity.

Art rested a hand on her shoulder. For long, drawn-out moments, neither of them spoke. They remained as they were, wrapped in a mutual wonder of discovery.

Dixie exhaled a long, deep sigh. Art knelt down beside her, sipping his coffee. His eyes took in her profile, the pert, upturned nose and flawless skin. The silken cloud of coppery hair. "You want to stay another day? It would only take a few minutes to unload again."

She shook her head, breaking the enchantment. "I've got to get back. It's been great, though."

"It could be more great, more often." His voice came out low and husky. Tempting. "All you have to do is kick back and let it happen."

Dixie knew she should stop the conversation. The cajoling was becoming a habit with him, the subtle pressure. "If I kick back too far, I'll find myself out of a job. Herb and I have a pretty heavy load right now. We all do."

"So you get canned." Art made his voice light. "It isn't exactly like you'd starve to death. If I had your kind of money—"

"You are beginning to sound very much like my mother, Art."

"Well, the lady has a point. In your position I would—"

"You'd what?" She tossed out the dregs of her coffee as they both stood up. "Quit flying, maybe?"

"Of course not. I love flying, but I'd sure as hell quit crop dusting for a living. It would take me all of three seconds."

"I love my work."

His voice took on a faintly sarcastic edge. "Yeah, better than anything."

She faced him and put a finger across his lips. The act was

tender but her voice was cool, her green eyes guarded and challenging. "Don't say anymore, Art. Don't spoil it, okay?"

He finally shrugged, smiling amicably. He kissed the tip of her nose. "You're the boss."

But as they walked toward the plane, they both knew that to some degree the romance of their trip had been spoiled.

As the lumbering Stearman lifted into the sky, both Art and Dixie took one last look at the peaceful valley below. It was a beautiful world, a montage of green and blue, yellow and brown, of fragrant pines and abiding peace. But both of them knew, too, that they needed more. They needed to *live* life, taste it, drink the full cup, bitter or sweet, in big, giant gulps.

Investigator Herb Woodall sat sprawled in the living room of his Scotts Valley home. It had been a lazy, hot weekend, too hot to put much effort into anything. Exactly the kind of weekend he enjoyed.

"Wanna play soccer, Daddy?" Amy, his six-year-old daughter, appeared at his elbow. "Mommy said you would play with me, 'cause we need to practice for the big father-and-daughter game. She says you need the exercise too. She says it would be good for you to 'stir around' a little."

Herb yawned widely and poked his head around the high back of his easy chair. His wife stood not ten feet behind him, resting her shoulder against the arched doorway of their dining room. Janice was wearing a pair of white shorts and a cotton halter top. Her body was tanned to a golden finish from days spent in their garden, a tan that had deepened a good two shades over the weekend. In Herb's opinion she was also wearing a Machiavellian grin on her pixie face. He looked back at his daughter.

"It's awful hot out there, baby. I wouldn't want you to get sunstroke."

Amy donned the special expression that transformed her into a mini version of her mother, an expression Herb had come to fear. "You know what I found out, Daddy?" she asked in her young/old voice. "You know what Mommy and I watched on educational television?"

Herb felt a groan building in his solar plexus. He didn't want to ask. "No, Amy, what did you and Mommy watch?"

Amy's flaxen brows came together in a frown of concentration. "Well, you see, our human bodies have a 'cooling system.' The way it works is—"

"Hey, Amy!" Herb capitulated. Leaping from the chair, he scooped the ball from his daughter's hands. "I've got a great idea! Let's *pla-a-a-y* soccer!"

He dribbled the ball around the room, making soft thunking noises against the carpet. "Boy, am I ready! This ol' cooling system of mine is kicking right in. I can feel it . . . under my arms . . . on my forehead . . ."

Amy giggled, all little girl again, as he spun like a dervish, dancing and dribbling past Janice. He growled under his breath. "You'll pay for this."

He went madly on, through the dining room and kitchen, into the tiled foyer. His dribbling grew more feverish. "Yes, indeed, I can feel it . . . the water's rushing down, gushing from my ol' cooling system!"

Running at his heels, Amy squealed with laughter. "No, sir, Daddy! You're a great big fibber! Your system can't work yet! The house is too cool from the air conditioner!"

But his system *was* working. In spite of the air conditioner he was already beginning to perspire. He dreaded the hot blast of air he knew would hit him the minute he opened the front door. Throwing Janice one last martyred look, an appeal that met with no sympathy whatsoever, he pulled the door open and came to an abrupt halt.

Pete Willis's large frame loomed there, almost filling the doorway. His finger was poised just above the doorbell. Upon seeing Herb holding the soccer ball, with Amy and Janice right behind, he smiled. But it was only a surface smile, a half apologetic shadow smile. "Hi, Herb. Looks like I came at a bad time."

The grin Herb returned was completely, sincerely genuine— the smirk of a reprieved felon. "Not at all, Pete. Come out of the heat. There's beer in the fridge." He handed the ball to Janice and ruffled Amy's hair. "Yeah, I think a beer would cool my system right down."

He ignored the hostile stares of his family as he motioned Pete into the kitchen. A moment later he heard Amy muffle a "Rats!" A closet door opened and shut as the soccer ball was laid temporarily to rest. Janice entered the kitchen with a good-natured smile.

Pete looked at her. "Sorry if I'm barging in. I should have called before coming."

"Don't be silly, Pete. You're always welcome." She went to the refrigerator. "Sit down, both of you. I'll pour the beer. Actually, Herb is grateful. You saved him from sunstroke."

Herb kissed her playfully on the cheek as she passed in front of him, but as he sat down at the table, looking across at Pete, his face sobered. The other man looked unshaven and rumpled. Grim.

Pete was a tall, extremely handsome man. Having been on the force for less than two years, he was also the newest member of the homicide team. As a rookie cop he had been severely wounded, both in the shoulder and the leg, and he still suffered a slight limp from the bullet wound. He was a good cop. But he was also a grateful cop. Dixie had been his field supervisor on the night he was wounded. She had killed a man that night. Pete owed her his life, and it was debt he refused to forget. In his eyes she was the perfect cop. The perfect woman.

"How goes it, Pete?" Herb asked the question rhetorically. From looking at Pete's face, it was easy enough to guess that his niece was still missing.

Janice put beer and mugs down in front of each man, pouring one for herself as well. Her eyes mirrored concern and sympathy as she reached over and touched Pete's forearm. "Your niece hasn't come home yet?"

Pete shook his head. He rubbed his face, grinding a fist into one of his tired red eyes, and then took a deep drink of beer. He put the mug down carefully. His hands were shaking. "Look, I know you can't do a damn thing, Herb. Maybe no one can. But it just seems to me like nobody gives a shit."

"Isn't Bruner working the case?" Once again Herb knew the answer, but he also knew that Pete needed to talk.

"Have you got any idea how many cases Bruner is working these days?" Pete's voice rose an octave. "Besides, I told you already, I told Brew that Gretchen is *not* a runaway."

Herb was Pete's friend, but he was also a cop. And now, without meaning to or even realizing it, he took a cop's tone and line of reasoning. "But she did have an argument with her mother, with your former sister-in-law, right? Brew told me that the mother admitted she and Gretchen had not been getting along very well.''

Pete shook his head adamantly back and forth. "No way! I know Gretchen, Herb, and I'm saying it for the millionth time—that little girl was not the runaway type. So she had a fight with her mom—it doesn't mean a thing, not to me. All teenagers have disagreements with their folks from time to time. Kids go through stages. You know how it is, Herb." His voice was taking on an edge of desperation. "Amy may not be there yet, but you can remember how it was for you, can't you? You didn't always like what your folks had to say, but you didn't run away, did you? *Did you?*"

"No, Pete, I didn't run away, but I wasn't a teenager in nineteen eighty—"

The phone rang, and Herb got up, grateful for the interruption. All three of the people sitting at that kitchen table knew the facts, the grim statistics. And Herb prayed that Pete was wrong, prayed that pretty, blond Gretchen Willis *had* run away.

"Hi, Herb, it's Tony."

Hearing the voice of his superior, Herb straightened slightly. "Yeah, hi, boss. What's up?"

"I tried to reach Struthers, but she's not home. I know you and she are pretty tight with Pete Willis. I don't suppose you've seen him this weekend."

Herb's glance slid to Pete and then quickly away. He turned his back toward the table. "Yeah, I have."

Lieutenant Anthony Di Franco was quiet for a moment, waiting for him to elaborate. When Herb remained uncommunicative, he picked up the cue. "He's there now?"

"I suppose you could say that." There was something in Di Franco's tone that told him to keep it straight. The leuy wasn't angry, or did not seem to be. He just sounded worried.

"Good, I'm glad he's with you. Look, Herb, you've got to talk to him. He's tipping over the line here. He went over to Bruner's a couple of hours ago; bothered the guy on his day off. Started badgering Bruner about the case on his niece. From what I could gather, it all started out okay. Brew knows Peter is worried out of his skull, so he tried to soft-pedal it. But from what I can gather, Willis got pushy, all flustered and overexcited. Started raising his voice and waving his arms around. Brew finally ended up cussing him out, almost *throwing* him out of the house. He called his own leuy, who just called me.''

"Oh, lordy.'' Herb said the words softly.

"I see you're getting the picture. See what you can do, will you? Talk sense to him, because if you don't, I'll have to—and I would hate to do that. If necessary, convince him to take some time off. He has plenty of T.O. on the books.''

"I'll do what I can.''

"Make it good, Herb. Comp time is a helluva lot better than *suspension time*.''

Di Franco hung up. A few seconds later the dial tone sounded into Herb's ear. He spoke to it, keeping his voice light. "Okay, then, see you later.''

Pete watched him return to the table. "Di Franco?''

"Yes.'' Herb eased himself into a chair. He picked up his beer mug. He sipped, and then licked foam from his upper lip. "Listen, Pete—''

"He told you what I did, huh? I really fucked up, Herb, I know that.'' He looked at Janice, flushing. "Sorry, Jan. Guess my manners have fallen by the wayside these days.''

She waved his apology aside. Janice Woodall was used to cops and accustomed to their occasional frustration.

"Pete, you've got to get this into some kind of perspective.'' Herb made his voice hard. "You're a good cop, and a good investigator, but you're human too. Everyone knows how rough family problems can be. Take a few days off. Time has a way of— ''

"Goddamn it, Herb, this isn't just a family problem!'' Pete stood up, nearly knocking his chair over. "Haven't you been listening? Gretchen did not run—''

Herb was also standing now, leaning across the table, chin forward. "Well, you sure as hell better hope she *has* run away, because if she hasn't, chances are she's—''

"Herb!'' Janice's voice stopped him, but his thoughts, the unspoken words, hung in the air.

Pete shuddered, and sat down heavily. "She is so pretty. She's like an angel, Herb, a little goddess. When she was younger, I used to plan birthday surprises for her, things a father would normally have done. My brother was such a rotten shit. He ran off and left them, just like he did me after our folks died. He treated Sally like dirt even before she got pregnant, but on the night Gretchen was born, the bastard split altogether, just up and left Sally without anyone, and little Gretchen without a daddy. I love her like a sister, Herb, maybe even like my own kid.'' Pete's voice was beginning to break. He fumbled at his hip pocket. ''Did I ever show you her picture?''

Herb felt like his guts had turned to lead.

Pete pulled out the school snapshot and held it up. His hand was shaking worse than ever, quivering violently, blurring the image of his niece.

Janice stood and came around the table. ''It's okay, Pete. Everything is going to be fine, you'll see.'' Her voice was soothing. ''Gretchen will come home soon, and you'll be mad at her for a week. It's going to be fine.''

Let it be true! she thought.

Pete was nodding, bobbing his head up and down, trying to laugh. ''You're right, of course. I've been acting like a real dummy, I guess, just an uninformed Joe Blow citizen.''

Once again he started rubbing at his tired, unshaven face, washing away tears he did not want them to see. ''Shit! You just wait until that little stinker gets home. When I get my hands on her, I'm gonna . . .''

The words trailed away and he swallowed hard. Janice bent, putting both her arms around his broad shoulders.

It was just too much. A sob ripped through him. He put his face into his hands and wept. Above him, for one long, poignant moment, Janice and Herb stared at each other. Then they both looked away.

Dixie listened to ring after hollow, unanswered ring as she tried to make contact with Pete. She had been calling all evening. After landing at the Watsonville Air Field, she and Art had lingered over a late lunch, prolonging their weekend together, both trying to mend the strain in their relationship by pretending it did not exist. But now she wished that she had come straight home. Pete Willis was very special to her, as a fellow officer, and especially as a friend.

Not that she didn't find him aggravating at times. If there was anything that made Dixie uncomfortable, it was a misguided sense of gratitude, and Pete had a very bad case. But he also possessed an old-fashioned brand of honor and chivalry that she found charming, if occasionally amusing. Next after Herb Woodall, Pete was her favorite cop.

"Still can't reach him?" Patrick asked. Dixie's grandfather, and her housekeeper Reversa, had been worried all day.

Dixie shook her head. "Herb says he was there earlier, and it looks like he may not be thinking straight. If he's not careful, he's liable to find himself in real trouble with the brass."

"Meaning Di Franco."

She put the phone down, finally giving up. "I don't know—Herb says the leuy is understanding enough for the moment, but if Pete doesn't get his act together—"

She still had her hand on the phone receiver when it rang. She jumped slightly and then lifted the receiver. She didn't have time to say hello before Pete's voice came on, an excited, agitated voice.

"Dixie? Is that you? Are you there?"

"I'm here, Pete. I've been trying to call you all evening. Where are—"

"They've found a body. I just heard it over the police-band radio I keep in my truck. I went to the scene and they won't let me—"

"Hold on a minute, Pete. Let's start from the top. Where are you?"

"I just know it's Gretchen . . . I just know it!" His voice was cracking. "I know it, Dix. It's her body! A young white female . . . blond. There are two beat units there, but they won't let me on the scene! I thought you and Herb were supposed to be on call tonight. How come you aren't here? Call in, Dixie, make them—"

"Stop it, Pete!" Dixie nearly yelled into the phone. "Listen to me!"

There was a a few seconds of relative silence on the other end of the line, but Dixie could hear him breathing heavily. "Okay," he finally answered. "I'm okay, Dix, really. I just want—"

"I want you to do me a favor, Pete." She cut him off again. "I want you to tell me where you are, and then I want you to stay put, and I do mean *planted*, until I can get there. Do you understand? Herb and I don't go on call until midnight, but I'm sure I'll be able to find out something. You just stay there. Are you listening to me?''

"Yes."

"So where are you?"

"Out in the east foothills, just off Quimby Road. I came back to the gas station at the intersection of Quimby and White to call you." He sounded calmer, but only slightly. "You'll come?"

"Right away, Pete, just stay where you are. Get back into your truck and wait."

She hung up and looked at her grandfather. "You were right, Pop, he *is* in trouble, teetering right on the edge."

Going to the closet, she donned the old fatigue jacket once more. There was no time to change. She also picked up her handbag, an incongruous creation in pale mauve peacock leather, and headed for the door.

Reversa came in from the kitchen just as she was leaving. "Now just where do you think you're—" Upon getting a good look at Dixie's face, she let her scolding remain unfinished.

"Do me a favor, Pop," Dixie said. "Call Herb and tell him I'm code three, figuratively speaking, of course, to the intersection at Quimby and White. Tell him Pete is there."

CHAPTER 3

THE WEEKEND WITH Art had all but evaporated from Dixie's mind as she maneuvered the sharp curves along Bear Creek Road. She concentrated on each turn and on reaching her friend before he made a mistake that could ruin his career—a career she knew without doubt he cherished as much as she did. No one but another cop could understand what it meant to be out on the streets, often alone, trying to help life make sense.

The idealism wore off quickly, of course—or had for Dixie. She did not fool herself. She was not a social worker. She would not save the world by doing her job well. She was just one woman in a male-dominated profession dedicated to making the world safer, if not completely sane.

To anyone who did not know her well, Dixie would have seemed a woman at odds with her background. A world of wealth and privilege. An inheritance from her maternal grandfather had assured her a life of leisure. Looking at her resumé, at the education from Stanford University and her former Saint Francis Wood address in San Francisco, few could know her true origins.

But Dixie never forgot that she was also the granddaughter of Patrick Casey Flannigan, a San Francisco foot cop, and the daughter of James Francis Flannigan, slain in the line of duty.

After her father was killed, her mother had remarried, and

in so doing, returned to the socialite world of her own youth. Rose Klien Flannigan Marks no longer wanted to see the ugly side of life, to know that things were not always safe and happy. She married Franklin Marks, gave birth to her son Ryan, and gave even greater energy to trying to direct the lives of her children. To her great frustration, her daughter did not always take such direction well. Dixie's original preference for the study of law soon gave way to a major in the Administration of Justice, classes in criminology and police science. The two women had battled almost constantly, sometimes in silence and sometimes loudly, with Irish tempers flying. Finally, after a miserably failed marriage and myriad attempts to make her mother and stepfather understand, Dixie had made her choice.

She was one of the first women hired as regular police officers by the nearby city of San Jose. And if her career path had been often scattered with obstacles, it had also been satisfying in the extreme. The men she worked with, Herb and Pete in particular, were like a family to her. Together they shared the challenge and excitement, the occasional boredom and frequent frustration, with a companionship she found nowhere else. There was little, if anything, she would not do for either of them.

The traffic was light along the freeway leading down into the valley. She took the quickest route possible through the lower east side of the city and had almost reached her destination when Herb caught up with her. He winked his headlights several times to get her attention. She pulled to the side of the road.

Herb parked and came quickly to her car, the modest looking but expensive BMW she had purchased to replace her wrecked and beloved old Jag. She rolled down the window. "And I thought *I* was breaking the sound barrier. Come on, turkey, get in. I do believe we have a friend in need."

"In trouble, too, unless he cleans up his act."

They both breathed easier upon seeing that Pete was still waiting, hunched behind the wheel of his Ford Bronco. It seemed impossible that he could look any worse than when Herb last saw him, but he did. Pete wore three days growth on his face, and his normally well-groomed blond hair was on end.

He almost stumbled from the truck when he saw them, and began pointing toward the foothills before they could hear what he was saying. He jerked open the door on Herb's side. "She's up there. They found her, dumped, right off the edge of the highway!"

Herb got out and let him into the backseat. Pete didn't notice the look that passed between his friends.

"Well," he said impatiently. "What are you waiting for—let's go!"

Dixie *went* all right. She pulled into the parking lot of the small adjacent shopping center and cut the motor. She and Herb turned at the same time, but she kept all hint of the frustration she was feeling from her tone. "We'll go, Pete, but first we need some information. We're not just barreling in on a crime scene without knowing at least a few particulars. You know better than that. Now, I want you to take a long, deep breath and start from the top. Why are you so sure that your niece has been found, that it's her body?"

"Gretchen did not run away." Pete repeated himself in a surly monotone. Great waves of guilt were washing over him, guilt he could share with no one—not ever. The only thing that could possibly help now, help make it right again, was to see Gretchen alive, smiling at him as she had all her life. But he knew it would never happen. Knew it in his guts, with all the instincts a cop had for finding the rotten underbelly of the world.

Herb was growing impatient. "Pete, you've said that a hundred times. We understand you being upset. What I don't understand, what *we* don't understand, is why you seem so convinced all of a sudden that she's been . . ." He tried to tiptoe around his own fears. "Why you think something bad has happened to her."

Pete looked Herb in the eye. "Because that's what *you* think, and you've been at it a hell of a lot longer than I have. After I left your place, I couldn't quit thinking about it." He knew how tired he was, and he spoke slowly, forcing himself to articulate each word clearly. The effort was obvious. "I went home and tried to sleep after I saw you and Janice. I really tried. But after a while I got up and changed clothes. I thought I would go over and see Sally again, my sister-in-law. I think she's . . . well, I keep feeling like there's something else she could tell me. Anyway, I got into the damn truck. I just had a C.B. installed a couple of weeks ago, and I automatically tuned into a police band. I was a block from home when dispatch put the call out. And then I knew. It has to be Gretchen. The description, everything matched.''

He looked from Herb to Dixie. "You know how these things work, damn it! I don't want that to be Gretchen up there, but if it is, there isn't any time to spare. If someone . . . someone has . . . hurt her, our chances of catching him get less with every hour.''

Pete was growing agitated again. "I tell you the I.D. was right on. I've got to get up there. I just know . . .''

Once more Dixie and Herb shot each other a look.

"You can't *know* anything, Pete,'' Herb said. "You're so damn tired you can't even think straight. But it won't hurt to go up there, take a drive by the scene. If it's in our jurisdiction, Delaney and Brooks should be there already. They're the ones on call until midnight.''

"We'll go, but only on one condition,'' Dixie said, turning stern green eyes on Pete. "You will stay right where you are—in the backseat of this car.'' He started to say something but she cut him off with a chop of her hand. "I mean it, Pete. You either promise to stay put, or I swear I'll turn this buggy around and take you home with me right now. Even if Herb has to handcuff you.''

Herb's eyes widened slightly. At any other time the comment would have been laughable. Pete Willis was a very big boy.

"Okay, I won't get out.'' Pete also knew that she was dead serious. At any other time, he, too, might have smiled, but now all he felt was a terrible dread.

The three officers were silent as Dixie guided the car up Quimby Road, through the last fringes of the city's poor east side and on into the foothills, where the homes grew gradually larger and more luxurious before the landscape thinned into hillside.

By the time they spotted the flares and flashing lights, they were at the far east edge of the city limits. It was an area comprised of a crisscross of city and county jurisdictions. In addition to an ambulance, there were five patrol cars and one unmarked vehicle at the scene.

"Four of those units are from the S.O.," Herb said. "Looks like this one belongs to the Sheriff's Office. Our guy must be giving a courtesy assist."

Dixie nodded, slowing, easing around the protruding tail of the ambulance, which had no doubt been dispatched by the country coroner's office. Pete looked at the orange-and-white wagon, his face going pale.

A deputy appeared at the roadside, khaki-colored uniform crisp in the glare of Dixie's headlights. He lifted an arm, using his flashlight to motion them by. Dixie followed his direction, but once her car was past the congestion, she pulled onto the shoulder.

"Remember what I said," she reminded Pete as she opened the door. "Don't even budge."

He didn't answer. He was twisted in the seat, his body leaning stiffly toward the rear window, straining his eyes to see past the twirling red bubble-gum machine lights of the patrol cars.

"Why don't you both stay," Herb suggested. "I'll go back and check it out."

Dixie hesitated only a moment and then nodded, closing her door again. Herb reached back and patted Pete's shoulder before leaving the car. It was like touching a statue, a cold chunk of cement.

"Make it quick," Dixie said. Her stomach was twisting into big, painful knots.

The deputy who had directed them was coming back. Through her rearview mirror, Dixie saw him converse briefly with Herb and then continue walking toward the car. He frowned as he flashed a beam of light into the backseat. "I spoke to your partner, Sarge, and I let him pass as a courtesy, but this isn't city jurisdiction."

"I realize that, Deputy . . ."

"Kory. Deputy Don Kory."

"Yes, Deputy Kory." Dixie shook the hand he offered. "I know we're tripping into your territory here. We appreciate the courtesy."

The young officer kept sliding his gaze into the backseat. Pete didn't even turn. It was as if he did not hear the conversation taking place.

When Dixie offered no further explanation as to their interest, Deputy Kory began to probe. "This fella showed up here earlier"—he tilted his head toward Pete—"and I've got to tell you, he wasn't the soul of courtesy. Downright pushy, in fact."

"Investigator Willis has been under considerable stress." Dixie didn't like discussing Pete as if he was no more than a coat tossed over the backseat, and again she refused to elaborate.

"Looked about half wild," the deputy continued. "Came screaming up here in that fancy Bronco of his, jumped out holding his badge in the air like he was making a dope bust or something . . . he pushed right past me. I didn't appreciate his attitude."

"Don't blame you." Dixie wished he would back off and disappear. She could almost feel how tightly Pete was coiled, wound up like a yo-yo just waiting to spin out and walk-the-dog right over someone's face.

Seemingly the deputy seemed satisfied that she was on his side. He straightened and looked over his shoulder, where the road dropped away to a steep hillside. "Not a pretty sight, I'll tell you. Enough to gag a maggot."

Dixie inwardly winced, and tried to flash a warning with her eyes, but he was not looking at her. Her hands clenched the steering wheel.

"The victim, or what's left of her, looks like she was probably sexually assaulted. Maybe before she was killed, maybe after. Strangled, most likely. Another sicko on the loose."

Great waves of tension rolled over Dixie, emanating from the rear seat. Pete still had not turned, but she could almost feel his reaction.

Deputy Kory leaned against the car, folding his arms across his chest, settling down for a nice exchange of tidbits. "Yeah, she was partially undressed, jeans down around her ankles . . . blouse ripped."

"*Jeans?*" Pete slowly swiveled his upper torso. "Did you say jeans?"

The deputy seemed startled by the sound of Pete's voice—a low, rasping growl—as if he had almost forgotten that Pete was there. He bent to look through the window again. "Yeah, jeans. You know, those 501's all the kids wear, and a red cotton blouse. Socks, but no shoes. Probably lost those while she was still in the creep's car, or maybe they got knocked off while she was being dumped down there, like so much garbage.''

"Pete?" Dixie looked at him closely.

He seemed not to hear. Scooting up on the seat, he brought his face almost nose to nose with the deputy. "She was blond, though, right? A pretty blond girl in her teens, right?"

The deputy instinctively leaned away. There was something about this guy in the back seat, he decided. Cop or no cop, he had a glazed, scary, half-hinged look about him. "Yeah, she was blond and young, too, as far as we can tell—which ain't easy, figuring she's been down there awhile. Probably over a week. And in this heat we've been having—"

A sound came from Pete. Not a word. Or a sigh. Or a groan. Not any sound readily identifiable as human. Rather, he seemed to exhale a great gulping, bellow's belch, a long, drawn out *whooooosh* of air. Gretchen had only been missing four days.

Deputy Kory looked at him in surprise, but just as he was about to renew his probing, Herb returned to the car. He looked weary and a bit green around the gills, and he still held the handkerchief he had used to cover his nostrils, protecting his stomach and the lining of his nasal membranes from the smell of decay. To Herb Woodall the stench of death, especially a violent death, seemed the ultimate humiliation. It was an odor he had smelled many times during his career, and one he would never grow accustomed to—or forget.

"The girl down there is not Gretch—" he began, as he slid into the front seat. But seeing the expression on Pete's face, he left the sentence unfinished.

"A real mess, huh?" Deputy Kory asked through Dixie's open window. Then he got another look at Pete, and backed off for good.

Pete Willis was beginning to shudder all over, his big frame quivering like a California quake.

CHAPTER 4

TOUR GUIDE GRADY Summers walked down the last flight of stairs, happy that his work day was almost at an end. At the moment he was sick to death of tourists. But he loved the old mansion, the place folks now called the Winchester Mystery House. It was no tourist trap either. The beautiful old place really *was* full of mystery—*real* mystery.

Grady had never been a man to believe in spooks, and he still wasn't. But for him the house seemed full to overflowing with the essence of its creator, Sarah Lockwood Pardee Winchester, the woman of his dreams. His fantasy lover.

Each day, as Grady led throngs of big-eyed tourists through the huge, rambling mansion, he thought of Sarah—who and what she had been, what she had suffered—and he loved her even more. Knowing that it was silly to love someone long dead did not change a thing. Grady could not give her up. He loved her, and that was that.

The place had been on television several times and was a bona fide historical monument, a downright enthralling tourist attraction. You could see the Mystery House advertised on giant billboards from coast to coast. Just the way Sarah had built it—and kept building it night and day, hammers banging and saws sawing, with no let-up for over thirty years—was enough to make people shake their heads in wonder. The stairs that led up to nothing, hallways that jagged around and stopped without warning, doors opening into vast nothingness, or blank walls. The five-and-a-half million dollars used to build it, in an age when most folks only made a dollar and a half a week, gave a body pause too.

It some ways it was a rat's maze, but Grady never thought of it that way, because it was so darn beautiful. Just as he was convinced Sarah had been.

As usual, Grady had come in early that morning. He liked arriving before anyone else. Sometimes he even got there before Mr. Martin, his boss. It was okay, though, because everyone recognized Grady Summers. The security guard who quit making rounds at eight in the morning. The grounds keepers. Someone always let him in, because they knew how he felt without him saying a word. He would go in and sit in the front garden, looking at the statues, smelling the flowers, looking at the trees Sarah had brought in from all over the world. Each morning he would come sit on a bench in the front garden, next to the sea serpent fountain, pour himself a cup of coffee from his big stainless steel thermos, and pretend that the house belonged to him—and to Sarah, of course. It was a make-believe time. He knew that. Just his habit of daydreaming gone wild. But he did it all the same. And he couldn't quit doing it. He didn't want to.

Sitting, he would look up at the mansion and pretend he was walking up to the big front door, paying a romantic social call. Sarah never allowed visitors in, but she opened the door for Grady, and standing in the foyer, kissed him as soon as the door was closed. She and Grady were in love. They would go to one of the many parlors then and sit and drink tea, always holding hands. They would make their wedding plans. And Grady would tell her again and again how much he loved her. He would help her, convince her not to be afraid anymore.

Grady Summers knew that if he had been given half a chance, he could have convinced Sarah that none of it was her fault. Not the death of her husband, and especially not that of her pretty little girl. He would convince her that the spirits were not angry. The spirits of all those Indians and other folks, killed by her husband's guns, the rifles his own daddy invented. The souls of all those dead folks haunted poor little Sarah, and just thinking about it made Grady sad.

Another thing Grady especially liked to pretend was that the mansion was just like it used to be, sitting out in the country, surrounded in the springtime by orchards of snowy-blossomed trees and old-fashioned roads, with only an occasional wagon rumbling by, and hitching posts instead of cement sidewalks, and no cars making their stink and honking their horns. It was easier for him to pretend in the morning, early, before rush-hour traffic started. Then, if he kept his eyes just on the house, just on the beautiful trees and flowers, he could pretend that the Town and Country Shopping Center wasn't right on the other side of what was now Winchester Boulevard. That there wasn't a giant, domed, four-screen movie theater right next door, with its asphalt parking lot just across from the one the tourists used.

Whenever possible he also avoided the rest area which had been set aside for all the hundreds and thousands of tourists who came to look at Sarah's house each year. It was a pretty area, too, all planted with silk oaks and lantana, with drooping whisper-pink fuchsias and lemon-yellow hibiscus. But it was just too darn close to the snack bar and the gift shop. Even though it made Grady felt guilty, because he liked all the other employees so much, he wished those buildings gone.

The only modern intrusion he tried not to think about at all, because it made him feel hypocritical, was the fancy mobile-home park beside and behind the mansion. Grady paid a lot to live in that park, just so as he could be close to where Sarah had once lived. He knew he shouldn't be there, but it made it easier for him to come early in the morning and stay late at night. It made him feel like he was doing something special for Sarah herself.

But not on this day. This had been one of those days he hated, a day filled with the wrong kind of tourists. Some visitors he liked a lot, the kind that showed a genuine interest, the ones who gave little cries of sadness at the terrible tragedy Sarah had known, at all she had suffered—the ones who knew enough to see the beauty of what she had done in spite of her eccentricity. But his great frustration were the other kind, the ones he was forced to be polite to, to take through Sarah's private domain whether he liked it or not.

34   *L.V. Sims*

The tourists Grady never called *visitors* hardly ever asked questions. They were too busy making fun.

What a crazy old bat!

All that money! What a waste!

For crying out loud, would you just look at that, Ethel! Was that old broad nuts or what!

They gawked and scoffed and wouldn't have known anything fine if it came up and bit their noses off. For them, Grady wished there *were* spirits. Evil spirits that would frighten their pants off.

This day had brought too many of them, and Grady Summers was plumb wore out from being polite. It was his fifth tour, his last, and he was leading the worse batch yet. The kid, especially, a little boy about six years old, was driving him nuts.

"Look, Mommy, look over here!" And over here was almost always somewhere the little brat didn't belong.

Grady frowned as the boy jerked open a cupboard. "Please stay away from there, son." He gritted a smile and pointed toward one of the clearly posted signs. "It says you mustn't touch. These things are old, and if everyone touched, pretty soon this fine house wouldn't be worth looking at anymore. Then all the other folks that come visiting would be real disappointed. So, like I told you a while back, *please* don't touch."

"Can if I want."

Grady looked at the boy's mother, who gave him a weak shrug.

"Shame, Billy," she said, "be a good boy and do what the nice old man tells you."

Billy slammed the cupboard door shut as hard as he could and favored Grady with a view of pink tongue.

The kid had been at it from the first step of the tour. Up roped-off stairwells. Ducking around corners. Flipping switches. Pushing and shoving his way to the front. Rushing ahead. Falling behind. Through the carriage house and bedrooms. The many parlors. The Séance Room. The Room of Fires. The Crystal Room, with its ornate, golden-flecked wall covering. Billy had paused there to pan for gold, scrape at the walls with dirty fingernails. And he did it all while his mother admonished in her soft, long-suffering voice. From time to time she would give Grady a *I know he's a nuisance but isn't he just too darling* look of apology.

Grady smiled one more time. The tour was almost over, and he was determined to keep his dignity intact to the very end.

"And this is the front door," he continued, "another example of the fine stained and mullioned windows Mrs. Winchester had shipped through Tiffany's. You will notice its design, the daisy flowers and leaf patterns, the colors. Every three years or so all of these windows must be taken apart, piece by piece, and scrupulously cleaned to preserve their beauty."

"That's dumb," Billy said.

"Now, if you'll just step this way, we'll enter the ante-room. From there you will see first the Morning Room, and then the Grand Ballroom."

Next after Sarah's bedroom, the room in which she had died, the Morning Room was Grady's favorite. He could so clearly picture her sitting there, a cup of tea on the table beside the tiny Victorian sofa. He saw the flush of her cheeks, and her silver-gray hair wound into an elaborate coiffure atop her head as she furiously scribbled some new plan for her ever-burgeoning home. He could see, too, just a spark of fear in her bright eyes, fear that the spirits would do exactly what she believed they had communicated to her. If the building was ever finished and the workmen's tools laid to rest, Sarah believed she would instantly die.

Tourists were prevented entrance to the Morning Room by a velvet barrier rope, the kind once used in theaters, for fear the carpets, floors or furnishings would be damaged.

"Yuk!" Billy pinched his nostrils with his fingers. "This place stinks!"

"Moving right along the ballroom now . . ." Grady did in fact move along, rather quickly, for he, too, had noticed the odor—an odor that had grown stronger with each passing day. Billy was not the only one who had wrinkled his nose.

Rats. Grady's other nemesis. The damn varmints got be-tween the walls and died every now and then, causing a terrible smell. But in a house like this one, with walls and ceilings and floors to be so carefully preserved, it was nearly impossible to find the little buggers. This time it was beginning to smell like a whole nest of the pests had expired. Even Grady had to admit that it was getting mighty rank. His own nose twitched with disgust as he guided his group back across the anteroom to the Grand Ballroom, the one in which a ball had never taken place. A sad, beautiful room with an oaken parquet floor and a huge Claugh and Warren pipe organ, which the solitary and reclusive Sarah used to play in the middle of mournful, sleepless nights.

Grady had just started talking when Billy interrupted again.

"Oh, yuk, Mommy," he said in a voice Grady thought would pierce his own brain. "There's a ghost in that closet over there!" He pointed back toward the Morning Room. "It's a lady ghost. She's naked and she's flying right off the floor, but boy does she *stink*!"

"Now, now, Billy, how many times has Mommy told you not to tell fibs. Please, be a good boy. We'll be all done in just a while and then I'll buy you an ice cream."

But Grady was already rushing back, for from where he stood, he could still see the Morning Room on the far side of the anteroom. The velvet cordon rope was still swinging back and forth, evidence of Billy's illicit intrusion—and beyond, the closet door, standing open.

Grady could see something else, too, something his eyes almost refused to comprehend. Blond hair scattered with wilted flower petals. A neck too long to be real. Very, very long. A body tattooed all over in crusty black designs. It had to be a joke, a macabre prank, but Grady knew that it was not. The smell told him. Now that the closet door was open, it was sickening sweet, foul and overpowering. From somewhere behind him a woman screamed.

Grady had turned a deathly white. "Please, folks, stay back . . . just move—"

"Oh, my God!" Billy's mother was right at his elbow. She had spoken in a whisper, almost a prayer. Her eyes bulged, and then she, too, began to scream, a high, shrill, siren wail of horror.

CHAPTER 5

DIXIE AND HERB were the on-call team for the week, and Di Franco had staggered their hours to help keep down the overtime being put in by the rest of the investigators. Summer, especially one as hot, humid, and smoggy as the one they presently suffered, made for a heavy homicide season. People were uncomfortable, tempers were short, and all too often alcohol was used as a thirst quencher. Over the past month family squabbles and barroom brawls had caused a heavy case load.

And as luck would have it, with the air-conditioning on the fritz, tempers in the Police Administration Building were little better than on the street. At three-thirty in the afternoon, as Herb and Dixie came on duty, the other investigators were finishing paperwork. Everyone was frazzled and edgy.

Lieutenant Di Franco, closed in the glass cubicle that served as his office, was wreathed in a cloud of blue cigarette smoke. Sweat stains showed beneath his arms, and his tie was loosened. His voice could be heard out in the squad room.

"How long, then? I tell you, my guys are frying up here! How in the bloody hell can we work in conditions like this?"

Herb smiled across his desk at Dixie. Over the past months she and Tony Di Franco seemed to have quietly, tentatively buried the proverbial tomahawk. He respected her as a cop

37

and as a detective, even if he would have preferred that she work someplace else. He still did not approve of female cops, least of all in his unit of command, but figured—better Dixie than any of the forty or so others. For her part, Dixie knew his feelings, ignored his chauvinism, and settled for being one of his *guys*.

Pat Delaney and Bill Brooks, the senior homicide investigators, were going through a stack of photos. They were both sweating, wearing expressions of irritable boredom. Delaney had a cigar clamped between his teeth, jutting from his face, a quiescent extension of his character. Delaney was an old-time cop. Blunt. Rasty. And extremely effective.

Pete Willis had still not taken Herb's advice. He was still working, a partner to Jake Spatlin. But for the past two days he had caused no more commotion, made no more waves. He did his work, and if he showed none of his normal enthusiasm, neither did he neglect his responsibility. He did not mention his niece. But each day as he came in and prepared to go off duty, he paid a carefully polite call on Steven Bruner.

Both Pete and Jake were still out in the field.

Doty Bangor, the homicide secretary, sat behind her typewriter. As usual, by early afternoon she'd caught up on her work. Putting her leisure to good use, carefully concentrating on each stroke, she applied blood-colored polish to her long fingernails. Her full lips pursed with each flick of the tiny brush. Also as usual, she wore clothing as seductive as she could without being called to task for inciting a riot. On this day it was a cleavage-exposing white cotton sundress with fire-engine-red patent leather belt and matching sling pumps.

"I swear," she drawled in her best southern accent, "it's simply too hot to live in this place!" She dried her polish by waving her hands just above the plunging neckline of her dress.

Jake Spatlin entered the room just in time to hear her. He was alone.

"You can bet your ass on that one," he said, "and you'll note, Ms. Bangor, that I didn't say *sweet*."

Doty stuck out her tongue. While Dixie and Di Franco had made a truce, Jake and the sexy Alabama-born secretary maintained their personal little war, a running battle that both seemed to enjoy a shade too much.

The tall black officer pulled his tie down and addressed no one in particular. "You know what I'm going to do? I'm putting in for a transfer to Narco. I just saw Cavanaugh out in the hall, and do you know what that jack-off was wearing?"

No one answered, nor had Jake expected them to. He preferred it that way. He enjoyed answering himself. "That asshole has on a pair of Bermuda shorts! Can you believe it? Bermuda shorts and a friggin' Hawaiian shirt! Undercover cops used to go sniffing out dope in dark holes, wearing scratchy old beards and black shirts. Now it's cocaine from the poor little rich kids—and Cavanaugh gets to wear fuckin' shorts!"

"Well, hey, Spatlin, I thought you people were used to hot weather—environmental evolution and all that." Doty was still concentrating on her nails, but her blue eyes were half shut, and a definite smirk tugged at one corner of her mouth.

Jake turned dark, lambent eyes on her, pointedly fixing his gaze on her chest. "Only if we wear loinclothes and chuck our spears. Say, baby, you want I should come dressed undercovery style tomorrow? I'll wear my loincloth just for you, crawl right under your cover, and chuck my spear—"

"Take a flying leap, Spatlin." She screwed the cap on her nail polish. "And don't you just wish!"

The phone rang and Doty answered. She spoke a few words and then transferred the call into Di Franco's office, never taking her eyes off Jake.

Herb spoke to Dixie in stage whisper. "Don't tell anyone, partner, but I think those two have had a case of the hots . . . for each other."

Dixie's chuckle was accompanied by laughter from the other detectives in the squad room. Jake and Doty opened their mouths to yell mutual disclaimers, only to be cut off by Di Franco.

The leuy walked into the room wearing a scowl. "Let's hope it's just the hots, *period*. The last thing we need around here is a lot of screwing around. To me, it's just like incest. You don't do it with your own. Or if you prefer, good sheepdogs don't kill sheep close to home. Either way, screw around in my unit, and you're out."

It was a common warning, and everyone knew it was really a snide aside aimed straight at Dixie. Di Franco still did not know her well enough to realize that she had never dated another police officer, not in all the six-plus years she'd been on the force.

He continued into the room, walking toward Dixie and Herb. "You'll all be glad to hear that maintenance assures me we'll soon have our air-conditioning back, tomorrow latest. Of course, they told me that yesterday, and the day before."

He handed Dixie a slip of paper, then mopped at his face with a large white handkerchief. "This just came in, Struthers. Lots of luck. One of the tour guides over at the Winchester Mystery House smelled a very bad smell, if you get my drift." His slightly pugged nose wrinkled accordingly.

Herb groaned. A body left for very long in the weather they now suffered would be ripe indeed. He hated ripe bodies.

"Are there black-and-whites already there?" Dixie was already on her feet, picking up one of the large purses she always carried to work. She slipped the strap over her shoulder.

"Yeah. Two units responded to the call. They're still at the scene, clearing tourists, taking care of crowd control with help from the security guard who works there. The press are probably en route, too, if they haven't already arrived. I called the coroner's office and the tech detail. They'll 1087 with you at the scene."

"Is the victim male or female?" Dixie asked.

Di Franco met her eyes. "Female. Young. Blond."

She turned to Jake, who was already back up on his feet. The squad room had grown suddenly quiet. "Where is he?"

"Down in Juvenile, pestering Brew."

"Find a way to keep him busy for the next hour or so. Away from radios and phone. We'll call as soon as we can."

"Probably just another false alarm," Herb said, hoping like hell.

Dixie didn't answer as she followed him out the door.

CHAPTER 6

DIXIE HAD SEEN many dead bodies. All shapes, sizes, ages. Herb had seen more. But nothing in their combined experience prepared them for what they saw at the Winchester Mystery House.

From outside, the mansion was beautiful. A giant gingerbread confection with fish-scale shingles, gables, and balustrades. A witch's cap tower, set amidst trailing passion vines, was only one of the many embellishments of the roof. Turrets, opaque-glass skylights, and finial-tipped cupolas formed a maze of swirls and angles against the pale blue afternoon sky.

But it was not the alluring exterior of the fabulously bizarre house that Dixie and Herb had come to see, or even the interior. They were there to see one tiny closet, a cubicle that held a sight so terrible, so gruesome, that even Dr. Jason Wittenhaur, the head coroner, was not wearing the infuriatingly smug smile he always showed them when a victim was discovered.

Wittenhaur had reached the scene before them and had already been inside, visually examining the body, but touching nothing. The pathologist greeted Herb and Dixie at the door, minus the usual macabre twinkle in his eyes.

He was puffing away, concentrating on the briarwood bowl

of his pipe. "These gentlemen don't think I should smoke inside, but I'll be damned if I won't. It's this or a handkerchief soaked in gasoline. The smell of gasoline makes me puke."

The two men he was talking about stepped forward. One was young, no more than thirty, and the other sixty, at least. Both men were pale. The youngest made the introductions.

"I'm the manager here," he said, "David Martin. And this is one of our guides, Grady Summers. Grady has been with us since the house opened to the public. He's the one unfortunate enough to discover what . . . what was in that closet."

"*I* didn't," Grady corrected. "That little snot-nosed snoop did." He was in no mood to be courteous now. He was sickened. Angry. Appalled at the desecration that had taken place in Sarah's house.

David Martin looked troubled. "Yes, the mother is already threatening to sue. She says her little boy has been traumatized by what he saw in that closet."

"I don't know why you keep working around the word, young man." Wittenhaur had not completely lost his bite. "It is not a *what*, it's a *who*. The body of a human being, with a name. A girl. A very young girl who has been carved up like a relief map, disemboweled and mutilated."

David Martin looked like he would throw up, but Wittenhaur was irritated, and when he was irritated, he could also be relentless. "It's okay, son, go ahead. Blowing a few chunks will make you feel better."

The young man swallowed several times, his face going even more bilious. But he also set his jaw stubbornly. He looked the pathologist in the eye. "I know you're not happy about the pipe, sir. But I can't change the rules just for you. There is no smoking allowed in the house. It's too old, too valuable to risk a fire."

"Anyone set fire to Sarah's house, I think I might kill them." Grady had mumbled the threat under his breath, but Wittenhaur turned and looked at him. The two old men stared at one another for a long time, and then the first thing even remotely resembling a smile fleetingly claimed Wittenhaur's blue eyes. He knew a match when he met one.

"Well, if I can't smoke, guess I'll use a hanky, without

gas." He looked at Herb and Dixie. "You'll need them, too, I promise."

Herb didn't argue. He pulled a large white handkerchief from his pocket in readiness for what he knew would be an unpleasant experience. If Wittenhaur had a problem, Herb figured everyone else would probably faint and fade.

Dixie thought about the small lacy bit of froufrou in her purse and inwardly groaned.

Grady Summers reached into the hip pocket of his slacks. "Here you go, miss, if you don't mind, that is. Hasn't been used."

Dixie took a small spray flask of Channel from her purse and looked at the old man. "Do you mind?"

"Not at all." In spite of his present agitation, there was an appreciative twinkle in Grady's eyes. "Might even keep it as a souvenir."

Dixie sprayed the perfume liberally over the handkerchief and held it in one hand. The sweetness filled the carriage house. She looked at David Martin. "Shall we go?"

"I'll take you around to the front entrance. We don't use it normally, because of the damage it might cause the window in the door. It's worth thousands of dollars. But if you and your people can be very, very careful—"

Wittenaur exploded. "Well, why didn't you say that in the first place, instead of leading me around like a rat in a maze? I must have walked a mile to get to the front of this house!"

David Martin and Grady Summers favored him with malicious smiles.

The parking lot adjacent to the mansion had been cleared, but that did not prevent rubbernecking by stagglers and early theater goers. Two uniformed officers kept the ghoulies back with the help of the security officer employed by the Mystery House. Employees, originally asked to wait in the visitor's rest area, were finally released to go home, but only after Herb had secured a list of their names, addresses, and phone numbers from David Martin. He and Grady Summers were the only regular employees who remained as the body and the crime scene were examined.

While rank, as the sweet-and-sour smell of death always was, the body of Gretchen Willis, dead for over a week, was only a shade worse than normal. Still, Dixie and Herb, as well as members of the homicide tech team who arrived shortly afterward, did wear the protective nose coverings. To Dixie it was the state of the body, the horror of having to look at it, that made the smell seem so sickening. It was as if the little boy had opened a gate, letting out all the noxious vapors of hell.

In reality, the interior of the mansion was comfortably cool, and less deterioration had occurred than might have in another setting. But that took away none of the shock. Dixie and Herb followed Dr. Wittenhaur into the Morning Room, with David Martin and Grady Summers trailing well behind. Neither of the employees completely entered the room, not far enough to get even a passing view of the closet.

Herb stood staring up, his eyes sick above the handkerchief. "I knew it," he whispered. "Deep down in my bones, I knew."

"Get to a phone," Dixie said. "Call Jake and ask him to break it to Pete. We're stuck here, and if he doesn't, someone else will. He'll hear it on the damn news. Also tell him to sit on Pete if he has to. Under no condition is he to come here. Tell Jake to do whatever is necessary. Let the men out front know. Most of them would recognize Pete, but give them a description anyway. Maybe Mr. Martin can show you to a phone."

Herb felt the urgency in her voice register throughout his own system. Pete might be a cop, but there was no way he could see this. *No way!*

David Martin nodded, led Herb into the foyer and through the front door. Herb was glad to go, to be given a little time to compose himself before having to see it all again.

Dixie stood very still, not even feeling the presence of Jason Wittenhaur beside her. She stared up at the sacrilege that had once been Gretchen Willis.

The closet was perhaps six feet in length by four feet in width. As was true throughout the old mansion, an odd mixture of cubbyhole architecture combined with expensive frivolities immediately struck the observer. In this case a pair of lovely stained-glass windows of elaborate pattern had been fitted high into the closet walls. They were lovely, done in muted shades of sea-foam green, softest peach, pretty pink. Jeweled patterns of light bathed the corpse.

The body of Gretchen Willis had been hung from an overhead water pipe. After death. Her face was not blue, nor her tongue protruding. She had not been strangled. But her pale neck had stretched like taffy. It was nearly two feet long, with flesh rotting and breaking away. A few more days delay in discovery would have found the body in two pieces, but as it was, Gretchen appeared almost to be dancing, tiptoeing through the gore of her own disemboweled entrails. A macabre ballet. Her body had also been twisted, revolved backward on a broken neck. A witch's death.

Most disturbing, however, were the geometrics carved into her naked body. Wide strips of flesh had been cut away. She had been literally carved in some sort of occult symbolism. Her right breast bore a four-inch Egyptian ankh, and the left, a much larger swastika. Her back was a series of dots, hearts, and arrows, which formed an obvious pattern but held no immediate significance for either Dixie, Jason Wittenhaur or Herb. Her upper thighs and arms bore smaller designs—spirals, snakes, and daggers plunging into hearts. Lividity had turned her lower arms and legs a putrid black, but the cuts, the designs, the multiple signatures of a deranged mind, were clean, congealed into black scabs against waxy, white skin. Crystallized drops of semen had crusted on her inner thighs, indicating that Gretchen Willis had either been raped or making love shortly before her death.

"They brought her through the window," Herb said, showing Dixie a small smear on the sill, previously hidden by the tassled damask drapes. There were other bits of blood in the Morning Room, minute flecks on the lacy sheers beneath the drapes, and a few on the floor. But there was nothing, no pools nor even large droplets, to indicate that the body had been bleeding profusely.

"There's no way yet to know for certain how long after the actual killing she was brought, dragged in here," Wittenhaur said. "But from the semen and the lividity in her extremities, I'd say not too long. My guess is that she was semi cleaned up. Given a bath, so to speak." His voice was muffled by the handkerchief he wore over his lower face, but his eyes were, surprisingly, suspiciously wet looking. "Probably so the artwork could be done with maximum precision."

Dixie and Herb knew the estate would have to be covered from stem to stern, grounds included, but thanks to David

Martin, no search warrant was required. Sergeant Blair Farnham, senior officer on the technical detail, was only too happy to assist by taking one of his men to comb the grounds, sheds, and outbuildings.

The murder of Pete's niece, and the subsequent discovery of her body, seemed to Dixie to have had an unsettling effect on all concerned. Cops who normally got through the day, through their jobs, by way of black humor, were silent. No one wanted to look. Everyone wanted to be gone, and as quickly as possible. While David Martin led the two-penny tour outdoors, Grady took Herb through the interior.

Not long before her death, Sarah Winchester had partially upgraded the gas lighting in her home for electricity, most often using the same elaborate and expensive fixtures, but with a single control box. It made the going much easier, except in those places untraveled by tourists—the attics and basements, as well as that part of the house closed up and unused after the great earthquake of 1906, a quake with an epicenter even closer to San Jose than to San Francisco. Going through that part of the mansion, Grady used great care, and cautioned Dixie and Herb to do the same.

"It frightened her to death," Grady said. "She was trapped in her original bedroom, you know. Not crushed, but buried alive, until her employees came back and dug her out. It took hours." Standing in the oldest part of the house, he shined a flashlight around at walls half crumbled away, floors exposed in places. "Watch your step now. The house is safe in most areas, and this has been shored up enough to protect the super structure from caving in, but it's dangerous to move around up here—except for Sarah's spirits, of course."

"Do you believe in those spirits, Mr. Summers?" Dixie asked, with no predisposition in her voice. She had already decided that she liked the old fellow, no matter what he might believe.

"Call me Grady," he said. "Everyone else does. I've been here so long, I think *I'm* becoming a historical landmark. As far as your question goes, whether I believe or not doesn't make a thimbleful of difference, Sergeant Struthers. The important thing was, *she* believed, bless her heart. That's all that counts. She had lost her husband and her little girl. She believed the spirits had taken them as a punishment for all the people killed by the Winchester rifle.''

He took them on from attic to cellar, until they could no longer tell front from back, south, north, east, or west. The enormity of the house was staggering, and the fact that Grady never got disoriented seemed a kind of minor mystery in itself. Dixie and Herb were dumbfounded by the distance they had to cover. Dumbfounded and worn to a nub.

''There's lots to it all right,'' Grady said, watching the expressions on their faces. ''Try to imagine cleaning it, maintaining it, keeping it in good order.'' He smiled gently and shook his head. ''This old house has 160 rooms, 10,000 windows, 2000 doors, fifty-two skylights, forty-seven fireplaces—thirteen of them wood burning—forty bedrooms, forty staircases, thirteen bathrooms, six kitchens, three elevators, two basements, and one shower.''

The detectives ran out of breath just listening to him. As they continued on, for just a while they were able to lose themselves in what they saw. No expense had been spared in building the house. Frescoed ceilings, embossed and varnished Lincrista Walton wall coverings, marble fixtures, and handmade ceramic tiles were predominant throughout. There were rooms that Dixie especially loved—the many tiny parlors, the Chinese bedrooms, and the Hall of Fires were Sarah sought relief in her old age from the crippling pain in her limbs.

But there were discomforting oddities about the house, too, manifestations of a deeply troubled mind, a mind delving constantly, relentlessly into the occult: the Blue Séance Room, for example, with its spiraled floor, with thirteen hooks for thirteen different colored ceremonial robes. The repetition of that superstition invoking number showed itself over and over again.

''That was one of the things that made Sarah so different,'' Grady said, avoiding the word peculiar. ''There were certain things she just did to death, like her daisy patterns and spider-web windows, and the number thirteen. She even signed her will thirteen times.''

Still, of all the rooms in the house, none was more charming than the Morning Room, the one so evilly defiled by Gretchen's killer. The dainty Victorian furnishings, the small fireplace with its mahogany facade, the oyster-colored damask draperies and ivory undersheers had made the desecration in the closet all the more chilling.

It was nearing two in the morning as Grady stood with Dixie and Herb in the final room, the main-level Venetian Dining Room. Dixie looked up, admiring the frescoed ceilings, the glowing, richly carved woods, and the craftsmanship which seemed so discarded, so alien to the present modern age.

"It's beautiful," she said, with Herb nodding assent. "So much of this old house is beautiful, almost *beckoning.*"

Grady smiled, the first genuine smile of the long night. "I could see you felt that way. Now maybe you can understand why I stay here, why I keep working like I do. I could've taken my pension and lived off my Social Security long ago. But I just can't. Sometimes I even get a little crazy, start thinking the place is mine."

He walked them out, almost rushing them through the gift shop, a place he obviously though incongruous to *his* house, and taking them into the parking lot. There, to Dixie's and Herb's surprise, Jason Wittenhaur still waited.

"I'll leave you now, then," Grady said. "I live right down this little narrow street here. It dead-ends at the mobile-home park. If I can help you anymore, I'll be more than happy to oblige. Sorry about that youngster. A terrible thing to happen in Sarah's house . . . in *any* house."

"I don't think it did happen here," Wittenhaur said, approaching them. "I still think the body was brought in, unless of course you've found evidence of the contrary?" He looked at Dixie, who shook her head.

"They didn't find anything in the outbuildings either, or on the grounds." Wittenhaur said. "There are lots of things I won't know until I perform the autopsy, but if you're interested, I do have some speculations." Dixie did not send Grady Summers away, nor did the old man leave. He stood listening intently. "For one thing, I don't think those carvings on her body were for real. I mean, that's not what killed her, if my guess is right. She was killed by stabbing, maybe even a frenzied stabbing—a rage unlike you and I have never seen. I think there's a damn good chance we'll find much deeper wounds beneath the others. My first guess was a broken neck, but I have a feeling now that I was wrong. That might very well have been done after the fact too."

Dixie shook her head. "But why?"

"*That*, my dear young lady, is for you to figure out. And in that I wish you luck. Quick luck."

Grady looked suddenly tired and ill. He lifted a hand in farewell and walked slowly toward the end of the street, disappearing through a set of metal gates leading into the mobile-home park.

The only other person in the parking lot now was the security officer. A tall man who stood beside his car, waiting patiently. Dixie nodded, and Herb walked over to the man.

Wittenaur still made no move to leave, and Dixie looked at him questioningly. He was smoking his pipe again, drawing deeply on the stem, exhaling long thin wisps of aromatic cherry tobacco smoke.

"You know, Sergeant, my wife always wants to know what I've been up to. She's been married to me long enough to see the interest in most of my cases. But I'm not about to tell her what I saw here. Jane wouldn't sleep for a month if I told her all of it. We have a granddaughter, a pretty little blond granddaughter about the same age as that girl. I've been at this a long time now, and not many of the things I see get to me anymore. But this one did. Dead children get to me. I can take anything else, make fun, joke when it makes me feel better"—a faint quirk tugged at his lower lip—"or when I run into someone like your partner over there, someone who can't see it's all fate, with no escapes allowed, not when a body's time really comes. But this thing . . . this *evil* does something to me, makes me want to hang up my smock and go fishing until my own turn comes. I hope you get the thing that did this."

Thing. The same word had come to Dixie's mind.

"I do autopsies all the time," Wittenhaur said. "There are all kinds of tests now. Technology has gone further than you can imagine. But there is nothing, not one blessed thing in the human brain, in the science of genetics, to explain how every once in a while a baby is born deformed . . . with something missing, some invisible something to differentiate it from real humans. That's what you're looking for, Dixie."

It was the first time he had used her first name. "You're

not looking for a human being. The body that did this is walking around, stalking the streets, and it has no soul."

The way he said it sent chills up Dixie's spine. He nodded and walked to his car. He drove away slowly.

"Mr. Martin is right, there's no other way, no other time it could have been done," the guard was saying as Dixie approached. "The alarm system was down for almost three days. They called the service number and informed them so they could let me know to keep a sharper eye than usual. I don't know that it's ever happened before, but I can see how it would. I don't like computers much, and that's the kind of system it is. A keypad with a special code."

Andy Wilson was a tall man, good-looking, with blond hair and a thick mustache. Unlike many of the men employed by private security-patrol companies, companies with notoriously low pay scales, he looked spruce and professional, even without a gun. The only obvious weapon in his basket-weave belt was a nightstick. His tan uniform was well pressed, right to the epaulets. His voice was low and well-modulated, with just a faint southern overtone. And even standing as he was, in the darkness, with only a fluorescent streetlight illuminating his rugged features, Dixie decided he was a man most women would find attractive. Appearing to be in his late thirties, he had broad shoulders, narrow hips, and arms that obviously saw a good workout several times each week. He turned a quick smile on Dixie and then fixed his full attention back on Herb.

He looked familiar to Dixie, and it took her a moment to realize why. Quick or not, it had been just the sort of smile she had always liked best—boyish. The kind of smile owned by all the men she cared for most. Art. Herb. Pete. She spent a brief moment wondering about herself. Perhaps, she thought, she had some kind of mother complex.

Dixie's face sobered. One thing was certain: one of her favorite men, Pete, was going to need all the mothering he could get, probably for quite some time.

"How often do you check the place?" Herb asked. "Are you employed strictly by the Mystery House?"

"No, of course not, that would be more expensive than most small companies can afford. West Side Security Patrol is getting pretty big. I handle this place, Town and Country, across the street, and a couple of other individual businesses.''

"Do you have access to the mansion, Mr. Wilson?" Dixie asked. "I mean, if you absolutely had to get in, could you?"

"Yes, but that's only happened once. Some kids tried to sneak in a few months ago. They set the audible alarm off. I chased a couple of them, but they got away. It didn't really matter. The main thing was to get them off the property before they did any damage."

"Boys? Girls?"

"I couldn't tell for sure in the dark. Boys, I think. Anyhow, I just reset the alarm after I went in and checked the old place out. It's real creepy in there at night. If I hadn't known the floor plan, I could have been lost for years. You know, like the guy in the song who disappeared 'neath the streets of Boston, the man who never returned."

Yep, Dixie thought, thirty-nine or forty years old at least. It was an old song.

"The gate there." Herb pointed to a break in the hedge running along the north side of the mansion, the one closest to the parking lot. The gap was filled by a high Cyclone gate. "I see it's kept locked."

"Just with a padlock, not all that hard to get past. But between that and the two lines of barbed wire on the top, it's pretty discouraging. I come by about every thirty to forty-five minutes. Besides, even if they did go over, the house alarm would go off if anyone tried to get in."

"But someone obviously did get in while the alarm was out of service," Herb said. "Or at least that's my bet. The walkway from the gate makes a beeline to the front porch. Straight as an arrow."

Wilson nodded. "That's my theory too. I was off that night, but Danny Garcia was on, and he makes me look lax. Whoever did that girl in must have picked the lock right after Danny did a check. Taken her in and killed her."

"We've pretty well established that she wasn't killed here," Dixie said. "Just dumped."

The security patrol guard winced slightly. "Not in such a nice way from what I hear. Glad I didn't have to see it."

"You should be," Herb said. "It will make sleeping one hell of a lot easier for you."

As he and Dixie left, driving slowly back to the police department to pick up their individual cars, neither had much to say. The night was soft and warm with the lingering touch of summer. Dixie had her window down. She rested her head on the back of the car seat. Even city air smelled clean to her at the moment. Any air but that inside the closet of Sarah Winchester's Morning Room.

After dropping the squad car at the police garage, Herb walked Dixie to her car. She almost had the door open when she saw Jake Spatlin. She lifted her hand to wave, but dropped it again when she saw the expression on his face.

"I know it's after three in the damn morning," he said as he got to them, "but I was afraid you might still think about paying Pete a sympathy call. Don't."

The thought had been crossing both their minds, but they didn't have a chance to ask why they shouldn't before Jake told them.

"If he wasn't my partner, my friend, I would have been scared to death of him tonight, no scooby-do. He was just on his way out when I caught him, and if you think I didn't have to sit on that hunk of honky muscle, you're wrong. He went wild, man. Took me and Delany both to stuff him into one of interrogation rooms and keep him from charging over to your scene."

"Poor Pete," Dixie said.

"Poor Pete, my ass!" Jake said. "Like I said, I know he's got it rough, but the way he fought, and then after we got him calmed down, the way he sat there staring at me with those marble-blue eyes of his—it scared the hell out of me. Brooks finally went out and got a bottle of Jack Daniels, which he almost had to make him drink at gun point. It finally got to him, though. Delaney took him home and put him to bed not more than twenty minutes ago. And by the by, I don't think you two are on his list of best friends anymore, not tonight, anyway. I'm sure you'll get back on the list tomorrow. Just wanted to warn you to stay away until he cools down."

They thanked him and watched him go to his own car, a hot-red Corvette.

●   ●   ●

Dixie was relieved to go home, though even the long drive up through the mountains, pine-scented and pleasant as it was, could not remove the stench of murder from her nostrils. And it was not just a physical smell she imagined clinging to her clothing, adhering to her hair. To her the murder of Gretchen Willis was the kind of vile stench that remained with one for a lifetime.

Working previous cases, not knowing who the murderer might be, she had nevertheless had a *feel* for them. Man. Woman. *Human*. But no such vague image filled her mind now. No image at all, just a terribly disturbing premonition, as if a dark shadow hung over her and the city she served. A menacing, faceless, formless essence of evil. It was not a feeling Dixie liked, and mixed with it all, with the memory of the dead and horribly mutilated teenage girl, was her sympathy, her worry for Pete.

Arriving home, she found herself still uneasy and more than faintly depressed. She was also dead tired. It was nearly three in the morning, and she knew she would have to be back on duty early the next day. The gory murder of Gretchen Willis had all the earmarks of becoming a splashy and spectacular case. Splashy for the press. Investigatively challenging. Spectacularly demoralizing. Clearing it as quickly as possible, catching the killer and putting the case to rest, was urgent.

Reversa Green, the woman who had happily, protectively served Dixie throughout her childhood, had left a note in the kitchen indicative of her personality:

Missy—Food is in the microwave, which we paid good money for so you could eat. Turn it on. EAT!   R.

The bossy tone of the note, and the well-loved face it brought to mind, caused Dixie to smile. Tired as she was, she followed the instructions, eating as much of the homemade gumbo as she could—which was not much at all. She was just putting the spoon down when she heard footfalls on the stairs. A moment later her grandfather's bedraggled form entered the kitchen.

Patrick squinted up at the wall clock. "Lord a mercy, girl, it's almost time to get up. You taking up the bad life?"

"Hardly, Pop." Dixie saw the dead girl, knowing all at once what *bad* really meant.

Wider awake now, Patrick noted the pallor of her face. He had been a cop long enough to recognize her particular shade of pale green. "Got a rough one, did you?"

She nodding, pushing her bowl away. Patrick picked it up and carried it to the sink. "Anything I can do, mouvereen? I may be too old for the street, and bit rusty, but I still have a pair of mighty sharp ears."

Dixie stood up, shaking her head, surprised at her sudden reticence to talk it out. During her years on the force, and especially on the homicide team, she thought she'd seen just about everything. She had developed a strong stomach. She could view a postmortem without wincing. She had striven for and thought she had attained a certain professional objectivity. But at the moment she felt neither strong nor objective. The brutalized body of Pete's niece, with all the overtones of ritualized sadism, horrified her.

Moving stiffly, every muscle and sinew crying for rest, Dixie walked with her grandfather to the bottom of the stairs. She stopped, turning to him. "You know, Pop, sometimes the world seems . . ." Her voice caught, and she swallowed several times.

Patrick gently pulled her to him and wrapped his arms around her.

That was all it took. For the first time in a very, very long time, Sergeant Dixie T. Struthers broke down and wept.

CHAPTER 7

THE HOUSE WHERE Gretchen Willis once lived was small, a neat little tract home in a subdivision that was one of the first installed in the south part of the valley, the beginning of the urban boom necessitated by the mushrooming electronics industry. The yard in front of the house was also small, but well kept, the lawn trimmed, and bordered along one side by a bed of yellow marigolds and black-eyed Susans.

Sally Nelson sat in the living room. Pete, clean-shaven now but still red-eyed, held her hand. The shades were pulled. A large fan circulated warm, stuffy air around the dim room.

"None of this makes a bit of sense, Sergeant Struthers." The bereaved woman looked from Dixie to Herb. "You can ask Pete. Gretchen was a good girl, with sound morals. She would never have taken a ride with a stranger, I know she wouldn't. Her Uncle Pete had warned her too many times. Gretchen knew the . . . the kind of things . . . the sort of things that can happen to girls if they . . ." Her voice trailed away and she choked off a sob.

"I know this is difficult, Ms. Nelson, and I apologize for having to ask questions at a time like this, but the sooner we get information, the sooner we'll be able to find the person who . . . the quicker we'll solve this case. Please try to bear with us. We'll keep our questions as brief as possible."

Sally Nelson nodded and swallowed hard, taking a deep breath. Dark half-moons of fatigue stood out beneath her eyes. Her lips were thin and pale. She wore almost no makeup, and at the moment certainly bore no resemblance to the photograph of her daughter, her only child. Gretchen had possessed a cloud of curly flaxen hair and wide blue eyes. Her mother also had blue eyes, but much more pale. A dull, watery blue. Her hair, a nondescript shade of mouse-fur brown, was parted in the center and fell into a straight line to the bottoms of her ears. She was a small woman, and very thin. Her shoulders were lifted slightly in tension and suppressed grief. Her entire body posture seemed taut, drawn like a poised slingshot.

"To start with, we will need a list of her friends." Dixie held a small notebook in her hand. "Addresses, too, the ones you have, and phone numbers."

Sally looked quickly at Pete, then shifted her body slightly. "I know this will seem strange, especially for a girl like my Gretchen, but she didn't have many friends. By that I don't mean I didn't know her friends, either. To my knowledge there just weren't any."

"None?" Dixie brows arched a fraction, but her tone remained neutral.

Gretchen's mother shook her head. "No, none. That was one of the things we argued about. If Gretchen had been different, or even like I was in school"—the woman flushed—"I could have understood. I wasn't pretty, and I was shy, painfully so. But even I had friends, two or three girls to share secrets and giggles with. But Gretchen . . . well, she preferred being alone. With her looks and personality, she could have had a houseful of friends. But she didn't. Believe me, Sergeant, I don't know of a one. Kids just never came by the house, or called. There was one little girl, Priscilla. She and Gretchen grew up together. But even Priscilla wouldn't speak to Gretchen anymore. Not even Priscilla."

Dixie looked at Herb. His face mirrored her own nonplussed expression.

Except for the whir of the fan, the house was quiet, filled with an empty, almost eerie sadness. Pete had fixed a quiet, steady gaze on Sally.

"You should have been pleased that she was selective,"

Pete said, obviously struggling to keep his tone from becoming accusatory. "She found nothing in common with most kids her own age. She was bright. It makes sense. But I'm sure there were some friends, Sally. At school. Think about it."

"I have thought about it, Pete." She looked at her former brother-in-law with adamant, defensive eyes. "Gretchen had no friends." Dixie slowly closed her notebook, avoiding eye contact with Herb, whom she knew was wearing the same nonplussed expression as she.

"Mrs. Nelson," Herb said, "was Gretchen upset about anything lately? Did she complain of anyone mistreating her in any way at all?"

"Only me." The woman's voice was filled with regret. "Oh, God, if only I hadn't nagged at her so much! But I couldn't help myself. I wanted the best for her. All kids need other kids, or at least I've always thought so. And with her . . ." She hesitated and then plunged on. "Frankly, with Gretchen's attitude, I was afraid she might never have friends again."

"What in the hell are you talking about, Sally? What attitude?" Pete cut in. His expression was dark. "I've never met a sweeter kid in my life!"

Sally Nelson turned sad eyes on him, eyes that now held a spark of anger. "Oh, bless you, Peter, but you saw what you wanted to see, and what *she* wanted you to see. I wish I could lie to you now that Gretchen is gone, I really do. But the truth is, she was a bit stuck up. More than a bit. She was so bright, so pretty . . . I used to accuse her of being incredibly conceited, and I still think that was true. Judgmental, too, especially of me. I know it sounds rotten to say. Maybe it was my fault. Maybe yours, too, Pete. We always told her how special she was, how exceptional. We've been doing it for years. Pretty soon I think she got to believing it in a big way. She got to thinking she was just about the most special person in the whole world."

Pete's eyes seemed to glaze over. His face settled into lines of granite. When she finished speaking, he stood up and turned his back on her, giving his full attention to Dixie and Herb. "I'll walk out with you."

It was a broad hint to leave, and his friends acquiesced and

got to their feet. Just before following him from the house,
Dixie looked back over her shoulder. What she saw was a
small, inconsequential-looking woman. Sally's head was lowered, drooping like a wilted flower on the stem of her neck.
Both of her hands were now clasped in her lap and she
appeared to be weeping. She looked sick, sad, and very much
alone.

Pete's grief, on the other hand, seemed to have been
replaced by outrage. Once he was outside and beyond earshot
of Gretchen's mother, he turned on his heels to face his
friends. "She's lying!" The words erupted from him in a
quick, angry spurt. "Don't ask me why. I know Sally loved
Gretchen; no one could *not* love her. She was a beautiful,
sweet little girl. But something is wrong here. Very wrong.
Sally is hiding something, and I can't imagine what or why.
I'll talk to her when I go back in. Just leave it to me, okay?"

"Take it easy, Pete." Dixie put her hand on his forearm.
"I know you're upset, that both you and your sister-in-law
are in pain."

Pete nodded, but his face remained hard. He turned, walking back into the house with determined strides as Dixie and
Herb got into their unmarked car.

Dixie started the motor and Herb turned the air conditioner
on high, but she didn't pull away from the curb. "You know
what we need here?" she asked.

Herb nodded. "Yeah, a little objectivity. Gretchen remains
very elusive, don't you think?"

"Too much so. She could not have been friendless, not
altogether. But she probably wasn't the angel Peter describes
either. I think what we really need is a kid's eye view."

Herb reached into the briefcase sitting next to his leg and
pulled out the snapshot of Gretchen Willis. He studied the
picture for several moments and then passed it to Dixie. "She
was pretty."

It made Dixie's stomach churn to look at the small heart-
shaped face, the deep blue eyes surrounded by thick, sooty
lashes. Seemingly guileless eyes. Though she tried to push
aside the gruesome image of the partially decomposed corpse
of Gretchen from her mind, she couldn't.

"I could understand all this a lot better if Gretchen looked
like *that*."

Dixie looked up to see Herb tip his head forward, indicating a teenage girl walking up the street.

"Yikes!" Dixie gasped her agreement. The girl was barefoot, and she half sauntered, half danced along the sidewalk. She wore shorts and an oversize sweatshirt, both in heat-absorbing black. In contrast, her skin was like milk, without a hue of California tan. Her face, an even more ghastly pale than the rest of her body, was heavily garnished in vivid cosmetics, her eyes ringed in black, the lashes gooey thick, her lips magenta. Even from where they sat, Dixie and Herb could see the iridescent blue-and-purple eye shadow. She looked like Vampira's daughter with carnival glass eyes. Sunlight sparkled off the diamond, real or simulated, that had been pierced through one of her nostrils. Her ears had been likewise mutilated, often pierced, bedazzled with a variety of studs and dangled baubles. A gold cross dangled from one ear, and what appeared to be a long silver charm bracelet from the other. But most startling was her hair. Dixie had never seen a coiffure as bizarre, or as unbecoming. Both sides had been buzzed, clipped to the scalp, leaving only a long flopping mane at the top, a swath no less than eight inches long, dyed jet black and striped in a dull fluorescent purple.

To their mutual surprise, the girl threw them a bright smile and approached their unmarked squad car.

"Ye, gads," Herb muttered, but he rolled down the window and smiled back. It was not easy. Kids who looked like this one made him fear for the future.

"You guys cops?" Her voice was unexpectedly pleasant.

"Sure are. Why do you ask?"

"Well, I just figured, what with Gretchen being murdered and all. God, that's really creepy!"

Sitting behind the wheel, Dixie dipped her head slightly, the better to see. "You knew Gretchen?"

"Sure." The girl was hopping from foot to foot now. "Damn, this sidewalk is hot! Guess I should put on some sandals. Shit!"

Herb turned and reached over the seat, opening the rear door. "Here, get in if you like. It's hot as Hades out there."

"Might as well get used to it, I guess." She giggled. "Dad says that's where I'm headed—straight to hell in a hand basket. 'Course, I never could figure out what a hand basket

looks like.'' All the same, she slid into the backseat. She
crossed first one leg and then the other, massaging the soles
of her scorched feet. Her fingernails were long, sculptured
with acrylic, and bloodred.

"I'm Sergeant Struthers, and this is my partner, Investigator Woodall.'' Dixie smiled, trying to concentrate only on the
girl's eyes. ''And your name?''

''Priscilla. Priscilla Smith. I live just up the street.'' At
odds with her outward appearance, her voice and smile were
sweet, and very young. ''Gretchen and I used to be best
friends.''

''Yes, her mother told us.''

''Yeah, you know, like when we were little, in elementary
school and junior high. Absolutely best friends. *Totally*
together—all the time.''

''So what happened?'' Herb asked. ''Did you go to different high schools or something?''

Priscilla shook her head and shrugged, still rubbing one
foot. ''Nope, we go—*went*—to the same school. We just
didn't get along anymore, not at all. I can't be friends with a
snob. I hate snobs.''

''Was Gretchen Willis a snob?'' Dixie had the most wild
urge to take out a handkerchief and wipe off the child's face,
to see what she really looked like.

''Well, I guess I shouldn't say it, because if I do, then that
means I hated Gretchen, doesn't it? And if I hated her, maybe
you'll think I killed her.'' The dramatic idea evidently struck
Priscilla's funny bone, because she giggled.

''We wouldn't think that,'' Herb assured her, ''but we sure
could use your help. There are a few things we need to know
about Gretchen.''

''Why don't you ask her mother?'' Priscilla's smile turned
sly, almost mean.

''You know how that goes, Priscilla.'' Dixie tried not to
sound patronizing. ''Parents aren't always the ones who know
their kids best.''

''Totally true!'' Priscilla literally cracked up now, hooting
with laughter. ''Sally wouldn't know anything if it came up
and bit her on the ass!''

Her laughter slowly died away. ''Gretchen's mom *wouldn't*
know anything about her. She, Gretchen, hated her mom

worse than anyone. She *always* did, even when we were little.''

''Why?'' Herb thought of his wife and daughter. Somehow, this turn of conversation made his insides hurt.

The teenager in the backseat shrugged again. ''Because she thought her mom was ugly, totally unsexy, and mean. She told me that's why Sally was divorced, why Gretchen had no father. She hated her mom for that. She thought Sally was kind of stupid, too, which I guess she is. Lots of adults are stupid. They think they know everything, every fucking thing, and that's *really* stupid.''

Being stupid adults, neither Dixie nor Herb responded to her comment. Instead, Dixie redirected the conversation. ''Who was Gretchen's best friend in school? She was so pretty, I guess she had lots of friends.''

''No way. The kids hated her, just as much as I did. You see, Gretchen wasn't a very nice person. She thought she was better than everyone else. Prettier. Smarter. Mostly smarter. Smarter than her mom. Smarter than me. The only one who could stand her was Tony Castellano. He and Gretch *might* have been friends. Seems to me like they walked together from class to class once in a while. But he's as bad as she was, so that doesn't count much. Everyone knows he's nothing but a fag, a *drama-geeky* fag.''

Dixie and Herb exchanged a look that mutually, silently agreed not to ask. And when little additional information seemed forthcoming from Priscilla, they drove up the street about half a block and dropped her in front of her house.

''By the way,'' she said, just as she was getting out. ''My friends call my Prissy. You can, too, if you want.''

''Thanks, Prissy.'' Dixie reached out to shake her hand. ''We really appreciate your help. Maybe we'll see you again.''

Once more, fleetingly, a sweet smile shone from beneath the garish mask. ''Maybe.''

After she disappeared inside an almost duplicate version of the Nelson home, Herb rested his head on the back of the car seat, letting out a long, deep breath.

''Lord, Lord, Lord,'' was all he could say.

School had been in session for less than a week. The corridors were a crush of young humanity as students passed from first to second-period classes. Rushed, intent on making class before the bell could ring, the mixed bag of students at Graham High seemed oblivious to all else. The two homicide detectives were crunched together, jostled and pushed, irrespective of their superior age.

Help! Dixie pantomimed the word, gripping Herb's arm for dear life. But within minutes, as if by magic, the hallway was clear. A bell sounded with only a few trotting stragglers caught behind.

A sign just above the detectives' heads read ADMINISTRATION OFFICE. They entered, shaking out their crushed clothing and bodies as they went in.

The principal, Lawrence Stokes, was a tall, dignified man with a patient, beatific smile. Crow's-feet meshed the corners of his light gray eyes. He shook hands and offered them a chair in his office.

"Homicide you say? In that case, I assume you're investigating that horrible Willis thing. Terrible. Just terrible. Gretchen was one of our finest students. I don't believe she's ever gotten so much as a B on her report cards, not in all her years of schooling. A straight 4.0 average. Very difficult. Very unusual."

He opened his top drawer and pulled out a file. "I thought you might be paying us a visit in the course of your investigation, so I've pulled Gretchen's file. She was offered a scholarship, you know, from Stanford University. A humanities scholarship. She was all set."

He riffled through the file, flipping pages, a faint scowl stamped on his face. "Such a shame."

"May I?" Dixie asked.

He hesitated for only a moment. "Yes, of course. I've already called Ms. Nelson, Gretchen's mother. She has given verbal consent to your examination of the records. But then there's no reason why she shouldn't. It's a spotless record. Exemplary."

Dixie and Herb viewed the file together. The examination took little time. There were no juicy frills. No record of misconduct or psychological counseling. Just transcripts, test scores, and similar documents, along with inoculation and health records. A test administered during Gretchen's freshman year listed her I.Q. at 168. In one regard, at least,

Gretchen had been right. She *was* smarter—smarter, according to statistics, than ninety-nine percent of the American population.

According to tests, thought Dixie, who had herself attended Stanford and knew her own I.Q. scores topped even those of Gretchen Willis. Dixie placed very little significance on such testing. She had met more than one unbalanced, unstable, downright unpleasant so-called genius in her time.

She handed the file back to Mr. Stokes. "Thank you. We appreciate your cooperation. Is there anything else you can tell us about the girl, anything at all—who her friends were, teachers or students who might have known her well?"

"Not really, I'm afraid. She was a pretty girl, but to my knowledge she wasn't much of a joiner. I often saw her in the school library during lunch break, always studying, and always alone. I can even remembering thinking how odd it seemed, especially with looks like hers."

The principal absentmindedly patted the front of his suit coat, then reached inside, feeling pockets. "Damn," he muttered. "I keep looking for my pipe. Mind you, I gave it up almost two months ago. Old habits and all that."

Dixie and Herb stood, and he did the same. "There is one teacher who might be of some help, a Ms. Banks," he said. "I've heard her speak of Gretchen often. She adored the girl, couldn't get enough of teaching her, from what I gather. She used to talk about it in the faculty lounge. And there are the other G.A.T.E. youngsters. That's our gifted and talented group, Sergeant Struthers. Most of them are in accelerated classes so they tend to know one another. If you like, I can check through their schedules and arrange for you to speak to those who most often had classes with Gretchen."

"That could help a great deal," Dixie said. "Please, let us know when it can be arranged."

They were almost to the door when Herb spoke. "One other thing, Mr. Stokes. There's a male student here, I think, maybe a member of your school drama group. A boy named Tony?"

"Oh, that would be Tony Castellano. He's been our star performer for the past couple of years. Tony is also gifted. A very bright young man." Stokes's brows knitted. "Surely you don't think *he* is involved in this gruesome business."

"Not at all," Herb assured him. "We simply heard that he and Gretchen were friends. Every little thing helps. We'll interview him at the same time as the others. I don't suppose there is any way to talk to Ms. Banks right now?"

The principal made a brief phone call to another office and then turned his pleasant smile on Dixie and Herb. Each teacher was given one free period for paperwork, he told them, and as good fortune would have it, Susan Banks was right in the midst of hers. He led them through several now placid corridors and into the faculty lounge.

At one table sat a woman in her late thirties. Though she was attractive, there was a faintly haggard air about her.

"I can't begin to tell you how Gretchen's death has affected me," she said, after introductions had been made and Stokes departed. "I've hardly slept a wink since the news reports started. My God, I still can't believe it. Not Gretchen." She looked on the verge of tears.

"Please sit back down," Dixie said. "We'll try not to take too much of your time."

"I'm willing to give whatever time you need." The teacher's voice grew stronger, adamant and angry. "Anything I can do will be little enough. I just hope you catch the . . . the . . . the *slime* that killed her. Whoever it was deserves the most hideous punishment!"

She had been grading test papers, which she now stacked neatly to one side. "So, what is it you need to know?"

"Anything you think might be helpful, Ms. Banks," Herb said. "Like for instance—"

"You can call me Susan."

"Thank you, Susan." His gaze and his smile warmed as he put his country-boy charm into gear, a ploy that often worked well for him when interviewing women. Dixie leaned back in her chair, letting him take the lead. "Now tell me, Susan, what were your impressions of Gretchen? Anything you noticed would help, even your feelings. Did you know her well?"

"Oh, yes, I'd say so. Better than I do most of my students. But then, I don't care to know many of my pupils, not personally. Such a waste of valuable time." She smiled at Herb's slightly startled expression. "Don't look so shocked, Investigator Woodall. Obviously you don't have any teenage children. Of course, you wouldn't have. You're not old enough. Take a good look around this school. Watch most of the youngsters. They're a pretty sorry bunch, I'm afraid."

"They looked pretty normal to me. Just kids, if you know what I mean."

"Oh, I *do* know, and that's exactly it. *Just kids.* Ordinary, everyday kids who do only what they're forced to do and no more. They will get by, and eventually they'll become just your everyday, garden-variety adults."

Herb decided that he might have difficulty keeping his charm in place. The woman was beginning to make him feel like an ordinary, run-of-the-mill head of cabbage.

"I'm a little surprised you chose teaching as a career, Susan, seeing you feel that way."

"I *love* teaching," she assured him. "And I'm damn good at it. My pupils *learn.* They learn, or out they go. I won't waste my energy or my talents on wastrels. And then there are those special few students like Gretchen, who make it all seem worthwhile. I just can't tell you what kind of talent and intelligence that girl possessed. She had an analytical mind and a special gift for research, especially in someone so young. Why, she spent hours each week in the library. She was not just bright—she believed in working hard as well. You won't find another student like her in a thousand, maybe five thousand. All I can tell you is that in over a dozen years I've never held another student in such high esteem." She made that sound like a distinct honor and privilege. "Gretchen made me feel humble, grateful that I had the opportunity to share my knowledge with her."

Dixie was beginning to feel nauseated. It was being smeared on just a bit too thick, she decided. No one, young or old, could be that exceptional.

The teacher looked near tears. "Oh, God! I tell you, it makes me so furious that some maniac could come along and snuff out so bright a light! My poor, poor Gretchen!"

"There now." Herb reached out and patted her hand. "We'll find the person who did this terrible thing. Never you fear."

Her hand was immediately withdrawn, snatched away. She pulled herself primly straight. "Don't patronize me, Investigator Woodall. I am not some foolish old maid who teaches because it's the only option open to me. I chose my profession over and above everything, including marriage. I have something to offer, something I think is rather special, no matter how conceited that sounds."

Herb, who now realized that he had sorely underestimated his quarry, flushed, feeling like an entire vegetable patch.

"How about Tony Castellano?" Dixie asked. "I understand that he and Gretchen were friends."

Susan Banks's lower lip curled downward. "The Castellano boy's intelligence doesn't hold a candle to Gretchen's. He's bright enough, I suppose, but he's also manipulative—gets by to a great extent on his looks. And as for him and Gretchen being friends, I didn't know they were. Now, if there is nothing further . . ."

It was obvious that the teacher's cooperation had evaporated. Her facial expression was closed tight, her body posture rigid.

"No, nothing, Ms. Banks," Dixie said. "Thank you for your time and help."

The detectives rose to leave, but just before turning away Dixie gave in to curiosity. "Would you mind one more question, a personal one?"

Susan Banks's eyes narrowed slightly. "That would depend upon the question, of course."

"What do you suppose makes a very few youngsters so special, so *gifted*?"

"In the opinion of most scientists and educators, Sergeant Struthers, it can be many things, or combinations of things. Environment. The influence of parents and teachers. And, of course, genetics. In fact, I believe that was probably why Gretchen was so advanced. She had the magic formula. She was an only child, which allowed her more than the normal amount of attention. If you've met her mother, then you know the other ingredient is there as well. Ms. Nelson—I believe she uses her maiden name—is an exceptionally bright woman. I never met Gretchen's father, of course, but she had seen pictures of him. She used to talk about how handsome he was. I've met her uncle. He's intelligent, in addition to being a very good-looking man. Quite polite and well mannered. He used to come to school meetings from time to time, and it was quite obvious that he loved Gretchen very much."

"Then, of course, there have been certain *teachers*." Dixie leveled a green-eyed gaze on the other woman, and was rewarded with a small, tight smile.

"Yes, Sergeant, certain teachers indeed."

Dixie and Herb left the faculty lounge, both silent until the door clicked shut behind them. Herb looked at Dixie, wearing an expression of mild surprise.

"Exceptionally bright?" He repeated. "Sally Nelson?"

Dixie continued walking, hoping they would not get caught in another crush. "Sometimes, Herbie, my boy, the exceptionally smart thing to do is not to appear *too* smart."

"Don't call me Herbie, Dix," he grumbled, half distracted. He was still feeling like a giant clod. "You know I hate that. You call me that again and I swear I'll use your middle name—while we're in the squad room."

"Herbert Woodall, don't you dare!" Dixie's exclamatory squeak was not feigned. To have the name she so hated bandied about the police department was her secret nightmare.

Herb grinned, feeling instantly better. He loved watching her get excited; it turned her eyes a lighter shade of green and made her upturned nose bounce up and down. He opened his mouth to tease her again, but quickly snapped it shut as the bell sounded. "Ye gods, Tulip," he yelled, "let's split!"

The detectives beat a hasty retreat from the corridors of Graham High School, with Dixie mumbling heated invective at Herb's back.

The Police Administration Building was cool at last, and as a result, more investigators seemed to be at their desks, doing everything they possibly could by telephone. A mountain of backed-up paperwork was being slowly whittled away. Dixie and Herb took the opportunity to go over crime-scene photographs, all in living color.

"Thank God we didn't have to watch the autopsy for this one," Herb said, his eyes scanning the slick photos. "I hope Pete never sees these."

"He will," Dixie said grimly. "You can bank on it—if not now, then at the trial."

"When is he coming back to work?"

"Day after tomorrow, I think. The service, such as it's going to be, is this evening. Ms. Nelson wants no funeral.

Just an hour or so for her and Pete by the casket. And then the burial tomorrow.''

"Think we should go?"

"Pete says no." Dixie was looking at her own set of pictures, rubbing her forehead as she spoke. "I talked to him on the phone last night, offered any help he might need. But he says that for right now the best thing we can do is stay clear. He's afraid his sister-in-law is going to come unglued if she has to see anyone else. Reporters are hounding her to death.''

Steve Bruner walked into the squad room. He looked around the room, his gaze finally coming to rest on Dixie and Herb. He approached slowly, his posture almost apologetic. "You got the Willis case?"

When Herb nodded, the Juvenile detective perched on the corner of Dixie's desk. "I don't suppose Pete's around?"

"No," Herb answered, "but he'll be back in another day or so. Spatlin needs him, and *he* probably needs to get busy again. Therapy.''

Bruner nodded. "What I really came in for is to . . . well, to tell him I'm sorry. I feel like a heel.''

"There was no way for you to know, Brew." Dixie liked the man. Steve Bruner was a hard-working dick. Overworked. A good, methodical cop with an impossible case load. "Pete understands, I'm sure.''

"He was half crazed when he came to my house. Unshaven. Red-eyed. He nearly scared the hell out of my wife, and she's used to having a bunch of nutty cops around.''

"He was half sick with worry," Herb said. "As it turns out, he had good reason.''

"Not *half* sick, Woodall. I'm telling you, he was right over the edge. Whacked out. But it's like you say—as it turns out, he had good reason. God, what a mess. You got any leads yet?''

"Not a one.''

"Well, for what it's worth, I did run across something.''

Dixie and Herb both snapped to attention.

Bruner looked at them and shrugged. "Don't get your hopes up. It's probably nothing. It's just that I couldn't quite buy it, all that about her having no friends. That's what her mother told me when I took the initial report. I mean, for cryin' out loud, I've been at this a long time. I've seen all kinds, and I'm telling you, the ugliest, meanest, weirdest kids in the world have *someone*.''

"And?'' Herb was leaning forward in his chair. The same disclaimer had been running through his head.

"Gretchen Willis had a hangout.'' Bruner looked a trifle smug, enjoying building a little suspense.

"Don't screw around,'' Herb growled. "If you had seen that girl's body, you would know this case isn't one damn bit of fun, Brew.''

"The library. Gretchen Willis spent a good deal of time at the main branch of the library. For sure she was there on Thursday nights. Every Thursday, from what I gather. Is that any help?''

"How did you find that out?'' Dixie asked. "One of her teachers mentioned her doing research in a library, but we figured she meant the one at school.''

"Probably did that too,'' Bruner said, "but I'm talking about the big one. A kid in her neighborhood told me.'' The Juvenile detective shook his head. "If you want to see a weird one, you'll have to see this kid. She'll give you the shudders for sure.''

"Priscilla Smith.'' Dixie and Herb said the name in unison.

"Yeah, that's her.'' Bruner stood up. "Prissy the Punker. Have you ever seen anything like her in your life?''

"I think I'd take a bullwhip to Amy if she wrecked herself like that,'' Herb answered, and did indeed shudder at the very thought. "Or better yet, a washcloth.''

"Prissy the Punker.'' Dixie chuckled. "That's cute, Brew.''

"I'd like to take the credit, but it's the nickname she gave me. I was doing a canvas of the immediate neighborhood, right after I went out to talk to Gretchen's mother. I knocked on the screen door of this one house and up pops this kid, like a jack-in-the-box. Made me jump. I guess she was lying on the living room floor watching television. 'Hi,' she says, just like some kind of goofy commercial, 'I'm Prissy the Punker. You lookin' for me?' '' Bruner wagged his head. "A real creepy kid.''

"We can question her when we go back to the school tomorrow,'' Herb said. "After a few interviews with the *gifted*, Prissy might offer a little comic relief. You're sure it was the main library, Steve?''

Bruner nodded. "According to Priscilla Smith it was. When I told her that Gretchen Willis was missing and that I was trying to locate her, she seemed to think it was a big joke. She giggled and asked me if I had checked the library. At first I thought she was just being cute again. But she says Gretchen Willis took a bus down there every Thursday afternoon and didn't come home until after the place closed. That would be at nine o'clock at night. A dangerous time to be hanging around a downtown bus stop."

"And did you check?"

"As a matter of fact I did, after Pete Willis paid his little visit to my house. I didn't really have time to chase red herrings, but since it was Pete's niece, I decided to go a little out of my way. The place is huge, of course, but I made a round of each floor, just on the outside chance she might be there. I didn't see her, though, or many other kids for that matter. But then I really didn't expect to, what with it being the last week of summer vacation."

"Did the Smith kid say Gretchen went down even during the summer?" Dixie asked.

"She didn't say one way or the other. She just said every Thursday."

Herb looked at his watch. "We've got time to go down there if you want, Dix. It's after three. Maybe someone who works the evening shift will remember seeing Gretchen, or even give us a line on some of her friends. I go along with Brew on that one—the kid had to have friends."

"I hope it helps," Bruner said, coming to his feet. "As for me, I'm leaving this joint on time today. A few more phone calls to make, and then I'm gone."

He looked around him, hunching his shoulders slightly. "The cool's just great ain't it?"

Dixie and Herb watched him stroll from the room. Even wearing a sport jacket, he was frisking his arms. Someone had obviously jacked the air-conditioning system into high gear. The building was growing frigid.

CHAPTER 8

THE MAIN BRANCH library building was a typical Silicon Valley structure. Four stories high, it was an edifice of arched concrete and big tinted-glass windows. Escalators slid silently from floor to carpeted floor. The carefully climatized air smelled clean, if it smelled at all. But somehow the whole place made Dixie long for her childhood days when, as a high school student, she rode a bus to the San Francisco City Library. She had always loved the less than perfect lighting and the shelf upon towering shelf of thick, musty tomes. Even the library in her stepfather's home, and the one in the rambling southern-style mansion owned by her Grandfather Klien, had held more magic than this one. Dixie felt a twinge of sympathy for modern youngsters and their clean, stark, sanitized world.

"I read an article not long ago," Herb commented, "in one of the architectural magazines. It said things are changing these days, a sort of backlash in building design, I guess you could call it. Architects are returning to the older ideas again. You know, the ones with 'style and grace.' " It was as if he had reached out and plucked the thoughts from Dixie's mind. Obviously he, too, had visited libraries from another era.

Such mental telepathy was becoming more and more common between Dixie and her sandy-haired partner. The longer they worked together, the more often they seemed to be on the same wavelength.

Almost like an old married couple, Dixie thought, chuckling aloud as she remembered their initial, very mutual animosity.

A young woman approached them. She spoke in a soft, lazy voice. "Do you need help?"

After identifying herself and Herb, Dixie showed her a picture of Gretchen Willis.

"Oh." She made a circle of her mouth, staring at the photo as if mesmerized. "This is that poor girl who was found at the Winchester Mystery House, huh? Jeez, what a rotten thing. Disgusting."

Her eyes were avid, brimming with curiosity. "I've read all about that place. I bet it was creepy finding her there, huh?"

"Not very pleasant," Dixie replied dryly. "Do you remember ever seeing her here, like on a regular weekly basis?"

"Not really, but then I wouldn't. I'm just part-time. The woman normally here is on vacation. Did you ask the check-out counter?"

Dixie nodded. She and Herb had covered most of the regular employees, a floor at a time. One man, who did indeed sit at the computerized checkout counter, seemed to remember seeing Gretchen Willis from time to time, but he didn't connect her with a particular day, or with anyone else.

"So," Herb said as the girl, sensing that no other information would be forthcoming, left them alone again, "another blind alley."

"I guess, but we'll come back to see the regular reference librarian all the same—especially if nothing turns up tomorrow."

"You know, Dix, this is really beginning to bug me. She *had* to have friends. Not just because she was Pete's niece, or because she was smart and pretty. Because she was *human*, for God's sake."

"Something will turn up. It always does. Meanwhile, I'm going home. Art's supposed to be coming for dinner. I wish I was more in the mood. I haven't been feeling very social lately, not since this thing started."

Herb noticed none of the usual enthusiasm in her voice when she mentioned Art Cochran, and after they had returned to the car and were en route to the police department, he gave her a long sideways glance

"Everything okay with you and Art?"

"Sure." Dixie kept her voice light. "We just don't always find the same subjects interesting. He's a crop duster and a stunt pilot. I'm a cop. Not exactly the most compatible careers in the world."

Herb continued to look at her. "Hmm."

She did not look away from the road. "Do me a favor, Herb?"

"Anything."

"Don't start."

"I got a call from your mother today."

They were sitting on the long back porch, with no light except what came through the kitchen windows. Reversa and Patrick could be heard indoors, wrangling away. Poke's massive head rested on Art's knee. It had been a pleasant meal. A nice visit with no heavy overtones.

"She called *you*?" Dixie could not mask her surprise.

Art's smile shined in the darkness. "Yes. I could hardly believe it myself. If anyone had asked me, I would have said Rose didn't care for me much."

"She doesn't dislike you, I'm sure. How could she? She's only met you two or three times."

What Dixie did not say aloud was that in all probability Rose Klein Flannigan Marks, her indomitable mother, did not like him. Rose never cared for Dixie's friends. Or, rather, she *disapproved* of most of them. If she had made a personal call to Art, it was with some scheme in mind.

"Well, anyhow, the old girl called," Art continued. "She wanted to know if we would like to attend a party at the end of the month, the twenty-eighth, I think she said."

Already in a prickly mood, Dixie felt unreasonably irritated. "What party and for what gala occasion?" she snapped. "And if she wants me, or us, to come somewhere, why didn't she come right out and ask *me*?"

Art took a sip of coffee, watching her over the rim of his mug. "Which question shall I answer first?"

"Sorry, Art." She was instantly contrite. The case was making her jumpy, on top of which, her mother always seemed to bring out the most unattractive side of her personality. "It's just that you don't understand how my mother works. I love her, truly and deeply, but most of the time she drives me right up a tree."

"Don't suppose I could drive you over here onto my lap?"

Her cheek dimpled as she threw him an impish smile. "Not until you tell me what Mother has cooking. I know her; she always has *something* up her sleeve."

Art hesitated, then spoke in a rush. "A birthday celebration for your fath—" He corrected himself at the last moment, ". . . for your stepfather. Now close your mouth, Struthers, and just listen for a minute, will you?"

Her smiled had vanished. "Whatever you say."

"Look, Dixie, I know the two of you don't particularly get along, but he's going to be sixty years old. Ryan is his son and your little brother. Why not bury the hatchet, even if it's just for kid's sake?"

"I'm telling you, you don't understand, Art. There is no hatchet. I don't hate Franklin Marks, and I'm sure he doesn't dislike me either. We simply have nothing in common. He looks at the world through lofty, green-colored glasses. *Money green*. There are other things more important to me. A lot more important. Franklin and I just don't look at life the same way. You wouldn't like him, Art, I promise you that. He would make you uncomfortable."

But the words had no sooner left Dixie's mouth than she knew they were untrue. Nobody made Art Cochran uncomfortable. He didn't care about the opinions of others. That was just one more of the many things she liked about him.

"I'm not thinking of your stepdad so much as your mom. She really wants you there. And so does Ryan. Franklin Marks is one of the things you and he have in common, right?"

"Do you want to go?" She didn't want to discuss her family life with him.

"Sure, I guess so."

"Black tie and all? Because that's what it's going to be."

He hesitated.

"Well, come on, Art."

"Oh, what the hell. Want to fly up in the Stearman?"

Even in the semidarkness Dixie could see the devilish

sparkle in his blue eyes, the darling naughty-boy smile. "Only if you think you can set it down in Franklin's front yard." She laughed. "Never mind. I take that back. You might try."

"Come over here," he growled, patting Poke off his lap.

Dixie went gladly, curling into his lap, snuggling her head up under his chin. He was such a comfortable man. A man she enjoyed being with and talking to—except about one subject. There seemed always to be the one unspoken taboo. At times, like lately, she needed to talk about her work, and the case that was so constantly, so relentlessly on her mind.

"Oh, Art, there are times when . . ." Her words and the thoughts they represented trailed into silence.

He held her, running a warm hand up and down her back, smelling the sweet perfume of her hair. He was almost afraid to speak, for fear of breaking the spell. Lately, with the strain creeping into their relationship, he had felt he was walking on eggshells. It was not a feeling he liked. Fear of any kind went against his nature. But then, Dixie was like no woman he had ever met. He wanted her. Permanently. Completely. And he was smart enough not to say so.

"I'll be glad when this case is over. It's giving me nightmares—such a *dirty* case," she said, letting him know that even now he did not have all of her. Testing him.

I don't want to hear about the damn case, he thought. *I love her, but I hate her work. Not a fun job. Definitely not fun.* "How's Pete doing," he asked, trying to sound interested.

"About as you might expect—angry and devastated. Having someone you love killed is bad enough, but Gretchen was mutilated. Pete is ripped up. He looks terrible. He wants this case solved, wants to see the killer brought in—yesterday."

"Understandable." Art's stomach muscles were tightening.

Dixie pushed a little away from him. "Art, I hope you're not being patronizing."

The kitchen light suddenly snapped off, leaving them in total darkness.

"I'm not being patronizing, Dixie. Promise. I just feel too relaxed to think about mayhem."

He pulled her back and kissed her. The warmth of his lips temporarily put all else from her mind. "Sometimes, I think I love you, Art Cochran."

"We're getting closer." He kissed her again. Longer and harder. "Next, you'll *know* you love me."

She nuzzled his nose, remembering their earlier conversation. "Don't try to use your wiles on my mother, me darlin'. That wicked little Irishwoman has something up her sleeve, and if you don't fall in with her grand plan, she might cut you up and eat you for Sunday brunch."

"Maybe she's going to try to trick me into marrying her daughter." Art's voice was low.

Dixie shook her head. "Nope. The only way she would do that is if she thought you could make me give up what *I* do."

A shaft of moonlight broke through the surrounding pines, lighting Art's face. Dixie quickly kissed him, pretending she had not seen his eyes.

Just before going to work the next morning, Dixie picked up the ringing telephone to hear her mother's voice chirp into her ear. The call would not have been a surprise in any case, since Rose called every week. But this one was more predictable than usual, especially after her exchange with Art the night before.

"How are you, dear?" Rose's voice radiated a forced good cheer.

"Uptight, actually," Dixie answered, hoping against hope that her mother would take the hint. "You've caught me just on my way out the door."

"You sound tired."

She did it every time, zeroed right in on the truth.

"I am, a little." Dixie did not add that she was having bad dreams, terrible nightmares.

"Oh, yes, I read about that gruesome case of yours. It hit the *Chronicle*, and the *Examiner* too. Really, darling, I don't see how you stand it. All the blood and guts, day after day, week after week."

Rose's chirp was beginning to scratch like a broken record on Dixie's nerves. *Peck, peck, peck.* "I stand it because I'm paid to stand it, Mother. That's what I do for a living, remember?"

"It would be hard to forget," Rose quipped. "But for once I didn't call to nag at you. Have you seen that nice young crop duster of yours lately?"

Somehow, to hear Rose refer so sweetly to Art, gave Dixie cold chills. "Yes, last night, as if you didn't already know. I got your invitation."

"Wonderful! We'll be expecting you then."

"We'll try to make it."

"Now, Dixie, don't start, please. I can hear that stubborness creeping into your voice already."

"Well, maybe it wouldn't be if I knew what *you're* creeping up to, Mother. Why the sudden interest in Art?"

"Not so sudden. I'm interested in any young man you see for such an extended period of time. That is a mother's perogative, don't you think?"

"I suppose." Dixie could not shake her suspicion that dangerous currents were swirling about beneath the convoluted workings of her mother's brain.

"So you'll come?"

"If this case I'm working on is cleared, maybe."

"At the risk of sounding like a harpy, I will remind you that it is hardly necessary for you to work at all. Your Grandfather Klien saw to that. You don't have to go and earn your bread, so to speak."

"Yes, I do, Mother. I have to very, very much, especially right now."

"Out saving the world, are you?" There was more than a faint hint of sarcasm in Rose's voice.

"No, just a little tiny part of it, when I'm lucky." Dixie sighed, wishing she could save one particular friend from the pain she knew he was suffering. "I have to go, Mother. I'm late."

"All right, dear. Just don't be late to your father's party." She spoke quickly, giving Dixie no time to respond. "Bye-bye."

"Good-bye, Mother."

"And Dixie?"

"Yes?"

"I love you."

A soft click sounded in Dixie's ear.

CHAPTER 9

THERE WERE ONLY a dozen students who had consistently shared classes with Gretchen Willis. And of those, only a few had more than casual, nondescript comments about her. She was *nice*. She was *quiet* and *shy*. She stayed pretty much to herself.

One girl was faintly critical. "Sometimes, just once in a while," she said, half apologetically, "Gretchen could really hurt a person's feelings. I don't think she meant to be mean or anything. She was just kind of well . . . stuck up, you know? She was real smart, but I think she knew it. Knew she was extra smart and pretty."

"Like maybe she was better than other people?" Dixie suggested.

"Yes." The girl blushed as if ashamed to slander the dead. "Exactly like that, but not always. Most of the time she was just quiet, but you got the feeling she was always watching you, listening to everything you said."

Another student, Ronald Gibson, was more forthcoming. He seemed completely at ease, and was the epitome of a future California yuppie. Bright, blond, and good-looking, he wore expensive sneakers, a cashmere v-neck sweater over a button-down oxford shirt, and a pair of jeans that had been faded to perfection.

"She was a really *rad* chick." He used the teenage slang facetiously, showing Dixie and Herb a row of white, very even teeth. "She was awesome-looking too. Extremely. But she was also a space cadet."

"Space cadet?" Herb looked confused.

"Sure, way out on Pluto somewhere, if you know what I mean. I know that I maybe shouldn't say anything, since she's dead and all, but it's kind of creepy when you stop to think about it. The way she was killed, I mean. Gretchen was really into that stuff. *Culty.* So I have to admit I wasn't shocked out of my gourd or anything when I read about her in the paper."

"You thought she might get killed?" For the first time since they had started interviewing the students, Dixie felt they were being given some hint of direction, the shadow of a clue.

"No, of course not. But the way she got killed creeped me out. It matched her personality. Do you know she did a whole term paper on that kind of stuff for Banks's class? A World Cultures project. She called it 'The Celtic Heritage,' I think, but what it really was was Druid beliefs, and what followed— you know, witchcraft. She really got into it too. Drew out diagrams of these weird shapes, gave recipes for potions even. Talked about the Old Ones and how they used to go into their Scared Groves, feeding the earth blood and all that garbage. Everyone was getting a little sick, even if it had probably taken her hours and hours to do it all. I shouldn't knock it, though. Old Ms. Banks popped an A for that one. And she almost never gives a perfect grade."

"Gretchen was into witchcraft?" Herb asked, feeling the first tinglings of a lead.

"I don't think so, not really. You would have had to know Gretchen. A thing like witchcraft would have been too primitive and uneducated for her. In class once, after she did that report—in fact, I think it was the next semester—she talked about how 'metaphysical phenomena' existed, really existed, and how it had to be properly used by the 'whole brain.' She said it could be directly correlated to religion, but not as it was practiced by the 'mundane.' How's that for spacey? If you want my opinion, I think she was on the road to firing up her own private cult. A new variety."

"Did you know Gretchen well?" Dixie asked. "Date her perhaps?"

"No." The boy answered slowly, no longer flip. "I tried once, because even though she was a little out to lunch, she was pretty, with a body that could make a guy go crazy. So I did ask her out, but she just looked at me with those big blue eyes and asked how I would feel about an out-of-body experience. She creeped me out, the way she looked at me, like maybe she was already out there somewhere."

Of the G.A.T.E. students, they held Tony Castellano until the very end, hoping that last would prove best. On that score they were disappointed. The boy was more than just good-looking. Older in appearance than his seventeen years, he had the kind of face most women would turn to stare at. He wore a polo shirt in a light shade of aqua which complimented his olive complexion as well as showing off a beautiful, carefully encouraged and maintained physique. He moved like a dancer, slowly and gracefully, but completely without feminine overtones. Rather, there was a subtle power in this stride, all masculine. His voice was well-modulated. He spoke proper English and kept his thick-lashed eyelids half lowered, never quite meeting their eyes.

Herb began the questioning. "Hi, Tony, sorry to take you out of class."

"I don't mind." The boy sat down at a front desk in the empty classroom.

"We hear you're a big star in drama here at Graham." Herb's voice sounded patronizing, even to him.

"I'm not a big star as long as I'm only acting at Graham High School."

"Is that what you want to be, an actor?"

"Maybe. Someday. After I've finished college and had the right kind of training. To become really good, you have to have a good coach, and an agent. It takes time—and a lot of luck." He did not use his hands when he talked. The small animation he exhibited was accomplished only by inflections in his voice. No body language at all.

"We need to ask you a few questions about Gretchen Willis," Dixie told him. "We understand that you two were friends. You know what's happened to her?"

"Yes, it's terrible, but someone must be mistaken. We weren't friends, not close friends, anyway. We just knew each other."

"You didn't occasionally walk her from class to class, or have lunch with her?"

The sooty lashes flicked up and then dropped again. "We walked to class together sometimes. From Trig to History, that sort of thing. *Together*. It wasn't like I was walking her to class. We had some of the same classes, that's all." A pulse was beating hard at the cleft of his throat, clearly visible beneath his open collar. "I was sorry to hear about what happened to her. Gretchen seemed like a nice kid."

"What sort of things did you and Gretchen talk about, Tony?" Dixie asked her questions quietly, as quietly as he answered.

"Not much. She was pretty shy. Once, I remember, we discussed Ms. Banks, our World Cultures teacher. That's a history class."

"She and Ms. Banks seem to have been quite close."

Tony Castellano's eyes opened wider again, and this time they stayed that way. "Gretchen *hated* Ms. Banks. Everyone does. She's a bitch."

"But she gave Gretchen an A in her class, and she speaks—"

"So what?" The boy was now clearly irritated. "Gretchen *earned* the grades she got from the old bat. Banks always picks a pet, and it's usually a girl too. Last year it just happened to be Gretchen Willis."

"You never went with Gretchen you say? You never met her away from the school, never went anywhere together?"

Tony stood up. He looked at his watch and then smiled. "I already told you, I hardly knew her. We certainly weren't boyfriend and girlfriend. I'm sorry that someone killed—that she's dead. But I hardly knew her." He looked at Herb. "Can I go now? I'm missing my P.E. class. We're pressing today, and I need the workout."

After he had been excused to leave, Herb turned to Dixie. "Do you buy that one?"

She shook her head. "No, but I'd give my right arm to get a little more verifiable corroboration about his relationship with Gretchen. So far all we have is the hint from Priscilla Smith, and frankly I don't think she is the most reliable—"

A voice echoed into the room. "Mr. Stokes says you want to talk to me." Prissy's head poked through the door.

Both Dixie and Herb jumped in their seats. It was almost impossible to hide being startled.

"Speak of the very one," Herb mumbled under his breath.

The floppy mane of black-and-purple hair no longer hung down on Prissy's forehead. She had obviously "dressed" for school, spiking the ridge of hair into a fan, cockatiel style. She wore high-topped tennis shoes in fluorescent green with thin black socks and leggings. A spiked wristband graced one arm, and a copper bracelet the other. Her long, oversize shirt of green-and-yellow flannel hung nearly to her knees, multibelted in black leather and chain. She still wore her outlandish earrings, but had added a spiked collar, a bowser torque, and a wide variety of plastic beads and base-metal baubles. She jangled as she bounced into the room.

"Hello, Priscilla." Dixie swallowed her urge to laugh. "How are you today?"

Prissy slouched into one of the desk chairs. "It's a pisser being back here. I hate high school. But I keep talkin' to myself. One more year, I say, one more friggin' year."

"So you're not going to college?" Herb asked.

"Oh, yeah, I'm going all right." She giggled, and chewed harder on the wad of gum in her mouth. "I'm going to the college my dad recommends, his old alma mater—the school of hard knocks. He likes the idea of me going to that school."

"Actually, it's a better school than many," Dixie said, without returning her smile.

"I suppose this is about Gretchen. I saw Tony leaving. Looked pale as a ghost. Guess having to talk to you brought *him* down to earth. What a geeky fag!"

"You don't like him?" The question came from Herb, who had the feeling that in actuality she liked him very much—or had at one time.

"I already told you, I hate geeks, especially the ones in drama class. They're so phony they make me sick." She looked around the room and folded her arms across her chest. "In fact, I don't like any of the kids you've been talking to in here. They're not all in drama, but all of them are stuck up and phony—just too good for the rest of us lowly types."

"Prissy, how do you know that Tony and Gretchen were

friends?'' Dixie concentrated on the girls eyes to keep from being distracted. ''He says they just knew each other from the classes they shared, and that's all.''

''Yeah, like from kindergarten. Tony went to the same elementary school and junior high that Gretchen and I did. He's had lots of classes with her. Lots. Maybe they weren't boyfriend and girlfriend. I didn't say they were for sure, did I?''

''No, you didn't.''

''You know, it's not like I'm glad Gretch is dead or anything.''

''I'm sure you're not. The thing is, Prissy, we're having a real problem with our investigation, and we need your help because you're one of the few people who seems to have known Gretchen at all.''

''Not anymore. I mean, we haven't been friends since we were young, like since forever.''

''But you seem to know how she was, what kind of person, the kind of things she did.''

''Word gets around.'' Prissy gnawed the edge of one long fingernail. A loud snap sounded as the acrylic cracked.

''Like, for instance, about the library? Right after Gretchen turned up missing, you told Sergeant Bruner that she went to the library a lot.''

''Yeah, and I didn't mean *the* Library, either. Did you know there's a club downtown called that? It's neat. Every Thursday is punker night. They let kids in too. If you're not old enough to drink, they just stamp your hand. Neat, huh?'' Prissy giggled again. ''Neat name. When your folks ask you where you're going, you just tell 'em to the library. I used to tell my folks that. I'd tell them I was going with Gretchen. That way if they called to check up on me, her mother would back me up without realizing it. That happened once. Dad thought he could trap me. He called Gretchen's house and asked for her. But guess what? She was at the library!''

Dixie and Herb both knew of the club, and even of the special punker night, but it never occurred to them to connect such a place with Gretchen Willis.

''So, did Gretchen go there sometimes too?''

''Of course not, especially not on Thursdays—not anytime, I don't think. Not even on regular nights. But it was great, that's all, the fact that she just happened to go to the real library every Thursday. Made my life a little easier.''

"Who did she go with?"

"Alone, probably. She usually took the bus. I don't know if you've found out yet, but Gretchen wasn't very popular. These phonies you've been talking to probably won't say that, but it's true. Gretchen was too stuck-up to be popular, and that's pretty damn stuck-up. She was even too stuck-up for the rah-rahs—you know, the cheerleader types. She was even too stuck-up for them. What a fuckin' hypocrite!''

"Why do you say that, Prissy. Why was Gretchen a hypocrite?''

Prissy shrugged and her face closed up like a clam. "No reason.''

"There must be some reason," Dixie insisted. "You've called her that more than once.''

"No, it's just that she acted so all *goody*." Prissy's eyes were suspiciously bright, as if she might be fighting tears. "And good people don't treat other people rotten, do they?''

One single tear spilled from her eyes, leaving a pink rivulet in her dead white makeup.

"So, what do you think?" Dixie asked. "Except for finding out about Gretchen's unusual special class projects, I feel like we're still dancing on square one.''

"Make it square one and a half," Herb said. "I think Priscilla Smith was right about the Castellano kid. I think he and Gretchen were tight. Maybe even going together.''

"Me, too, but our Prissy the Punker is mistaken about him being a fag. Tony Castellano is not gay. I sensed some very strong drives in that young man. Very strong. And all beneath the surface. He's hiding something, no doubt about it, but it could that he's just frightened. It was a frightening kind of murder. I have to admit that it's getting to me, causing me a few lost hours of sleep. I keep seeing that body, and Pete's face.''

"Join the club. I'll be damn glad when this one is over.''

CHAPTER 10

Tony Di Franco met them as they entered the squad room. He was wearing his suit jacket, straightening his tie, preparing to leave for the weekend.

"Glad I caught you two," he said. "I need a quick update on the Willis case, something for the press. How's it coming?"

"At the moment, it isn't," Dixie answered, putting her purse and briefcase on her desk. "Just a couple of very nebulous leads."

"For instance?"

"Nothing concrete, Tony. I mean, certainly nothing you would want released to the media. Like I said, very nebulous at this point. There is a boy, maybe a boyfriend, and we have some reason to think that Gretchen Willis may have been involved in some sort of cult, possibly even trying to start a new one all her own. But we certainly can't be positive. If it wasn't for the condition of her body, we probably wouldn't even bother to check it out."

"How would you feel about me just hitting the surface of the occult thing? The reporters are hounding me, and you never can tell, a story like that might even flush something out of the woodwork."

"I don't suppose it would hurt anything," Dixie finally answered, "but don't blow it out of proportion. Remember, I said 'may have been involved.' The only thing we know for sure is that she had a more than passing interest in the metaphysical.''

"So what?" Pete Willis entered right on the tail end of her sentence, and he wasn't really asking a question.

With the exception of Jake Spatlin, all the detectives on the homicide team were in, and they turned at the sound of Pete's voice. He was wearing a black suit.

Dixie took a step toward him, but the dark expression on his face stopped her in her tracks.

"Gretchen was a nice normal kid, just a bit brighter than the average, that's all." He addressed his comments to Dixie alone. "Actually, she was a lot brighter. Don't go throwing any extra crap into this case, Dixie. Please, just don't."

He turned bloodshot eyes on Di Franco. "And I'd appreciate it very much, sir, if you don't give the press any extra bones to chew on. Things are already miserable enough."

Di Franco cleared his throat. "Hello, Pete. Glad to see you're okay. How about coming into the office for a couple of minutes."

Pete followed their superior without looking at Dixie or Herb again. His shoulders were hunched and he moved slowly, as if he were in physical pain.

"He shouldn't be here," Herb said, as Dixie settled herself at her own desk. "He looks like death on a soda cracker."

Dixie nodded, but before she could comment further, Jake walked in. His eyes went to Di Franco's office and then to Dixie and Herb. "He's back to work already?"

Delaney and Brooks got up and walked over to Dixie's desk. Pat Delaney spoke around his cigar. "Look, it's probably not too cool for us to congregate like this, jawing about Willis and his problems. Too much like a hen party. I suggest we get together somewhere, and the sooner the better. Pete called me today, asking all kinds of questions about the case, things he knew damn well he shouldn't ask. I smell trouble brewing."

Jake shot a quick, almost furtive glance at his watch. "I'm up for it. What say we all meet at the Baron Hotel in about an hour? In the coffee shop?"

Dispersing as quickly as they had gathered, Delaney and Brooks went back to their desks, drifting out a few minutes later, seemingly leaving for the weekend. Jake Spatlin hung around longer, waiting for Pete to exit Di Franco's office. He need not have bothered.

Pete left the lieutenant's office, closing the door deliberately behind him. He left the squad room without a word to or glancing at anyone.

"I'll go along with Delaney on this one," Jake told Dixie and Herb once Pete was out of sight. "My partner looks like a walking stick of dynamite. Still spooky."

Herb nodded. "I don't think I've ever seen him walk by Struthers without giving her one of his puppy-dog smiles."

"Knock it off, Herb." Dixie respected Pete and wanted no reminders of the debt he still thought he owed her. It had been an incident in the Dunkin' D Donut Shop. She had killed a man that night—in police vernacular, had "made her bones." For Dixie it was nothing to joke about.

"I wasn't wisecracking, Dix," Herb said. "Just making light with a heavy subject."

She looked up, saw Di Franco motion to her, and headed toward his office with a sense of relief. The last thing she needed at the moment was a verbal dual with her partner.

Herb watched her go with mingled feelings. There were times when the pert, green-eyed detective irritated him beyond belief. She was a great cop, a damn good investigator, but she was also a headstrong, stubborn woman. Outrageously beautiful. Feminine without pretense. A *rare* woman.

He knew that her first weeks in the homicide bureau had been difficult. He remembered her as she had been, all business, ultra reserved, right down to the way she dressed. Business suits. A bun on top of her head. He remembered, too, thinking that she wasn't bad-looking—just a bit overly prim and proper. But something had happened not long after he started working with her. Something spectacular. Almost overnight she seemed to stop caring what the other investigators thought of her, or whether or not she fit into the austere, unacknowledged mold expected of female police officers. In short, she seemed to give up all pretense of trying to blend in with her male colleagues.

Remembering the metamorphosis, Herb smiled. They had been investigating a bizarre murder, the death of a beauty salon proprietor named Charles Bouchard. Dixie had trans-

formed herself that night, changing in what seemed the twin-
kling of an eye from a straightlaced "lady" into an auburn-
haired bombshell. And she had not reverted since. Any stranger
looking at Dixie would have been more likely to dub her a
model than a cop. She dressed and carried herself with a
verve previously unseen in the hallowed halls of the SJPD.

The coffee shop at the Baron Hotel was a favorite Code 7
stop for police officers. Much too favorite, as far as the brass
were concerned. Time and again officers had been warned to
thin it out and not congregate. It looked bad to see five
black-and-whites in the parking lot at the same time. But the
warnings never carried weight for very long. The food was
too good, especially at half price—a small gratuity appreciated
by officers on a tight budgets, but equally abhorred by Police
Chief Quinn. Quinn ran a tight ship and a clean department.
He ordered memos sent. They were heeded for a week or two
and then ignored.

But the detectives sitting in one of the large booths in a far
corner of the restaurant were in plainclothes. Except for Dixie
and Herb, they were all presently off duty. They liked the
food well enough to pay full price.

Amidst the restaurant sounds, the muted clatter of dishes,
and the hum of conversation around them, they discussed the
dilemma of Pete Willis.

"He's gonna get his ass in trouble if we don't watch him,"
Delaney said. "I can see it coming. Pete loved that kid like
she was his own—loved her maybe too much."

"I would be exactly the same way," Bill Brooks argued.
"If a thing like that happened to one of my kids, even a niece
or nephew, I'd be spitting fire, sticking my long nose right
into the middle of things."

"Yeah, and you'd find yourself reassigned too," Delaney
answered. "We've got to find some way to settle that boy
down. He needs to be close enough to know things are being
done. Otherwise he'll pop a cork. But we've also got to keep
him from following in behind Struthers and Woodall."

He looked across the table at them. "More important, we
need to keep him from getting in front of you. It'll be bad
news if Pete gets to this guy before you do. That happens,
he'll become one of our cases."

Dixie nodded and took another quick sip of her coffee. "Part of the problem might be solved easily enough. Pete's name came up while I was talking to Di Franco." She looked at Delaney. "You're right, Pete is in a bad frame of mind. The leuy says he nearly begged to have the case signed over to him, even though he knows damn well it's impossible. Or at least he would know if he was thinking straight—which he isn't. Pete is making the boss real nervous."

"So he's getting reassigned?" Herb asked. "God, Dixie, that will tear him up. Pete was so proud when he made the unit."

Dixie shook her head. "Di Franco isn't taking action, not yet anyway, but he wants to keep Pete on whichever shift we happen to be working, which is swing relief right now. Di Franco thinks that will help, keep temptation down. We can't afford to have Pete dogging our trail. It will be Jake's job to mind the leash."

Thinking of his active love life, Jake Spatlin groaned, but not loudly nor for long. "Oh, what the hell, they'll just have to wait."

"Who'll have to wait?" Brooks fell into it, giving Jake just the opportunity he wanted.

The tall black man grinned. "All those little nurses down at the County Hospital of course. Now I'm talkin' some *sweeet* stuff, no scooby-do. Why, just last night—"

"Give us a break, okay, Spatlin?" Dixie rolled her eyes but was not really offended. Long ago she had learned that if she wanted the acceptance of her peers, she would have to develop a thick hide. "Let's just get on with it. Herb and I have other fish to fry. We're still on duty, remember?"

"Yeah, well, I don't mind nights for a while, is what I'm saying. Chances are we'll get enough to keep us plenty busy. That might make it easier for me to keep a leash on the kid." Jake sobered. "I like Pete. He's a good man, a good investigator. I feel for the man."

Herb cleared his throat. "Try not to care too much. Don't let him talk you into any stupid moves."

"What's that supposed to mean?" Jake looked offended. "Do I look like a rookie to you?"

"Stow it," Delaney growled. "Remember Smitty Saunders? A few years ago? Some guy molested his little girl and he went nuts, nearly got his hooks on one of the suspects—the wrong one. Got his ass shipped out of the Sexual Assault Unit in double time. Lucky he didn't get fired. He wasn't a rookie either. Neither was Harley Dayton, his partner. Both of them almost bit the dust over that little episode. That's what happens when a cop's family gets victimized. It's just—''

"Okay, okay. I don't need a lecture, Papa Bear." Jake turned dark eyes on Dixie. "I feel like you could help out with this more than anyone else. Why don't you collar him, Dix? You're the one person he might listen to. Everyone knows how he feels about you, how grateful he is.''

Dixie flushed slightly. "What do you want me to do, Spatlin, remind him?" She shook her head. "Nope. We'll *all* work on keeping Pete out of trouble. As much as I hate saying it, I don't think he should be allowed to read the reports. We've got a couple of new leads, and I don't want Pete coming in behind us to muddy the waters. Keep him away from all written reports. Herb and I will keep our notes with us or under lock and key.''

After everyone nodded, she turned her attention back to Jake. "What have you got going right now? Anything absorbing?''

The other investigator shook his head. "A bar stabbing, with plenty of witnesses. Pretty straightforward stuff. We just have to put our hands on the suspect, but it might keep us a little busy for the next few days. I'd drag it out longer if I could, but I don't want our suspect to split. I don't think he will. Too stupid. I'm pretty sure he's still here, over in the deep east side somewhere. Like I said, a few days work, tops.''

"Then for those days at least, Herb and I have a clear field.''

Once more nods went around the table, and for the next several minutes conversation swung to other things. What none of the investigators noticed was the lone man sitting at a smaller table on the far side of the coffee shop. He held a newspaper in front of his face, watching the homicide dicks over the top edge with a pair of weary, grief-and-guilt-stricken eyes.

CHAPTER 11

HERB WALKED INTO the quiet squad room alone, and to his surprise, found Doty Bangor still there. She was holding a mirror in one hand, fluffing her curly blond hair with the other. When she saw him, she pursed her lips. "Well, howdy-do, if it isn't Herbie the hunk. Lost the little woman, did we?"

"Only temporarily. She's visiting the cat box." Herb smiled at the disgusted look she threw him. "What are you doing here, besides lying in wait for some poor unsuspecting rookie?"

She was just about to answer when the phone rang. Doty picked it up as a matter of habit, but realizing that she was off work, her sultry southern voice held an edge of impatience. After listening for a moment, she put the caller on hold, still holding the receiver. "Herbie," she drawled, "this lady wants to speak with Sergeant Struthers. Would you mind taking it so poor little Doty can, like split? I'm late, I'm late, for a very hot date."

"Ah-ha, so some unsuspecting rookie is going to bite the dust! And who, pray, is the lucky young fellow?"

"That's none of your business." She smiled seductively. "But I don't mind giving you a tiny hint. He's not a rookie, not with the slim pickin's from that last academy class. I've temporarily switched to investigators. You want I should put your name on the list?''

"Alas, I think my wife would object, but I think I know just the man, a long, lean detective who would probably give his very soul. I heard somewhere that Jake Spatlin has been eating his heart out to—''

Doty slammed the phone down on the desk, stood and snatched up her handbag. "Fuck you, Herbie. Now, take this damn call!''

Herb pushed the button and lifted the receiver, waving good-bye as Doty made her exit and threw him an obscene gesture just as she rushed out the door.

"Investigator Woodall.'' He spoke into the telephone. "May I help you?''

"I'm not quite sure,'' answered a hesitant feminine voice. "The card I'm holding says Detective Sergeant D. T. Struthers. It's about . . . about the little Willis girl—the one who was killed?''

Herb reached for pen and tablet. "My name is Investigator Woodall. I'm Sergeant Struthers's, partner, Miss . . .''

"Ms. Jackabcin. Lillian Jackabcin. I work at the downtown library. The girl who helped out while I was away gave me this card. I've been out of town, you see. My mother has been ill. But I read about that terrible thing in the paper when I came back. I thought I had better call.''

"You knew Gretchen Willis?'' Herb jotted down the woman's name.

"I may not have known her well, but I recognized her name and her picture at once. I tell you, it made me want to cry. She was a regular at the library, she and her friends. See what happens when children meddle in dark, evil things— things beyond human understanding? Oh, it's just terrible!''

Herb's pulse picked up, giving him that small spurt of adrenaline he always felt whenever he knew he was on to a good lead. "We appreciate you calling, Ms. Jackabcin. The best thing would probably be for us to come and speak to you in person. Maybe I could make an appointment now?''

"That will be fine, I'm sure. In fact, I'm working until nine this evening. I don't suppose you and your partner could come by? I live in Gilroy, you see, and it's such a long way for me to come—''

"No problem," he assured her. "We can be there in less than fifteen minutes. Say about eight?"

"That would be perfect, Investigator Woodall, just perfect. Good bye."

After she hung up, Herb sat staring out the window, wrapped in thought. He didn't see Dixie come into the room, and when she lightly tapped his shoulder, he nearly jumped out of his skin.

She laughed at the scowl on his face. "A little nervous, are we?"

"Cripes, Dix!"

He was glad to see her back to normal. He loved her laugh, and her smile, and her bright, inquisitive mind. He told her about the call, and saw the answering light of excitement in her green eyes.

"Let's move it, partner," she said, "and keep our fingers crossed that this is the break we've been waiting for!"

Friday evenings were quiet at the library. Few patrons sat at the reading tables on the second floor, but Lillian Jackabcin was at her desk, going through a card file, looking every straight-spined inch like a stereotype of her profession. Her long salt-and-pepper hair was twisted into a tight knot on top of her head. She wore gold-rimmed glasses and little if any cosmetics. Her dark suit covered a white blouse, which was buttoned neatly to her neck and garnished with an old cameo brooch. Her most startling feature was a pair of large, kindly blue eyes, eyes that shone with sadness as she stood to shake hands with Dixie and Herb.

"I've hardly been able to concentrate on my work," she said. "Just thinking about that little girl makes me want to cry. Have you any idea yet who could have done such a savage thing?" She shivered. "So horrible!"

"We have a few leads, Ms. Jackabcin," Dixie answered, "but nothing solid. We're hoping you might be able to help."

"Anything I can do, of course." The woman nodded, straightening her posture even more. "I've always thought of myself as a good citizen. That's one reason I called, but also because I care. Why don't we sit over here at a table?"

Leading the way to a round reading table, she motioned to

another employee—the same young woman who had talked to Herb and Dixie on their first visit—to take her place at the reference desk.

"I swear," the librarian murmured, "I don't know where they're coming up with the part-time help these days. That child hardly ever reads, much less visits a library when she isn't working. A bit lazy, too, I'm afraid. But then, most youngsters are nowadays, don't you think?"

Dixie and Herb gave polite if vague acknowledgment to this pronouncement and then began the interview, first getting her name, address, and telephone number.

"How well did you know Gretchen?" Dixie asked.

"Obviously not as well as I thought, or would have liked to, but I did talk to her quite a bit, to all of them, the ones I used to think of as 'the gang'." She laughed softly at the emphasis she put on the last words. "I always thought of them that way. Watching them often reminded me of how things used to be, way back in the *old* days. You know, back in the forties, when I was a girl in college. A whole group of us, our own *gang*, used to meet each week at the library. That was our own idea of a good time, doing homework together and then going out for a root beer or a Coca-Cola at the drugstore."

"So Gretchen and her friends came often?"

"Every Thursday. They didn't always arrive at exactly the same time. Jimmy was usually a bit late. But they always left together, just before closing time. They were usually smiling and whispering, you understand, so as not to disturb anyone. Not like some youngsters who come in here. I pictured Gretchen and the others going out somewhere for root beer and hamburgers. Such nice children. If only they hadn't . . ."

Her voice trailed away and sadness once more replaced the nostalgia in her eyes. "I tried to tell them how dangerous those books were, how very unhealthy. I've always been for freedom of the press, mind you, but there are certain unsavory kinds of literature I feel very strongly about."

"What sort of literature, Mrs. Jackabcin?" Herb asked.

"The *evil* kind. I know most people would laugh at me, but I don't think some of the hocus-pocus on those shelves is hocus-pocus at all." She indicated a section of shelves right behind her. "Witches and warlocks. Voodoo and Egyptology. Druids and necromancy. Such things should not be subjects for ridicule. Demons are real, Investigator Woodall, whether most people think so or not.''

For the first time the librarian seemed defensive and on guard. She looked at the detectives warily. "The Lord tells us to beware of such things. If the Bible says there are demons among us, then there are.''

"But Gretchen and her friends didn't believe?''

She looked straight into Herb's eyes. "That's just the problem—at first they probably didn't, but later I'm sure they *did*. They were just children, young and impressionable, and they were investigating forbidden things. Everytime I walked past the table, this very one, I saw the books they had spread around them. Terrible books. *Wicked*.''

"Can you give us an example?''

"I can do better than that. I can give you many.''

She stood and lead the way into a tall row of shelves.

"If this isn't blasphemy, I'd like to know what is is!'' Her soft voice shook with indignation. "I've spoken to my superior more times than I can tell you about these horrible tomes being put in the religious section. The very idea is an insult!''

She tapped along the rows, hitting some books, avoiding others. Titles jumped out at Dixie and Herb. *Baron Samedi, the Man in Black. The Old Religion. Wisdom of Darkness. Osiris and Isis: an Eternal Love. Chants, Spells, and Amulets*. The volumes went on and on, from witchery to tarot cards, palm reading, and communication with the spirit world. Voodoo and Egyptology. Mythology and Wicca. All sandwiched in amongst the *Kabbalah*, the *Holy Bible*, and *The Book of Changes*. The list seemed not only endless, but often incongruous.

"Those children were playing with fire.'' Ms. Jackabcin reiterated. *"Hell fire!''*

"Did you try to tell them?'' Herb asked, keeping his voice as calm and natural as hers was agitated.

"Not at first.'' She shook her head. "You have to be careful in a job like mine. I really do try to mind my own business, and that's helping our patrons find the sort of books they need, for whatever reason. Then, too, at first it was obvious that those youngsters—or at least some of them—were working on school reports.''

"How many of them were there?''

"Four. Two boys and two girls, one of them being Gretchen, of course."

"And they were all working on reports?"

"I thought so. I helped them at first, although, as I told you, I disapprove of such books. But after a while I realized that they were truly interested in what they were reading. They sat for hours sometimes, always orderly, but excited by the things they found in those awful books. I became worried about them. I even prayed that God would close their minds to such evil."

There were real tears in her eyes, bright silvery drops which gleamed brightly behind the lenses of her glasses, as she led the detectives back to the table.

Once seated, Dixie leaned back in her chair. Important pieces were beginning to fall into place at last. And with each piece, it seemed more certain that Gretchen had been enthralled with the occult. Not just metaphysics, but the down-home nitty-gritty of spooks and spirits. But unlike the tormented Sarah Winchester, the quest of Gretchen Willis had ended in quick, violent death and mutilation.

A picture of Pete's tortured face flashed through Dixie's mind, but she resolutely pushed the image aside. Pete, who wanted only to think of his niece as a sweet little girl, as his little goddess, would be infuriated at what the investigation into her death was beginning to unearth. But no matter how badly she wished to protect and soothe her friend, the investigation had to take its true course. And the sooner it was ended, the sooner Pete could begin to heal.

"Tell us about Gretchen's friends, Ms. Jackabcin." Slipping one hand into a pocket of his sport coat, Herb switched on the tape recorder he always carried. The tiny machine, smaller than a pack of cigarettes, allowed him to get all the information they needed without making the people they interviewed uncomfortable. Only Dixie used pen and tablet, and usually only when she preferred a touch of nerves.

"Yes, I knew who they all were. I make it a habit to know our regular patrons whenever possible. It makes coming here more personal to be greeted by name. I get them from the computer at our front desk." Lillian Jackabcin tucked a stray hair back into her bun. "Like I've already told you, there were four of them. Wendy Nakamura was the prettiest, even prettier than Gretchen. So lovely with her mixed blood. Exotic is the word I always thought of when I saw her. And then there were the two boys. Jimmy Baldwin and Anthony Castellano.''

Herb and Dixie shot each other a quick look as she said the last name.

"Every one of those children were bright, and so good-looking." She sighed. "I was sorry when they quit coming—just when I felt they might be starting to accept me, to listen to me."

Herb's eyebrows raised a fraction. She noticed and smiled at him. "Oh, yes, I finally started talking to them, telling them how our Lord felt about the dark and evil sayings in those books. I knew they were searching, you see, looking for something solid in their lives, and I wanted to help them."

CHAPTER 12

DIXIE'S WATCH READ just a little past eight as Herb drove out of the library parking lot. By mutual agreement they had decided not to put off until Monday what should be done with all due haste.

Tony Castellano was their target, and the route to the Almaden area of the city was a long but very straight shot. Once there, sitting in the large circular driveway in front of the home Tony shared with his mother, Herb looked through the car window and whistled.

The first thought that leapt to mind was *BIG*. The Castellano home sat on the highest peak of a semicustom housing development nestled in the rolling hills of Almaden. And though the tract itself, grandly dubbed Royal Vista Estates, might have been semicustom, the home built by Anthony Castellano, Senior, for his wife and son was custom all the way. A 5200-square-foot payoff.

The Castellano's were Catholics of the old ilk. They were not divorced—simply separated. And the woman who answered the door was incredibly beautiful. In early middle age, Asunta Castellano had a figure like Sophia Loren, below a Madonna's face. Her nose was Roman, but finely chiseled. She had a full, soft mouth, and a pair of violet-colored, sooty-lashed eyes. A whisper of gray had dared touch her temples, but only served to make her long, thick, jet-colored hair more startling. She was wearing a lounging robe of white silk.

"It is a little late, officers. Do you think that perhaps this could wait?" Her voice was deep and sultry. She had an accent.

"I wish it could, Mrs. Castellano," Dixie answered, "but I'm sure you can understand the urgency involved in an investigation of this kind. We feel that Tony may have vital information that will help us very much."

She hesitated, and then opened the door wider to let them in. Herb almost stumbled, still trying to recover from the first awesome sight of her. He felt giddy as the smell of her perfume wrapped about him, tickling his nostrils with beckoning wisps. Dixie jabbed him in the ribs, grinding her elbow deep and hard.

"I'll go get my son," Mrs. Castellano said. "He may already be asleep."

After she had disappeared, leaving the detectives in a peach-and-cream-colored living room, Dixie turned on her partner. "Wake up, jerk, beauty is a transient thing. Besides, if you don't snap out of it, I'm going to snitch you off—you know, send a little bird to perch on Janice's shoulder."

"No fair, Struthers." He pouted and then smiled. "Easy to see where the kid gets his looks, isn't it?"

"I'll say. Wonder what papa looks like."

"Shame on you. He's a married man."

The jibes were cut short as Tony followed his mother into the room. He was rubbing his eyes, wearing only his pajama bottoms, but Dixie had the impression his drowsiness was about as genuine as his disclaimer of friendship with Gretchen. He yawned widely, showing a pink clean mouth and perfect teeth. His eyes were just a bit too bright to have opened only moments before.

Standing beside his mother, with his smooth muscular chest exposed, Tony Castellano looked like a young god—to his mother's goddess. The Queen and the Heir Apparent of Royal Vista Estates.

"Hello, Tony." Dixie offered a hand he completely ignored.

He flopped down on the long silk sofa, gathered a throw pillow into his arms and crushed it against his upper abdomen. "I'm tired, and I don't know what you two want. I've already answered your questions."

The way he said "you two" gave Herb and Dixie all the status of worms.

"We know you answered, Tony," Herb said, "but this time we're hoping you might try doing it with a little more honesty."

Mrs. Castellano said nothing, but she left the room so swiftly that Herb and Dixie stood without speaking, expecting her to return momentarily.

"She's calling Dad," Tony informed them with a big grin. "She always calls him when there's trouble. And he always comes."

"Good," Dixie said. "I'm sure he'll understand the importance of your answering our questions."

"I've answered them the only way I can, Sergeant Struthers. The ony way I will."

"This time without skipping any pertinent details, like meeting Gretchen and your other friends at the library every Thursday evening."

Tony's face didn't change, but he was squeezing the pillow tighter. "So I went to the library. Lots of students go there."

"Not to study the things you and Gretchen did. Why didn't you tell us she was your girlfriend, Tony?"

"Anthony does not have a girlfriend." Mrs. Castellano reappeared as if by magic to answer for him. A light coming through the doorway behind her showed an outline of her voluptuous figure, the shapely line of thighs and calves, the indentation of her narrow waist, the swell of her breasts. "With his lessons in drama and dance, with all the homework, he has no time for dating."

"You knew Gretchen Willis, Mrs. Castellano?" Dixie asked.

"I've seen her and her mother at school meetings. An unusual pair, if I remember correctly. But the girl was pretty. She and Anthony have gone to school together for years, and of course they know one another. I see nothing unusual in that. My son has many friends. It is my observation that many young girls think well of him."

Her eyes went to her son, and she smiled in a way that made Dixie very uncomfortable. A smile that somehow conveyed more than pride.

Tony looked back at her, and tears suddenly filled his brown eyes. "I'm tired, Mother. I can't understand why you got me up for *this*, to let these people accuse me of something I don't know anything about." His voice had changed, taking on the petulance of a ten-year-old. "They came to the school and pulled me out of class, just because I know that girl."

To the total and appalled amazement of both detectives, he began to shake all over. "I . . . I . . . can't stand it, Mother! I've been having terrible dreams! Ever since they started asking me questions it's been worse! I feel sick!"

Asunta Castellano went quickly to her son, gathering him into a pair of soft, round arms.

"My poor Antonio," she murmured. "All you have to do is tell them you know nothing. They are kind people. They will listen, I'm sure. Just tell them the truth."

"But I *have*!" He buried his face in her chest, pulling his legs up onto the sofa and nestling into her like an infant. "Please, Mother! Gretchen was young, just like me! What happened to her is terrible! I can't stand it! You know how I am about that! I can't help it!"

Mrs. Castellano was running her fingers through her son's dark, curling hair, caressing his back, rocking him. Looking at Dixie and Herb, she lifted her shoulders in a helpless shrug. "You can see how it is, officers. Anthony is not like other children. He is very high-strung. He is seeing a doctor about a morbid fear that plagues him, a fear of *death*." She actually made the sign of the cross over her son's head. "Terrible in one so young, don't you think?"

"I think your kid is full of—"

Dixie put a hand on Herb's arm just as the front door opened. A man walked in who could not have resembled the two handsome people on the sofa less. He was short and round, tanned from working outdoors, and barrel-chested. But his clothes were expensive, a pair of white linen slacks and a blue silk shirt. And Herb was certain that if he continued to wear the gold chain around his neck, Antonio, Senior, would die a hunchback.

"What the fuck are you doing in my house?" Castellano greeted them. His eyes shot to the sofa and narrowed. "How dare you come in here and upset my family?"

"We have questions that need asking, Mr. Castellano,"

Herb explained, more patiently than he was inclined. "We believe your son might have the answers. It's only routine."

"Take your fucking routine somewhere else!" The man looked like a bull, pawing the earth and snorting through flared nostrils. "You want answers, give my attorney a call. You want in my house, bring a fuckin' search warrant!"

He walked back to the big double doors and pulled one open. "Get outta here!"

There was no legal recourse, and in fact no solid reason to obtain a warrant at all without further evidence. Dixie and Herb left, both wanting to do a murder of their own as the door slammed shut behind them.

Herb stood glaring at nothing in particular, seething. But Dixie was more interested in the yelling she heard from inside the house they had so hastily vacated.

"What in the hell are you doing," Castellano yelled. "Get up from there!"

Asunta's voice was much softer, but Dixie could still hear it clearly. "See how you are," the woman said. "You act like an animal! You treat your son no better than one of your workers! Can't you see that he is ill?"

"All I see is his face in your tits!"

Tony was sobbing loudly.

"See!" His mother also began to yell now, in a good, hearty Latin bellow. "You want to live with me? *Ha!* You know nothing of love! You are a beast! An animal! We hate you!"

Herb was listening now too. He looked at Dixie with round blue eyes. "Holy shades of Oedipus," he whispered. "I'd stake my life on it!"

Dixie nodded. "And live to a ripe old age."

CHAPTER 13

PETE SAT HUNCHED in the dark interior of his Bronco. The radio was not playing and his C.B. was silent. For now, he was off duty, his last evening off before Di Franco and the rest of the squad put their hooks into him.

He was parked several houses down from 10 Linda Loma Drive, the house where Gretchen had grown to maturity. *Almost.*

He was sleeping little these days, grabbing an hour early in the evening and then a couple more just before going back to work. Each day he went to the police department, investigating a variety of unchallenging cases with Jake Spatlin, keeping his appearance up as much as possible. He would continue the routine, but with one difference now. He would keep his mouth shut. He would ask no more questions, not of anyone.

Why bother? The rest of the squad was shutting him out, turning their collective backs on him. Even Dixie. She was the one who hurt most of all. He could not believe how she acted, how she refused to help him. She never came right out with it, never said she no longer trusted him. Instead she gave him vague, meaningless answers to straightforward questions. She smiled, but her eyes held shadows.

Just thinking of how Dixie and Herb had deserted him,

made Pete hurt all over, ache deep down inside. Ache even
more than he already did. But he had come to a decision,
finally. If they would not confide in him, it would work both
ways. Nothing for nothing. He would take care of things
himself.

Dixie and Herb were out in left field. They had taken a
wrong turn. He had heard enough, read enough in the
newspaper, to see what direction they were taking, and it was
all wrong, stupid. They were trying to make Gretchen look
like some kind of kook, when what she had really been was a
beautiful girl with an intelligence level that made most other
people look like idiots. She had been a great kid. And just
because she had been murdered, butchered by some pig of a
slime, they were off chasing a bunch of wild leads, a school
of red fucking herrings.

All that bullshit stuff about ghosts and goblins! *A cult.* The
whole idea was ridiculous. A false trail, planned in advance
by the killer.

Pete kept his eyes glued on Sally's house. Sooner or later,
if he was patient enough, he would find the lead he was
looking for—*right here*, doing just what Dixie and Herb
should be doing. And the first thing was to learn the identity
of Sally's visitor, the man he was convinced had been in the
house that night when he came to talk to her about Gretchen.

He had tried to tell Dixie. If she had just listened, she would
have known that Sally was too general, too downright evasive
about her arguments with Gretchen. And if there was nothing
wrong with the guy she was seeing, if her new boyfriend was
straight-arrow, why keep him a big, dark secret?

Pete believed in his own instincts, the ones now telling him
that he was on the right track. He had been here for four
nights already, and he would keep on forever if necessary, no
matter what they did to him at the department. Sally was
involved with someone, and he intended to find out whom.

Tipping his head against the back of the seat, he half closed
his eyes. Without meaning to, or even wanting to, he remembered the day Gretchen had been born. The county hospital,
the drab-looking rooms filled with other women on welfare or
who had no money for a private hospital. Sally in a bed,
looking for all the world like the hippie she was, holding the

tiny bundle in her arms. Drew standing four feet away, long, greasy hair to his shoulders. Frowning.

In those days Sally had been a true flower child, a little Earth Mother who had wanted nothing more than to continue doing what she had been, trailing Drew all over the place. Until she saw Gretchen's face, held the little girl baby in her arms.

But Drew had not been a hippie, just a bum who had come back and lodged himself temporarily so that Sally could have the kid, a kid she now insisted on keeping no matter what Drew said. She sat there in bed, smiling weakly at Drew, with the baby nuzzling for milk.

Pete had watched them, and even at fourteen years old he had known that it was a replay of the same old story. After the folks had died, Drew had hung around for a while, restless, angry to have the responsibility of his much younger brother. He held onto the little east side house for about six months, and then lost it because he refused to work steady, refused to make the payments. And even though Pete walked on eggshells, keeping his grief to himself, he could not always stay on the right side of Drew's temper. Finally, as he had feared, he ended up in a foster home.

And then Drew had come back, picked Pete up, and let him live in the grubby apartment he and Sally shared. Pete had not cared how grubby it was. He had a family again. He liked Sally. There was going to be a baby.

Pete had spent night after night lying awake on the roll-away bed, making believe it was all going to come out right—pretending he and Drew and Sally would start making a real home, that it would be just like before the folks were killed in a car crash.

But on the day Gretchen was born, Pete had seen all the dreams come crashing down. After they left the hospital, he had tried to talk to Drew, tell him how it could be, if he would only try.

Drew had hit him in the mouth, giving him a chipped tooth, and then he had split. Really split. Forever.

Sally had kept Pete with her for as long as she could, but he knew how hard it was, and after less than a year he, too, left. Working at night, going to high school in the daytime, and then college, he had managed somehow to keep a roof over his head and make adulthood. His impetus had been Drew. He, Peter Jacob Willis, had become everything his older brother was not. Decent. Respectable. A law-abiding citizen. A police officer.

And, of course, there had always been Gretchen. Smiling, blond Gretchen. His little goddess, the child he worshipped. The single bright, shining jewel in his life. And in all the years that he had spent loving her, only once had they disagreed about anything. Only once!

Pete straightened and rubbed his eyes. Reaching into his shirt pocket, he pulled out a penlight and shined it on his watch. It was after ten.

Putting the light away, he looked up the street again. There had been no movement in or around Sally's house. The lights had gone out about half an hour ago.

Maybe the guy was married, Pete thought, deciding to give it another hour. Maybe that was the only reason Sally kept her lover under wraps. Perhaps it was just that simple. But married or not, the man might have known Gretchen. He might have looked at her with evil, greedy eyes. He might be a nut.

The street was quiet. From time to time a car would pass, but not often. Pete checked the rearview mirror every few minutes, but his eyelids were growing heavy. He had gone too long without enough sleep.

When he first spotted the girl walking down the street, he hardly recognized her. When he had asked Gretchen why she and Priscilla Smith were no longer friends, she had said only that the other girl had "changed." That, Pete now saw, was an understatement.

He squinted, hardly able to believe his own eyes. Prissy had changed, sure enough. To Pete she looked like something or someone right out of a circus sideshow. A *freak*. He frowned and felt a stab of regret, a sadness tinged with disappointment. He had liked the kid and felt badly that she and Gretchen no longer hung around together. But to see her now, how she had turned out, made him shake his head.

Priscilla Smith was walking slowly, doing a lackadaisical skip, skip, hop down the street toward her own house.

She shouldn't be out alone this time of night, Pete thought, even though the sight of her would scare most guys to death.

She shouldn't be out walking the streets alone at night. Not after what happened to Gretchen.

He watched her and tried to equate what he saw—the avant garde Mohawk, black clothing, and spiked jewelry—with what he remembered of Prissy. The equation did not compute.

She had been a pretty little girl. Not as pretty as Gretchen, of course, but dark and lively and delightful in an eager-to-please sort of way. A nice little kid. He remembered taking her to movies and to the zoo with Gretchen. The only problem he could remember was a bit of youthful competition for his attention.

Pete smiled, remembering Gretchen's one tiny fault. When it came to him, she did not like to *share*.

Prissy was almost directly across the street from him now. She did a little whirl and then walked on, nearing her front door.

If Gretchen had looked like Prissy, Pete decided, he might be better able to comprehend all that had happened. Punkers could be bad news. But Gretchen had been nothing like what he now observed of Prissy.

He shook his head again and wondered if she was high on something. The way she was moving, almost dancing, seemed even more odd, incongruous, considering her bizarre outward appearance. She was acting almost like a heroine from some old movie. The heroine on cloud nine because she had just been kissed by the boy of her dreams, by her own Prince Charming.

Just as she went into her own house, headlights appeared in Pete's mirror. He scooched down as the interior of his truck was lighted. A van went by, a scuffed yellow, with no windows in back. A peace sign had been spray painted in black on the rear door. Pete watched it through the top of the steering wheel, narrowing his eyes as he saw that it also had no rear license plate.

He was just about to turn on his motor, to follow, when a second set of lights showed up behind him. Lower. Moving slower. Gliding along the quiet street. At first he thought it was going to pass, but then another movement caught his eye. Sally's garage door was opening, automatically controlled either by the person in the car or by Sally herself.

The small blue compact passed by Pete, slowed even more,

and then turned into Sally's driveway, slipping quickly into the dark interior of the garage. The door closed.

It was all Pete could do to sit still for the next ten minutes. But he knew he had to wait—just long enough.

When he finally went to the front door, he banged loudly. The drapes moved, but a full two minutes more passed before the door opened.

Pete blinked in the sudden and unexpected glare of the porch light. Sally stood staring at him, her face dark with anger.

"Let him in," a voice behind her said. "Let him in just one more time."

CHAPTER 14

IT WAS SATURDAY. A free day. A time for leisure. But Dixie awakened without her usual sense of anticipation. The Castellano interview had been a total farce. Worse, she had once more been plagued with nightmares. And she still felt the exaggerated sense of urgency which was constantly with her. A terrible forboding.

She lay in bed unrested, but relieved to be awake and in control of her own mind again, a mind that seemed to run amuck the moment sleep claimed her.

She stretched and yawned, rubbing a pair of eyes she felt sure were puffy and bloodshot.

The recent bout of nightmares, while unsettling, was also annoying to Dixie, who had always considered herself too sensible, modern, and well-educated for superstition. The boogie man and his sack of spooky dreams were for children.

Children, like Gretchen, Tony, Jimmy, and Wendy.

The thought left her even more uneasy. Regardless of the direction this investigation was taking, she wanted to push aside the idea that people so young, so obviously promising and bright, could have perpetrated a crime of such heinous proportions. Kids could be selfish. Spoiled. Troubled. Even cruel. But no teenager she had ever met fit the mental image she had formed of the killer. The idea that Gretchen's friends, either collectively or individually, could have killed and so horribly mutilated her, was one Dixie dwelt upon only with reluctance.

A light tap sounded on her bedroom door. "Missy? Are you awake in there?"

"I'm awake."

"Well, then, you best pull your pretty bones up. That crazy Art is downstairs eatin' us out of house and home."

Dixie automatically looked at the clock and thought about the date, trying to remember if she and Art had made special plans.

"He says he never can get ahold of you these days," Reversa continued, a tinge of reluctant amusement in her voice, "and that he ain't goin' away until he gets a kiss."

Dixie smiled, but only faintly. Her mind was still mulling over some very ugly images. "Tell him I'll be right down."

She dressed slowly, trying in vain to improve both mood and appearance. She chose a full cotton skirt to wear, with a matching, loose-fitting blouse, both in a gay spring print. Her reflection gave credence to her vision of puffy eyes. Two dark smudges beneath each let her know that she was indeed sleeping poorly, a fact she camouflaged with a light layer of cosmetics. She brushed her hair and pulled the sides back with a pair of ivory combs. By the time she entered the kitchen, she felt almost human.

"There's the winsome stranger," Art said, with what she perceived to be a slightly forced joviality. "Morning, sleepyhead."

She smiled and kissed him. "Good morning to you, too, but it's only nine."

Patrick took a close look at her, then looked quickly away, picking up the newspaper. "I do believe he's referring to the old adage about early worms and their birds," he said, "with emphasis on the *birds*."

"Watch that Art, Missy," Reversa added her own warning. "He's gone and sprouted another one of his wild hairs."

"Nothing wild about it," Art protested. "Just a nice little jaunt along the Big Sur—via the Steerman, of course."

Dixie poured herself a cup of coffee and sliced off one of Reversa's gooey cinnamon rolls. She said nothing. In fact, she was only half listening.

"Hey, you awake?" Art asked. "How about it?"

She looked at him blankly, and saw the beginning of a frown appear between his sandy-colored eyebrows. Her brain scrambled for a quick replay. "About the Big Sur you mean?"

"About going flying there with me. The weather is great, light winds. It should be spectacular. We can drop down in Monterey and grab a bite to eat, take a taxi out to the pier, maybe."

"It really sounds great, Art, but I think I'll take a rain check." She tried not to notice his disappointed look.

"So." He gave her a weak smile. "What *would* you like to do on this bright and sunny Saturday? Just name it, babe. A picnic in the woods? A trip to the beach? A quiet stroll up memory lane, reviewing those bygone days when we still had fun?"

"How about a trip to the library?" She had not known she was going to suggest it until the words popped out of her mouth.

Art, Patrick, and Reversa looked at her as if she were ill.

"I'm serious," she said defensively. "You asked what I want to do, didn't you? Okay, then, I would really like to go to the library."

Reversa got quickly to her feet and began clearing dishes as Patrick buried his face in the sports section of the paper.

"I don't suppose this has anything to do with your job?" Art asked. "With the case you and Herb are working?"

"It does, as a matter of fact, but that shouldn't keep us from having a nice day."

"At the library."

"Why not?" This time it was Dixie who forced a note of cheerfulness. "Actually, the books I'm looking for might provide you a bit of amusement. I'll tell you about it on the way. This is a very unusual case, Art. I don't think I've ever been so—"

"Spare me any colorful details, please." Art held up a hand. "I've read about all I can stomach in the papers lately. And spending the day browsing through any books that would have to do with what you're working on right now wouldn't provide me a drop of amusement."

Dixie was becoming irritated, and she felt a streak of stubbornness creep over her. But it was more than irritation or stubbornness that made her so persistent. It was her sense of urgency about the case. Time seemed to be rushing by, a precious commodity that she must use with all efficiency.

"Come with me, Art. You can go to another section, find something *amusing*. I'm sure you won't have a problem. Getting what I want shouldn't take too long. Then we can—"

Art stood up and finished the sentence for her. "Read together?"

"There are worse ways to pass the time, but that wasn't what I was going to suggest."

"I'm surprised." He was slipping into his scuffed leather flight jacket. "Look, Dix, I don't want to argue. If you feel like you need to work, I'll just be on my way. No hard feelings, okay?"

"I'm not working, Art. I just feel the need to do a little special research."

"Investigation," he corrected.

"*Research*," she repeated. "Just call it my own small, personal project."

To her surprise, he did not forego planting a kiss on her forehead. "You don't have to make excuses. I should have called before coming. Personal projects need personal care. What say you tend to yours while I tend to mine."

A quick burst of panic skipped through her. She could feel the rift between them, the differences in their interests and personalities widening. She forced herself to smile. "An equitable arrangement, I guess, but only until tonight. Do you want to take in a movie?"

"Which one?" There was just a touch of challenge in his eyes.

Dixie realized that she had no idea what movies were playing. The only articles she read in the papers related to her case. And except for the late news broadcasts, she almost never turned on the television. She gave Art a sheepish grin. "You pick."

She heard the sigh he heaved as he left the house, and for a moment she was tempted to call him back, recant, and skip the library altogether. That was until she remembered the small closet in Sarah Winchester's house, the closet with its high, stained-glass windows throwing colorful patterns over the corpse of a sixteen-year-old girl.

She stood on the deck watching Art drive away, once more only half aware that she raised her arm to return his wave. She started as a hand came down on her shoulder.

"A bit jumpy, are we?" Patrick was beside her.

"Art would probably put it a little differently," she answered.

Patrick gave her shoulder a squeeze. "He'll get over it, probably about the same time this case of yours is solved."

"I'm sure you're right, Pop, but what about the next time?"

He met her eyes. "Guess that depends on the two of you. Art is a fun-loving boy, and you have to admit that a messy 187 is no barrel of laughs. You take your work very much to heart, mouvereen, and I'm not faulting you for that. Just remember there's another world out there. A place where normal folks live nice, normal lives."

"A state of affairs that would soon deteriorate if no one got involved in messy 187 cases." Her tone was depressed, troubled. "You can't understand, Pop, not even as a cop. Not without seeing what Herb and I saw at that mansion. I have to find the man who killed Pete's niece, and *soon*!"

Even as she spoke, Dixie prayed that the killer was a man. Not a boy. Or a girl. Not *children*.

CHAPTER 15

DIXIE HELD THE computer readouts in her left hand and ran her right index finger along a row of books. Several of the volumes she wanted were missing, but most were there, titles clearly visible on each spine. *Voodoo on the Dark Continent: The Red Sects*, and *Baron Samedi, the Man in Black*, checked out by Jimmy Baldwin. *Local Loas and Veves* was missing now, but had been checked out by the Baldwin boy no less than three times. The address listed for him matched that of Wendy Nakamura, who had checked out *Greek Gods and Special Wisdoms*; *Chants, Spells, and Amulets*; and *Mythology and Magic*. From Tony Castellano's favorites, Dixie selected *Secrets within the Pyramid*; *Isis and Osiris: Eternal Lovers*; and *Age Old Madonnas*. The remainder had been checked out by Gretchen: *Warlocks, Witches and Modern Day Wonders*; *The Old Religion* and *Druids and Their Deities*.

There were other books as well: *Guides and Their Guises*; *The Loving Spirit*; *Elektra*. But Dixie wanted to focus her efforts on just those tomes that would give her not only information, but also symbolism.

She was just on her way to the escalator when Lillian Jackabcin approached. "Have you found what you're looking for, Sergeant?"

"Not really, Ms. Jackabcin, because I'm looking for a *who*, not a *what*, but this seemed like a good place to start. I obtained a list from the gentleman at your front desk; it tells me what books those youngsters were studying.''

"You're wrong, you *are* looking for a *what*. But here, let me help you.'' She took several of the heavy books Dixie was carrying, her face registering distaste as her eyes scanned the titles. "I'm sure you're taking a false path. None of those children would have killed Gretchen.''

They rode the escalator down together. "I hope you right,'' Dixie said. "The idea of anyone committing such a crime, much less a teenager, hardly appeals to me either.''

"They were simply searching,'' the other woman insisted. "They might not have understood everything I tried to tell them. Perhaps they haven't yet even accepted the fact that God, the one true God, wants them, wants their bright, young, shining souls. They may not have accepted *yet*, but they will in time. All except poor Gretchen, of course.''

She looked at Dixie with bright, zealous eyes. "Gretchen was *taken*, not by our Lord, but by evil. She was used as a warning to the others.''

"Did you tell the group that they were *chosen*, Ms. Jackabcin? Did *you* warn them that something bad might happen?''

"I talked to them, yes. I even quoted to them from the prophet, told them how it had been prophesied that in the last days the young would see visions. Jimmy and Wendy, all of them, were exactly those kind of young, just the kind God would choose to pour his spirit upon. I miss them all terribly, but I know I will see them again someday. They will grow wiser as time passes, and they will come back.''

Dixie listened and watched her, the soft expressive eyes, the longing voice. Lillian Jackabcin was obviously a lonely woman. A spinster, without children of her own. On the surface she seemed sincere and kind. Still, Dixie could not help wondering where one drew the line between zeal and fanaticism.

"So you spoke to them often, and you did warn them.''

"No, I prayed for them. I even worried about them. But I never believed for an instant that our Lord would allow the evil one to inflict such a terrible lesson.''

"You don't honestly believe that the devil did this, do you, Ms. Jackabcin?''

The librarian put the books she was carrying down at the checkout counter. She looked at Dixie with a sad, almost condescending expression. "Don't scoff, my dear. The devil takes more forms than you can possibly imagine. And he has helpers. Many, many helpers."

Dixie drove home deep in thought, giving Lillian Jackabcin more mental scrutiny than she previously had, but in the end she shook her head. If the librarian was mad, truly and wickedly mad, she would in all likelihood have condemned all four of the teenagers who met in her section every Thursday evening. A background check on the woman was in order, certainly, and perhaps even some surveillance, but Dixie felt certain such investigation would show only a woman alone. A nice, slightly too intense lady who read her bible nightly and attended a fundamentalist church each and every time the doors were opened.

In short, Lillian Jackabcin did not fit Dixie's image of a person who could have murdered a young girl as Gretchen had been murdered . . . but then, neither did anyone else.

Upon arriving home again, she employed her favorite tension reliever by donning a pair of shorts and working with Patrick in his vegetable patch. The two worked side by side, talking, mulling over what little Dixie and Herb had learned, but no experience they had collectively known shed a single ray of light on the death of Pete's niece.

"I hate to think how it must be affecting him," Patrick said. "I've been thinking how I would feel if . . . if it had been you."

Chills rippled up Dixie's spine. "Do us both a favor, Pop, don't let your imagination run away with you, okay?"

"And the same to you. I saw that stack of books you brought in, and so did Reversa. She's talking all kinds of mumbo jumbo."

Dixie started to laugh, but he held up his hand. "Careful now. Don't go making fun of what you don't know. She really is skittish, Dix. I've never seen her quite this way."

"I wasn't poking fun, Pop, even though you're the second person to say more or less the same thing to me today. I'll talk to Reversa, but not now." She was looking at her watch. "If I don't get dressed, Art may never speak to me again."

Passing through the living room on her way to get dressed, Dixie paused long enough to scoop the books from her small writing desk. She did not see Reversa standing at the kitchen door, or the frightened look on the black woman's face.

CHAPTER 16

DIXIE SAT IN bed with her legs pulled up, a book propped against her knees. She was pale as her eyes scanned the pages.

For a while at least, earlier that evening, she'd been able to put the work and worry to one side. Art had chosen carefully, taking her first to their favorite Mexican restaurant and then to a movie, a comedy. It had been a good film, and watching the screen helped provide some moments of true, spontaneous laughter—a good dose of therapy. The world was still a nice place. She was glad for the reminder, and grateful to Art for showing up without a pout on his face, an expression he too often wore these days.

But reprieve or no reprieve, her determination had not wavered. Even as she laughed at the antics of the actors on screen, in the back of her mind the sense of urgency lingered. The Willis case was not solved, and until it was, Dixie knew that she would not entirely relax, would not feel at ease.

Upon arriving home just after midnight, she had gone straight to her room, and after preparing for bed, looked at the stack of books awaiting her attention. She selected one with what she considered a relatively innocuous title, and began to read. Now she found herself sitting in her own bed with an upset stomach and the hairs on her arms prickling like needles on an aggravated porcupine.

The book she held, *The Old Religion*, was no child's tome, and certainly not a literary selection to induce peaceful dreams. Her eyes widened and her digestive tract bubbled aloud as she read of incidents originally recorded by some of the ancient historians—Strabo, Livy, and Tacitus.

Druid lore and practice exceeded anything she had imagined for gore and grist. Severed limbs and drinking goblets made of human skulls. Entrails hanging from the boughs in Sacred Groves. The contemporary author had traced it all, from the old beginnings to modern witchcraft, and Dixie cursed her own ability to read and transfer the written word into vivid living color.

She saw the ancient Celts, heads partially shaven and spiked with lime, bodies painted blue, at the festival of Dionysus, crying out to their bloodthirsty gods. Bodies ripped asunder in ritual sacrifice. Mother Earth drinking human blood. Savages staring at her from the pages of the book with bright and vicious kohl-ringed eyes, their arms and legs tattooed with serpents.

A knock sounded on her bedroom door, and the book went flying. She could barely voice permission for Reversa to enter.

It was almost two in the morning, and the housekeeper wore a bathrobe of thick pink chenille. There was, however, no air of drowsiness about her. She sat down in the small chintz-covered chair near Dixie's bed, looking acutely uncomfortable.

"You don't have to squeeze your healthy self in there," Dixie teased, patting the bed and wondering what could possibly have brought Reversa to her room at such an hour. But whatever the reason, she was suddenly glad for the company, especially from a body as down-to-earth as Reversa Green.

"I don't care if I get squeezed to death. I'm not comin' over there, not with all *that* wickedness." Dixie looked at her in surprise as she pointed at the books scattered around her ankles.

"Fact is," Reversa continued, "that's just why I'm here.

Couldn't sleep. Fact is, too, I wish you'd just get that trash out of my house.''

When it came to matters of cooking or cleanliness, Reversa always took verbal possession of the house. Obviously, she had relegated Dixie's latest reading selections to the latter category.

"Don't be silly, Reversa," Dixie chided, once more feeling the arch hypocrite. "They're only books. I need them for the investigation."

"You need *those* books like a hole in the head." Reversa's lip poked stubbornly outward, but her eyes were filled with worry. She pointed a long finger at one volume in particular, a small black book with bold red letters. She made a hawking noise in her throat as Dixie picked the volume up and read aloud.

"*Voodoo on the Dark Continent: the Red Sects.* Really, Reversa, it's all just—"

"Don't you be telling *me* what it is, little miss smarty pants. I wouldn't even put my hands on a book like that. Think I'm a silly old woman if you want, but that book, all those books you brought here are . . . are . . . *evil*—chock full of wickedness and black, dark sayings. Makes me shiver just knowing they're here. I'm a Christian woman, you know that, even if I don't go around praisin' the Lord from dawn to dusk—even if I don't go run to a church every time the door is open. I read my bible regular, Missy, and I believe what I read." Reversa's voice shook slightly. "For sure, I do wish you would take that trash right back where it came from, Missy, please."

"I won't keep them here long," Dixie promised, no longer making light of her friend's fear. "I have to do this, Reversa. Somewhere in these books I hope to find a lead that will help me solve my case. It's important. If I don't catch the man who murdered Pete's niece, someone else might die."

"You think those bad, trashy books might help you find the man who killed that youngster?"

"Possibly."

After giving it several long moments of thought, Reversa wagged her head again and expelled a long, worried sigh. "Well, then, I guess you've got to do what you think is right, but keep them away from me. I won't touch them, not even with a feather duster. Not one little touch, even if they get all moldy and covered with cobwebs.''

Dixie chuckled. "You have my word they won't be here long enough to grow anything."

Reversa stood up, groaning slightly, and stretched until her spine popped. "You need something while I'm still up? I don't like the look of you lately. Thought I didn't see them little black sacks under your eyes, huh? Never mind arguing with me either. I'm bringing up some cocoa with a dollop of brandy, and that's that—one for myself too."

Dixie did not bother arguing. While Reversa was gone, she stacked the books on the floor beside her bed. Then, as an afterthought, she shoved them all the way under, shielding them from view with the dust ruffle.

The hot cocoa, liberally laced with Napoleon, tasted delicious. Better, it sent a wonderful sleepy warmth through Dixie's system as she and Reversa sat talking about inconsequential matters. She yawned widely, and without realizing it, her eyelids fluttered shut. Reversa took the cup and saucer carefully from her hand.

The black woman stood for several moments, looking down at Dixie, the young woman she had all but raised. Brushing an unruly curl gently from Dixie's forehead, just as she had often done more than twenty-five years before, she smiled. "Whoever heard of a little biddy girl being a *poleece*!" She muttered the familiar complaint aloud, but in a whisper. "Ain't no bigger'n a popcorn fart!"

After switching off the lamp, she tiptoed to the door. From where she stood, with a wide shaft of light spilling in from the upper hallway, she could just glimpse a book title peeking from beneath Dixie's bed.

"Dark sayings," she grumbled as she softly closed the door. "Such black wickedness ain't gonna bring Missy no good!"

CHAPTER 17

UPON ARRIVING AT work on Monday, the first thing Herb and Dixie received was a summons to the leuy's office. As usual, Di Franco looked harassed, buried under a small mountain of paperwork. He held a cigarette between his teeth and squinted against the smoke. He looked up and nodded when they entered.

"I don't need it," he grumbled. "I just don't fuckin' need it. It's not enough everyone's gotta have a piece of me, now I get calls from snotty, big-shot attorneys tellin' me how to run my division."

Dixie and Herb took their seats without speaking.

"You interview a kid named Castellano?" he asked. "Some rich little pisser from Almaden?"

"Last night," Dixie answered. "We were just writing up the reports."

"Reports, reports, since when will I find time to read it? Anyhow, I got a call from the kid's attorney first thing this morning. He says we're harassing the poor boy, and that unless we intend to charge him, keep away. Seems his daddy is a big contractor and builder hereabouts. Big Castellano says Little Castellano is a very sensitive boy. If the kid gets a nervous breakdown on account of my investigators, Big Castellano is gonna file suit against the whole damn city."

"Oh, for Pete's sake," Herb said, "we didn't even—"

"Yeah, and that's another thing; seems Pete is still at it. His sister-in-law called in to complain that *she's* being harassed too. By him."

"We'll talk to him," Dixie said quickly, hoping to forestall any talk of transfer or discipline. "I think he's convinced that Sally Nelson is withholding information. He could be right. Herb and I will talk to her, smooth her feathers and also see if we can find out what Pete is digging for. We'll talk to Pete, too, and find some subtle way to tell him to butt out."

"Thought you had already covered that ground with him. I know I have."

"We'll cover it again."

Di Franco cast another baleful eye at the mess on the desk. "And the Castellano boy?"

"We might have some more homework to do there, but we won't push unless we have to."

"Do you think he's dirty?"

"No way of knowing at this point. Let's just say he doesn't come across straight."

"Okay, for now I'm going to let you play it however you have to in order to get the job done. But the sooner this one is cleared, the easier I'm going to rest. I'm getting nasty vibes about this case, Struthers, and I'm thinking maybe you and Herb are a little too involved. Too close to Pete, maybe? Don't lose your objectivity."

Both detectives murmured hasty agreement and rose to leave, anxious to be out of his office. Once the door had closed behind them, Herb turned to Dixie.

"The boss is right. It's a stinking case, and the sooner it's over, the better, especially for Pete. He keeps up the bullshit and he's going to end up without a job. Maybe we should pull in a little help to speed things along. That school report Gretchen did interests me. I wonder if any of the others did similar assignments. It's not the sort of thing most teachers would forget."

"Probably not. Maybe Delaney and Brooks can find time to check the different schools, do some of the scratch work for us. Why don't you ask? Meanwhile we can go see Sally Nelson, and then go to the Nakamura house."

Herb nodded, and went to speak to Pat Delaney.

Dixie returned to her desk. A large brown envelope was laying on her blotter, addressed from the coroner's office. Breaking the seal, she pulled out the postmortem report. Her eyes scanned line after line, then suddenly stopped and widened. She read the same sentence three times. Her face turned grim.

Herb looked up from the report he was holding, the one Dixie had waited to hand him until they were out of the squad room and in the car. Her eyes looked sick, and now he knew why.

"Do we tell Pete?" he asked.

"That isn't a decision I want to make on my own."

"Have you told Di Franco?"

"Not yet, nor anyone else either. I got the report after we left the leuy's office. So far the only ones who know are you, me, and Wittenhaur."

"Ah, yes, the cheerful cherub himself."

"If you remember correctly, he wasn't making any jokes at the scene on this one. I know you don't like him, Herb, but he's damn good at his job."

"It's not that I don't like him. I just don't like the idea of becoming one of his patients."

"Nor me." Dixie managed a smile in spite of what they had just learned. Herb's aversion to autopsies in general, and in particular those normally conducted with such good humor by the head coroner, was a standing joke between them. Wittenaur was all too often an abominably cheerful pathologist, and Herb felt about pathologists like many people did about snakes. Everytime he saw the coroner, he broke out in a case of cold chills.

But as Dixie had said, the man was very good at his job. Amidst the terrible damage inflicted by abdominal wounds, the fetus—the small, marble-sized seed of humanity in Gretchen's womb—might easily have been missed by a less scrupulous pathologist.

"This says she was between six and seven weeks," Herb said, "just far enough along to know, or at least suspect."

"And if she did know, it's likely she would have informed the father."

"Tony Castellano or Jimmy Baldwin."

"Two pretty good guesses," Dixie said.

"If that fetus had been bigger, we probably wouldn't have to guess. The head ghoul and his gang could have run tests to prove paternity."

"I called Wittenhaur. According to him, we might still have been able to, even with a fetus at that stage of development. Some of the new technology allows them to narrow paternity down to a ninety-five percent certainty. But with the stab wounds sustained, there was damage to the fetus, too, and contamination from Gretchen's own blood."

Herb looked down at the report again. "I see he was right about the other too. About the depth of the wounds."

Dixie nodded, her expression almost distraught. "Yes, she was stabbed all over the place, slashed or punctured deeply at least twelve times. As far as Wittenhaur can tell, the art work was all done after the fact."

"Just for fun."

Dixie started the car and pulled out of the police garage. "I doubt it. The symbolism is very ritualistic, but confusing too. From what I'm learning, there's a little bit of everything. Voodoo. Witchcraft as it was practiced long, long ago. I hope. Greek and Egyptian myth and magic. A hodgepodge. Some of it is downright phallic, but not all. Or not that I can make out. Those books I checked out of the library are brimming over with nightmare material. The same books checked out by you know who."

"*Our gang*," Herb quipped. "I still think it could have been done for fun, though, or rather as a little joke on us."

"To make it look like something it wasn't?"

"A nice gory trail intended to lead us to all the wrong people. Those kids bother me, Dix. I'm having one hell of a time believing they could have done a job like that, especially since a lot of the work was obviously done on a *corpse*. We haven't talked to them all, but it's just the *idea* of it, Dix; it bothers me. Castellano is a real little asshole with an overinflated sense of his own importance. But I can't picture even him hacking away at a body like that."

"It wasn't hacked, not in the end, anyway. Those doodles were very neatly cut. Artistic, if you can stomach the word in association with what we saw in that closet."

"But done over the top of other wounds," Herb reminded her. "As camouflage, maybe? It's just a thought."

Dixie sighed. "Yes, and a good one, but it puts us right back where we started. Those kids are what we have. If none of them are guilty—and I feel the same way you do about that—then we have a big fat zero again. We're missing something."

They drove aimlessly along the streets, both thinking, neither speaking for a long time.

"So, are we going to tell Pete or not?" Dixie finally asked.

"I'm afraid he'll pop a gasket," Herb said. "He's already borderline."

"God, I hate this!" Dixie smacked the wheel with the heel of her hand. "I agree with you, but I feel like a traitor, almost like I'm sneaking around behind his back. He calls me, pretending that he just wants to shoot the breeze but saying almost nothing. Waiting for me to tell him the things he wants to know. I can hear his questions hanging in the air between us. For the last couple of days he's hardly spoken to me at all. I'm sure he's getting the message, I just wish it was the right one. I swear, Herb, I can *feel* the pain coming from him!"

Herb reached across and gave her shoulder a rub. "I know what you mean, kid, but remember *why* we're keeping things from him, will you?"

"So, you're sure we shouldn't tell him about the pregnancy?"

"Not a hundred percent, just a gut-level reaction."

"Okay, then, if that's the way we're going to play it, I say we keep it under wraps all the way."

Herb looked at her. "You mean you don't intend to tell anyone?"

"Not at this point."

"Not even Tony Di Franco?"

She shook her head. "The leuy has plenty of reports to keep him busy—he said so himself. Why add to his work load?"

Herb groaned. *"Ohboyohboyohboy!"*

The electronics firm where Sally Nelson worked was a duplicate of others all over the valley. Clean, modern, and given over to the gods of high tech. As secretary to one of the vice presidents, she had her own office, complete with personal computer. An overpowering spray of flowers sat on one corner of her desk, and several cards, along with a picture of Gretchen which neither Dixie nor Herb had previously seen. It was posed to look like it had been shot in a forest, with Gretchen perched on a log, holding a white flower—a gardenia—up near her face. She was breathtakingly beautiful.

"People have been so nice," Sally Nelson said. "My boss sees that I have fresh flowers twice a week. The people I work with send cards."

"I'm sure it helps," Dixie said.

"In a way, but it also hurts." She got up and poured Dixie and Herb each a cup of coffee. "There comes a time when you want to let it quit hurting, to not be reminded anymore. This was . . . was worse than just the . . . the normal kind of thing. People are not forgetting as quickly, but I'm sure they will in time. Once you've found out who . . . who . . . Oh, I'm sorry, Sergeant Struthers. It's still terrible! There are times I don't even know what I'm doing!"

Feeling useless, but wanting to comfort the woman, Dixie took the Styrofoam cups from her hands, murmuring silly platitudes which she knew Gretchen's mother had heard a hundred times in the last week. Meanwhile, Herb looked at the cards, straining to see the signatures of sympathizers. Most he didn't recognize, but there was one, and he wondered at it being in the office and not at Sally Nelson's home. Casually he picked up and read the sentiments. Just as casually Sally Nelson lifted it from between his fingers and propped it back in place.

She sat down at her desk and gestured for them to sit across from her. She blew her nose on a tissue, and sighed deeply. "I know you're doing all you can to get this horror over," she said. "But I might—I say *might*—find it easier to deal with if Pete would quit hounding me to death. I've always cared about Pete, loved him almost like a younger brother, but I think he must be losing his mind. He seems to forget who I am, that *I* was Gretchen's mother. He acts as if . . . as if I'm somehow responsible, just because she and I weren't getting along well. He doesn't understand how it can be with a teenager, raising one *alone*."

The unmistakable tone of bitterness was back in her voice,

the same tone Dixie and Herb had heard the first time they interviewed her. "Gretchen never did understand—my being divorced, I mean. But Pete did. He knew what his brother Drew was like. He knocked Pete around plenty when he was a kid. Beat the living tar out of him, with me screaming interference the whole time. So now *I'm* the bad guy? He thinks *I'm* not upset? I just don't understand."

"Pete hasn't been himself with anyone lately, Ms. Nelson," Dixie said. "I know that doesn't help much, but we're all hoping he'll begin to get over it soon, enough to quit blaming the world for the actions of one sick and deranged individual. Getting this case over as soon as possible will help more than anything—and that's *our* job. It's especially hard on Pete because we can't let him be involved. Very hard for a cop like Pete. A good cop."

"Well, if he's so damn good, tell him to stick to the rules, and I don't think that includes hanging around outside my house, spying. And certainly not banging on my door at all hours, accusing me of whatever pops into his sick mind. I'm not the only one involved, Sergeant. There are others, friends who don't deserve this kind of treatment as a repayment for kindness."

"Like who, Ms. Nelson?" The question came from Herb.

"Like I don't think that's any of your concern, Investigator Woodall."

Herb reached out again, slowly, and touched the sympathy card with the very tip of his index finger. He quoted the handwritten sentiment he had seen inside. "All my love, darling, all the comfort my arms can bring. Yours forever, S.B."

Sally Nelson colored, her gray eyes angry to the point of tears. "My personal business has nothing to do with your investigation. God knows I've been patient. Pete has gone through Gretchen's room, through her things, time after time. I found nothing in the least unusual, and neither did he. I've answered his questions and yours. I've told you everything I know that might help. But now I would appreciate it if you would both leave. It's like your boss says, I don't deserve to be harassed. And if this idiocy doesn't stop immediately, I'm going to file suit against the whole police department, the whole damn city. I have a right to privacy!"

Herb stood. Dixie remained sitting. Sally Nelson looked at her with glacial patience. "Yes, Sergeant?"

"Just one comment, Ms. Nelson, and one more question. Gretchen *did* have a boyfriend. That's a fact. Do you know who he might have been?"

"No, I do not, but since Pete seems to have known my daughter so well, I suggest you ask him."

Herb and Dixie left without further words. Once they had gotten back into the car, with Herb taking his turn at the wheel, Dixie said, "Maybe a change in tactics *is* called for. Maybe we should tell Pete, or at least test the waters. See how his frame of mind is holding up."

"You, or me, or both of us?"

"I'd like to try," Dixie said. "As much as I hate having it that way, he seems to see me as Mama Bear."

"Well, have at it, then, Mama. I can't say I hate to miss it. I still think he'll come unglued."

Herb pulled out onto the street, automatically heading the car for the southern end of town. "Well, are you going to ask or not?"

"About the card, you mean? I don't have to. *S.B.*, a.k.a. Susan Banks, teacher *extraordinaire*."

"Either you're too damn smart for your own good, Struthers, or we've been married too long."

Ms. Banks was putting her classroom materials away for the day. She looked up as Dixie and Herb entered, then shoved the last stack of test papers into her briefcase.

"I would really like to stay and chat," she said, without feigning a drop of sincerity, "but I have things to do."

"Your cooperation would help, Ms. Banks," Dixie said. "Either that or we can take you downtown."

"On what grounds? Refusing to be harassed by a bunch of overbearing, nosy cops? I don't think so, Sergeant."

"You think wrong, lady," Herb said. "I'm sure your secret admirer called you, and she's right—what the two of you do in the privacy, etcetera, etcetera, is your own business. On the other hand, if you did not want your privacy spread around the school, and if Gretchen was going to do that spreading—a juicy little tidbit that would not do your career or your reputation a bit of good—it's quite possible that you would want her out of the way. Right?''

The teacher snapped her case shut but made no move to pick it up. Her posture was still defiant. "Right, Investigator Woodall, the tidbit, as you call it, would do my career irreparable damage. I care very much about what I do for a living. Don't you? Gretchen *did* find out that her mother and I were . . . close. She was not happy about finding out. She and her mother *did* argue about it. That's what you want to know, isn't it?''

"What we want to know," Dixie answered for Herb, "is who had a motive for killing Gretchen Willis. It would seem that—''

Susan Banks paled. "You're wrong. Nothing could have made me harm one hair on Gretchen's head. After she found out, or at least until she turned up missing, I stopped seeing Sally. We both agreed that it was the best thing, not for us, but for Gretchen. The child was already upset, finding growing up difficult, a brilliant mind in a child's body. She was floundering badly, and neither Sally nor I wanted to make it worse.''

"What was it about maturing that Gretchen found so difficult?" Dixie asked. "Did she confide in you, I mean before she learned the truth?''

"To some extent. She was at an age when she needed a father, a male image to look up to, more than just a doting uncle. She wanted to know who her father was—not his name, but what kind of person he was, why he had left her. She talked about finding him. That's happening a lot these days. You see it on the news all the time. An adopted child hunts and hunts until they find the natural parents. There is something sad and desperate about it, I think. Gretchen may not have been an adopted child, but that's the way she felt about finding her father—obsessive. Not unnatural, perhaps, but very hard on Sally. Gretchen wanted answers that Sally refused to give her.''

"You say refused. Does that mean she had answers and simply refused to give them to Gretchen?''

"To some extent, for the child's own good. Her father was the last thing she really needed. Drew has popped in and out a few times over the past few years, though never often or for

very long. A day or two, tops. Once he came from Canada.
Another time from Wyoming. Almost always from a jail or
prison of one kind or another. He didn't give a fig for
Gretchen, or Sally either. He only came a few times during
those sixteen-and-a-half years, but each time he wanted money.
Never even asked to see his own daughter. Sally didn't want
Gretchen to know that. As far as she was concerned, Gretchen
belonged to her. She refused to even consider the fact that her
daughter also had half of Drew's chemistry. Half of his
genetic makeup.''

"When was the last time Drew Willis came here? Was it
recently?''

"No, almost a year ago, in fact. He went to Sally's office,
but she was sick that day, so he went right over to the house.
Thank God Gretchen was here at school. When Sally refused
to give him anything, he made threats, said he would come
back and see Gretchen. In short, Sergeant Struthers, he black-
mailed Sally. I'm sure he would have tried the same thing on
Pete if he thought he could have. But he steered clear of his
brother—the *cop*. I'm sure that was smart, because as much
as Pete loved Gretchen, he would probably have beat Drew
nearly to death. Regardless, Sally gave Drew five hundred
dollars the last time, over half of what she had in her savings
account, and he left town again. He promised he wouldn't
come back.''

Susan Banks's face mirrored total disgust. "He even tried
to get Sally to sleep with him before he left—and he lied
through his rotten teeth. He will come back, sooner or later.
He always shows up again, like a bad penny. And he almost
always uses the same ploy. He sweet talks, and when that
fails, he blackmails her about Gretchen. Then he tries to
make it all up by offering her the thrill of his *services*. He's
an animal, but then''—she looked at Herb without apology—
"most men are.''

She picked up her briefcase. "If you think I killed Gretchen,
you're wrong. I loved her. Still, if you think I did, take me
now. I know where I was on the night she died—right here,
attending a meeting, with 120 other teachers from this school
district. Several of us went out for drinks afterward. But be
my guest. Take me in. At this point I'm beginning not to care
one way or the other. I'm not quite as bad as Sally. I'm only

in the closet because of my students. Otherwise, I would be happy to scream my love for her from the rooftops.''

''Does Pete know?'' Herb asked.

''He does now. He has since last night, when he came pounding on Sally's door like a lunatic. He was really foul, called us names that I don't think he ever used before. Said we had corrupted Gretchen, that Sally had, and that he would never forgive her, that *now* he understood why Drew had deserted her. He was crazy, I'm telling you.''

The teacher walked to the door, knowing full well that neither Dixie or Herb would stop her. She turned just before leaving. ''If you want my opinion of Pete Willis, he was overly attached to Gretchen. Unlike him, I won't make dirty accusations, but he was far too fond of the child. He called her his 'Little Goddess.' Sometimes I think Gretchen actually believed him. But neither Pete nor anyone else could compensate for the fact that her father had deserted her. No one.''

''Poor Pete,'' Herb whispered after she was gone.

''I agree. It seems he just keeps getting it. One shock after another,'' Dixie said. ''But then, he needs to slow it down. He was wrong last night. He can't keep this up. If he does, he's going to lose his job—and his job is about all he has left. And his friends, if only he knew it.''

''Try telling him that when you talk to him tonight, Dix. I'll still come with you if you want.''

Dixie shook her head. ''No, my chore. But I will tell him, if he'll let me.''

''He may not,'' Pete warned.

''Yes,'' Dixie said. ''I know.''

CHAPTER 18

ARRIVING AT THE Nakamura home, one was not struck by any of the Castellano magnificance. Rather, from the outside, it was like many other homes in the upper-middle-class Willow Glen area. Older. Conservative. Traditional. And very, very neat.

A lovely Japanese pine sat in the front yard, just a trifle off center, twisting graceful arms over a lawn that looked as if every blade of grass had been hand measured and matched. Stones lined a pathway of redwood cross sections leading to a shady front porch.

Wendy had answered the door, still dressed in her school clothes. A dress with ruffles and lace, a design hardly in keeping with the modern teenage fads. She had invited them in—a portentous beginning for what both detectives hoped would also be a more productive interview.

A view from the foyer showed a living room to the left, and in the rear of the house, a spacious family room. Looking through the sliding patio doors, Herb and Dixie could see a large pool and spa, an area as neatly landscaped as the front, but far more lush. A manicured jungle.

But they had only just arrived and were still standing in the tiled foyer when Wendy's father arrived. He was a courteous man, but stiff. Herb gave an inward groan of apprehension.

132

Directed by no more than a nod from Edward Nakamura, his daughter led them into the living room.

Wendy Nakamura was a petite, beautiful girl, an exquisite combination of two cultures. Her face at first glance was obviously Oriental, but each feature was softened slightly, altered by her maternal ancestry. Her eyes, Mongolian-curved but round and wide at the outer corners, were gently tilted and a soft doe brown, with golden flecks around her pupils. Her hair was straight and fine, falling nearly to her waist, a waterfall of chestnut-colored silk. More than any other feature, her lips were Oriental, a classic rosebud of a mouth which pouted slightly and yet bore no trace of petulance.

It was a very *sexy* mouth, Herb decided, feeling a bit guilty at the thought. The girl was only fifteen, after all, nearly two years younger than her peers at the library gatherings. Still, somehow, in spite of her youth and diminutive size, Wendy gave the impression of adulthood. Her body was fully developed, a perfectly proportioned miniature. And at any other time, Herb felt sure, her eyes would have held a gentle humor; the knowing, slightly amused expression he had often noted in Oriental women.

There was, however, no trace of mirth on her face at the moment. She looked frightened, plain and simple. She sat on a sofa with both delicate hands clasped tightly in her lap.

The Nakamura home was elegant in its simplicity combining, as did the girl herself, the best of both worlds. Edward Nakamura sat in a chair nearby, wrapped about in calm silence. With virtually no expression on his face, he nevertheless managed to look stern. His eyes rested contemplatively on his daughter. He did nothing to interfere with the police interview.

Mrs. Nakamura, Herb and Dixie learned, had passed away some five years earlier. Her picture sat on the mantle of the fireplace. She had been a pretty blond woman, with inquiring blue eyes and a pert, slightly askew smile.

"So Jimmy Baldwin only used this address for the library, in order to have a card?" Dixie affirmed the information Wendy had already given.

The girl nodded. "Yes, it's almost impossible to be in a library every week and never check out a book. Especially for Jimmy. He . . . we all liked to read, to study. That was the

thing we had in common. Jimmy preferred our main library to
the one in Santa Cruz. The other is closer to his house, of
course, but . . . but . . . he liked coming over the hill . . .
you know, meeting each week to . . . to . . .'' She searched
for a word, and finally settled on the most innocuous. ''. . .
to study.''

''He drove over?'' Dixie had already taken down Jimmy
Baldwin's address. ''He has his own car?''

''No, he doesn't have a car.'' Wendy's eyes slid toward
her father and then quickly away. ''Probably he took the bus.
I'm sure he must have. The depot is only a block or two from
the library, isn't it? Really, I never asked him.''

Somehow, without any real change in expression, Mr.
Nakamura's face managed to settle into lines of granite.

Dixie closed her notebook and put it away in her handbag.
Her voice became more personal, less official in tone. ''Look,
Wendy, we know you must be very upset about Gretchen.
I'm sure I would be if one of my closest friends had been—''

''Oh, we weren't close.'' Wendy hesitated. ''I mean not
that close. We studied together at the library. I liked Gretchen,
but we never—well, you know, we never hung around together. Just at the library, that's all. We went to different
schools and everything.''

''But you had mutual interests, right? You liked the same
kind of things, the same subjects, the same *study*.''

Wendy began to shift in her seat. Her hands were now so
tightly clasped that her knuckles had turned white. And though
Herb had said virtually nothing, he was beginning to feel like
a thug. There was something about the girl's eyes. She
looked like Bambi being pursued by armed hunters. Moreover, he knew Dixie. For all her gentle, persuasive tone of
voice, she was on the scent, moving in for the kill.

''I must say, Wendy, I find the interest you shared with
Gretchen, and Jimmy, and Tony Castellano, a bit unusual. All
the more so seeing how Gretchen died, how she was
murdered.''

Wendy jumped as if she had been shot. Tears rushed to her
eyes and spilled down her cheeks in a sudden and unexpected
torrent. For the first time since greeting Dixie and Herb at the
door, Mr. Nakamura seemed to lose his inscrutability. He

rose from his chair and quickly moved to stand in front of his daughter, almost completely shielding her from view.

"You are upset, Wendy, and overwrought. I think you have been studying too hard. Go to your room now and—"

"But Papa, they will think . . ." Her voice was soft and muffled by tears. "They, they will . . ."

"Wendy, stop this." There was a sharp edge to Edward Nakamura's voice, but whether in admonition or with a touch of panic was difficult to tell. "We will discuss this later, when you are more rested."

"I'm sorry, Mr. Nakamura," Dixie interrupted, "but we need very much to finish talking to Wendy. A homicide has taken place, and if your daughter knows anything that might help us—"

Nakamura turned around so fast that both Dixie and Herb were startled, leaning back in their respective chairs, away from the suddenly thunderous expression on the father's formerly bland face. "Is my daughter a suspect in your case, Sergeant Struthers?" He continued before she could answer, "Because if she is, I shall of course call my attorney at once. If she is not, then I must ask that she be allowed to go to her room. I will be most glad to speak with you when I return."

He held out a hand, which seemed from where Dixie and Herb sat to hang almost disembodied in the air for several long seconds before Wendy reached out and clasped it. Still weeping, she came to her feet. She moved tiredly, keeping her eyes on her father's face as she passed the detectives.

Looking at her, Herb suddenly wondered why he had thought she seemed mature. The expression on her face as she gazed up at her father was utterly childlike, vulnerable, mirroring perfect trust and perhaps a hint of adoration. She seemed to exhale a little moan, half hicupping, and laid her head on his shoulder as they left the room together.

After the pair had disappeared from view, Herb and Dixie looked at one another.

"Well, I'll be flipped," Herb muttered. "I would have sworn she was scared to death of the old man."

"Me, too, but maybe only with regards to Jimmy Baldwin. Maybe she isn't allowed to see boys yet."

Dixie was staring thoughtfully at the door they had gone through. "There's something about those two, I can't quite put my finger on it, something very special—a kind of touching closeness. It must be hard not having a mother in the home. I think Wendy was afraid all right, but probably just because of the whole library scene. I seriously doubt that her father knows what she and the other kids were up to there, what they were *studying*.''

"I still think he's a strange guy," Herb said, looking around at the room they were in, seeing things he hadn't noticed before. One wall was hung with a montage of photographs, all of Wendy, from toddlerhood through adolescence. And in each of them her father was at her side. Wendy, at five or six years old, obviously being taught to ski by her father; the two peeking over the lip of the swimming pool. Wendy, at what appeared to be a scholastic awards ceremony, accepting a bronzed plaque. Again her father stood next to her, looking at her rather than at the award, his stern face altered by a big smile. There were no less than a dozen pictures in all, and in all Wendy and her father were together. Traditional Japanese or not, it was obvious that Mr. Nakamura worshipped his daughter. The only photograph in the room not of them together was the one on the mantle of Mrs. Nakamura.

"The mother must have taken all of—" he started to say, but stopped short as Mr. Nakamura came back into the room. He entered quietly, his dignity and calm firmly intact. He sat on the sofa Wendy had vacated and looked at the detectives, Dixie first, and then Herb.

"My daughter has shown signs of great strain lately," he said. "I now understand why, and for that I thank you."

"You didn't know that Gretchen Willis had been murdered?" Herb made no attempt to mask his surprise.

"Yes, I knew of the murder, of course. Who could miss such terrible news? I did not, however, realize that she was one of Wendy's friends."

"Are we to assume then," Dixie asked, "that the Willis girl never came here?"

"No, she never did, but then that is not unusual. Wendy is a very studious girl. She does not socialize as many young people do. She knows that by working hard now, preparing for her future, she will achieve successs. Success brings leisure, all the more appreciated with maturity."

He was quiet for several moments, looking now at the pictures on the wall. "She is very American, is she not? So many nice things to do. So many opportunities." His chin came up slightly. "But she is also Japanese. She works hard at school and is conscientious. She will leave high school early, at the end of this year, and will hopefully enter Stanford University. Wendy has always planned to become a physician. Her grades are most important, and now, for the first time, she seems to be having some difficulty in school. It must stop. She must not be upset any further."

"We feel strongly that your daughter may be able to facilitate our investigation, Mr. Nakamura," Dixie said. "Not only would she be assisting us greatly, but talking about it, getting her friend's death into proper perspective, might very well also help her recover from the trauma."

"But she has already told you, Sergeant—she and the murdered girl were not close friends. They did not socialize. They were simply study mates when they encountered one another at the library."

"They saw each other every week, Mr. Nakamura. We know that for a fact. And do you know what they studied?"

His eyebrows raised ever so slightly in question. "Why, a variety of subjects I would imagine. Wendy carries quite a heavy class load, as I understand from the newspaper reports, did Gretchen Willis. They were both very bright stu—"

"The *occult*," Dixie interrupted. "Your daughter and her friend studied witchcraft and voodoo and all manner of other unusual subjects. Does Wendy have a class in hocus-pocus, Mr. Nakamura?"

The man's face was turning color, from calm gold to an angry red, but Dixie plunged on. "We have it on good authority that those young people, all of them, had more than a mild interest in some pretty gruesome stuff. They were not only interested—they were *absorbed*."

Wendy's father came to his feet. There was no longer any subtlety about him. He was angry to the point of shaking. "You may think me a foreigner, Sergeant Struthers, and so perhaps ignorant of your laws. I assure you that you are wrong. I am a citizen, a good citizen. I own a prosperous business and have most excellent attorneys."

He was already walking from the room, indicating the front

hallway with a sweep of his arm. The invitation for Dixie and
Herb to leave was abundantly clear. "In the future, if I can be
of help, I will be most happy to oblige. If, however, you wish
to question my daughter, one or more of those attorneys will
be present. Please be so kind as to give me notice of such
intention."

He stood silently, his arm still extended, until Dixie and
Herb left the room. Equally uncommunicative, he let them
out of the house and firmly closed the door on their departing
backs.

Herb looked at Dixie. "Di Franco is going to leap for joy.
So far we've interviewed two members of old lady Jackabcin's
little gang, and it's put two packs of attorneys on our backs.
Worse, the way I see it, we've hardly made an inch of
headway."

Dixie shrugged, but also felt despondent. "What the hey,"
she said. "Tomorrow we can shoot for number three. Baldwin's folks probably have a lawyer or two."

They were almost to the car when Herb noticed the white
van sitting in the Nakamuras' driveway. It bore a sign familiar in the valley, a single, artful sprig of bamboo, gold in
color and outlined in dark green. The lettering bore the name
Golden Bamboo Nursery.

"Holy shit!" Herb stopped in his tracks. "*That* Nakamura!"

Dixie, who had not been reared in the area, looked at him in
question. "What are you talking about? What Nakamura?"

"Never mind. Just get in the car and I'll give you a little
Japanese/American history lesson."

As they drove, he filled her in on what he knew of Wendy's father, a self-made man who could easily have afforded
to live in an area many times as posh as the Willow Glen
District. As he spoke, he remembered in more detail a news
article he had read several years before.

"I think of it almost every time I see one of those vans or
trucks," he said. "I'm surprised I didn't make the connection
earlier. He wasn't joking when he told us he was a citizen.
He was born here. His folks had a nice vegetable and flower
farm in what used to be a strictly agricultural area, right about
where IBM now sits. His folks were citizens, too, but *Issei,*
first generation in the States. His father was worried about the
growing tensions between the two countries, worried about

his wife and son. He put them on a boat and sent them back to his own parents for safekeeping. Guess when?''

"1941."

"You've got it. They departed from San Francisco early in October of that year. Edward Nakamura was only four years old. It took him one whopping long time to get home. Over eight years, not just because of the war but because there was no money afterward. When he finally got back, there was no farm either. It had been confiscated. Meanwhile, his mother had been killed in the bombings on Tokyo. His father was old and sick from his little stay in Poston, Arizona. Everything the guy has now, he dug up from scratch. And believe me, Dix, he has plenty. All the Golden Bamboo Nurseries, of which there are at least five or six, plus a vast multitude of private and industrial landscaping accounts. He's worth a fortune.''

"So, what it amounts to is that we have two big guns to deal with—*Big Castellano*, and now *Big Nakamura*. You're right. The boss is going to be *deeeelighted*.''

CHAPTER 19

PETE WAS NOT in the squad room when Dixie and Herb got back, and Jake informed them that he had gone off duty early.

"Said he wanted to visit the grave," Delaney said. "The guy may look normal, or nearly, but he isn't *healed*. Not by a long shot. How's the case going? Anything new crop up?"

"Nothing good enough," Herb grumbled. He did not look at Dixie, nor she at him.

Delaney chewed on the end of his cigar. "This is about the nastiest bit of business I've ever run across. Hope you put an end to it soon. Even my old lady is edgy, and that woman is a rock, best wife a cop could have."

A murmur of assent went around the room. There were a lot of edgy wives these days.

Dixie picked up the phone and dialed Pete. There was no answer, but she had plenty to keep her busy. Piles of notes to jot down, including the inclusion of several she had made from her home study course in the occult. Symbols that she had hand drawn, followed by reams of explanation. The rest of the detectives had already left when she finally handed Xerox copies to Herb. He leafed through several.

"Give me a break on this stuff, Struthers! You've got to be

kidding! Reading some of this crap is worse than *Hustler*! Worse than the grittiest smoker I've ever seen!"

"Ah." Dixie grimaced. "You must be referring to my Egyptian notes. Good old Apis and Hathor, lovely beasts."

"Really, Dix, I can't imagine you reading this shit. Cows and bulls, for crying out loud—with *people*!"

"To the people who worshipped them, those cows and bulls were only the embodiment, hosts for the gods they represented. Isis was Hathor, and Osiris—or Amon-Ra, if you prefer—was Apis, the bull. A cozy pair."

"Oh, great. I don't care who was what, it's damn gross." Herb held the paper in his hands between two fingers, like he might get burned. "And this other crap, the Druids. Real bad, Dix. It's a wonder you can sleep at night."

"I don't, or not very well. But some of it really is interesting. I've always had an interest in mythology, Greek and Egyptian both. Some parts are pretty sexy, too, Herbie." She grinned at him. "Lots of bed hopping. Mama with son. Brother with sister."

"Bull with virgins." Herb shook his head, not in the least amused. "I suppose you find all this voodoo stuff a real kick in the keester too."

"I see connections, believe it or not, between *all* those religions, or cults, or whatever genre you care put them in. Even voodoo. Poor Reversa, those books scare her to death."

"Reversa?" Herb laughed. "I didn't think anything could scare that woman."

"Neither did I." Dixie also smiled, but only faintly.

"Well, partner, I'm off." Herb stood. "If I'm late home again, Janice will *nag* me to death."

Dixie had tried reaching Pete by telephone, but without success. She finally decided to stop by his place on her way home. There was no doubt in her mind that he was feeling not only grief-stricken, but also neglected by his peers. His whole demeanor screamed it, and she knew that being slipped into his moccasins, she would have felt the same.

She drove slowly, passing his condo and then coming back. His truck was not in the driveway, but she had known it probably wouldn't be. He babied the sturdy four-wheeler,

giving it a spit-and-polish waxing no less than once a week.
She was sure its normal bed was in the garage.

After parking, she walked up the three stairs leading to his
front door and rang the bell. Hearing no movement on the
other side, she tried once more, then turned to leave. She was
almost back to her car when he pulled up.

The Bronco, his one-time pride and joy, was dusty, hub
caps and bumpers dull. She wished that Pete looked happier
to see her as he got out of the truck.

"Hello," he called, but with little enthusiasm.

"Hi, Pete."

He looked like himself, and yet did not. Still wearing his
workday suit, with shirt and tie, he nevertheless lacked the
usual spruce she had come to associate with his appearance.
Pete Willis was not only very good-looking, normally he was
neat as a pin. Dixie noted the unironed shirt and creased suit,
and did a mental shrug. Hard times had come to Pete, a
grieving time. He had a right.

Still, she hoped that the case would break soon. With each
day that passed, she worried more, slept worse, and prayed
harder for a solution. She wanted it to be over. Dreams
haunted her nightly, and if it was so for her, she could only
imagine what the endless hours of darkness must hold for
Pete. Her single solace was that he did not know everything.
He had only the newspapers and newscasts to keep him
abreast of the case. Grisly enough, but not half as bad as the
reality. It had to end, and soon. For Pete. For herself and
Herb. And most of all, for the next unsuspecting victim.
Dixie was unshakably convinced that the person, the *thing*,
that killed Gretchen would strike again.

"You have news for me?" Pete asked. His tone was not
rude, but neither was it hospitable. And certainly not hopeful.

"I have *concern* for you, Pete."

"Appreciated." He looked like he appreciated it the same
way he might a broken collarbone. "That's all?"

She bit back the retort that sprang to her lips, but she was
finding out what she wanted to know. Pete was in no mood
and no condition to be told of his niece's pregnancy. "Nothing solid," she answered.

Pete's face was hard. "Well, how about something liquid,
then, or anything. Surely you've made *some* progress. I saw

the envelope come in this morning—from the coroner's office, wasn't it?''

"Yes, but just the usual stuff. You've seen them before, Pete. Blood type. Weight. Height. You also know how a case like this goes, a rough one. You just keep it up, meandering around, pushing buttons here and there until somebody jumps, or until one of the buttons starts making a loud clicking sound in the back of your head.''

"That's bullshit, Dixie. I've been working with you for quite a while now, remember? You aren't so good at meandering. You *home*, Sarge, like a pigeon.''

"Not this time, Pete. Listen up. I'm telling it true. All we have this time is a small group of kids playing abracadabra. And to my way of thinking, they probably don't fit the bill, which is not to say I still won't give it the old college try.''

"Give it more than that. Give me their names.''

"Damn it, Pete, haven't you made enough waves? When you stick your nose into dark places, you run the risk of getting it punched. Wasn't last night enough?''

"Now it's your nose in the wrong slot, Dixie. That was family business.''

"Wrong. For the time being anything to do with the death of Gretchen Willis is *police business*. And I'm the police officer who's taking care of things. This is my case, Pete, and it's going to stay that way.''

Pete gave her a long, withering look. "Friends are friends, but business is business, right, boss? With you it's always work, isn't it? But that's good. Keep it up and you'll make lieutenant next Monday.''

Dixie wanted to slap his face, but she made herself remember what he'd been through. He was hurting. She could see it in his eyes, in the hunch of his broad shoulders.

"See you," he said, turning away from her and walking to his front door.

Dixie stood on the sidewalk until he disappeared, hoping against hope that he would come back to say good-bye, give her even a weak version of his good-natured and boyish smile.

There was no movement that she could see inside the condo. No drape flickered. No light went on.

She felt sad and hollow as she got back into her car and drove home.

CHAPTER 20

THE NEXT DAY seemed endless, a morning spent going over the few facts they already had, but facts that neither Dixie or Herb felt good about. Nor was there anything solid. Just a jumble of puzzle pieces, none of which seemed to quite fit. They talked to Wittenhaur again, who had more than his usual interest in the case. He also feared that the killer would strike again.

Early in the afternoon they had paid Grady Summers a visit, taking a tour along with another gaggle of his "bug-eyed scoffers," as he called them. The structured tour made the house no less interesting, Sarah Winchester no less mysterious. But Dixie and Herb found nothing new, nothing to further the investigation. Though it had only been just over a week since Gretchen's body was discovered, time seemed to be closing in on them.

They left for the Baldwin interview late enough to feel certain they would find Jimmy Baldwin home from school. Dixie and Herb were both quiet as they drove over the mountains. Dixie used the time to think, to analyze the sketchy information they had garnered to date.

That the teenagers had been at least dabbling in the occult in one way or another was a certainty. But whether their intent had been serious or simply a case of youthful, half playful curiosity, was questionable.

From what they had learned so far, Gretchen Willis had not been the frivolous, playful type. Ditto Tony. Ditto Wendy. All were serious students. All seemed to have been loner types, not given to heavy socializing.

"Did you get a chance to go over those notes I gave you?" Dixie asked after a long silence.

"You mean the *sexy* stuff?"

"No, dummy, the *symbol* stuff. Did you notice that it was all there? All the carvings on the body. The ankh, from ancient Egypt—very phallic. The swastika—from Greece. Dots and lines, daggers plunging into hearts—voodoo. Snakes, found both in voodoo and Druidism, in abundance."

"Druidism is witchcraft, right?"

"Yes and no. The Druids in their Sacred Groves provided the roots. I don't think there are many today who practice witchcraft, or Wicca, in the old way. Or I sure as hell hope not. But you have the right idea."

"Well, in answer to your question—yes, I did notice the symbolism. And that takes us right back to those kids, doesn't it?"

Dixie did not answer. She was too tired. Too depressed.

They both retreated into their own thoughts again, silent until they reached Rio Del Mar. It was a unique community, combining mountainous, pine-crested vistas with a long expanse of beach front. A small, tightly knit town, with a majority of homes set into the hills, overlooking the sunny, blue Pacific.

The Baldwin house had no fence or gates, but the driveway leading to it was so steep that it made Dixie's scalp tighten. A giant black-and-tan rottweiler met them in the wide circular driveway at the top. When the car stopped, the dog leapt up, barking and slathering against Herb's window.

"Hot damn," he yelped, "look at them jowls! Guess I'm going to skip this interview unless someone comes out here to soothe the savage beast."

Dixie also stayed firmly put, unconciously pushing down the lock on her side. "Makes Poke look like a regular pussycat, doesn't he?"

"*Down*!" Herb yelled, but the dog stayed and continued to bark. "Down, I said! *Je-e-e-sus*, will you shut up!"

Even with the windows up, the deep, chesty bark seemed to reverberate inside the unmarked car. Dog spittle and breath fog glazed the window. Dixie honked the horn, long and loud.

About two minutes later, a time stretch Herb thought must be two hours, a young man appeared at the rottweiler's side. He wore a tank top and a pair of long shorts. The outfit complemented his tall, lean athletic build. He was blond and blue-eyed. A Calfornia Boy. A quick word and a hand signal from him brought the animal neatly to heel.

"Okay, Herb, you can get out now." Dixie gave him an evil grin. "Women and children last. Age before beauty and all that."

"Thanks heaps."

The dog's owner greeted them with a wary smile, patting his beast on the head. "You looking for someone?"

Herb showed his badge and extended his hand while Dixie cautiously emerged from the car. "If your name is Jimmy Baldwin, we're looking for you."

The smile went a little lopsided. "You make me sound like one of those bulletins you see in the post office. Wendy called me. She said you would probably be coming. I guess I really expected you, even before she called."

"Do you want to talk inside?" Herb asked. He tried not to look at the dog, who now sat panting contentedly, as if in happy anticipation, pink tongue dripping copiously.

Jimmy stroked the dog's massive head again. "Don't mind Brutus. He's really gentle."

With a too studied expression of nonchalance, the boy looked over his shoulder toward the house. "Would you mind if I met you somewhere else? I mean, I'm not trying to be tricky or anything. It's just that my mom is kind of sick and, well . . . would you mind?"

Herb looked at Dixie and saw her nod.

"Sure, just name the place."

"Have you ever heard of Sister Snoots? It's a coffee shop down on the main drag, right next to the beach, beside the causeway."

"I know it," Dixie said. It was a place she and Art often

went to enjoy espresso on cool Sunday mornings. "We'll meet you there."

"In about fifteen minutes," he answered, turning and waving at the same time, walking swiftly back to the house. Brutus remained exactly where he was, but he quit panting. His teeth made a sharp clicking sound as his jaws snapped shut. Herb was sure his red-brown eyes narrowed a fraction.

"Exit stage left," he whispered, "and get the hell out!"

Seeing as how she had farther to go, Dixie moved with more agility and speed. She had just made the safety of the car when she heard Herb swear.

"Get back, you bloodthirsty son of a bitch!" A rip sounded as he jerked his right leg inside the car. He tried to slam the door, and the dog yelped. "I said get back, or I'll blow your brains out!"

Brutus did back off, shaking his great dark head to clear the pain caused by the door. Herb made his next slam count.

"I think you hurt his feelings," Dixie said. "In fact, he looks like he might even be crying."

"You know what, lady? I've never hit a woman before, but—"

Dixie cut him off with a giggle that turned to a nervous laugh as she drove down the driveway.

Sister Snoots was a local hangout, a second-story coffee house with a great view from a small rear balcony. The air inside reverberated with shades of Bach and Beethoven, the wonderful classical music adrift on the aroma of freshly brewed gourmet coffee. At any given time an aspiring author or two could be found snuggled into a corner, scribbling like mad on long legal tablets, chewing pencil ends, staring dazedly into worlds seen only in their own minds.

Dixie and Herb took seats out on the balcony. They ordered and then sat quietly, watching gulls drift over the dusk-painted Pacific Ocean. A vast sky was purple and pink, striped with wispy, lavender clouds. Neither of the detectives spoke for some time.

Dixie was the first to break the silence. "He looked like a poster model for the all-American boy."

Herb nodded, sipping a strong black Sumatra. "Apple pie all the way."

"It's hard to believe kids like the ones we've been talking to could possibly be involved in what we found at the Winchester Mansion—or, for that matter, in anything remotely resembling some of the things I'm finding in those books I checked out. Some of that stuff sets my hair on end."

"That must be pretty cute." Herb smiled. He was feeling more relaxed, soaking up the view and the tangy, salt-laden air, soothing his Brutus-jangled nerve endings. "Besides, Dixie, we haven't established anything for certain. We're still working strictly by braille, feeling our way along. At this point everything is pure supposition."

"Pretty damn good supposition, I'm afraid. I just can't get over how these kids look—how healthy and bright. I'm beginning to understand how Lillian Jackabcin felt."

Herb put his coffee mug on the table. "I'll grant you they appear to be a cut above average, but the key word there is *appear*. They all seem to come from good homes, or at least affluent ones. All except Gretchen. She's odd man out there, but otherwise she fits perfectly. They all have clear skins, and straight, white smiles. But so far they all have something else in common too. Trouble. Troubled minds. Wendy, Tony . . . As for the Baldwin boy, we don't know yet, but I would be willing to bet—"

"Officers?" Jimmy Baldwin stood at the rear door of the coffee shop. Brutus sat beside him, panting, grinning at Herb, who nearly knocked his coffee over.

"Excuse me, son, but isn't there some law over here against bringing animals into eating establishments?"

Jimmy smiled and, sure enough, his teeth flashed white and very, very straight. He patted Brutus. "I didn't bring him in exactly; I walked him through. Go on, Brutus, go over there and lay down. Down. That's a good boy."

The dog flopped into one corner, resting his jaws on giant paws, about three feet from Herb's feet and ripped pant leg.

"I take him for a walk every night," Jimmy said.

"So your folks think you're out walking the dog." Dixie took a sip of coffee and looked at him over the rim of her mug.

He met her eyes. "Yes, they do. Or at least my mom does. She isn't feeling very well, so I can't stay too long. I don't want her to be upset."

"Do you know why we've come, what we need to talk about?"

He nodded. "Gretchen."

Dixie put her coffee mug down. "That's right, Jimmy. You seem to be a member of a very small but select group. You are one of only three people who seems to have known Gretchen Willis well. She didn't have any friends at school."

"Except Tony."

"Tony Castellano?"

"Yes. They had classes together, I think. They were pretty tight."

"How tight? Boyfriend and girlfriend?"

"I wouldn't know about that, but friends."

"You mean to say that the four of you, two boys and two girls, met at the same place every week for over three months, and you don't know whether or not Tony and Gretchen were going together?" Dixie's right eyebrow arched a fraction, mirroring the obvious reservation in her voice.

"That was a *study* group, Miss . . . er . . . Sergeant . . . Struthers, wasn't it?"

"Sergeant Struthers and Investigator Woodall," she answered.

"Yes, well, like I said, we met there at the library. Except for Tony and Gretchen, we didn't know each other before. We shared a table and studied. We didn't stand between the rows of books making out." The answer was a bit pert, but the tone of his voice was not. He spoke quietly, with just the right amount of respect.

"But then that wonderful little volume on Baron Samedi isn't very romantic either, is it?" Dixie continued to study him. He began to flush slightly. "That was one of your all-time favorites, I believe. You checked it out three times."

"I . . . I . . . was doing a paper."

"In July?"

An edge of belligerence slipped into his voice. "No, not in July. My paper was due on the first of June, just before last year's finals. I got it in on time. If you don't believe me, why don't you check? It was for Mr. Knowles's class. Psychology Two."

"We already are checking, Jimmy. That's our job. And you *did* check the book out for the last time in July."

"Since when is reading a crime, Sergeant Struthers? I found the book interesting. When I was reading it as a project, I gave it a rush job. I went back and covered some of it again." He paused. "Not that I really have to explain a thing like why I check a book out of the library."

"You're right, you don't, and everything you say sounds perfectly reasonable." She gave him a slight smile. "Actually, I'm not trying to jump your case, Jimmy. We're investigators. That's what we're doing—*investigating*. We simply need your help. Any information you can give us will be appreciated."

Not once had he avoided looking into her eyes, and he did not do so now. "Please don't give me a pat on the head, Sergeant. I know I'm still a kid, but I'm not stupid. You're investigating, all right. You're investigating *me*. Gretchen was . . . killed in a horrible way. We were studying some pretty way-out stuff, and you and your partner think there is a connection. Well, you're wrong. What we were do— What we . . . the things we talked about and the books we read had nothing to do with what happened to Gretchen."

Herb spoke for the first time since the interview had begun. "You're right, son, we are investigating you. All of you. And you're giving us some pretty good reasons by not telling us everything."

"But I have told you—all there is to tell, anyway."

"Like why you went to a library almost thirty miles from where you live? Why you used someone else's address to check out your weird books. That's a long way, thirty miles."

"I wanted to be with my—" His mouth snapped shut as he realized his mistake.

"With your friends," Herb finished for him, "the ones you didn't know at all until you met them at the library."

"I *did* meet them there!"

Dixie could almost see the mental wheels turning as he tried to recoup credibility.

"I went over there once in a while because the library was so much bigger. There was more reference material, stuff you can't check out anyway.And then, after I met Wendy and Tony and Gretchen, I just went because I enjoyed going there more."

"Guess that's as good an explanation as any," Herb said. "But I still think that's one hell of a long way to drive."

Jimmy did not respond, and Dixie stepped back into the conversation. "You did drive?"

"I don't have a car. I took the bus a couple of times, but mostly I hitched. I always got a ride pretty quick."

"Your folks let you do that—hitchhike thirty miles every week, on a school night?"

The boy twisted in his chair. He answered slowly and with obvious reluctance. "They didn't know."

"How could they not? Where in the world did they think you were for so long?"

"At the library." He gave them a lopsided smile. "I didn't lie, I just didn't say which library. Mom goes to bed pretty early most of the time, so she didn't realize I was getting in a little late."

"A little?" Herb asked.

Jimmy ignored him. "And my father goes out on that night. He has some kind of meeting. He's never home early on Thursdays. Never."

Dixie thought she detected an undertone of bitterness in his voice, but she said nothing.

Jimmy glanced down at his watch, and now his face did mirror alarm. "Look, I've got to get home. My mother will worry." He came quickly to his feet. "Brutus, come."

"We still have several questions," Dixie told him. "Maybe we could—"

"I can't, really. I've got to go."

The dog was beside him as he turned to leave. He was almost through the door into the coffee shop when he stiffened. He stood there, did a little shuffle, and half turned, as if looking for an escape. But then his shoulders drooped and he stood perfectly still. Dixie got a look at his face and saw that he had gone pale beneath his tan.

"You little shit!" A low, menacing voice sounded, and a second later a man came through the door and out on the balcony. "Walking the dog are you? Boy, you were born a liar and you'll die a liar."

"I just stopped to get something to dri—"

The man brought a hand down on his shoulder. Even from

where she sat, Dixie could see the thick, hair-tufted fingers dig hard into Jimmy's flesh.

"Come on, son, you and I are going home." Mr. Baldwin was almost smiling. Something unpleasant, a sort of anticipation, lurked in his steel-gray eyes.

Brutus growled, low and deep.

Dixie stood, her mind working quickly, more on instinct than anything else. "Mr. Baldwin?"

The man looked at her and scowled, a frown that deepened as Herb also came to his feet.

"We asked your son to join us," Dixie said. "Hope that's not a problem."

The man's hand quickly left Jimmy's shoulder. "Is that so? And just why would you do that?"

Howard Baldwin was a large man, good-looking in a burly, ex-athlete sort of way. He had blond hair, graying, receding from a high forehead. He wore an expensive pair of slacks and a short-sleeved white dress shirt. The dark tie just below his collar had been loosened. After another moment of hesitation, he approached and gave them something just barely akin to a smile. Jimmy did not move, except to pat Brutus gently on the head. He seemed to be murmuring beneath his breath, soothing the animal.

"I'm Sergeant Struthers." Dixie extended her hand. "And this is my partner, Investigator Woodall."

"No kidding? Well, excuse me then. I'm Howard Baldwin." His face did a quick change, lighting as he gave them both a brisk salesman's handshake. It was a genuine see-what-a-nice-sincere-guy-I-am shake.

Dixie did not believe the shake or the phony smile.

"Sorry if I sounded a little gruff just now. My boy's got chores to do. You know how it is. And he told his mother he was just going out to walk the dog. She didn't know he was meeting you."

"He wasn't," Dixie lied, without being sure why. "We were on our way to your house anyway and just happened to see him coming down the street. It's been a long hard day, and to be honest, we decided to kill two birds with one stone." She indicated the table. "I was plain old dying for a cup of coffee."

Howard Baldwin turned, looking over his shoulder at his

son. "Come on over here, boy." He gave the kid a big cheesy grin. "Why didn't you just say you had to talk to these officers. Not in trouble are you, son?" He followed the question with a big, bluff har-har.

"He isn't in any trouble," Dixie answered for the boy, hoping she was not talking too fast. "Just something to do with an acquaintance."

Jimmy walked slowly toward them. His troubled eyes shot Dixie a fleeting look of gratitude and then quickly shifted to his father. His face was guarded, his posture tense. "I really ought to go back, Dad, don't you think? Mom needs help with dinner."

"We're done here anyway, Mr. Baldwin." Dixie picked up the check, and Herb plucked it from her hand and silently went to pay. "As it turns out, Jimmy didn't really know the other student very well."

A spark of doubt lingered in Baldwin's eyes. "Oh? And who might that have been?"

Dixie took a chance, putting just a faint note of suspicion in her tone, as if she were double-checking on Jimmy with an *adult*. "Tony? Tony Castellano?"

"Never heard of him."

"Yes, that's what Jimmy told us. He knows the Castellano boy, but not very well. Just another student he sees around from time to time."

"Well, I don't know the kid, but if he's a troublemaker, I'm sure my son would not be involved with him." The man was all good cheer again. The proud papa. "Jimmy is a good boy, Sarge. Gets good grades. Goes to church every Sunday. Minds his manners. That's the way he's been brought up."

Herb returned on the tail end of the conversation. Dixie noticed how he casually patted Jimmy on the shoulder as he passed, a gesture Mr. Baldwin did not see. Herb's own face was passive, but as the boy and his father left, he looked at Dixie and wrinkled his nose.

"Why the ca-ca face?" she asked.

"I just don't like that guy. There's something menacing about him."

They left Sister Snoots, walking slowly back to their car. With the nearing of autumn and the start of the school year, the beach crowd had pretty much evaporated. The weather was still warm, though, and local residents strolled along. Every now and then a jogger thumped by.

Herb looked at his watch. "Just like I said. We've been on overtime for almost an hour. You want to call it quits and grab a bite?"

Dixie shrugged. "Sure, why not. All this sand and foam makes me lazy. Works up an appetite, too. Not a great combination."

She looked up, away from the ocean and toward the nearby mountains. The homes nestled in amongst the trees winked at her, windows reflecting the sunset like lambent orange eyes.

"You know, Herb, when I was growing up in the city, I used to like looking at the houses, especially at night." Her voice was touched with nostalgia. She continued to look up at the hillside, a mild sea breeze ruffling her hair. Herb looked at her and smiled as she continued. "In San Francisco it's not like here, where people can live all spread out. There, it seems like every inch of space is used. Most people spend their lives living all stacked on top of one another. Above businesses. Over garages. In houses and apartments squished together like sardines. I used to make up stories.

"Pop knew how I was, a little weird I guess, and the two of us used to walk along main streets, or go down into Chinatown. He did it so that I could stare up at the buildings and think about all the hundreds and thousands of people that lived behind the windows. Behind white lacy curtains and sad, tattered drapes. All kinds of people. All colors. With every sort of romance and loneliness, happiness and problems."

She chuckled at herself. "Guess I'm more tired than I thought, rambling in my old age."

Herb followed the direction of her gaze. "Not rambling too far, maybe. All these kids in their nice houses—makes you wonder what their lives are really like."

Dixie gave herself a little shake and straightened her shoulders. Her eyes were no longer dreamy as they entered a small seafood restaurant. "I'm wondering, all right, about a lot of things."

The hostess seated them near a long bay window, and once more they had an ocean view.

"I'll tell you one thing I wonder," Dixie continued, "and

that's what we would find if we could peek through the windows of those kids' rooms.''

"Probably some pretty classy literature. You know, like *Full Moon Frolicks*, or *How to Make Your Next Cookout a Religious Event*. . . .''

Herb, will you be—''

"Or maybe, *Sing Along with Satan*—''

"Herb, this is not funny,'' she said, in spite of her smile.

"I know it isn't, Dix. I'm just not sure what you're getting at.''

"Well, it seems to me that if those kids were all so heavily involved in some kind of cult, there's bound to be evidence somewhere. On their persons. In their rooms. Wouldn't you think?''

"What, like a bell, book and candle you mean?''

"Yes. Something, anyway.''

"Don't tell me you're beginning to believe in spooks, Struthers.''

"No, but we're not finding much else. Doesn't that seem strange to you? All this hocus-pocus dominocus and what we see are three kids who look arrow straight. That's what I meant about their rooms. I'd give anything to look a little deeper into the way they spend their time. What their bedrooms look like. Inside their dresser drawers. I want some evidence that they were really doing what we think they were doing, having séances, sticking pins into little dollies, pouring chicken blood all over each other, something for crying out loud!''

Dixie started slightly as a shadow fell across her. She looked up to see their waitress. The woman was staring at her with wary eyes. "Uh, can I take your order?''

"Sorry,'' Dixie apologized, "I haven't looked at the menu yet.''

"Me either,'' Herb said, "give us a little longer. In the meantime, maybe we could get something to drink. Dixie?''

"Sure. A beer will do for me.''

The waitress marked it down on her little green pad. She was still casting Dixie cautious sideways glances.

"And I'll take some chicken blood.'' Herb grinned. "Straight up.''

•   •   •

Herb leaned back in his chair, dabbing at his mouth with a napkin. "Okay, Struthers, out with it. I can hear your brain clicking from here, and you've said hardly a word since I made the waitress throw up."

"You're a very funny man, mister." The same woman who had taken their order, perfectly sound of limb and color, plucked up his empty plate. "A real funny guy." She gave him a bark of laughter, Dixie's plate a disapproving look, and disappeared again.

Dixie's plate was almost untouched. She speared a buttery prawn with her fork, but instead of eating, she twirled it slowly around, looking at it without seeing. "I'm not clicking hard enough, partner, because I still can't come up with a thing. With the reactions we're getting from the parents involved, I don't think there's even an itsy-bitsy chance of getting close to any of those kids for a private conversation, much less a peek into their rooms. Much, much less taking a real good snoop.

"I think I'll go back to the library tomorrow," she said. "There are a few more books that I'd like to check out. Want to come?"

"Tomorrow is Saturday, Dix—the big game." He made a bright face. "Daddy and Daughter Soccer!"

"Oh, God, I almost forgot. Sorry."

"That's okay, I forgot to tell you that Janice invited Pop and Reversa to come along with you and Art."

Dixie said a poignant nothing.

"What's wrong, you can't make it?"

"Oh, *I* can, but I think Art will probably be busy."

Herb started to ask questions, then changed his mind. "Well, all the more reason to drag the others over."

"I won't have to drag Pop or Reversa. They'll jump at the chance. It's been too long since they've seen Amy."

"Forget Amy. It's me who's going to need a cheering section. Janice is umping."

"Uh-oh." Dixie teased him. "Thou art most surely in T-R-O-U-B-L-E."

The playful hassle Janice gave Herb was a standing joke, not to mention the difference in their energy levels: Janice, the gun-ho dynamo, to Herb, the lounge lizard.

"In that case maybe we better pull Pete in too. I need all the cheering I can get."

"You worried about me playing the old maid, Herb?" She said it lightly enough, but without looking at him.

Herb sobered instantly. "No matchmaking intended. I'm worried about our friend. He can probably use a little socializing."

She instantly felt ashamed. "Sorry, that was incredibly self-involved. I think things are getting to me."

"We all have a right once in a while." He decided to ask after all. "You and Art not flying so high these days?"

"Just the opposite," she said in a low, hardly audible voice. "I think maybe we've flown too high—for too long."

CHAPTER 21

THE CALL CAME at just after two in the morning. Dixie rolled over in bed and lifted the receiver before the shrill ringing could wake anyone else, but her mind was still wrapped in sleep. She kept her eyes closed.

"Hello." She croaked a whisper into the phone and then swallowed to clear her throat. "Struthers."

"Yes," said a male voice, "sorry to disturb you at this hour, but I need to speak to Sergeant Struthers."

"This is Struthers." She wanted the voice to go away.

"Pardon me, but I mean *Sergeant* Struthers."

Drowsiness made her grumpy. She scowled. "This *is* Sergeant Struthers. To whom am I speaking?"

"Oh, er . . . sorry, Sergeant, I didn't realize." There was another pause and then the voice continued, not quite so crisp. "This is Investigator David Gates from the Santa Cruz County Sheriff's Office. We've had what looks like a possible 187 over here."

She was coming awake now, but her eyes remained shut. She cleared her throat again. "Yes?"

"It seems a man has been killed by his own dog, or rather his son's dog."

Her eyes flew wide open and she sat straight up in bed.

"It would appear that the man, a Howard Baldwin, was

killed just a little before midnight. There were no witnesses except the boy, and I think it's very possible . . . well, there is a question of whether or not this was an accident. The kid has a black eye and he seems kind of shocky, you know?''

Dixie visualized Jimmy and how he had looked on the previous evening. Pale of face. Tense of body. She remembered, too, how large his father's hand had seemed as it came down on the boy's shoulder.

"He isn't talking to us." The voice on the telephone continued as Dixie stood up and pulled on her bathrobe. "He's shaking all over—won't say a word. It's weird. He's just sitting, staring off into space, shut up like a clam. I've tried talking to him several times. He's got questions to answer, but there may have been some special circumstances here. I don't want to take him in unless I have to. The last time I tried to talk to him, he went upstairs and brought down the card you had evidently given him. Are you a relative, or just a friend, or what?''

"None of the above, Investigator Gates." She held the phone on her shoulder as she tied the sash of her robe. "Are you at the scene now?''

"Yes, my partner and I got here with the tech team. They're going over things." His voice dropped almost to a whisper, indicating that there was someone nearby. "I don't mind telling you, Sergeant, this is a real mess. The guy's throat is ripped out. If the kid *is* responsible, he's in some very heavy-duty trouble. And like I said, he won't talk. Can you shed a little light?''

"Do you have any objections to my coming over? I assume you'll be there for a while.''

"Oh, we'll be here all right.''

"It will only take me half an hour or so.''

"See you then.''

The line went dead, and Dixie stood in the darkness, holding the telephone. She considered calling Herb, but quickly decided it was a bad idea. This was off-duty time, unpaid and unrequired. Herb had an obligation to his family, and a game to play with Amy in less than eight hours.

Quickly putting on a sweatshirt and a pair of jeans, she went into the bathroom. After washing her face and brushing her teeth, she ran a comb through her hair with quick, impa-

tient strokes. She left the house without any frills. Just a
wallet with identification, and the small chrome-plated nine
millimeter Walther PPK slipped into the waistband of her
jeans.

Poke greeted her with a sniff and a whine as she came
down the stairs. She patted his head just before letting herself
quietly out of the house. It was pitch-black outside, but she
knew her property so well that she could have made her way
to the car blindfolded. Across the high deck. Down the stairs.
Gravel crunched beneath her boots as she made her way to
the carport. The air was alive with pine. Crickets chirped.

The route of Rio Del Mar was almost deserted, and in just
over fifteen minutes she was gearing down to take the steep,
narrow road leading up to the Baldwin place. The large
two-story house sitting at the top of the hill was ablaze with
light and activity. Three patrol cars sat in the driveway, along
with two unmarked vehicles. Two attendants in white pants
and red jackets leaned against an ambulance, waiting to trans-
port the body of Howard Baldwin from the house to the
county morgue. Brutus was leashed to the door handle of one
of the regular patrol cars. He looked forlorn, his massive head
resting on the ground between his front paws.

The ambulance drivers looked speculatively at Dixie as she
emerged and walked to the house. A uniformed officer escorted her into a living room with high vaulted ceilings. A
massive natural rock fireplace dominated one wall.

"Sergeant Struthers?" A plainclothes detective greeted her,
holding out his hand. His eyes quickly took her in, noting her
diminutive size; curly, still slightly bed-ruffled hair; and her
figure. And though his eyes registered mild surprise, his face
remained unsmiling. Carefully professional. "I would say
welcome, but it hardly seems appropriate."

He tipped his head toward a long white sectional sofa
which monopolized another entire wall. The cushions were
splattered with dark crimson bloodstains, some so thick that
they still shone a damp glistening red. The body of Howard
Baldwin was still there, but it had been covered by a sheet.
The outline of the man's head was visible, and where his
neck would naturally have been, there was a large circular
bloodstain. One out-flung hand, curled into what more closely
resembled a claw, poked from beneath the macabre covering.

That hand, too, showed wounds, deep puncture marks. There were smears on the pale ivory carpet near the sofa. Several men, evidence technicians, were examining the area, taking samples of both blood and fibers.

Dixie looked at the mess and then away. "Where is the boy?"

"In the kitchen with his mother," Gates answered, "but let's you and I talk first, shall we?"

Dixie gave him a faint, fleeting smile. He was still looking at her with inquiring eyes, and she could almost read his mind: *This is a cop*? Throughout her seven years on the force she had grown used to the surprise, the doubt. "Anything you say, Detective Gates."

"Dave," he corrected, and smiled back. "Let's go into the next room."

Dixie followed him through a wide archway into a formal dining area, glad to escape the mayhem. He motioned her to sit, and then took a chair on the other side of the table.

"I warned you it was a mess," he said.

"And you think the boy engineered the attack?"

"I don't know that I would use that particular word, but yes, I think there is a better than even chance that he sicced Fido on his old man."

"Commanded the dog to attack?"

"Something like that. Of course, it's always possible the dog acted on its own."

"To protect Jimmy."

"Sounds great, except for one thing." Gates was softly tapping his fingers against the edge of the table. "Howard Baldwin had an argument with his son all right, but earlier in the evening, around eight or nine according to Mrs. Baldwin. At the dinner table. If another incident took place, she was not aware of it. She was sleeping, very soundly I would guess. You'll know what I mean when you meet her. Pretty heavily doped."

"You said that Jimmy has a black eye. I would call that a bit more than just an argument, wouldn't you?"

"Okay, call it a fight then—but the fact remains that it took place quite a while before that black beast ripped out Baldwin's jugular. It wasn't like he was hitting the kid right then or anything. Not that we know of. In fact, it looks like the old man was just sitting there, reading and having a highball. There was a book on the sofa near him. The damn thing looked like a half-eaten sandwich.'' Gates shook his head. "I can't see the dog just strolling through the room and going after him, not without good reason—not without being *commanded*.''

"Unprovoked attacks have been known to take place," Dixie said. "You read it in the newspaper every now and then.''

"Sure, but never by this breed. I'm a dog lover, Sergeant Struthers."

"You can call me Dixie.''

He smiled. "Okay, Dixie. So like I said, I love dogs, big or little, but mostly big. Rottweilers are a special breed. Protective and very expensive. They are also notoriously stable, not like pit bulls or even Dobermans. I've heard of a lot of pit bulls turning, and even a few Dobies—not many, but some. Never heard of a rottweiler going sour, though. Never.''

"Until now.''

"Until now—*if* that's what happened.''

"There's always a first time. My partner and I met good ol' Brutus yesterday afternoon, and he was a real barrel of laughs. Nearly took the leg off my partner's pants.''

"So you'd say the dog was vicious?''

"Let me put it this way—he seems to really *enjoy* striking a bit of terror. Maybe he's just playful.''

"I've met dogs like that." Gates chuckled, and then sobered. "Do you mind telling me why you and your partner were here? This is a bit out of your jurisdiction, and I noticed that you and I work the same detail—homicide.''

"Yes, my partner and I are working the Willis case, a teenage girl who was—''

"I've heard about it. From what I gather, that was another not-so-pretty.''

"Very." Dixie did not elaborate. "We were interviewing Jimmy because he was one of the girl's friends. Just routine.''

"How did he strike you. Nervous? Cocky?''

She shook her head. "No, very courteous and pleasant for the most part. A nice, open smile. He didn't want to talk to us here, though, said his mom wasn't feeling well.''

"An understatement, I think.''

"Well, that was the reason he gave, but I think there might have been another. We met him down at Sister Snoots. His father found him there with us, and the boy did a real change then. I got the impression he was scared, and I sort of bailed him out. To be honest, I got the impression that he was genuinely frightened of his dad.''

"Looks like he had reason. He's got a real, honest-to-Pete shiner, and his lower lip looks a little puffy.''

The detective straightened and leaned back in his chair. "I'm still unclear as to why the kid refuses to talk to me—or why he gave me your card, especially since you had just met. At first I thought you must be a relative or maybe a close friend. You know how people are, even when you pull them over for a ticket, they'll pull a name on you. Everyone knows a cop when they're in trouble.''

"Maybe I just have one of those faces.'' Dixie found herself smiling at him again, half wishing she had taken the time to make up her face. Her hair felt a mess, tumbling down over her shoulders. "Guess us big-city types just inspire more trust.''

"No doubt.'' He stood up. "You want to see him now? Let's hope he'll talk to you. There's something about that kid, something I can't quite put my finger on. The only word I can come up with is *victim*. I don't want to have to drag him out of here and put him through the ropes unless there's a valid reason.''

"Have you Mirandized him already?''

"Of course. I had to. And I'm sure that didn't help. As soon as you say 'You have the right to remain . . .' people get the idea you're going to throw them in the slammer.''

He opened a door and escorted her into the next room. It was a spacious kitchen, eating area, and sitting room. Casually furnished, the sitting area held rattan furniture, a small sofa, and two chairs. The kitchen itself was fully equipped, from microwave and compactor to an open-brick barbecue. Gleaming copper pots hung over the island stove. Leafy green plants, hanging garlic ropes, and naturally dried spices kept the air fragrant and homey.

Jimmy Baldwin sat on the small rattan sofa next to a pale blond woman. She was thin, undoubtedly under forty, but she nevertheless had old, weary, and artificially glazed eyes. Her lips were tightly compressed. Tears ran unchecked down her cheeks, and her head rested on Jimmy's shoulder. The two held hands.

The boy looked up as Dixie drew near. His face was stark, drawn tight with pent-up emotion, with tension—and maybe with fear. Maybe grief. Maybe.

Jimmy swallowed hard and gave her a wry, twisted smile. "Hello, Sergeant Struthers. Long time no see."

"Sorry about your dad, Jimmy."

The look he returned did not really change his expression, but his eyes altered slightly, going icy and turning inward. He nodded but did not answer.

Dixie felt the restlessness of the investigator at her side. Gates was looking at the boy, too, and Dixie wondered if he had also seen the slight change. One thing was certain, whether or not Jimmy had actually killed his father, he was not mourning.

"Do you want to talk?" She put the question to him in a low voice.

He looked from her to Gates and back again. "I . . . I don't know why I gave him your card, Sergeant. I'm not sure what . . . what I was even thinking. It's just that you helped . . . I mean when my . . ." He swallowed again, with difficulty. "You helped me when my father caught me at Sister Snoots. I don't know, maybe I thought you could help again. I'm not sure." He looked back at Gates. "He says I have the right to an attorney before answering any questions. He read me my rights, just like the cops do on TV."

She thought there was a faint hint of something resembling sarcasm in his voice, and once more his lips lifted in a joyless facsmile of a smile.

"Those rights hold, son," Gates said. "You do have the right to an attorney before questioning, but it would save us all a lot of time if you could tell us more about what happened here."

"What are you going to do to Brutus?" There was more animation in his face as he asked the question. Real worry. "He was only protecting me, you know. I've had him since he was a little puppy. He . . . he loves me."

His mother, who until now had not said a word, lifted her head slowly from her son's shoulder. She had a hazy look in her half-lidded eyes. Her speech was slurred. "I love you, too, baby. I love you, really I do."

Jimmy patted her hand and at the same time eased slightly away from her. "I know you do, Mom. Don't worry. Everything is going to be okay."

He stood up. "Can we talk, Sergeant Struthers? Just the two of us?"

Gates took the hint and stepped back a few paces, but he was still within earshot.

"I'm a police officer, Jimmy," Dixie told him, trying to put aside her personal inclination, the tug of sympathy that made her want to put her arms around him and tell him all would be well. He was like a little boy, a little tin soldier, trying to play general. A child who had, perhaps, always carried too many burdens, too much responsibility. But she kept her voice purposefully professional. "Anything you tell me can be brought into evidence, even though I don't work in this county. Do you understand that?"

"I understand." He sounded unutterably tired. "I still want to talk to you, but not here." His glance softly touched his mother and then slid away.

Dixie looked at Dave Gates and saw his nod of acquiescence.

"Jimmy?" Mrs. Baldwin reached out a hand, groping at the air. "Don't leave me, honey."

Jimmy knelt down in front of her and spoke as he might have to a very small child. "It will be all right, Mom. I'm not going anywhere, just to my room. Just for a few minutes. You rest now, and I'll be right back, okay?"

"I can't rest, honey, I need a pill. I really need one, Jimmy."

The boy looked at his watch and then went to a kitchen cupboard. For the first time Dixie noticed the lock. He took out two bottles and shook some pills into his palm. He gave them to his mother, along with a glass of water. She nodded and slumped back against the cushion, closing her eyes and sighing deeply.

Jimmy looked at Dixie. "She hasn't been well, not for a long time now." His tone was defensive. "You can see that, can't you?"

"I see a lot of things, Jimmy," she replied a note of sympathy creeping into her voice.

CHAPTER 22

SHE FOLLOWED HIM from the kitchen into a hallway that opened into the living room several feet farther on. A staircase rose from the opposite end, and Jimmy led her to the second floor. Several doorways lined the upper hallway, all closed except the last. Jimmy's room. It seemed ironic to Dixie that she was now, without any effort on her part, being given just the thing she wanted, access to the bedroom of one of her teenage suspects.

At first glance it seemed exactly the kind of room one might expect of a studious, athletic seventeen-year-old boy. Bookshelves and a built-in study area covered one wall, with posters tacked up on the others. What appeared to be a drafting board rather than an easel sat in one corner, and on it a large sketch pad lay open. Dixie stopped in her tracks, staring at the pencil drawing.

"Just call it a *Farewell to Gretchen*," Jimmy said. He went to stand by the tipped drafting board. He reached out with one finger and traced the lips of the girl he had drawn. The rendition was surrealistic, but with an all too recognizable touch of the familiar.

The background of the sketch was dominated by the Winchester Mystery House. Drawn just slightly askew, slanted and bizarre. The windows were dark, penciled in a way that left an illusion of eyes with tiny pinpoints of light for pupils.

As if entranced, Dixie stepped closer. She could not tear her eyes away from the drawing. Though done by the young man who stood next to her, there was nothing young about the picture. And the longer she stood in the silence of the room, gazing at the drawing, the more she saw. A ridge of chills crept up her back. What seemed like hundreds of tiny faces had been superimposed onto the structure Sarah Winchester had built so long before. Everywhere the eye traveled, there was a face. Some scowled, with lips drawn back, as if in a hiss. Others grinned sly, secretive grins, while still others simply gazed back. Sad. Waiting. Those faces were all the more unsettling for their subtlety. They did not leap out at the viewer. Half hidden within the structure of the house, it was as if they waited in patient, timeless quietude to be discovered.

Jimmy Baldwin also waited. Standing silently beside Dixie, he watched the fascination on her face.

She concentrated on that house for what felt like a very long time, because she didn't want to focus on the main subject of Jimmy's drawing. He was irrefutably an artist. He had managed to capture the likeness of Gretchen Willis only too well. Dixie thought of Pete and hoped he would never see the drawing.

Gretchen's face hovered in the foreground, or rather, her dual image hovered. Her face was split into three-dimensional halves. The right side closely resembled her photograph. A sweet, smiling face. Innocent. Youthfully vulnerable. The left mirrored fear and a horrible, naked agony. Her left eye was rolled upward, half buried in the recess of her skull. Her mouth was open and screaming. Blood dribbled down her chin. Her long hair stood up in a parody of dancing flames. In three of the four corners there were cowled figures, one tall and one short in each, obviously three couples. But in the fourth there was a single small girl, Gretchen again, alone and nude, with only a series of dots—an outline—beside her. Dixie touched the blank area with the tip of her finger.

"And what really belongs here?" She asked the question without looking at Jimmy. "Or rather, *who*?"

"I don't know. If I did, the picture would be finished." He

walked to his bed and sat down. He looked very tired, and suddenly very, very young. "She was so damn pretty."

"Was she your girlfriend?"

"I've already told you she wasn't."

"Wendy?"

"Not her either, not really. Although if things were different . . ." His eyes went to the picture again. "It's weird what happened to Gretchen, you know, because *she* was beginning to believe in all that stuff."

"What stuff?"

"Oh, the games we were playing, silly kid games that seemed funny at the time. I've thought about it a lot since she . . . since Gretchen was killed, and I don't think it ever was a game to her." He looked up at Dixie. "There really was something special about her, Sergeant Struthers. I don't know how to explain it exactly. It was like she really did have special power or something. We were all doing papers, special papers for different subjects, but ones we found we could all tie into what we at first called the 'weird shit' section. It made the assignments more interesting. Actually, it was more interesting than I think any of us expected. There are people all over the world who believe in what you call magic, hocus-pocus, whatever. It got to be a lot of fun—at first. Until we took things a little too far. And then, of course, there was old lady Jackabcin."

"I've met her."

"Well, then you know what I mean. We could really get her going."

"Are you trying to tell me that all those books, all the in-depth papers, that it was all just a way of making your schoolwork more interesting?" Dixie made no attempt to hide her skepticism.

"I'm telling you that's the way it started, at least for most of us."

"Who was the exception?"

"That's just it, Sergeant, *Gretchen* was the exception. She was always the leader. No one came right out and voted her in or anything, but she was our leader all the same. She was really smart, much smarter than me or Wendy or Tony. When we started playing games, having séances and stuff, she really got into it, she had us almost believing. I realize now that she picked us for friends on purpose. She had some pretty strange ideas. And she had her own reasons for digging into certain kinds of things.''

"Like what?''

To her surprise, he flushed a deep red. "I . . . I can't tell you that.''

"Look, Jimmy, someone in your little club, or whatever it was, went off the deep end. Over the edge. One of your friends is a crazy.'' Her voice raised. "Would you like to know exactly what was done to—''

"You're wrong!'' Jimmy was on his feet again, yelling into her face. "A kid wouldn't do a thing like that! None of us would have done that, not any of us, no matter how crazy we are! We were just fooling around. It wasn't until later that Wendy and I caught on to what . . .''

His voice trailed away in mid-sentence. He dropped back onto the bed. "You're wrong, Sergeant Struthers, I wish you would believe me. Whoever did that to Gretchen was not . . . not a kid. You can't get that crazy until you're all grown up. You're looking in the wrong place. It was an adult. Only adults—'' His voice broke.

There were more questions she wanted to ask, many, and she was tempted to probe further, but that was not what they had come up to his room for, and she did not want him to come apart at the seams. Nor did she want to alienate him. There would be time enough in another day or so. Jimmy Baldwin was going nowhere for a while, unless Dave Gates's suspicions proved unfounded.

"Do you want to talk about what happened here tonight?'' she asked him. "Did it have anything to do with Gretchen?''

"No, it had to do with my old man being a bastard.'' His voice was too quiet. He looked up at Dixie again. "I don't care if he was my father, and I don't care how it sounds. I don't care how many clubs he belonged to, and I don't care that he went to church every damn Sunday of his life. I just don't fucking *care*. No one knew how he was, what a rotten, stinking man, how he treated me and Mom. He was ruining my life, and he still will. He's going to kill my mother even though his fucking throat is ripped out.

"You want to know something, Sergeant? It's guys like

my father who really have power. Real power. *Bad* power.
He was . . . was . . . was . . .''

The boy's shoulders hunched. He hiccupped, and began to
cry in deep sobbing gulps. ''Oh, God, what's going to happen to Mom? What will happen to us?'' He was not talking to
Dixie so much now as to himself. He continued to weep,
hitting the bed over and over again with a clenched fist,
releasing the tension he had held in for so long.

Dixie let him weep for several moments before she sat
down beside him and put a hand on his shoulder. ''Listen to
me, Jimmy. I have no way of knowing what took place
between you and your father, but you need to talk. I don't
mean to me, or to Investigator Gates. You need to talk, and
you need rest. Is there a doctor I can call?''

He shook his head adamantly, wiping his nose with the
back of his hand. ''The only doctor we see is the one *he* sent
us to—a friend of his. You saw Mom, how she is. Dr.
Lawrence keeps her loaded all the time. Tranquilizers. Anti-
depressants. He helped my father keep her quiet. It kept her
out of Dad's hair, too, most of the time.''

He wiped his eyes and scrubbed at his face, pulling the
skin down taunt. ''I want to talk, Sergeant, but to you. I'll
talk to you.''

She felt suddenly uncomfortable. She did not know this
boy well, and yet there was something about him that reached
out and touched her, almost physically. The battered eye, the
wound on his lip, the blond hair falling over his forehead.
Jimmy was an odd combination of a little boy and young
man. Both terribly unhappy, maybe even mentally ill. He was
undoubtedly disturbed, and she wanted to help him.

''Are you sure?'' she asked. ''I've been straight with you,
told you how it is. If you decide to talk to me, it's just like
talking to Investigator Gates. I've got to take it all the way,
right down to reading you your rights again. It might be
better—''

''I want to tell *you*. Read whatever you have to, but let me
tell you what happened. If you think I need a lawyer, I'll try
to find one. Maybe you could even help me.'' He gave her
another of his goofy, lopsided smiles. ''Lawyers are like
doctors around here. The only ones I know think my dad was

tits. I don't think any of them are going to be crazy about lending me a hand.''

Dixie stood, purposely putting a little distance between them, mentally trying to regain her professional objectivity, forcing herself to remember that beyond his father's death, Jimmy Baldwin was also a potential suspect in the Willis case. She glanced quickly at the sketch and around the room. It was a large room, with furnishings and fixtures that did not denote parental abuse. The Baldwin home was one of obvious if not opulent affluence. A small color television sat on one shelf, a small stereo on another. Materialistically speaking, at least, Jimmy seemed to suffer no hardship. Those were the facts Dixie forced herself to concentrate on as she paced slowly back and forth, reading him his rights from the small laminated card she always carried in her purse. She did not need to read the terse speech. After being on the street a week, every cop knew the words by heart. But cases had been thrown out of court simply because a word was dropped, or an officer had no proof of reading.

"You have the right to remain silent," she began, ending, as usual, with, "Do you understand?"

"Yes," he answered, "I understand."

Dixie nodded and sat down on the stool near the drafting table, imagining that she could feel Gretchen's eyes boring unblinkingly into her back. "Where shall we begin?"

"I just want to tell you what happened here tonight, Sergeant. Just plain old tell it like it happened."

Dixie nodded again but said nothing.

"My father was still pissed when we got home from Sister Snoots. He asked a few questions, but not many. I was glad. I lie when I have to, but it's not my favorite thing. Anyhow, he pretty much left it alone. He did his regular thing, what he always did on the few nights he stayed home. He told me to get my ass in the kitchen and cook dinner, and then sat down on *his* ass and started drinking."

"Cooking dinner is one of your regular chores?"

"It has been for the last couple of years, the last year especially. Mom is pretty much just like you saw her most of the time. Dad didn't like strangers in the house, so . . . well, I did most of it. Cleaning. Cooking. And you can bet it had better be done right.

"Anyway, he—my father—didn't say another word to me until . . . until we had the first . . . argument. Until dinnertime, when he started chipping on Mom."

"So it started with an argument between your parents?"

"Not *between* them, Sergeant. My mother doesn't argue. She whines once in a while, but she does not argue. She hasn't got enough spirit left for that. Dad came to the table, took one look at Mom, and made a face. You know, disgusted, like she was just some piece of shit he had to tolerate. He had already had three, maybe four drinks. Heavy ones. My stomach was in knots because I could tell just by looking at him that he was going to be nasty. I was having a hard time swallowing. Any appetite I had just sort of evaporated."

Jimmy rubbed a hand across his stomach, as if the memory brought the knots back. "He started right in about how crappy everything tasted. I'll admit it wasn't great. Just hamburger patties with salad and baked potatoes. I overdid the meat. My father liked his pretty rare, and there wasn't a drop of pink.

"Next thing you know, he's yelling at Mom, saying how if she would get off her fat ass and be a decent human being, *she* could see that he had a decent meal once in a while. He kept it up, on and on and on, until Mom finally started crying.

"She may be loaded most of the time, but she still has feelings. I couldn't stand it, and that's when I did it. I threw my fork clear across the room and started yelling back at him."

A strange look came over Jimmy's face. "God, it felt good! I had never dared do anything like that before, no matter how bad he treated us. I've always been too scared. But something happened to me tonight. Maybe it was all the extra worry, talking to you about Gretchen. I'm not sure. But whatever it was, tonight I blew. Watching him, seeing Mom and the kind of half human she's turned into, I couldn't stand it anymore. I threw that fork, hard, and I told him exactly what I thought of him. I told him to shut up and called him a rotten bully bastard, a fucking hypocrite . . . every single thing I could think of."

He stopped talking. He sat staring at Dixie with glazed eyes, like he was seeing it all again. He was breathing heavily.

"Where was Brutus?"

He blinked several times. "Right there, laying on the kitchen floor. He didn't even growl until Dad hit me, knocked me off the chair. He jumped on me and started pounding. Brutus got excited then, started growling and barking. I had to yell at him to get back."

"And he did?"

"Yes, he moved away, but he kept growling. Deep down in his throat, you know, like he could hardly stand still. Mom was screaming and crying. I think the only reason my father didn't kill me right on the spot was because Brutus shook him up."

"Is that when your eye and lip got hurt? Had your father ever hit you before?"

This time he did not answer. He stood and turned his back to her. Her eyes opened wide as he began unbuckling his pants, but it was not necessary for him to pull them down very far. She gasped. His lower back bore several deep scars, thickly corded welts where a belt buckle had obviously bitten deep into his flesh.

He refastened his jeans and sat back down on the bed. "I've told you, Sergeant, my father was one hell of a nice guy. You've heard of ego? Well, dear ol' Daddy was blessed with a big one. All that charity bullshit, the 'giving of himself' that I know damn well will end up in the newspaper, was just his way of being the center of attention. When Mom couldn't stand it anymore, she went to their attorney. She was going to file for divorce. Fat chance! Dad's lawyer buddy called him up at his insurance agency while Mom was still waiting in the office. Dad got there in five minutes and took her straight to the doctor. And, of course, she was yelling and cussing all the way, causing a real scene. Actually, she was probably scared to death.

"Well, Dr. Lawrence took care of that quick, too, and he's been taking care of it ever since."

Jimmy's face turned stone hard. "Not anymore, though. No matter what else happens, my mother is going to get well now."

He expelled a deep sigh, and as he continued, his voice began to drone, turn into a monotone. "Everything might have been okay if my father had gone to bed after dinner, or if he had passed out. But he didn't do either. He went into the living room and just went right on drinking. Brooding. He acted like he was reading, but I don't see how he could have been, not with all that booze. I think what he was really doing was planning a way to get even with me. He loved to cook up great punishments. Beating me up was never enough. Not ever.

"I got the kitchen cleaned up and put Mom to bed just as quick as I could. Her room is right next to mine. And then I came here. Brutus came, too, of course. He sleeps by my bed at night."

"Always?"

There was just a brief instant of hesitation. "Yes, always. He's *my* dog. My grandpa, Mom's dad, gave him to me when he was just a pup. Over seven years ago."

"And he's been attack trained?"

"Trained, but not for attack. I took him to obedience school. He's smart too. He almost always does what I tell him, unless he's overexcited."

"Like tonight?"

Jimmy met her eyes. "Yes, like tonight. He was already restless. I've never known any dog like Brutus. He seems to pick vibes up from out of the air. Really. He seems to know exactly what I'm feeling every minute. Like when I'm happy, when the two of us are alone, walking along the beach or up in the hills, he romps and yips like a little puppy. He almost dances. Tonight, after I came to my room, he just laid there, staring at the door, whining and then growling. There was a lot of hate in this room tonight, Sergeant Struthers, an awful lot.

"I finally got hungry, though. So, after I was pretty sure Dad would be in bed, I went downstairs to the kitchen. But when I came down the hallway and saw there was a light still on in the living room, I just ducked into the kitchen without going through. Brutus had come out of the bedroom with me. I'm not sure why he wasn't still with me when I went into the kitchen. Probably just sniffing around, the way he does sometimes.

"I guess my father heard me get into the fridge. He called me into the living room. His eyes were all bloodshot and he was slurring. He was stinking drunk. He asked me what I was doing in this real low voice, and he was kind of grinning. All it took to get him started was for me to tell him I had come down for food because I was hungry. He's always saying I'm too thin, calling me skinny. That's how it started the second time. According to him, I'm ungrateful—a skinny, ungrateful little wimp—and how a guy like him got stuck with a fucking wimp for a kid he'll never know. I hated listening, standing there listening to his voice, but I'm used to it, and I'm not stupid. My face still hurt like crazy, and I didn't want to get hit again. I just stood there like the skinny, fucking wimp I was and I took it . . . until . . . until he started calling Mom . . . calling her names. He said I might think I was smart but that I didn't know shit from soda crackers about Mom . . . that she was a whore . . . that she was already pregnant when he . . . that she and I . . .''

He was talking in broken sentences, and very fast, unconsciously thrusting out his hands, as if to push the nightmare away. "It . . . it was too much. I couldn't stand it. Finally, I raised my fist. I yelled something, I can't remember what, and I really was going to hit him. But he came up too fast. He brought both hands down on my shoulders. He loves to do that. He squeezed, pinched the nerves there real hard. So hard. God, it hurt!''

His voice was growing high and shrill, and Dixie's professional facade fell temporarily by the wayside. "Slow down, Jimmy. Take it easy. Everything is going to be okay.''

It was as if he hadn't heard her. He went on, breathless. "That's when Brutus came charging in. He didn't even bark, not that I can remember. Suddenly he was just there, and he leaped between us. My father let me go, and I fell backward.''

"So you didn't intentionally set the dog on him?"

"No!" Jimmy looked tortured, almost as tortured as the macabre half of Gretchen's face in his sketch. "I may be a murderer, but I did not sic Brutus on him, not on purpose.''

Dixie's heart skipped a beat. He said he was a murderer, and her first thought was that if he had not killed his father, he must be referring to Gretchen Willis. A wide pit opened in her stomach. She got to her feet and walked slowly toward him, not wanting to believe it, and yet knowing that if he was the psychopath who had so mutilated, so desecrated, the body of his friend, that she must use all caution. She had to let him talk, must continue to appear sympathetic.

"We all do things, Jimmy," she spoke softly. "We do things and then we're sorry. You need to tell someone, talk to a doctor. You said you did not kill your father, and I believe you."

He stared up at her with tortured, unseeing eyes. "But you you're wrong. I *did* kill him, sure as hell. I just didn't set Brutus on him. I could have called him back, though. I could have yelled at him to stop . . . to quit. . . ."

He dropped his head into his hands, breathing in deep gulps, almost but not quite sobbing. "I *did* kill him. I *am* a murderer."

For no reason she could immediately analyze, Dixie felt a rush of almost overwhelming relief. She sat down on the bed beside him, putting an arm around his heaving shoulders. "Listen to me, Jimmy. You are not a murderer."

She wanted to go on, to tell him that all would be well, that he was not responsible. But she said no more, for there was no way of knowing how Gates might view the validity of his story, or how a district attorney might react. There was only her own gut-level instinct, which counted for nothing.

They sat on the edge of the bed. Close. Her arm still around his shoulder. In the distance, from downstairs, the sound of voices drifted up to break the silence. An automobile engine sounded from outside.

Jimmy came slowly to his feet and walked to the window. Brutus barked as the ambulance pulled away from the house. A foggy gray dawn lighted the sky, sifting into the bedroom.

Dixie also came to her feet. She walked to the shelves lining one wall and looked at the books. Jimmy did not turn. She tilted her head to read titles. There seemed nothing unusual, no volumes on the occult, no tomes stuffed with magical formulae. No bell. No candle. It was just the small library of a boy with above medium intelligence, textbooks and some of the finest modern fiction: *Lord of the Rings*, *Shibumi*, *The Fountainhead*. A good cross section. There were art books with subject matter ranging from history to application.

Dixie moved to stand by the drafting board, and looked at the sketch again. Her eyes quickly took in the image of

Gretchen Willis and then the house, the old mansion where a troubled and eccentric old woman had wandered the passageways, communing with her spirits. Once more she was drawn in, mesmerized by the horror of Gretchen's tragedy. Standing there in the soulful quiet of Jimmy's room, only half aware of the boy's still, statuelike presence at the window, she once more sought and found the strange surrealistic faces buried within the slanted framework of the house. So entranced was she that what felt like hours seemed to pass before the other oddity caught her attention. And she knew that what she saw was no coincidence. Dancing around the faces, cleverly worked into the structure of the huge rambling old house, were a series of symbols. Hearts, with daggers plunged into their centers. Ankhs, crosses, spirals, and serpents with long flicking tongues.

She turned, about to speak to Jimmy, but he was right behind her. She started, nearly gasping at the fixed stare of his eyes. He seemed almost trancelike, or perhaps only very, very tired.

"Tell me about these." She spoke low, almost whispering. With the tip of her fingernail she touched one after another of the symbols. Her eyes held a plea. "One of your friends has been murdered, Jimmy. Help me."

His eyes slowly left her face. He looked down at his own artwork. "It was a game, just a silly, childish game. We went there, sneaked in one night, just one, to play one of our silly games. We were going to have a séance and we were almost caught. We managed to split, and we never went back."

"The symbols, what—"

"Nothing, Sergeant, nothing at all. Just more games." His eyes were watering, but whether with fatigue or grief she could not tell. He touched the upper left-hand corner of his drawing, tracing the blank area behind Gretchen. "I don't know who this is, Sergeant. If I did, I would tell you. The rest is just what I told you—a private farewell to Gretchen."

A knock on the door caused them both to turn. Jimmy paled. A moment later the door opened. Dave Gates stepped into the room. He spoke to Dixie first.

"We're just about through down there. The tech team is packing up. I need to talk to the boy—if he *will* talk."

Jimmy looked at her, a question in his blue eyes.

She shook her head. "I can't advise you, Jimmy. This is a decision that has to be made by you alone."

What she wanted to say was, *Talk to me, kid, tell me what I need to know*, but she was treading in a thin gray area. The boy was worn to a nub of raw nerves. What he needed more than anything was to sleep, and then to get his own problems in proper perspective. She said none of this, however, and when Jimmy nodded, she gave no more advice.

"Can we go downstairs first?" Jimmy asked. "I'll tell you what you want to know, but if my mom wakes up and I'm not around, she'll be upset."

Gates led the way out of the room with the boy close behind. Dixie came last, casting a final look at the poignant black-and-white sketch. Once they reached the kitchen, Jimmy headed straight for his mother. He touched her shoulder, and she opened her eyes. She smiled up at him.

"There you are, my darling," she cooed in a fuzzy voice. "Help your favorite girl, will you? My head hurts something awful. I'm sure it's time for my medication."

CHAPTER 23

PETE TRIED TO act natural, to hide the pain churning his guts into mincemeat. He arrived at the soccer field exactly on time.

Dixie was not there yet, and he was glad. Maybe by the time she came he would seem more relaxed. Maybe he really could set some of the bitterness aside. He hated what was happening to him, to his feelings toward the people whom he had always considered his best friends. Even knowing on a conscious level that they were trying to help him did not alleviate his animosity at being left out in the cold concerning the investigation, kept constantly in the dark when he knew damn well the rest of the homicide team knew every last, grisly detail. All he could do was follow Dixie and Herb when his schedule permitted it, or lurk like a thief around Sally's house. And keep a keen ear open. As he intended doing today. If he knew Dixie as well as he thought, she would not be able to resist talking to Herb about the investigation. He intended to listen very carefully, covertly if necessary.

With each passing day, Pete's tension had grown worse. He could feel himself coming apart. Each day, somehow, he managed to get himself to work, to look quasinormal. But it was an act. A sham. His life was like one long, terrible dream. The waiting. The endless imaginings, waking and sleeping nightmares. And most of all, the guilt.

Gretchen had been dead for nearly three weeks now, three weeks that seemed like three hundred years. But the memory of his niece, with her sunny smile and teasing blue eyes was still vibrantly, painful vivid. For sixteen years she had been a major part of his life. He'd loved her as he imagined he would love a child of his own, maybe even more, but without the normal parental strains. He'd had the best of it. Because he had not actually lived with her, he was not forced to be her constant overseer, hadn't had to tell her what to do, where to go, what time to come back. He'd been her father figure, but he and Gretchen had also been friends, siblings, everything to each other. Too much, perhaps.

Since the age of nine or ten she had made it a habit to take the key he hid for her just inside the electrical switch box and let herself into his place. No less than twice a week he would come home to find she'd been there. A tiny bouquet of flowers would have been left on the table. A plate of cup-cakes. A special card. Small endearing acts that made him enter his house at night with a sense of anticipation.

Such was the level of their mutual trust and affection that never once in all those years had Gretchen doubted her wel-come. She came whenever she wanted, when he was there or when he wasn't. And for that reason Pete never brought a woman home, not to the place where he lived. He was an old-fashioned man, with old-fashioned values. Having had no home while he was growing up, he held the one he now owned as almost sacred. Gretchen was the only family he had left. He would not allow a stranger in, not until the day he decided to marry. And under no circumstances would he have caused his niece emotional trauma. He believed that adults should set the example—all the more reason for his present anger at Sally.

To Pete there now seemed not enough hours in the day. When he wasn't working, during every free moment he had, Pete investigated on his own—as best he could with the limited information he had—trying to find the fiend who'd murdered his niece. He was weary, and more weary from pretending to be otherwise.

He walked to a row of bleachers and took a seat. He did

not wave or yell at Herb, who was warming up, cavorting with Amy and their teammates out on the playing field. A fleeting smile creased Pete's boyishly handsome face as he saw Janice walking the sidelines, wearing the black shorts and white blouse denoting her status as referee.

Sitting quietly beneath a watery September sun, Pete watched Amy most of all. Seeing her long blond hair whip out behind her as she ran reminded him of Gretchen. But then everything reminded him of Gretchen these days.

In his mind's eye he saw his niece again, just as she had looked the last time he saw her. He'd come home to find her there, curled like a kitten on the sofa. There was no makeup on her face. Gretchen never really needed cosmetics to enhance her prettiness. Moreover, she knew he preferred what she laughingly referred to as her "Madame Lafarge" look. He had greeted her on that afternoon as he always did, calling her his "Little Goddess."

Pete had sensed something different about her that evening, an undercurrent of excitement, and he could still clearly remember the ripple of worry it caused. But it had only been a worry, a small one, not a terrible premonition. Not a warning of the horror about to claim her.

Sitting on the sofa, with the afternoon sun spilling through the window to light her hair, she had looked incredibly beautiful. Her eyes sparkled even more than usual. Her very skin seemed to glow. And not for the first time Pete had felt a pang of sadness at seeing how quickly she was casting off the mantle of pubescence. She was almost grown, a young woman—in love.

Love?

Pete found the idea upsetting, and put it from his mind. He wanted her to stay a girl forever, and instead her adulthood suddenly seemed to be rushing at him with dizzying speed.

On the surface there had been nothing particularly unusual about her visit, the last time they would ever spend together. Gretchen had slipped turkey pot pies into the oven and then sliced them both a huge wedge of the German chocolate cake she had made and brought with her. His favorite dessert. The only thing out of the ordinary was her suppressed air of excitement, and the small gift she had given him.

The gift. She had often given him small things, trifles she

could afford by saving her allowances. A book. A set of hair brushes. A new wallet. This time, just before leaving, she stood on tiptoe and slipped a chain around his neck. Some sort of good-luck charm, an Egyptian facsimile of the cross.

"For my favorite guy," she said, kissing him on the tip of his nose.

"What's this, a love charm?"

"Maybe." She had smiled up at him. "If I can't be your girl, then you better find one soon. Otherwise you're going to become one of those disgustingly crusty old bachelors, all set in cement."

"I'm still looking for someone as pretty and sweet as my little goddess." His hands had been on her waist. He had been saying the same thing since he was twenty-one and Gretchen seven, and he hardly expected her response.

"Why look?" she had asked, pressing close to him, kissing him again, this time on the lips. The kiss had not been chaste.

Now, sitting alone on the bleachers, watching Amy dribble and kick the ball, Pete felt the heat rush to his face as he remembered his reaction to Gretchen. He did not want to remember, not now or ever. He did not want to remember the night that had alienated her from him for almost two months prior to her death.

"Uncle Pete!" Amy had spied him and was waving madly.

The term of endearment from Herb's daughter had always been welcome, but now the words cut into his soul. He swallowed hard and lifted on arm, unable to call back. Slowly, taking time to get himself together, he worked his way toward her.

CHAPTER 24

BY THE TIME Dixie arrived home, Patrick and Reversa were already gone. A note on the table told her they had left for the soccer game—an event she'd completely forgotten until she walked into the silent house, greeted only by Poke.

She hurried upstairs, telling herself she was not tired, not weary to the bone. Forcing herself to concentrate on getting ready, she attempted to clear her mind of gruesome images. A hot bath, while slightly rushed, helped her relax. She yawned widely as she went into the huge walk-in closet in her bedroom, careful to avoid looking at the bed or succumbing to its invitation.

For having gone most of the night without sleep, she managed to paste herself together relatively well. The bath, a little makeup, and a casual khaki-colored safari outfit worked a minor miracle. That and a pair of dark sunglasses.

She was on her way out the front door when the telephone rang. She masked her surprise at hearing Pete's voice.

"Dix?"

"None other. You're at the game?" She had not really expected him to attend.

"Yes. Their team is ahead."

"Sorry I'm late. Maybe I'll be able to catch the last quarter."

"Herb won't be in it, I'm afraid. He's sprained his ankle pretty badly."

Unreasonably, she felt like a traitor. "Rough luck. Sure it's not broken?"

Pete chuckled, sounding more like himself than he had for weeks. "Nope, not according to the team doctor, but he says it's all your fault. He was so busy wondering where in the hell you had gotten to that he wasn't paying attention."

There was a brief silence, but when Dixie said nothing, he went on. To her surprise, he seemed not in the least annoyed by her reticence. "He says you can redeem yourself by coming to the house for some grub, *and* by picking up additional painkiller—namely, beer."

What she really wanted to do was kill her own pain with a long, deep, and dreamless sleep. "Will do."

"I'll see you in a while then."

She hung up slowly, wondering at the change in him, hoping against hope that he was finally beginning to heal. Her next thought was for Herb and *his* healing. That she was without a partner was certain. But for how long?

Sitting on Herb's wide back deck, Dixie was almost too tired to feel sleepy. Her mind was sluggish but, try though she might, she could not put the case from her mind. Moreover, knowing that she would be without Herb for a while, she needed his advice, or at least his point of view.

The afternoon sun was pleasantly warm. After sitting with Dixie and Herb for an hour or so, Pete had taken Herb's normal place at the barbecue grill. Reversa and Janice worked in the kitchen, but when Dixie offered to help, Janice had been adamant.

"Please, if you really want to help, just tend the bear. The man is impossible when he's in any kind of pain at all." She coated the complaint with a kiss to Herb's cheek.

"Well, it feels like it's busted into a jillion pieces!" he protested. Sitting in one deck chair, with his foot propped on another, he took a deep gulp of beer, sloshing the liquor down into his stomach on top of thirty milligrams of codeine. He gave Dixie a semifocused stare. "You wanna tell me now? Where'd you go in the middle of the night? A new beau?"

Pete was standing several feet away, and they both gave

him a quick, guarded look. He seemed completely absorbed in turning the huge steaks he had cooking on the grill.

She spoke in a low but normal tone. "Hardly. I got a call at about two this morning from the Santa Cruz County homicide unit."

Herb momentarily forgot his pain. "Don't tell me we've got another body with the same M.O. over there? If so, Gretchen was probably only the first in a series. It would be bad news to find out we've got a random killer. People would panic. Shades of Charles Manson."

"No, Herb, not another body, at least not one at all like Gretchen's. It was Howard Baldwin. Your friend Brutus ripped his throat out."

"Holy shit!" He nearly pulled his foot off the chair as he bolted upright.

"Keep it down, huh, Woodall," Dixie hissed from between her teeth. She looked at Pete again, but he still seemed intent on the grill. His back was to them.

"Sorry, but criminy, that made my belly turn over! Just thinking about that black beast makes the hair on my arms stand up. What a godawful way to go!" Herb took another long pull on his beer. "I don't suppose there's any connection to our case?"

"Not directly." She leaned back, relieved to reason aloud and get his feedback. Her mind had been wrangling away, picking at a solution she did not really want to consider, much less accept. "How much do you know about the gods, Herb?"

He blinked at her. His voice was getting fuzzy. "As in plural?"

"Yes, mythology, Greek and otherwise."

"Just what I learned in school. It's been a while. And, of course, your little *project*. So what are you getting at exactly? I'm a little drunk, I fear, and thou must be more clear."

"I agree, partner, about you being soused I mean. But then, I'm a little tired, and I'm coming around to my point by way of big circles. It's just that I keep getting a jumble of pictures in my mind, most of them not very pretty, and I've thought for a long time now that I was missing something very important. The proverbial snake waiting to bite. Last night, or rather this morning, I met one of the Santa Cruz

dicks at Jimmy Baldwin's house. I saw the mess Brutus made
of his dad, or enough not to want to see anymore, but I also
got a chance to have a longer, more productive talk with
Jimmy. He's a really talented boy, Herb. In his room there
was a drawing that he had done.''

"Ah-ha, you did gain access to one of the inner sanctums.''

"Yes, for quite a while, and seeing that drawing started a
new set of wheels turning.'' She tapped her head. "Similari-
ties are what we need all right—and not just in the weird stuff
those kids seemed to be into. Those kids had a whole crop of
things in common, especially Wendy, Tony, and Jimmy.''

"With Gretchen odd man out yet again?''

Dixie hesitated. "I sure as hell hope so.''

Herb was just about to ask another question when the
screen door opened and Reversa and Janice emerged from the
kitchen carrying bread baskets and plates of food which they
sat down on a long picnic table in the backyard.

Janice called to Pete, "How much longer?''

"Done to perfection,'' he answered. The steaks were neatly
stacked around the outer edges of the grill.

At almost the same time, Patrick and Amy appeared from
around the corner of the house. Having taken a tour of all of
Amy's favorite haunts, they returned laughing, hand in hand.

Amy came running up onto the deck. Herb winced as she
came near his foot, but she carefully sidestepped the chair and
went to put her arms around his neck. "Poor Daddy.''

"I'm just fine, peanut,'' he said, but the sympathy felt
great.

"Does your footy still hurt? Are the endolphins working
yet?''

"Endolphins?'' Herb asked, already wondering if he really
wanted to know what she was talking about.

Amy nodded sagely and donned her six/sixty-year-old expression. Herb groaned beneath his breath,and not just from
the pain in his foot.

"Yeah, Dad, you know—en-dol-phins. We watched it on
educational television.''

"Please, Amy, Daddy is—''

"Endolphins are those little things inside you that—''

"Endorphins,'' Janice corrected, wearing a wicked grin.

"Oh, that's it, endorphins. Well anyhow, they look like

little bugs." Amy formed her fingers into a facsimile of jaws. "They run around inside your blood and eat up the pain. All you have to do is—"

"Amy, aren't you hungry?" Herb patted her briskly on the head. "I'll bet if you eat all your vegetables, Reversa will give you some more of those chocolate crinkles she brought to the game."

"Yeah, but I want to tell you first—inside your brain is an endorphin machine. You can make 'em go and eat up the pain. Do it, Daddy. That way you can be a biggy-tough."

It was a name Janice used when she wanted Amy to be brave.

Herb's aching extremity felt like it was being sledged to a pulp. He took another long pull on his beer and showed a row of alligator teeth to his first-grade daughter. "I *am* being biggy-tough, darling. Now, why don't you just be a good girl and go eat."

"Well, are you going to?"

"Amy."

"But Daddy, aren't you going to make those nice little end—"

"Amy go eat!"

Amy leapt back, but then seeing the faces around her, smiled, pleased with herself. Not only had she provided her rather cranky father a bit of invaluable information, she had also managed to amuse his friends. Aunt Dixie and Pops were laughing hard, while her mother and Reversa chuckled. Even Uncle Pete was smiling.

There was little time that afternoon for Dixie and Herb to talk further, nor would it have been particularly fruitful if they had, for Herb was soon four sheets to the wind. By six o'clock, as a soft autumn dusk crept over the backyard, he was losing the ability to enunciate properly. Dixie was so tired that she, too, felt almost inebriated, but her brain kept busy in spite of her weariness. Try as she might, she could not put the Willis case on a mental back burner. Tomorrow she would call Herb and talk to him again. By that time she might have it all clear in her own head, along with a few pertinent facts.

As the sun lowered in the sky, they all stood up, preparing to go inside. Patrick and Reversa helped Herb to his feet. Pete scooped Amy into his arms, and as he did, she reached into his shirt collar and pulled out the small gold medallion he still wore on a silver chain.

"That's pretty, Uncle Pete," she piped, not noticing the pain on his face.

Caught by surprise, Dixie stared at the ankh. She smothered the exclamation that automatically came to her lips. The thing seemed to catch the last rays of sunshine, turning the gold metal to bloody pink.

"Yes," Pete answered Amy in a low, quiet voice, "it is pretty. And it was given to me by a very pretty little girl. A little goddess, just like you."

He turned a long, level look on Dixie, a look that, for just a moment, she imagined held a silent challenge. Then he smiled, almost himself again.

CHAPTER 25

"AND *I* SAY you're going to bed, young lady." Patrick scolded Dixie as she sat at the small writing desk in the living room. "Reversa is right. You look like a zombie."

"No wonder either," Reversa grumped, casting a wary eye at the stack of books, "what with all that wicked garbage laying around the house. My mama would have burnt it up by now. Think I might too."

"No you won't either," Patrick said. "Those have to do with a murder case. Besides, a book is only what you make of it—just words on paper, unless you choose to make it more. It's not Dixie's fault you were born half chicken."

"Why, you old coot!" Reversa doubled up one ham-sized fist and shook it in his face. "Since when is a Catholic paddy any better, what with all that—"

Dixie stopped the verbal assault by standing up. "Enough, you two. I capitulate—on both scores. I'll go to bed, and by tomorrow these books will be long gone. Now, how about a little peace?"

Suddenly she realized just how tired she was, and knew that Reversa and her grandfather were right. Tomorrow would be soon enough to jot down her scattered thoughts. Walking to the stairs, she dragged herself up and into her room. She didn't bother with a gown after she peeled off her clothes.

She just crawled between the cool, sweet-smelling sheets and fell almost instantly to sleep—only to dream.

Her eyelids fluttered as ghostly images danced around within the slumbering labyrinths of her mind. Symbols bounced like Ping-Pong balls through the chambers of her brain. She saw Gretchen's body, carved in gory detail with the same surrealistic characters Jimmy had so artfully drawn. She was running through the maze of corridors built by Sarah Winchester, being chased by fresh-faced youngsters dressed in robes, holding bright, bloody blades above their heads. They surrounded her, backing her into a giant spider web, and grinned wide, fang-toothed grins as the blades rushed downward.

Dixie sat up in bed, not remembering the nightmare, but perspiring profusely and struggling to catch her breath. She sat still for several moments, waiting for her heart to slow, and listening, wondering if she had been awakened by a sound. Except for its usual creaks and groans, the house sat silently around her.

"What a ninny!" She scolded herself aloud.

It was still pitch black outside her bedroom window. She flopped back down, but she knew it was useless. She had gone to bed no later than eight, and the digital radio clock beside her bed told her that it was five after three.

Seven hours was her usual allotment for sleep, and it seemed her body had no intention of making up for lost time. Her eyes kept coming exasperatingly wide open. After rolling from side to side and beating her pillow numerous times, she decided to give it up.

Sitting on the edge of the bed, she stretched, suddenly delighted with the quiet and the prospect of a few hours of uninterrupted leisure. After brushing her teeth and slipping on a light robe, she stepped into the upstairs corridor. The area more closely resembled a gallery—a wide loft beneath a high, open-beamed ceiling which gave a full view of the main living area below. As always, Patrick had left on a small lamp, with the three-way bulb switched on low. It was his own small act of superstition, one that he never really explained except to say that it kept the leprechauns at bay. Remembering Reversa's outrage the night before, Dixie smiled at the small eccentricity. In any case, it was a habit she liked.

As a child visiting Patrick, she had never awakened to a completely dark room.

Her slippered feet made no sound as she descended the stairs. She went into the adjoining kitchen first, beckoned by a slice of apple pie she knew was in the fridge.

Her hands were full as she came back into the living room, a plate balanced in one, with a tall, frosty glass of milk in the other. Both went flying as she was grabbed from behind.

Taken completely off guard, she had no time to cry out before a blanket came down over her head. Outside the blanket, an iron hand clamped her mouth shut. She felt herself half lifted off the carpet. She kicked her feet, aiming for the pair of shins she knew had to be right behind her. She tried to bite at the hand, but the blanket was suffocating. One of her heels made firm contact with a shinbone, but she had lost her slippers in the struggle and her bare foot carried little impact. Her assailant simply grunted and tightened his hold around her arms and shoulders.

She felt herself being half dragged, half carried backward. The darkness and the claustrophobia caused by the blanket were disorienting. She was not sure what direction they were taking, but she thrashed out with her legs, hoping to knock over a piece of furniture, hit a wall, anything to cause a racket or a loud thump. Her anklebone hit something solid, a wall or door frame, and she let out a muffled, barely audible yelp of pain.

Where was Poke? she wondered. Her heart beat faster with the fear that he had been injured or even killed. Her great frolicking wolfhound was no great shakes as a watchdog, to be sure, but he looked intimidating. And she was certain that Poke would never lie placidly by while she was being manhandled.

Her thump had brought no one. She was beginning to panic, afraid she would be dragged from her home with no one the wiser for hours. Terror gave her a burst of strength. She twisted sharply and then let her body go limp.

It almost worked. She slithered halfway down the torso of her captor, but the iron hand pressed harder, never leaving her mouth. The grip on her shoulders did slip, and she heard the man curse through clenched teeth as he bent at the knees to retain his hold on her.

Stiffening, Dixie snapped her head up and back, making contact with his jaw. She heard his teeth click sharply, but his grip tightened around her once more, harder than before. She felt as if her collarbones were being bent in two.

He stopped and pushed her tightly against a wall, using his shoulder to hold her still in order to free one arm. Her face was smashed against the wall like a pancake. She could hear him breathing heavily. He was a large man, and she could smell the male odor of him. A clean man who bathed in Ivory soap.

She felt him move and heard a door open. She tried to renew her struggle, but he increased the pressure on her body. She could feel his hips and the strength in his thighs. The hand he had been using to keep her quiet suddenly tightened even more. His fingers pried her jaws apart. He turned her and at the same time crammed a large wad of the blanket into her mouth. A moment later she felt the gag being tied in place, but he quickly plucked the blanket away from her nose, giving her room to breathe.

She was being wrapped about, swaddled like a woolen mummy. Knots were fastened, clamping her arms more securely than ever to her sides. Her feet, which she tried vainly to kick, were bound tightly together. When he finished with her, there seemed not a micromillimeter of wiggle room left.

Suddenly he moved away, leaving her to lean in futile fury against the wall. If she tried to move, she knew she would fall, a danger she minded not in the least. A nice 103-pound thump on the floor should bring someone, she decided, using her backside to hoist herself into open air.

A pair of large hands caught her before she had tumbled more than six inches. An instant later she felt herself lifted off the floor altogether. Air whooshed from her nose as she was slung like a sack of oats over her assailant's shoulder.

From that moment on, Dixie's most overwhelming emotion was one of outrage, tinged with humiliation. Beneath the swath of blanket her face burned a bright red, a shade that deepened as she was jostled along and then dumped quietly but unceremoniously into a closet. The smell of wool and rubber told her she had been deposited into the entry closet of the foyer, which was also the most distant place in the house from the upstairs bedrooms. She would have to do more than thump a few times to be heard by Reversa or her grandfather.

She was wedged in tightly, doubled almost in half. A soft click told her that the man who had bound and gagged her had also closed her in.

To Dixie, hours seemed to have passed since she cut herself the slice of pie, but reason told her that in all likelihood it was still no more than three-thirty in the morning. She lay in the blackness for several minutes, ears strained, listening. The house was once more silent, save for the occasional settling creak.

Dixie began trying to maneuver her body into a position that would at least allow her to get her legs into an upward position. With that accomplished, she could bang on the closet door or one of the walls with her bare heels. She was perspiring heavily now, her own breath wetting her face. Her back ached, and she grunted, trying to unpretzel her legs. By bending them even farther, she could just barely touch one set of numbed fingers to her ankles. But bound about by the blanket as she was, any attempt to unfasten her bonds was futile. She silently cursed.

By working her way around until her back was pressed against the inside of the closet door, she had just about scooted down onto her back when she heard a stealthy footfall on the oaken parquet floor of the foyer. She clearly heard the front door open and, after a brief pause, softly click shut again. At almost the same moment came the castanet sounds of claws on the floor.

Poke!

Her first emotion was one of relief, followed quickly by annoyance that the idiot beast had obviously waltzed right by the stranger.

Poke immediately began sniffing at the bottom crack of the closet door, whining and pawing for all he was worth, which in Dixie's opinion was not much.

It took several more minutes for her to finish scooting onto her back, and longer yet to work herself back around. Had she not been so damnably hot and angry, she might have laughed at herself. There she was, at four o'clock in the morning, swathed upside down like a cocoon, mucking her head through Patrick's old boots and galoshes. Sergeant Dixie T. Struthers. Police Officer *extraordinaire*!

At last, with her posterior toward the door of the closet, she heaved her legs back and pummeled with her heels just as hard as she could. Poke began barking in his deep, husky baritone.

Dixie's ankles were beginning to feel battered when the closet door was finally thrown open. Her legs and lower torso tumbled into the foyer.

"Dixie!" Patrick cried. "Oh, my God! We thought someone was knocking! Back, Poke, that's a good boy!"

Dixie wriggled about like a giant, woolly worm, grunting her outrage. Poke sniffed at her covered head, mingling his panting breath with her own.

"Oh, lordy!" Reversa's voice merged with Patrick's mumbled exclamations as he hurried to untie her. She had been covered with the mohair afghan normally draped over the back of the living room sofa. Her assailant had obviously then dragged her into the kitchen, for she was bound with dish towels that had been tied together.

"Da-a-a-mn!" She literally screamed the word when her head was at last uncovered. She chafed her wrists, sending blood back into her fingers. *"Damn, damn, damn!"*

Patrick was sputtering questions, his face still puffy with sleep. Reversa stood behind him with wide, shocked eyes. Dixie got up shakily, rubbing the small of her back. Poke licked her hand, and she turned furious, accusing eyes on him.

"Get away from me, you wretch!" Poke backed up and tucked his tail between his legs. "I swear you aren't worth the food you eat!"

The dog whined and crouched lower, rolling his eyes upward in mute appeal.

"Oh-h-h," Dixie threw her hands into the air, *"cat crap!"*

She left the foyer, going into the living room and then on to the kitchen. She paused at the doorway, stepping over the spilled food. Her glass of milk had soaked into the carpet.

Behind her Reversa knelt and began cleaning up the mess. "Always said that dog was one good-for-nuthin' hound. Eats like a horse too."

Patrick followed Dixie. "What in the hell happened? What in the bloody blue blazes did anyone—"

"I don't know!"

"But *why*? Do you think this has anything to do with the case you're working on?"

"I don't know!" She knew she was yelling, being unreasonable, but she couldn't help herself. She felt rattled and disoriented. "Look, Pop, I don't know what happened, and certainly not why. All I know for sure is that . . ." Her knees went suddenly weak. "I've got to sit down."

Rushing to the large, round, oak table, Patrick pulled out a chair and helped her sit. He took a deep breath. "It doesn't matter, mouvereen, not right now. You just stay put. What you need most at the moment is a neat shot of the Irish."

Going to the pantry, he bent and pulled forth a bottle of White Horse. After pouring two fingers of the amber liquid, he brought it to her, urging her to drink.

She sipped and felt the warmth spread down her throat and into her stomach, but she had to sip three more times before she quit shaking. Patrick stood silently next to her, watching her face closely.

"Are you okay?" he finally asked. "I mean to say, are you *hurt*?"

"Only my dignity." Her face was still flushed from the heat of being wrapped up in the blanket, but her cheeks pinked anew. "I can't believe that happened, Pop! I stumbled right into a damn burglar, for crying out loud!"

"So what were you supposed to do?"

"Pay a little closer attention, for one thing. I woke up. Obviously something made me wake up. A noise, probably. I wasn't using my head. I thought I had just had a nightmare or something."

Poke's giant cowlicked head came through the door, but he kept the rest of himself out. He cut his eyes apologetically at Dixie, who glared at him.

"Get out of here," she growled.

"And get outta my way," Reversa added, coming through the doorway. "Move your big, hairy self, Poke, or I'm gonna take the broom to your hide!"

Patrick was looking at Poke, too, frowning. "Come here, boy."

The dog slinked in, almost on his belly. His thick tail beat mournfully against the floor as he licked Patrick's hand and whined.

"I'm not so sure we aren't leaping to conclusions here," Patrick said, looking intently at Poke. "I can't see him, friendly as he is, letting a burglar walk right into the house, or I should say *break in*, not anytime, much less in the dead of night."

Dixie shook her head. "Well, that was sure as hell no friend." The drink was taking effect and her tone was less adamant, but she still had no use for Poke. "It hardly matters now. The main thing is to find out whether I came down before he had a chance to get anything. I want to know how he got in here too."

Together she, Patrick, and Reversa started taking inventory, beginning at the back of the house and working forward, examining doors and windows as they went. They checked for jimmied locks or breakage. At the same time, they looked for any missing valuables. The furniture, fine and old though it was, had obviously not been the thief's target. Not with the house occupied. That sort of thing was usually done in full light of day, moving van and all, while residents were sure to be away.

No, they decided as they went from room to room, the thief had not been after emptying the house, but rather after the smaller, easier to tote items. Perhaps he had even had an accomplice waiting outside. No doubt patting Poke on his big, friendly head.

Reversa gave careful scrutiny to kitchen and dining room, checking to make sure all china, silver, and small appliances were still in place. They were.

"You probably came down too soon, Missy," she said. "Caught the devil before he had time to put his sticky fingers on things."

Dixie said nothing. A very unpleasant thought was beginning to niggle at her. She went on, looking closely at every window, frowning. They finally found the point of entry. In a far corner of the living room, a single pane had been neatly cut from one of the windows, a single square of mullioned glass cut right at the edges and suctioned out. The quick, sharp sound had in all likelihood been what shook Dixie from her nightmare. From that point it had been easy enough for the intruder to reach in and lift the window latch.

"I'll go get my kit," Patrick said. He still kept all of his old equipment—paraphernalia from his days as a San Francisco cop. He disappeared up the stairs, returning with a small black suitcase, more cumbersome than the one Dixie owned, but far more picturesque. A gift from his son, it was made of soft black elk hide, with bronze fixtures and corner guards. A treasured remembrance of Dixie's father. While upstairs, he had also retrieved his quiescent half-smoked cigar from a bedside ashtray—the one Reversa kept trying to throw away.

He clamped the cigar between his teeth. A pair of gold wire-rimmed spectacles were perched on the end of his nose as he knelt, opened the case, and set about dusting for fingerprints.

Kneeling there in his checkered woolen bathrobe, with the lamplight glancing off his full head of silvery hair, he made an endearing sight. And even in her agitated state of mind, Dixie could not help feeling a rush of love for the old man.

Reversa groaned and grumbled about the smoky-gray smudges being left on the windowsill, frames, and walls immediately surrounding the point of entry. "Hope you don't expect *me* to clean up that awful mess. You sure you know what you're doing there? Just looks like a bunch of dirt to me."

For once, Patrick ignored her. He squinted closely at his work. Dixie knelt beside him, but as she had feared, there was nothing to disclose. No prints. Not even a smudge. Her unpleasant suspicions were mounting by the moment, but she left them unspoken until they finished going through the remainder of the house. Nothing was missing, and except for a couple of opened kitchen drawers—from which the man had obviously extracted Dixie's bonds—and the upset milk and pie, nothing seemed out of place. Dawn was just breaking as the trio returned to the living room.

"Well, I guess we should be grateful," Patrick said. "You must have surprised the bugger real good. Too bad you didn't scare him to death."

Reversa wore a troubled frown. "Maybe he wasn't a thief."

Patrick and Dixie looked at her.

"Maybe he was a *kidnapper*." Her face showed true fear. "Or one of those *rapists*!"

She clamped a hand over her heart and sank down into Patrick's favorite wing chair, the one he had been about to take for himself. She stared up at Dixie. "Oh, Missy, didn't I tell you about bringing all those evil books into the house? It's bad luck!"

"Oh, Reversa," Dixie chided her gently, "if that was the case, I would be spirited away."

"Don't say it, Missy! Please! Makes this old heart of mine go plumb wild with fear!"

Patrick rolled his eyes, although the same thoughts had secretly crossed his mind, at least about the kidnapping or rape. Thoughts too terrible to contemplate. "Oh, for the love of Mary, woman, be done with all this mumbo jumbo. It was a sneak thief and no one else."

"A perfectly strange sneak thief, whom Poke allowed in without so much as a bark," Dixie mused in a slow, quiet voice. "A thief who bound me up—not too roughly, come to think of it—and then waited a good five minutes after locking me up before leaving the house, all while Poke pawed at the closet door. And yet nothing seems to be missing."

Her face was flushing again, her anger returning full force. She went quickly to her desk. She looked at the books and the folder full of notes and photographs on the Willis case.

Dixie made a mad dash for the stairs and ran up them two at a time. "I'll kill him, that's what I'll do!"

Patrick's eyes widened. "Wait, darlin', what's going on here?"

Bolting up after her, he called out again, "Hold there, girl. What's gotten into you? Dixie? Answer me, girl!"

Reversa was not far behind, and as she and Patrick arrived on the landing, they could hear her cursing. The angry and entirely unladylike exclamations poured from the open door of her bedroom.

Patrick and Reversa stood staring at each other, mouths open, completely baffled. An instant of silence was followed by the loud slam of a door.

Dixie stood in her closet, so angry that she could hardly see, much less decide what to wear. She jerked a pair of blue jeans from one shelf and a cotton-knit pullover from another.

She did not bother with any of the usual fripperies. A pair of panties, but no bra. A pair of suede boots, but without socks or nylons. She pulled the brush through her riotous coppery locks so hard and so quickly that her eyes watered. She skipped makeup altogether. She neither knew nor cared how she looked.

In the short time it had taken her to dress, Dixie's vehement oaths had simmered into an angry silence which still boiled beneath the surface. She needed no cosmetics. Her cheeks were deep pink, and her eyes glittered like emeralds. Brilliant and flint hard.

Her grandfather was still waiting on the landing, no longer looking confused. Poke sat on haunches beside him.

At the sight of her pet, Dixie's glare softened a bit. She stooped to ruffle both his ears. "Forgive me, old boy. I've been a real dope."

"Look here, Dixie," Patrick said, "I think I know what you're thinking, but why don't the two of us sit down and think a little more? Don't go off half cocked. In the morning—"

She thrust her finger toward the downstairs windows. "It *is* morning, Pop, and I have to go."

"Whoa, now, girlie. Reversa's down making coffee. Just hold your britches on for a few more—"

She went quickly down the stairs and through the living room, almost at a run.

Patrick made no attempt to follow her. He just stood wagging his head and clucking his tongue, knowing that once his headstrong granddaughter got something so firmly in her head, talking would be futile.

Dixie was still shaking as she nearly leapt into her car; shaking so badly, so enraged, that it took three jabs before she finally managed to get the key into the ignition. The engine roared to life. A spray of gravel kicked up behind the BMW as she left the driveway and headed for the main road.

She took the hairpin turns of Bear Creek Road with dizzying speed, trees and leafy ferns flashing by in what seemed a long flash of variegated green light. Ten minutes passed before her breathing finally began to slow.

In equal proportion her foot lightened, easing on the gas

pedal. She felt lightheaded and then, finally, almost detached. The anger she experienced slowly cooled. Hardened.

She had nearly reached the highway, the wide ribbon of asphalt leading into the city, when she slowed almost to a stop.

Guiding the car onto the shoulder of the road, she sat for several long moments. She let her vision range out over the view, the sprawling metropolitan valley below, the valley and the city she served. The world that took such a large and sometimes painful slice of her life. Finally, making a tight U-turn, she slowly drove back home.

CHAPTER 26

"THIS IS A rough one, Struthers."

Lieutenant Anthony Di Franco and Dixie sat across from one another. They were in his office, and had been for well over an hour. He was looking at her speculatively, rubbing his chin. Her face was calm and determined. What needed saying had already been said, the decision virtually made, per Dixie's request. But he asked one more time.

"You're absolutely sure you want to do this?"

"I'm absolutely sure that I have no choice."

Their eyes met, and Di Franco came as close as he ever had to giving her a spontaneous smile. "This might not be the best time in the world, Struthers, but do you mind if I say something? Without getting your tail feathers all ruffled?"

She was automatically wary. "Guess I won't know until you say it, Lieutenant."

"Relax, I'm not going to delve into your sex life."

"You're telling me." A wry quirk at the edge of her lips took the bite out of her retort.

"I didn't want you in this unit, Struthers. Okay, okay, so you can drop the eyebrows; I know I'm not revealing any big secret. Female cops still make me nervous, you included."

"Thanks for the vote."

201

"Don't be flip, lady, because that's just the point. I want you to know you have my vote, for what it's worth to you."

Dixie laughed. "Sorry, Tony, it's just that you look so darn surprised—like you just gave yourself a terrible shock."

"I *am* surprised." He had the good grace to flush slightly. "But I'm also glad. You've got a rough row to hoe with this Willis thing, and I just want you to know you have my support, however it goes. You're a good cop, Struthers."

They were both embarrassed by the compliment, and Di Franco rose quickly, going to the door. He did his usual bellow into the squad room. "Spatlin!"

Jake cupped a hand to his ear. "Is dat de boss man a callin'?" He was talking to Pete, but it was Doty who shot him a pert answer.

"Reverting, are you?"

"Cut the crap and get in here, Jake," Di Franco said. "You want to be a comic, apply for Eddie Murphy's job."

Jake sauntered in, looking at Dixie with undisguised curiosity—hoping against hope. Everyone knew she would have to have a new partner until Woodall healed. At a nod from Di Franco, he closed the door and took a chair.

"I'm sure you know we're one man down," Di Franco began. "Woodall had an accident."

"Playing Pele." Jake nodded, and tried not to smile too widely at his little joke. To show his glee at coming up with Herb's partner would be bad form.

"Struthers here, as you also know, is still hip deep in the Gretchen Willis thing. Normally she could go it alone for a short while, but not now. She needs a partner."

Jake struck a serious and sober pose. "No problem, sir."

"Glad to hear it, Spatlin." Di Franco stood up again. "I know you don't like working alone either, but let's hope it won't last for any extended amount of time."

Jake's mouth fell open and he gave his head of couple of good shakes, sure he had missed something. Or maybe his hearing was on the wane. "Work alone? What in the hell are you talking about?"

"I'm putting Pete with Dixie."

"*Pete!*" Jake could not keep his voice from cracking. "Hey, man, what kind of scooby-do are you pulling here,

Leuy? Pete's niece was the victim in this deal, or have you forgotten? I thought the whole idea was to keep him clear.''

"Changed my mind." Tony Di Franco may have softened slightly in his attitude toward Dixie, but he had not lost the ability to look threatening. He was glowering at Jake, letting him know he was stepping over the line.

Jake did not miss the message. He stood up and shifted from one foot to the other, trying to swallow his anger and disappointment.

"Look, sir, I'm not pitchin' a bitch—I just don't understand.''

"You don't have to, but I'll explain all the same. Pete seems to have settled down, and this is important to him. Think how you would feel, Jake, if someone offed one of your relatives, especially the way it was done to his niece. Wouldn't you want to get a hand in?"

"Yeah, I guess, but—''

"Well, I'm sure Pete Willis feels the same. We've been keeping a pretty close leash on the kid. As long as he keeps his act together, manages to keep his cool, I think we ought to give him a chance to help bring in the scumbag who killed the girl, don't you?"

Jake wanted to gnash his teeth. More than that, he hated really understanding—which he did. Ever since Struthers and Woodall broke their first big case, Jake had experienced a giant hankering to pull D. T. Struthers as a partner. A female cop and a black cop. Two minorities. A friggin' *great* team. Great combination. Great press. Jake did not *want* to understand. He wanted to work with Dixie!

"So let's hope Woodall heals up soon." Di Franco headed for the door. "Regardless, you can have Willis back as soon as this case breaks, Herb or no Herb. Promise.''

"Could be soon," Dixie put in. "There are a couple of leads that might pan out. Sorry for the inconvenience, Jake.''

He looked at her and nodded. "No problem.''

He straightened his shoulders and left with a show of dignity he did not feel. When he returned to his desk, Pete looked up at him with a question in his eyes.

Jake jerked a thumb toward Di Franco's office. "Go get 'em, kid. You got a new partner, but don't settle in too tight. Her main man is coming back.''

CHAPTER 27

PETE WAS STILL suffering from a state of mild shock. Or, perhaps, not so mild. He wondered how blatantly the surprise had shown on his face as he stood in Di Franco's office. Dixie had spoken very little, and he wondered whose idea the temporary reassignment had been. He suspected that it had been Dixie, and the thought made him edgy and nervous. He listened to her talking now, and felt like his heart was beating somewhere in the pit of his stomach.

". . . Dave Gates says they aren't going to file charges," she said, concluding her comments on the Baldwin case.

"So the kid is going to skate?" Pete had listened without interrupting. "This Investigator Gates doesn't have the last word. You don't think the Santa Cruz D.A. will charge him?"

"I think it unlikely. Jimmy claims that the dog attacked on its own. I called Gates early this morning, and he says the boy was telling the truth about the dog not being trained for attack. Also, the injuries sustained by Jimmy, all the scars, not to mention the mental trauma, make it hard to feel super sorry for Howard Baldwin. I sure as hell don't."

Dixie was driving, weaving easily in and out of the downtown traffic, heading toward the main library.

"Rough way for a kid to live," Pete said, who knew it better than most.

"Yes. I think the mental scars are the most painful ones, especially for a boy like Jimmy. He struck me as a very sensitive young man."

"Sensitive," Pete repeated. "As in high-strung? Excitable?"

"Could be. We both know it's impossible to tell a potential murderer just by looking, Pete, but I would be very surprised to find out that Jimmy Baldwin killed Gretchen."

"She never mentioned his name to me, not once."

"Maybe not, but they *were* friends. There was a group she hung around with. I think I told you that. She met them every Thursday night at the library. At closing time they left together."

"So if they were such great friends, how come she never talked about any of them?" Pete was beginning to get that dogged look on his face again. Bulldog stubborn. "Gretchen and I were close, Dix. If these kids were really close friends, someone she actually hung around with, went places with, I would have known."

They were riding through the downtown area, moving easily through traffic that had thinned from the early morning rush. Dixie pulled the car into a parking lot adjacent to one of the new business high-rises which seemed to have been air-dropped into the civic center over the past two years, a giant edifice of gold-toned glass windows. She wore sunglasses that she did not bother to remove as she cut the engine and twisted in the seat to face him.

"Look, Pete, we talked about this in the *leuy's* office, but I think we better cover it again. If you're going to work this case, it has to be with some objectivity. The personal perspective can be helpful, even vital, but not all-inclusive. You *thought* Gretchen told you everything, shared all aspects of her life with you, but she obviously did not."

He started to interrupt, but she made a quick chopping motion with her hand and frowned. "Whatever you're going to say, don't bother, Pete. Let's just make a few ground rules, okay? If I want a personal point of view, I'll ask for it. Otherwise, I expect you to stick to the investigative facts. Got it?" There was no nonsense about her tone, and no smile on her face.

Pete flushed a deep red. Dixie had been his first regular patrol supervisor. As a rookie, fresh out on the street, he had resented taking orders from a woman. But then she had saved his life, dissolving the resentment to something very akin to worship. Once he joined the homicide team, their respective ranks had seemed of minimal importance. Sergeants and investigators worked side by side throughout the detective bureau. They became partners. In most cases rank was only a secondary consideration. But Dixie was asserting the prerogatives of her rank now. He looked at her, unable to see her eyes through the dark glasses. He saw only a hard-nosed detective sergeant. His friend, the beautiful woman he had so often seen both off duty and on, seemed to have disappeared.

"Yeah, I've got it, Sarge." He gazed at the front windshield, his jaw jutting slightly forward. "I'll keep my personal views to myself."

"Unless I ask."

"Unless you ask."

She gave him a curt nod and started the car. Just before pulling onto the street, she reached into the backseat and picked up a thick manila folder. It was stuffed with papers and held together with several rubber bands.

"Take this home with you tonight." Her face was bland. "All the reports and crime-scene photographs are there, along with notes on the interviews Herb and I conducted, along with a few *other* notes you might find interesting. The coroner's reports are included. Familiarize yourself with them."

Pete's heart was bouncing around in his belly again. He couldn't look at her.

"I'm warning you, Pete," she continued, "don't go charging off on your own. I can't say it emphatically enough. If you go through the material I've given you, and think we haven't covered it thoroughly enough, speak up. Otherwise, stick with the official investigation."

"I get the message loud and clear, bwana." His tone was only slightly sarcastic. "No histrionics . . . no cowboy tactics . . . no personal vendetta. I hear and obey."

"That would make me happy."

She pulled out of the parking lot, traveling only a few more blocks to reach the library. Pete was silent all the way. He kept running his palms up and down the folder he still held on his lap.

"Just leave it in the car," she said after parking the car again. "It will take you hours to read through it all. It's reading I think you should do alone, in private."

After getting out, she walked to the back of the car and unlocked the trunk. "If I don't get these books back today, they'll be overdue. Mind giving me a hand?"

He looked into the trunk at a pile of books. His brows raised a fraction. There were no less than twenty now. Not only books on the occult, but several volumes on psychology. He cocked his head to one side, trying to see the titles.

Dixie stepped in front of him. "Come to think of it, I'll probably need both of your hands."

She was right—it took both of his hands and arms, as well as her own, to deliver the books in one trip. The man at the book drop glanced at the books and then up at Dixie, nodding in recognition.

"Get through them all?" he asked.

"Enough to get the information I needed. This one was particularly good." She held up a small, gray, bound volume entitled *The Elektra Complex, A Modern Tragedy.*"

"I haven't read it myself," the man said. "Maybe I'll give it a try."

To this Dixie said nothing. She walked deliberately to the front door and saw Pete's hesitation. His eyes went to the escalator and then back to her. He seemed confused, as if he had expected her to go up and not out.

"Yes, Pete?"

"Oh, er . . . well, that's all, huh?"

"Why, did you want to check out a book or something?"

Once more his face colored. "No, not really, just thought *you* might want to, since you're obviously such a regular patron these days."

Under other circumstances Dixie would have found it strange that Pete did not talk once they got into the car, that he did not ask where they were going or what she had planned for the remainder of the day. But she already knew the answer. She felt the waves of discomfort radiating from him like heat from a potbellied stove. She forced herself to talk, carrying on a carefully courteous, one-sided dialogue about nothing.

By the time she pulled to a stop in front of the Nakamura home, her own nerve endings were beginning to unravel.

Pete went through his lumbering, disoriented routine again as she bypassed the walkway leading to Edward and Wendy Nakamura's house and knocked instead at the house next door.

An elderly man answered and squinted at the badges they showed him. He identified himself as Mr. Patterson.

"We are conducting an investigation, Mr. Patterson," Dixie began, "and would appreciate it if you could answer a few questions."

He was at least seventy, with a mass of creases on his face. "What sort of investigation?"

"Just routine," she evaded, knowing that ninety percent of the time the evasion worked. "We'll be talking to your neighbors as well."

"About what?"

"Are you well acquainted with the Nakamuras?"

"They live next door, have for years—even before Nakamura got stinko rich."

"Is it a quiet household?"

"Sure is. That man won't hardly carry on a conversation, not even in his own front yard."

"And the girl."

"Pretty little thing, even if she is a half-breed. My wife has passed on, but we used to know Wendy when she was no more than a baby. She and her mom came over to visit with my late wife every now and then. That was before Mrs. Nakamura died, of course. Too bad about her, passing on and leaving such a young one. But then, maybe it's all for the better, if you know what I mean."

"I'm not sure I do, Mr. Patterson," Dixie answered.

The old man's face hardened a bit. He looked from Dixie to Pete. "I know how it is these days. Everyone is supposed to look the other way and pretend anything folks want to do is okay. They say what they think is expected instead of what *is*. But I'm too old to care about that stuff. If people ask me a question, I tell 'em what I think, and what I think is, people ought to stick to their own kind. Ed Nakamura may not be black, but he isn't . . . well, he isn't white either. His wife was lily white, blond as she could be. Confusing for their little girl, I would think. My wife and I used to talk about it, how Mrs. Nakamura liked to come for coffee, visit, and how you could hardly get a word out of her husband. A strange match, if you want my opinion. Wendy is pretty much the same way now. Real Japanese, minds her manners, but keeps to herself.''

''So you don't hear a lot of noise from there, like loud music and big groups of teenagers?''

''Nope, none at all that I can remember. Never had reason to complain. Not since Mrs. Nakamura died.''

''There were disturbances while she was still alive?''

''Oh, nothing big really, just the regular stuff, like all couples. A fight now and again. Maybe it was a little worse, what with them being so different, but that was a long time ago. If I remember right, most of their disagreements had to do with how to raise Wendy. That's why I said what I did, you know, about it maybe being better this way. Now that her mom's gone, she's just plain Japanese. No halfway about it.''

As Dixie and Pete went from house to house, covering the ones next to and across from the Nakamura residence, they found the same basic theme repeated. In each instance the interracial marriage was mentioned. And Mr. Nakamura's wealth. And how quietly he and Wendy lived. Of them all, however, Mr. Patterson seemed the only one who remembered disharmony in the Nakamura marriage, or who looked on such intermarriage as even slightly objectionable. To everyone else, Edward Nakamura and his daughter seemed to fit the Japanese stereotype. He was hardworking, industrious, and quiet. Wendy was pretty, bright, studious and, of course, quiet.

It wasn't until after they rounded the block, checking at the houses behind Edward Nakamura's neat single-story, that an odd note sounded. A warning knell that made Dixie sick to her stomach.

The warning came from a young, soft-spoken woman with a personality as far as one could imagine from the gossipy neighbor type. The woman's name was Dora Billings, and she was smiling when she came to the door. But at the mention of the Nakamuras her eyes grew troubled and her cheeks colored.

''Oh, don't tell me something has happened!''

Dixie and Pete shot each other a quick look, and she suddenly realized that she had perhaps jumped to conclusions.

"I'm sorry," she half stuttered. "It's just that I thought . . . well, that he had . . ."

"Mrs. Billings, is there something we ought to know?"

The woman looked to the left and right, as if someone might miraculously appear to pull her out of the soup. "I really shouldn't say . . . Oh, now what have I gone and done!"

"Perhaps we could come in, Mrs. Billings. If you know something that can help us, we would appreciate your cooperation."

She hesitated only a moment longer and then stepped aside, holding the door open to them. She insisted that they have coffee, but Dixie had the impression she was stalling, avoiding talk about the subject that had obviously upset her so much.

At last she sat down. "I don't know quite how to say what I think I should say without sounding terribly dirty-minded, Sergeant Struthers, but it's about the people you were asking about, the ones who live just behind me."

"The Nakamuras."

"Yes, the Japanese man and his daughter. There isn't a mother living there, too, is there?"

"No, no mother. She died several years ago."

"Oh, so he's a widower." She stared down into her coffee cup. "I wish that explained . . ."

Her voice trailed away, and then she looked up and met Dixie's eyes. "But it doesn't explain why a man and his daughter would bathe together, does it?"

"What do you mean, bathe?" Dixie asked. She saw Pete come forward slightly in his chair. "Are you saying that you saw into their bathroom window?"

"No, but they have a spa in their backyard, a big one in the far left corner, just on the other side of the fence and below our bedroom window. We can hear it running sometimes, and that's how this all started."

"When you say a spa, I'm assuming you mean a hot tub. You saw Mr. Nakamura and his daughter in the spa together? Unclothed?"

"I believe that is a rather common Japanese custom," Pete said, his shoulders relaxing slightly.

"That's what I've been telling myself, and I'm still trying, wanting to believe I'm wrong. Honestly, I would rather have it turn out that I just have a rotten dirty mind."

Dixie gave her a reassuring smile. "Well, I doubt you have a dirty mind, Mrs. Billings, but it is possible that you simply misconstrued something you saw. Why don't you start at the beginning."

"Well, like you say, I've been hoping that it's all a terrible misunderstanding."

"About two and half months ago, after summer really set in, I woke up because it was so hot. I had the windows and the sliding door open. It didn't help much. I could hardly sleep anyway, and they had the spa on, bubbles and all. It was quite noisy. Finally I just gave up. I was tossing and turning so much, I was afraid I would wake my husband. I went out and sat on the little balcony that's just outside our bedroom."

Mrs. Billings's face was beginning to flush again. "I just opened the screen and went to sit without turning on the light. I was only wearing a light gown. I knew no one would see me, because with our bedroom being upstairs and the lights all out, I was in shadow, under the overhang of the roof. I just wanted to sit and cool off, and I had only been there for a short time when the spa was turned off. It was nice and quiet. Just a couple of moments later I saw something move in the Nakamura's backyard, a kind of flash. You can't see much in that yard, not even from our balcony, because of all the plants. Just the back door and a real small part of the patio. But it was the girl I saw, the one you called Wendy. The little Japanese girl. She ran into the house, from the spa I'm sure, and she wasn't wearing anything. I didn't think anything bad at first. After all, I was sitting outside in a shorty nightgown. In fact, I smiled, thinking how we never know who's watching us."

She looked at Dixie and Pete. "I wasn't spying, really."

"We know you weren't, Mrs. Billings," Dixie said. "Please, go on."

Pete shifted in his chair, and Dixie suspected that he wished the woman would not go on at all.

"Well, like I said, I saw the girl first. I thought she had been out there alone, cooling off. And then I saw her father. He . . . he didn't . . . wasn't wearing anything either. I didn't even know their names, not until just now, but I knew that they were Japanese, of course. Ever since that night I've been trying to make excuses for not doing anything, not saying anything to anyone."

"Maybe it is just as simple as you think, ma'am," Pete suggested. "Just a cultural thing, completely innocent."

Dora Billings shook her head. "That's just the problem. I didn't think it was innocent. I felt guilty, too, either way."

"What do you mean, either way?" Dixie asked the question. Covertly she was also still watching Pete, even more closely than the young woman they were interviewing. Her new partner seemed suddenly very alert.

"I felt guilty for having such—well, such a dirty mind. But I also felt guilty for not saying anything. I haven't even mentioned it to my husband, but I'm almost certain that it was not innocent because of what I heard later." She took a deep, shaking breath. "You see, Sergeant, I've turned into a snoop since that night. I just couldn't get it out of my mind. There have been several times now, late at night, when I've heard their spa go on. Twice I've gotten up, put on a robe, and gone down into my backyard. I . . . I stood up close to the fence, trying to listen . . . and to see."

Her face was fuchsia-colored now, and her eyes watered with embarrassment. "I couldn't see anything. There are all those leafy plants, and most of the time, with the sound of the spa, the bubbles, I couldn't hear anything either. Except once. I heard them one time, quite clearly."

"Maybe Mr. Nakamura was not with his daughter," Pete injected. "Maybe the girl was out on that particular night. Maybe her father had company, a lady friend."

Mrs. Billings blinked her eyes and swallowed. "No, it was the girl, the one who lives there. I've seen her before, during the day, several times. And I've heard her voice too. It was definitely her."

She looked at Pete, as if she was almost afraid to continue, afraid he did not believe her. But Dixie gently prompted her again. "Go ahead. You were worried about the girl, so you went in your backyard to find out if you were right. You heard something . . ."

"Yes. This was maybe three weeks ago. The girl was crying. I still couldn't understand anything because the father—both of them, in fact—were speaking Japanese. The girl's voice was so soft I don't think it would have made much difference anyway, even with no bubbles, even just sitting there in the hot water. She was crying, like I said, and at first her father seemed angry. But after a while his voice lowered too. I'm not quite sure how to explain what I heard, Sergeant Struthers. Even though they were speaking another language, I heard—and I *knew*. He was talking . . . well, his tone of voice *changed*. He was soothing her and . . . and eventually he . . . well, I heard . . . I know certain sounds when I hear them. They were making love . . . having sex."

The young woman was nearly in tears now, and her voice rose an octave, becoming almost belligerent. "I don't care if I seem like some nasty old gossip or not, I know it's the truth—in here!" She tapped her sternum emphatically. "Whatever's going on in that house is all wrong. *Sinful*. And it's against the law too. If I could have proven it, I would have called you already. Maybe that's why you're here. Maybe fate sent you."

"Maybe," Dixie agreed. She stood up.

Pete followed her example with a dark, troubled face. His eyes were hooded.

"Please don't feel as if you have done something wrong, Mrs. Billings," Dixie said. "You've helped us a great deal, and we appreciate it."

Coming to her feet, the woman made a depreciating gesture. "I feel terrible, and I hope you realize that I can't swear to anything."

"It still helps, gives the investigators a place to start." Dixie handed her a business card. "If there's anything else, if you see anything more, or remember something you left out, please call me."

Dora Billings gave the card a casual glance and then her eyes widened. "But this says *homicide*!"

"That's right, we're investigating a case involving one of Wendy Nakamura's friends."

"But . . . but . . ." The other woman stuttered.

"But a crime is a crime," Dixie said, touching her arm. "You've done the right thing, Mrs. Billings. Perhaps you were correct in saying that fate sent us here. If what you believe is true, Wendy Nakamura very much needs help."

Pete followed Dixie back to the car. She looked at him and saw that he could not meet her eyes. "You take the wheel this time, partner. Take us somewhere quiet, a place where we can talk. You choose the place, Pete, and you talk. I'll listen."

"I don't know what you're talking about, Sarge." Pete's voice was not quite steady. "I don't have anything to talk about."

Dixie opened the passenger door. "Oh, let's hope you do, Pete. Let's hope so very much."

Pete got behind the wheel. His face was pale and sick.

CHAPTER 28

———————————————————————————
———————————————————————————

PETE CHOSE HIS own home, and he drove there in utter and complete silence. Dixie watched him from the corner of her eye. Having passed the last several hours with him, observing him and his jitters at close range, she knew that at least some of her suspicions were well-founded, and yet she also prayed that she was wrong. Pete had been a member of her team in one way or another for almost as long as he'd been on the force. He was her friend.

Dixie clenched her teeth, pushing sympathy aside. She was a cop and so was Pete. They both knew the rules, and that's the way it had to be played. Hardball.

She had never been to his condo, not inside, and as they entered, she looked around, more than a little surprised. This was not a typical bachelor's pad—or at least not what most women would have expected. Dixie had always pictured Pete in a more Spartan environment. Clean, perhaps, but utilitarian.

His home was masculine. No ruffles or frills. But the colors, both on the walls and in his furnishings were soft. Blues and grays with a touch of white here and there. A light, bright place to live, with lots of throw pillows and deep cushions. No dirty dishes littered the bar separating kitchen from living area. She could see into his bedroom. A king-sized water bed was neatly made, covered with a thick blue and charcoal-colored comforter done in a geometric design. The only incongruity was the large, messy stack of what appeared to be photographs on his night table.

Most surprising to Dixie, and one of the personal touches that reached out and touched her, was the oversize brandy snifter in the center of a low chrome-and-glass coffee table. Half filled with water, it floated a single gardenia. The pungent fragrance of the flower scented the air. There was but one picture in the living room, a large, expensive, and beautifully finished photograph of Gretchen, the same one she and Herb had seen in Sally Nelson's office. Wearing a frothy white sundress, surrounded by green, with the flower close to her face, Gretchen was smiling. There was a mingled essence about the picture of innocence and sensuality.

The photograph and the single floating flower in the snifter had transformed Pete's living room into a shrine.

Dixie stared at Gretchen's beautiful blue eyes and wondered what it must be like for Pete, loving her and knowing she was forever gone as he sat looking at her picture night after night.

"This is nice," she said aloud, referring to his home, trying to keep her voice pleasant, to give them some sense of normality.

"I've always thought so. I like having my own place. It may be only a condominium, but to me it's *home*."

"I would imagine that's important to you, isn't it?"

He didn't nibble at the sympathetic bait. "As much as it is to anyone, I guess."

He put down the folder Dixie had given him and took off his sport coat. He carried a six-inch Smith and Wesson in a black leather shoulder holster. "Can I get you a cup of coffee?"

Dixie did not often feel the need for a drink. She did at the moment, but she simply nodded, wishing they were not still officially on duty. In fact, she sadly realized, she especially was very much on duty.

"I'll be just a minute," he said, disappearing around the short breakfast bar and into what was obviously the kitchen. She heard the rattle of utensils, but the moment he was out of sight, Dixie moved, heading for his bedroom like a laser beam. She knew what she would find, but she could not smother just a tiny spark of hope.

Quickly, she lifted the stack of photographs she had spied beside his bed.

She was angry at herself for the tears of disappointment that filled her eyes as she leafed through them. Photographs of reports. Photos of crime-scene photos. Her stomach felt sick.

"Do you ever stop, Sarge?" Pete's voice sounded from the doorway. "Are you always a cop, always an investigator? Or do you turn into a human being when the moon gets full?"

"Screw you, Willis," She faced him and removed her sunglasses. "I see you haven't quit *investigating* either. But now you do it illegally, you steal from your friends. What about you? Do you ever stop?"

"Not where this case is concerned."

"You should have, Pete. There was a point at which you definitely should have—namely, at breaking into my house. It wasn't even your case, not then."

"Bullshit!" His voice exploded into the room. He was shaking all over. "It *is* my case. How could it not be? I wanted—"

"This is *my* case, Willis, and I trust myself to do it right, even if you don't. You have one helluva nerve burgling my house! You're goddamn lucky I didn't blow your head off!"

He leaned forward, his huge frame towering above her. His face was thunderous, contorted with anger. "I asked you, both of you! Herb wouldn't give me diddly shit, not so much as a stinking crumb! Hell, Dixie, everyone in the department knew more about this case than I did, and no one, I mean *no one* wants that fucker who killed Gretchen like I do!"

"You're a grade-A, number-one ass, Pete. We were trying to protect you. So what do you do—go and commit a felony!" She was screaming into his face, and her next words turned him ghostly pale. "Want to know what I think, Willis? I think *you* were the father of that baby Gretchen was carrying!"

"Shut up, Dixie. I mean it, you better just—"

"What are you going to do, Pete, hit me? Kill me?"

If he had been shaking before, now he was unglued, cracking apart at the seams. But Dixie no longer cared. Her own rage removed both courtesy and caution.

"You might as well," she yelled, "that way we can add homicide to your rap sheet. Burglary! Assault on a police officer! Theft! Illegal intercourse! Incest!"

The blow came out of nowhere. She did not even see him raise his arm before he delivered an open-handed slap. Her mouth filled with the taste of blood as her head snapped. She staggered backward and fell across his bed.

Pete stood there, as if in shock. Peter Jacob Willis, who had never hit a female in his entire life. Who had never even considered doing it—especially not *this* female. Not Dixie T. Struthers, the woman who had saved his life. The woman he had often feared he might love.

She laid perfectly still. A bright drop of blood showed at the corner of her full lips. Her copper-colored hair was spread in disarray behind her head, with a few stray tendrils clinging to the damp of her cheeks, damp caused by angry tears she was not aware she had shed. Her green eyes glistened.

Pete was still breathing heavily. He blinked and shook his head like a dog with a burr up its nose. He held out his hand, half in supplication, half as an offer of assistance.

Dixie ignored both gestures. Coming to a sitting position, she wiped at her mouth with the back of her hand and then looked at the smear with disgust.

"Dixie, I . . ."

She stood and brushed past him, going into the adjoining bathroom. There, she turned on the cold water and began washing her face and hands, dabbing at the edge of her mouth with a cloth.

Pete appeared behind her. "I didn't do it, Sarge."

"What's that, Pete? Which crime? I suppose you didn't break into my house, attack me, and truss me up like the proverbial fatted calf."

"You know that's not what I mean."

She met his eyes in the mirror. "I want to believe you, Pete. I don't think I've ever wanted anything so bad in my whole life."

"I loved Gretchen. Really loved her." Pete's voice was firm and his gaze did not waver. "Not the way she wanted me to, and I'll admit that she made it pretty damn hard on me. I'm human, Dixie, and she was growing into one of the most beautiful women on earth. That's the way I thought of her. She . . ."

His voice faded and he rubbed a hand over his face. "Do you suppose we could sit down? I really need to sit."

She gave him a half-crooked smile. Her lip was beginning to swell. "Not me. I feel fine as frog's hair."

Pete looked at her face and colored to the roots of his hair. "Dixie, I—"

She relented. "Never mind, Peter. Could you just get me something to drink? And I don't mean coffee. We went off duty three minutes ago."

In admitting what she knew the best of men would have had difficulty admitting, Pete unshakably convinced Dixie that he was telling the truth.

"I felt the chemistry," he said, taking a deep draught of the beer he had opened for himself after pouring Dixie a stiff scotch. "I don't think that's so weird, even if I did feel guilty as hell. Looking back, I realize that she had been testing her newly acquired little wiles on me for quite some time. And I don't think that's unusual either. Little girls grow up. Their fathers or brothers are usually the men they love best. They do things innocently, completely unaware that they're posturing, swaying, rubbing like kittens. They just do it, all in innocence. But Gretchen did know, I think, at least toward the end.

"She was really bright, Dix. Maybe that was the problem. Maybe that kept her from having as many friends as other, more normal kids."

Dixie, who had by now formed her own opinions of Gretchen's character and level of innocence, refrained from comment.

"The way I figured it, I had three choices. I could reject her outright, get angry with her, stop letting her come around. I don't think that would have been good, Dixie. It would have ripped her up. I did turn her away, but I didn't reject her. I thought she knew that. I bent over backward to make it clear. My only other choice would have been to give in to the chemistry, and then go out and eat the barrel of my 357 the next morning." He grinned wryly. "Somehow that didn't seem like such a great option either."

Whether Pete knew it or not, he was describing a common

crossroads in many father/daughter relationships. But few
fathers either recognized, acknowledged, or admitted that
basic flesh-touching-flesh chemistry was no respector of family
relationships. All too often a father thrust into such a situation, appalled by his own humanity, reacted on either a
conscious or subconscious level by pushing his daughter away,
becoming overly strict and critical. According to many psy-
chologists, the result was rebellion on the part of the adoles-
cent girl. Anger and hurt for all concerned.

And then there were the other few—the unhealthy men.
That tiny percentage of sick fathers who stepped over the
social and moral line.

Pete had been the closest thing to a father Gretchen would
ever know. Father. Brother. Imaginary lover. Dixie was glad
that he had not stepped over the line.

"There were little things," he continued. "Like I said,
when I think about it now, I realize that she had probably
been testing me for a long time. We would go to the beach
and she would have me rub lotion on her. Nothing unusual in
that, right? I had been swabbing her down with lotion since
she was a month old. But it was different, and I knew it.
Little by little I just quit buying into the games, games which,
like I said, I thought were innocent. She was only a child. I
felt a little guilty sometimes, because I couldn't help but see
her, how pretty and sexy she was getting. But I was proud of
myself, too, because I thought I had handled the whole thing
pretty damn well. She was going through a stage, and I had
managed to help her without hurting her. But that last
time. . ."

Pete closed his eyes, almost groaning with the memory.
"God, Dixie, she caught me off guard. She came over and
we had dinner together. It was something we both liked to do.
Eat here. Talk or watch a little television. An awful lot of the
time we just sat in the same room and read, or listened to
music. Once in a while, when she and Prissy were still
friends, they would both come over. I would take them out
somewhere, to a movie or to play miniature golf, that type of
thing. I think Gretchen pretty much preferred our twosome,
though, and of course, after she and Prissy had a parting of
the ways, that was the way it stayed. Just me and Gretchen."
He was getting off the track, talking in circles to keep from

remembering that last night with his niece. Both he and Dixie knew it.

"What happened, Pete?" She asked the question softly, hating to see the twist of pain on his face.

"She threw herself at me." Pete sounded as if he would strangle on the words. "I would give anything to put it some other way, but I can't. She gave me this—" he pulled the chain out from under the collar of his shirt—"and then kissed me—more than kissed. She wrapped herself around me like a rubber band, and she did it in a way that made it impossible to laugh off. There was nothing funny about the situation. It was terrible, Dix. I found myself kissing her back, and then I pushed her away. Hard. She wouldn't let go, and I had to nearly knock her down.

"Oh, my God, my God! I'll never forget how she looked. She started crying, hanging onto my legs." Pete was crying himself. Tears ran down his face. "She kept . . . kept talking crazy, saying how she wanted to have my baby, and that if I really meant what I said, that if she was my little goddess, I would want her the same way she wanted me. There were other things. I can't remember every word, probably because I did my best to put it all out of my mind before she . . . she. . .''

"Easy, Pete." Dixie wanted to hold him, rock him back and forth like a baby, but he was sitting too far away to let such an action seem natural. His body was rigid with grief, and the last thing she wanted was to give him another bad memory. "It wasn't your fault, Pete. It absolutely *was not*."

"You may be right, my friend, but there's one thing I won't forget as long as I live, and that's Gretchen's face. How she looked up at me. And how she finally ran out of here, like she never wanted to see me again." His face was drawn and pale. "She never did either. I never saw Gretchen again. Not alive."

Pete ground his next words out from between clenched teeth. "I want the animal that killed my niece, Dixie, the same animal who I'm sure made her act like she did that night by getting her pregnant. She was desperate, but I had no way of knowing then that she was going to have a baby."

"She wasn't, Pete, not then."

He stared at her. "How could that be? Why would she act that way?"

"Because she loved you and just did not know how to handle the feelings she was having. She loved you, Pete."

His face grew more stark. "I want the man who killed her, Dixie, the man who got her pregnant. I *want* him!"

There were things she wanted to say to him, to tell him about his niece, but she decided it could all wait. "We'll get him, Pete. Or them. Whoever killed Gretchen."

He nodded and then fell silent for a long time. And while Dixie's heart ached for him, in another way she felt wonderful, literally exhilarated by the overwhelming sense of relief at finding out that Pete was innocent of the darkest crime, the worst that she had suspected of him.

She finally broke the silence herself. "Pete, I want you to listen to me. You have to know that you're in no way responsible for what happened to Gretchen. Surely you realize that she was troubled. Accept that much, at least. There was no other way for you to deal with what happened between the two of you."

"So you believe me?"

"Yes." She answered with the single affirmative. No addenda.

The look of gratitude Pete shot her was all too familiar. She groaned. "Oh, my God, whatever you do, don't start looking at me like that! Honest, Pete, you don't owe me a thing." She grinned, and then scowled fiercely. "Unless you ever put your big mitts on me again, or come slinking into my abode in the dead of night. In that case you won't have to be grateful to anyone for anything, because I'll kill you. Slowly. Painfully."

He raised his hand in a Boy Scout gesture. "You can do it inch by inch."

"As Jake would say, 'No scooby-do, partner.' "

"Boy does that sound good to this felon. Want another drink?"

"Another would put me under the seat. I've got to drive home and put an ice pack on this." She indicated an inflated lower lip. "Oh, quit looking at me like a chicken-killing hound, Willis. I've been hurt worse."

His chagrin dissolved into a boyish grin, the first she had seen on his face in a very long time. "I remember."

He walked her to the door. Just before leaving, she put a hand on his arm. "At the risk of having you hit me again, and having to likewise do you in, there's something I want you to do for me."

He lifted his brows in question.

"I want you to read my notes all the way through, especially the last ones, the ones you haven't seen yet. More than that, I want you to try doing it with an open mind, okay?"

"Will do."

"My observations may not go down so great," she warned. "You're not going to like a few of my conclusions."

He frowned. "I don't care for a few I've already read, but I'll at least try to understand how you reached them. That good enough?"

"All I can ask."

Pete walked her to her car and watched her drive away. He felt myriad emotions, love and gratitude not the least among them. But he felt leaden as he walked back into his own living room and picked up the thick manila folder. Then, taking a deep breath, feeling almost like a cop again, he began to read. And the more he read, the deeper his frown became.

CHAPTER 29

THE CASE WAS far from solved. Even so, Dixie drove home that
night with a vast feeling of accomplishment—and relief. Pete,
while still bent on bringing in the killer, was beginning to
recover from what she viewed as an illness. Perhaps it had
been his striking her, an act so completely out of character,
that began to snap him back to reality.

She gingerly fingered her lip. A wry smile flitted across her
features. It had been a painful prescription, but one she was
happy to fill if it helped cure Pete.

As she pulled up to her house, she smiled again, wider,
and then winced as she felt the edge of her lip tear. There was
a small car taking her place next to Patrick's battered Chevy
pickup. A shining bronze-colored Mercedes 450 SL convert-
ible. Franklin's high school graduation gift to Ryan.

The sound of her arrival brought her half brother out to the
deck. She hurried to him, stepping happily into his bear hug.
She laughed. "No doubt the Grande Dame herself has sent
you, to keep up the pressure."

Ryan nuzzled her neck and squeezed until she squealed in
protest. "Nope, came on my own, and for my own good
reasons."

Dixie looked over his shoulder and received another surprise. Art was standing just inside the front door, hovering in

the shadow of the foyer. His face looked incredibly good to her. Too good, she decided, as Ryan put her back on her feet. She forced herself not to smile too brightly.

"Ah-ha," she mumbled. "De plot do thicken."

Ryan put an arm over her shoulders. "No plot, sis, just an honest desire for two things. Stunt flying and getting to know this guy a little better. Seems to me he's been hanging around in the wings for quite a while."

Art was moving toward them now, and she knew he was within earshot.

"Yes," she said, "quite a while—but not much lately."

Art did not take the bait. Instead he bent and kissed her lightly. His eyes widened as she winced, and when he saw the reason, his brows lifted a good inch. He backed off a pace. "I can see I'll have to be a more regular visitor in the future. My stand-in is a little rough."

Ryan turned and looked at her more closely. "Jeez, Dix, what bulldozer *have* you been kissing?"

"Believe it or not, I'm just clumsy. Wasn't paying attention and opened the car door right into my own face."

"Well, ask me if *I* believe it, Missy T.!" Reversa filled the doorway. "I certainly do not, not for a minute."

Dixie rolled her eyes heavenward. "You never believe anything I say when I'm late for supper."

"You've got that one right. Now get yourselves out back, all of you. The old paddy says those steaks he's burnin' out on the barbecue pit are just about ready. My part's done too. The best part. Now come on!"

An obedient trio followed her through the house and onto the back veranda, where a table had been set and laden with salads, cottage fries, and several rich, crusty desserts. Eating Reversa's cooking was a far cry from the fare served in the Marks mansion, and Ryan gave a greedy cry of delight. At nineteen, cucumber sandwiches, soufflés, and noncaloric patés de blahs held little appeal.

"Reversa," he said, sidling up to the scowling Juno, "have I told you lately that I love you?"

"And butter wouldn't melt in your mouth, boy. Don't go greasin' my ego, cause I've got you down for dishwashing, no matter." A pleased smile nevertheless creased Reversa's face. She was fond of any healthy appetite, and Ryan's in particular.

"You just going to stand there chipping your teeth all day, woman?" Patrick called from beside the barbecue pit. "Or are you going to bring me a platter?"

The air was aromatic with mesquite-grilled New Yorkers, and dusk was just beginning to fall as they sat down to eat. It was a pleasant meal, with the strain between Dixie and Art relieved by the gregariousness and easy banter of the others. Ryan chattered about college life at Stanford. Patrick and Reversa kept up a token quarrel.

After they had all finished eating, Dixie stood and began clearing dishes. Ryan stopped her. "Didn't you hear the boss? I've got K.P. duty. I suggest you and Art just kick back. Of course, I'll need Pop and Reversa. I would get bored if they stopped the show now."

The hint was taken instantly. Within what seemed a matter of seconds, the table was cleared. The good-natured bantering resumed indoors, leaving Dixie and Art alone on a pair of deck chairs. The last lingering rays of September sun had turned the sky purple, with tufts of purple clouds drifting overhead.

Art decided not to beat about the bush any longer. "I've missed you," he said.

Unsure of how to respond, of how she really felt, Dixie changed the subject. "So, Ryan is taking up dips and dives, is he?"

"Yes, and I think he'll be good at stunt flying too. That kid has nerves of steel—just like his sister."

"His sister's nerves aren't so hot these days, I'm afraid."

"Oh?"

"She has been a little distracted, perhaps even *snappish*?"

No disclaimer was forthcoming. "I guess we all have our days."

They sat in silence, but after several moments Art reached out and took her hand, turning it palm up, looking at it as if to read her fortune. "Want to tell me about that lip now?"

She thought for a moment and then told him the truth. "Pete clipped me."

He dropped her hand and sat forward. "The bastard really has come unglued!"

"Funny as it sounds, I think hitting me helped. This thing with his niece has really ripped him apart."

Art wore a menacing scowl. "I'll show him what ripped up is. What he needs is a long stint of R and R, but not until I show him how to treat a lady."

"He already knows how, Art, and I would appreciate it if you keep the whole thing under your hat. I purposely pushed Pete to the wall. He needed to blow, and I needed information. We both ended up satisfied, and my lip doesn't hurt bad enough for me to be sorry."

"Anything for a fellow officer, right?"

"Anything for a *friend*."

"I wonder if that includes me."

"I hope so."

The tension was there again, rebuilding the invisible wall between them. Once more Art was beginning to feel angry, and helpless to tear it down. "I've always thought we were friends, Dixie. Maybe I was wrong."

She looked out at the garden Patrick so carefully tended, at the trees and the beautiful gloaming sky. It was a good life she lived, a satisfying life, in spite of the occasional horrors of her job. She met his troubled blue eyes.

"You are not wrong, darling." She spoke endearments rarely, and this one very softly. "But friendship is a two-way street. There are certain things a friend, a true friend, would never ask."

"Will you marry me?"

Dixie's eyes flew open. It was her turn to sit up straight. "What in the hell kind of question is that!"

All at once Art started laughing. He could not help himself. She looked shocked. "Evidently *that* wasn't the wrong thing to ask, thank God. But maybe not the right thing either?"

"Arthur B. Cochran, is this a joke?" She was blushing with confusion, as well as feeling more than a little apprehensive.

"Oh, for crying out loud, who knows!"

He stood and pulled her up beside him. His arms went around her waist, and he looked down into her face. He gently kissed her nose. "All I know for certain is that I love you. Beyond that, nothing seems important at the moment. I haven't been able to think straight for days."

"I love you, too, Art." She had never told him before, and

an odd kind of fear shot through her as the words came out of her mouth. Her heart was hammering against her ribs at an unreasonable rate. "For now, though . . . for now can we just . . ."

He stopped the stuttering with another kiss, also applied gently, a tender balm.

As his lips moved to her ear and then down the smooth column of her throat, leaving a trail of delicious goose bumps in their wake, Art also felt a tremor of premonition, fear for the commitment he had just made. He had never met a woman he could not, given sufficient effort, forget. And of all the beautiful, stubborn women on earth, Dixie Tulip Flannigan Struthers was the one he wished to forget most of all. He wanted to hoist her from the waking and dreaming labyrinths of his mind. He wanted to purge her—and instead he had just asked her to marry him. Without thinking things out.

Coming to her house with Ryan, Art had intended to lay down an ultimatum. Instead, he had proposed, and he did not know whether to laugh or cry.

He still wanted her to leave police work—*or else*. And that was what he had intended to tell her.

He found the hollow of her throat and buried his lips there, inhaling the sweetness of her flesh, feeling the beckoning warmth of her body—praying that his one potential ally would come through. All his bets were on Dixie's mother.

Oblivious to everything save the urgent physical message he was telegraphing through her nervous system, Dixie wrapped both arms around his neck. She kissed his temple, his cheek, until he once more lifted his head. She sought his lips, ignoring the pain his kiss caused. She was oblivious, too, of his silent plea.

In the kitchen, as if the invisible fire on the veranda was a palpable, crackling thing, Ryan, Patrick, and Reversa looked at one another. For once the latter two shared a conspiratorial smile.

Only Ryan turned away from the back door and the poignant all-telling silence. Frowning, he thrust his hands back into a sink filled with suds and dirty dishes.

CHAPTER 30

"*INCEST!*" HERB BOLTED upright in his recliner, sending the book he had been holding onto the floor.

"Herb, really!" Janice looked around in alarm. "Amy will hear you!"

He lowered his voice. "Are you sure?"

"I'm not saying for absolute certain," Dixie said, her voice coming through the receiver. "All I'm saying is that it's an avenue to be explored. One more thing our little *gang* may have had in common. We've been seeking connections that would provide a motive. Pete and I have been doing some checking, and we're coming up with more than we know what to do with."

Dixie was sitting at her desk in the squad room. She looked at her temporary partner. Pete was at the computer terminal, checking backgrounds on a list of names they had composed.

"Wait a minute," Herb said, suffering a mass case of frustration. "Back up, woman. My ankle might be out of commission, but as far as I know, my brain is in gear. You're losing me."

Dixie leaned back in her desk chair. The squad room was quiet. She and Pete had put in a long, hard day, and they were the only ones still on duty.

"Like I said, Herb, it's an avenue we've decided is worth

exploring. It seems pretty certain that the Nakamura girl has been sexually abused. Proving it might be tough, because the witness probably wouldn't hold up in court.''

"But she's straight, the witness I mean?"

"We feel sure that she is."

"Edward Nakamura." There was a tinge of incredulity in Herb's voice. "Hardly the M.O. one would expect, is it?"

"Why not? You and I both know that particular crime runs the gamut. Dock workers and doctors. Rich and poor. Social status seems to make no never mind to the average ol' child molester."

"Yeah, but Nakamura is *Japanese*, almost of the old world variety."

"The same thought ran through my mind, but since when is it a new world crime? We're all guilty of stereotyping, Herb, even when we don't want to, and I think that's what we've been doing. As for Nakamura being old world, he married a 'round-eye,' didn't he?"

"I hardly think that qualifies him as a monster, Dix."

"No, but we've found pretty good reason to suspect that he's had intimate relations with his teenage daughter."

"This is really sickening, Dixie. One of the nastiest cases I've ever come across. I'm beginning to wonder how much dirtier it can get before it's over."

"Me, too, but there's more dirt on Mr. Nakamura. You told me that he has a rather successful gardening service."

"A *very* successful one. I think he has something like a hundred employees."

"One hundred five to be exact, and some very impressive accounts. Homes all over Los Gatos, Saratoga, and Monte Serreno. That's without even counting his main source of income, the commercial contracts. Let me run another of his contracts by you, just for fun."

Herb was one step ahead of her. "No, let me guess. Old Sarah's house?"

"You've got it."

"*Jeez, Louise!*" Herb breathed. "Do you think he's our man?"

"A possibility, at least. Could be that Gretchen found out what was going on and needed to be shut up. Pete seems to think it's a good bet. He's chomping at the bit to bring the guy in for questioning."

"And you?" Herb was straining at the bit to get out of the damn recliner and go to work.

"I want to check Nakamura all the way," Dixie answered. "Like I said, I think this"—the word felt dirty on her tongue—"*incest* business may be a significant thread. Sunday morning I laid it all out again." She refrained from mentioning Pete's clandestine visit. "I spread all the notes out on the living room floor. I must have sat there staring at them for two hours. Witchcraft. Spooks and goblins. Druid sacrifices and voodoo. Greek gods and ancient Egyptians doing it with bulls. That was on the one side, things I had picked up from the books Gretchen and her buddies checked out of the library. I read them, too, but in the beginning I was only looking for leads, hoping to track down exactly why Gretchen had been murdered and mutilated like that. I wanted to find out what all the symbolism stood for. And on the surface it all seemed a conglomeration, a mishmash of beliefs all rolled into one horrible murder. But remember what I told you, about how all the ancient gods, or most of them, interconnect? How even the Judeo-Christian beliefs have some pretty strange roots?"

"Yeah, Struthers, you've been a real barrel of laughs lately."

"Well, just bear with me, partner, because that's the way my mind works best sometimes, especially when I'm dead tired. It works in circles, big ones that get smaller and smaller as I go. And I was tired, more tired than you can imagine."

"So, I'm listening." He ignored Janice's pantomime to get off the phone and rest.

"Those four kids are the only solid leads we've got, Herb. I sat there in the gray morning light looking for connections. Even on the surface there were quite a few. By almost anyone's standard, all four of those kids were nice-looking. All had some pretty heavy-duty family problems. They were of supposedly well-above-average intelligence. They all seemed to have been dabbling in the occult, a rather impressive variety of occult beliefs at that—and *that* was the rub. Why would they be? Even given the almost certain fact that they're all troubled, why would they be so interested in what most people consider a bunch of hocus-pocus? Given their collective intelligence, I didn't think it matched, not unless I was missing something.''

"Maybe the Baldwin boy was being straight with you,'' Herb said. "Maybe they were just playing around. A game. Like the one that was so popular with college kids for a while—*Dungeons and Dragons.*''

"That game went awry a couple of times, too, if I remember correctly. But I think it's possible that this one gave someone the perfect ruse, a bright red herring for our dragnet.''

"And you think it's one of the other links, like something in one of their family situations?''

"That was where I found the other similarity,'' Dixie replied. "With the exception of the Baldwin boy, each member of the group lived with a single parent. And from Gretchen's point of view, Jimmy Baldwin might as well have too. I told you how it was with him, so think about it. Tony and Asunta Castellano; Wendy and Edward Nakamura; Jimmy and Betty Baldwin. Sound like *couples*, don't they?''

"Shades of Oedipus again, but that leaves Gretchen odd man out, unless . . .'' Herb's stomach did a giant flip-flop, and he could not finish the sentence.

Dixie looked back at Pete. He was still pressing buttons on the computer. The screen cast an almost eerie glow on his face. He was frowning.

"I think you have it, friend,'' she told Herb, lowering her voice. "Shades of Oedipus *and* Elektra, and it's exactly what I came up with.''

"Oh, no, Dixie, tell me this is a joke. We've known Pete for an awful long—''

"It was a joke to him, Herb, but I'm sure there was nothing funny about it to Gretchen. I've already checked it out. I had to.''

"That must have been hard on Pete.''

Dixie touched her lip, but said nothing of the altercation with their mutual friend. "You could say that, more than a little, but he came up clean.''

"Doesn't surprise me a bit.'' Herb tried not to let the relief come through in his voice. "Have you had a chance to check the others? Really check?''

"In progress, partner. In fact, that's the reason we're still here. We couldn't reach Nakamura until a little over an hour ago. He's agreed to meet us here for an interview. We told him we wanted to abide by his wishes about not upsetting Wendy any further. He sounded amicable enough on the phone, in his own cool, courteous way."

"If he's our man, you can bet he'll show with an attorney."

"My thought exactly. Coming down here with an attorney is no proof, of course, but it would give us one more thing to mull over."

"*Damn!*"

"What's wrong, is your foot hurting?"

"No, my pride. I hate this, Dix, sitting here, not able to help. It's driving me bonkers."

"I miss you, too, *dear*," Dixie purred. "Get well soon."

Herb growled and hung up.

CHAPTER 31

DIXIE LOOKED AT her watch and then at Pete. He was still staring hard at the terminal screen, his brow knitted into furrows. She stood and walked toward him. "Have you come up with something?"

He turned, and for several seconds she thought he had taken a giant mental step backward. He looked dazed, his eyes taking her in without really seeing her. But the glazed look disappeared almost instantly. He shook his head, punching the return key and clearing the screen just as she got to him.

"Not much," he answered. "Anthony Castellano, Senior, has been busted for duce once. Of the kids you interviewed at the high school, only two have been arrested for illegal substances. Priscilla Smith was one of them, she got pinched on an ABC violation for being in a bar. Her folks evidently let her cool her heels at the hall for a couple of days. She was also under the influence. Too bad. I liked the kid when she and Gretchen used to hang out together. But like I said, no big deals so far. I'll pull the full reports tomorrow."

"Nothing on the other adults? Susan Banks or Lillian Jackabcin, in particular?"

"Clean as a whistle, which doesn't necessarily mean anything, of course. Edward Nakamura and Howard Baldwin were also clean, and we know they were a couple of real nice guys.''

"Sergeant Struthers?" Edward Nakamura stood at the door. He was wearing khaki-colored work clothes—perfectly pressed and immaculate, with an oval shaped Golden Bamboo logo just above the left pocket. On the pocket itself was a small plastic badge which read: EDWARD NAKAMURA, LANDSCAPING ARCHITECT.

"Yes, Mr. Nakamura," Dixie greeted him, holding out her hand. "Thank you for coming down. Please, have a seat."

He sat in a straight-backed chair. She sat at her desk while Pete took the place normally reserved for Herb.

"As I told you and the other gentleman who came to my house, Sergeant, I'm glad to help in any way I can—just as long as my daughter is not upset."

"Wouldn't want that," Pete mumbled, but he managed to trim any trace of sarcasm from his tone.

Dixie began the questioning in a crisp, routine manner, reaffirming that Wendy had been at home during the hours Gretchen was believed to have been murdered.

Mr. Nakamura made a great show of patience as he answered each of the questions again. Yes, Wendy had been at home. No, she could not have left without his knowledge. Impossible. Wendy was a good and extremely obedient daughter.

"You're sure she could not have left the house," Pete asked, "not even by way of her bedroom window?"

"Certainly not, not without my knowing. I usually retire late, and I always check on her."

"That may be, but kids have a way of pulling the wool over their parent's eyes at times, even normally *obedient* kids."

"Not my daughter." Nakamura's expression did not alter, but his tone hardened. "Wendy *does not* disobey me, or question my authority."

"Not ever?"

"Not since she was very, very young."

"Why do you suppose that is?" Dixie asked. "There are very few perfect children, Mr. Nakamura."

Though his posture was already straight to the point of being stiff, Nakamura's shoulders squared a fraction more.

"She has been raised differently than most American children, in the old way, the way my own grandparents raised me, with rules and a sense of order. Duty."

"And fear, perhaps?" Pete was delighted to play the heavy. He did not, he decided, like the man. Edward Nakamura may have come to his wealth the hard way—old calluses on his hands attested to that fact. But those narrow hands were now immaculate, with professionally buffed and pared fingernails. His haircut had cost no less than thirty dollars. He was a very smooth and cool customer, so slow and graceful in his gestures that Pete found him almost effeminate.

"Why should my daughter fear me?" the man asked.

"I'm not saying that she should—I'm asking you if she *does*."

"Not to my knowledge."

"And your knowledge takes in most of Wendy's activities, Mr. Nakamura?" Dixie asked. "You knew, for instance, that she and her friends, the ones she met at the library every Thursday evening, shared a deep interest in certain, shall we say, *unsavory* matters? Occult matters for one, and—"

"Don't be ridiculous, Sergeant. You mentioned this before. I tell you Wendy is much too intelligent for superstition, old or new. Whatever you have learned, or think you have learned, can be explained, I assure you."

"Did she ever ask you questions concerning the Winchester Mansion, Mr. Nakamura?"

"No, and there is no reason why she should."

"Except that you hold a contract there, I believe, for all the grounds services."

Edward Nakamura was holding his own, not turning a hair at the mention of his business affiliation. "I bid for and receive many contracts. My men trim lawns at the mansion, prune trees and flowers. The interest I have there is concerned solely with fulfilling my obligations. To my knowledge my daughter is not even aware that I have such a contract. Certainly she has never expressed any interest in my business affairs, which do not concern her."

"We have reason to believe that she and her friends attempted to conduct a séance there."

"Ridiculous." Nakamura's lower lip curled slightly. "If

you insist, I will ask Wendy about this nonsense, but I assure you—"

"How well do you know really know your daughter, Ed?" Pete was tipped back in Herb's swivel chair. He looked at the Japanese man with hooded eyes. "Or maybe I should put it to you another way—do you *have* knowledge of your daughter, Mr. Nakamura?"

The English subtlety was obviously not wasted. For the first time since his arrival, Edward Nakamura moved, twisted in his chair as if the seat had grown a bit too warm. Tiny spots of color suddenly appeared on each high cheekbone. "I will pretend that I do not understand such a question. I will do this for the sake of your career."

"My career will survive your lack of pretense. What we're after here is honesty."

"Please forgive our crudity, Mr. Nakamura." Dixie sounded sincerely contrite. "There are questions we simply must ask. In the course of our investigation we found it necessary to question certain of your neighbors. One of them has observed you and Wendy in the backyard of your home."

"Butt naked," Pete added.

The man's face had gone completely red now, almost puce. "You are a most ignorant man. You know nothing of my cul—"

"I know sex sounds when I hear them, turkey, and so does your neighbor."

Nakamura came swiftly to his feet. "This discussion is finished. You have brought me here on false pretenses. If you have any further questions, you may ask them with my attorney present."

"Will he know why your daughter has no friends?" Nakamura was stalking to the squad room door as Pete continued to hammer questions at him. "Will he know why one of the few friends she had turned up dead and mutilated at a place you have special access to, *Mister* Nakamura? Did Wendy tell her friend something that you did not want known?"

Just before thrusting himself into the corridor, the other man turned. His face was twisted with rage. Or fear. His lips pulled back from his teeth and he hissed. "I took due note of your name, Investigator Willis, and it is very obvious to me that you should not be working in your present capacity. You have lost your good sense and have—how shall I put it?—a *personal* axe to grind. My sympathy for you has disappeared, however. We shall see how your axe does against a pair of rather sharp pruning shears.''

He was gone then, nearly vanishing before their eyes. Pete made a hawking sound of disgust deep in his throat. ''Turn him over to S.A., Dixie. This case belongs with the Sexual Assault dicks. They'll have Nakamura out of that house in less than forty-eight hours if they sweat him right, attorney or no attorney.''

''You don't think he's good for the other . . . for Gretchen?''

Pete shook his head. ''Nakamura is just a wimp who gets his sexual kicks from dominating his own kid. A no-balls, chickenshit wimp. But I don't think he's murdered anything, except maybe his daughter's spirit.''

''What makes you so sure, Pete?''

He shrugged. ''Call it instinct, something *you* helped teach me.''

She smiled at him. ''So what does your instinct tell your tummy about this time of night? Want to grab a bite?''

''I don't think so, Dix.'' He smothered a yawn and stretched before coming to his feet. ''We've got another long one tomorrow, and what I really need for a change is a full night of uninterrupted zees. Can I take a rain check?''

''No problem.'' Dixie waved as he left. She glanced at the overhead clock and realized, with a start, that she was late for a dinner date with Art. Quickly, Dixie put her reports away, locked the desk, and left the building.

CHAPTER 32

PETE DROVE FROM the police parking lot slowly. He saw Dixie's car pass. Her coppery hair caught the breeze from an open window, flying about her face like tongues of flame. But for once Pete was unaffected by the picture she presented. In fact, he now saw Sergeant Dixie T. Struthers only as an obstacle to be put safely to one side. He breathed a sigh of relief as her BMW disappeared from view.

His eyes opened wider and he snapped to attention. His face settled into stony lines of determination. Everything that he had felt when Gretchen was first found murdered—the pain and rage, the gut-boiling need to tear someone apart—was back, but this time it was worse. A new dimension had been added to his agony, one that made it almost impossible for him to hold himself together in front of Dixie.

Shame pulsed through him. Sitting in the squad room, listening to Nakamura, Pete had wanted to scream. Edward Nakamura was a criminal. To Pete the man was slime. But only that. Just a small sliver of refuse that needed purging from society and from the life of the daughter he had victimized. Nothing more or less.

But Pete knew for certain that the Japanese man had not killed Gretchen. The knowledge made him want to rage and weep at the same time. The computer had told him everything he needed to know. The letters, strung into glaring words, had literally glowed up into his face, nearly strangling him. He had experienced actual physical pain, a burning sensation in the fingertips he had used to press the computer keyboard. And he had felt indescribably filthy.

Pete's blue eyes stared straight ahead as he drove down Taylor Street. The gargantuan Valley Fair Shopping Mall was busy with late-night shoppers as he made the turn onto Winchester Boulevard. He did not rush. There was no need.

Pulling his Bronco into Town and Country Village, he selected a parking slot that faced the boulevard and the Winchester Mansion. He cut the engine and sat there for several moments, watching the mansion, with its circle of thick green hedges. He also had a clear view of the adjacent parking area.

The car was there, as he somehow knew it would be. The white-and-gold quasipatrol car for the Westside Security Patrol Service. But no one sat behind the wheel.

Pete continued to watch and wait. Ten minutes ticked by. Fifteen. Andy Wilson did not return to his vehicle.

Pete left his truck, locking the door behind him. The habit of caution came automatically. A policeman's caution. He crossed the street legally, walking to the signal light, pushing the pedestrian button, and waiting for the green. He moved neither slow nor fast, drawing no undue attention to himself. He was just a tall, good-looking blond man wearing a quiet, gray business suit. A white shirt and tie. A man on his way to see a film. With a gun that felt incredibly heavy in the holster secreted under his left arm.

He gave not a minuscule of thought to Dixie now, or to her warnings. Now more than ever, he knew that this case was his alone, as it had been from the very beginning. For the first time since his niece's disappearance, Pete Willis realized that the moment he was even now living had been somehow preordained, written in some invisible book of human destiny, a book filled with dark sayings, penned in human blood.

Once beside the mansion, he melted into the deep shadow of a hedge, keeping low. Moving with stealth.

The Cyclone gate leading from the parking lot into the grounds was unlocked, as he knew it would be. He opened it quickly, careful that the padlock did not rattle, and then swung it back into place.

Traffic noise destroyed the silence of Sarah Winchester's rambling gardens. The statuary stood in expectant silence. The musical fountain had been turned off for the night. But the smell of fresh-cut lawns, of autumn roses and other perennial flowers, mingled in the dark, wrapping Pete in sweet aroma as he hurried up the walkway and onto the huge front veranda.

Trying the front door and finding it locked, he moved to the right, beneath the stained-glass closet windows which had danced color over Gretchen's mutilated corpse. Pausing at the first old-fashioned, double-hung window, he strained his eyes to see if the latch was securely fastened, but the darkness was too dense, the veranda roof abetting the night. All he could make out were the frame against a backdrop of sheer lace curtains.

Taking a penknife from his pocket, he wished for the tools he had employed during his last burglary. But when he had broken into Dixie's house, he'd planned well in advance. With true malice of forethought.

Pete's lower lip curled in a rueful smile, a smile completely without mirth, at the thought of yet again playing the felon.

Slipping the knife blade between upper and lower frames, he felt for the lock and found it tightly fastened. He went to the next and found it less secure. A little pressure and a few jiggles with the blade allowed him to slide the bottom pane upward.

He knew that the window by which he entered was the same one used to drag Gretchen's body into the Morning Room, but he was unprepared for the impact the sight of that room had upon him. His eyes adjusted to the dark, and he could see more clearly than he had anticipated. The room seemed to jump and sway around him. The small fireplace. The feminine Victorian sofa. The closet door, now tightly locked against curious little boys. He recognized every detail from the crime-scene photos he had originally stolen from Dixie.

Pete swayed on his feet. He reached out, grabbing at anything to steady himself as a wave of nausea surged through him. His fingers clutched at one of the silvery brocade drapes. His knees sagged, and as he fell, his elbow clipped a small brass lamp. The ornate fixture wobbled crazily and then tumbled off the table, hitting the oak floor.

To Pete the clatter of metal against wood seemed to reverberate through the old house like a warning clap of thunder. He was on his knees, his breath coming in labored gasps. Perspiration beaded his forehead. He knelt there, struggling to push away the visions that came to him, the vivid mental pictures of Gretchen. Alive and well. Laughing. Crying. Begging him for something he could never give. And, finally, hanging from a pipe, neck elongated, body horribly mutilated. *Dead*.

Gritting his teeth until the muscles in his jaw rippled, he got to his feet. The house was silent around him. Lights from the parking lot threw colored patterns through the windows of the ballroom across the hall, casting an eerie glow. Pete could see Sarah's old organ sitting silent, ivory keys yellowed to a dull patina.

He was breathing with less difficulty as he stepped over the red velvet barrier rope. He waited, listening, and then moved into the foyer. Pressing his body against a wall, he waited again.

A creak sounded ever so faintly above his head, followed by another and then another. Soft footfalls from the upper floor. He looked up and his eyes narrowed to slits. He slowly pulled his gun, ignoring the icy chasm that simultaneously opened in the center of his chest, sending rivulets of chill into his bloodstream. He headed for the back of the house.

There was no predictable path for him to follow. It was like being a rat, caught up in a maze of false trails. He knew that he had passed through some areas as many as four times before he finally found a set of stairs that led him to the second story. At times he was forced to creep through total, musty darkness, feeling his way with an out-thrust foot or hand.

Every now and again he would see a dim light, and cautiously round a corner to find another window, a small spot of brightness to lead him on to yet another maw of black.

Hours seemed to have dragged by when he at last started up a narrow, enclosed stairwell. His palms were sweating. The butt of his gun felt hot and sticky.

He reached the top and began testing his way again. He had not gone far when he heard what he was sure was laughter. A high, distant note, tinkling along the darkened corridor like a disembodied spirit song. Pete frowned as the hairs on his nape lifted.

Unsure of which direction the sound came from, he moved forward. He could not be certain whether he was headed east or west, toward the front of the house or the rear. He took short, careful steps, stopping every few seconds until he finally reached another door and, beyond, a mullioned spider-web window. Moonlight spilled in, showing him a small, unfurnished room with an alcove in one corner. Another corridor jagged away to the left, obviously one of the more heavily traveled tourist routes, for his hands found another of the velvet ropes.

He did not expect the furnished room to appear so quickly. Stepping around yet another corner, he saw the flicker of a candle. And the bed. And the girl.

She was nude from the waist up, her lower torso covered by Sarah Winchester's white-and-blue patchwork quilt. Sitting boldly in the bed where Sarah had drawn her last breath. The girl pulled back her head and laughed again. At close range it was no longer an eerie, tinkling melody, but a kind of chuckle. Lower and more throaty. Evil.

In the wavering candlelight her eyes were dark, malevolent pools. Her red lips pulled back from her teeth in a cruel smile.

"Welcome, *Uncle* Pete. We heard you come in."

The shock of seeing her froze Pete in midstride, and by the time he realized they were not alone, it was too late. Pain burst through his head. He twisted half around to see eyes boring into him, a pair of deep blue eyes—very like his own. That was the last thing he saw before he sagged unconscious to the floor.

CHAPTER 33

_____
_____

"WILLIS CALLED IN sick," Jake told Dixie as she came into the squad room the next morning. "Sounded like he had a stinking head cold."

Dixie put her purse down on her desk. "This just isn't my week. Two partners down and none to go."

"I know the feeling," Spatlin answered. His head was down and he seemed absorbed in paperwork. "But if you need a sidekick, I'm up for grabs. Just until Pete mends, of course. Or Herb."

"I hate to put you out, Jake. You don't have anything going?"

"Nope. Closed my most recent case yesterday. There's a very unhappy immigrant worker right now. America, the land of opportunity, has opened her ever-luvin' arms and welcomed the little sucker—right into the county jail. How's the Willis thing going? I haven't read any of the recent reports, especially not since the need to protect our fair-haired boy, my own dear partner, evaporated."

She wondered if he was being sarcastic, but when he looked up, he was smiling pleasantly. "No kidding, Struthers, all I've got going now is the same junk we all keep in our back desk drawers, the John Does with no connections, no roots, and no one that cares enough to help. I work them when I can, knowing damn well I'm going to have to file them as unsolved sooner or later.''

"In that case, the help is welcomed, along with the company, of course. I'm heading over the hill to Rio Del Mar, to see the Baldwin boy again. I'll catch you up on the way.''

Jake was ridiculously pleased, but decent enough to feel guilty about his elation over Pete's illness.

"He really sounded lousy,'' he told Dixie as they left the building. "A rotten cold and a sore throat.''

Dixie's lips quirked. "Too bad he doesn't have a dog. He could be all cured by tomorrow morning.''

Jake looked at her like maybe he had missed something.

"*Vooo-doooo*!'' She shook an imaginary rattle in his face and did a small jig. "No kidding. That's the voodoo cure for sore throat.''

"I've heard about the crazy stuff you've been getting into, Struthers, but don't go laying your bullshit on me.'' Jake was grinning. "Are you trying to tell me that some of my great-great ancestors thought owning a dog kept them from getting a sore throat?''

"Nope, hair sandwiches.''

Jake smacked his head a couple of times. "Either you lost me again or you've gone over the edge. Did you say hair sandwiches?''

"That's what I said.''

"Well, lady, I've heard of hair—''

"Don't be nasty, Jake!'' She tried not to grin. "This is serious medicine to the people who believe in the power of *loas*, the voodoo spirits. They believe that if you get a sore throat, you can transfer it to your dog. You just pluck one strand of hair out of your head—stop laughing, Jake—put it on a single slice of bread—I said stop laughing—fold it in half and feed it to Bowser. Next morning you wake up feeling fit as a fiddle, but Bowser doesn't bark so good.''

Jake didn't follow instructions well. He was laughing, wiping at his eyes. "Struthers, anyone ever tell you that ladies with red hair go over the edge at a certain age? Just the age your at, I think. But if it will make you feel any better, we can stop down at the pet shop and buy Pete a bow-wow. He probably has the bread, and God knows he's got the hair.''

"Naw," Dixie said. "I like Reversa's cure better. A hot toddy and a bowl of chicken soup."

"Reversa?" Jake's brows raised in question.

"Just a friend." Dixie was still a very private person, and with the exception of Herb and Pete, she intended to keep it that way. "A friend who makes the best chicken soup I've ever tasted. It would probably help Pete even more than the hair sandwich."

"Well, why don't you just tuck little Petey into beddy-bye and spoon feed him while you're at it?" Jake was definitely delivering a dig now, but his expression kept it a joke.

"Not a bad idea." Dixie shot him a look. "Anything for the fair-haired boy—*or* a friend."

The difference in Jimmy Baldwin was startling, but the change in his mother was nearly unbelievable. Though she still did not look really healthy, neither did Betty Baldwin in any way resemble the woman Dixie had seen on the night Howard Baldwin was killed.

Dressed in a turtleneck sweater and a pair of slacks, she at least gave the impression of having gained weight. Her hair was styled and her face made up. But above all, her eyes were clear—unclouded by the ingestion of tranquilizers and narcotics. Her hands still shook and her voice quavered slightly—unsteady, as her nervous system took the battering discomfort of withdrawal—but her speech was no longer slurred.

When Jimmy opened the front door, he at first looked surprised, perhaps even uncomfortable. But then he seemed pleased. There was unmistakable pride in his posture as he ushered them into the living room. His mother rose from a pretty flowered sofa, a replacement for the one on which her husband had met his death. She smiled timorously as she shook hands with both Dixie and Jake.

"Jimmy told me how kind you were, Sergeant Struthers. Everyone has been kind—even many of Howard's friends. People from all over town brought food to us after the funeral. We're very grateful."

Dixie looked around the room, wondering at the absence of Brutus, both indoors and out.

Jimmy seemed to read her mind. "Brutus took a little

holiday. Mom paid to have him flown to La Crosse, Wisconsin. That's where my grandfolks live. By now he probably has all Grandpa's cows giving cottage cheese instead of milk. I miss him, but he's going to have to stay away for a while. Because of the article in the paper, you know. It wasn't bad for Mom and me, but Brutus came out looking real bad, like the meanest, most vicious dog ever born.''

"I'm glad to see you looking so well, Jimmy," Dixie told him, knowing she was about to maneuver the conversation in a particularly unpleasant direction. "Investigator Gates obviously saw what kind of young man you are. I wish my own case were going as well."

"So do I, Sergeant Struthers, because I want it to be over—*all* of it." Jimmy's voice changed. A touch of the old sadness returned to his eyes. "Mom and I are both seeing a special doctor now—Dr. Zolbrod. She's a really nice lady, one who reminds me a lot of you. Mom and I know this is a healing time for us. It's not easy, especially not for Mom, but we're going to make it, start a new life as soon as we can. Brutus might not even have to come back here at all, because if and when Dr. Zolbrod thinks it will be okay, we're going to sell the house and move to my grandparents' farm. They're getting older now. We all need each other."

Jimmy hugged himself with his arms. "But this business with Gretchen is still hanging around inside my brain, all mixed up with the other. I know I'll never completely forget, but I would like for it to at least feel *over*."

"No more than we would, Jimmy, and that's why we're here."

"I told you I can't help you, Sergeant Struthers." Jimmy had been sitting on the sofa beside his mother, but now he stood. After pacing back and forth several times, he sat back down, this time in a chair nearby. "You were nice to me. Really nice. You believed me when I told you the truth, so if I *could* help, I would. But I can't."

Betty Baldwin moved uneasily, her face full of worry. "Don't start lying now, Jimmy, not for me or anyone else."

"Be quiet, Mom!" He didn't yell, but there was terrible strain in his voice.

Jake Spatlin, only newly informed of recent developments

in the case, went for broke. "The sergeant already *does* know, Jimmy. She knows all about you and your mother."

"No, she doesn't!" Jimmy did yell this time, throwing Dixie a glare that combined hostility and pain. He suddenly looked near tears. "You may think you know, but you're *wrong*!"

Betty Baldwin possessed a Dresden complexion, but seeing her son's agitation, she blushed to the roots of her hair. Her eyes were watering. "Sit down, Jimmy, *please*!"

He went to her at once and then obeyed. He picked up her hand, chafing it nervously between his own as she began speaking again. "He is telling the truth, officers—not about what happened with his friends, perhaps, but about what's taken place between the two of us."

She reached out and brushed a stray lock of hair from her son's forehead. "I'm the one to blame. I was so . . . so weak, so dependent on Jimmy. After the doctor started giving me . . . after *I* started taking so many drugs, I just leaned on him all the more. I was so afraid of Howard. I wanted to escape, but I didn't know how. Looking back, the truth is I probably didn't have the nerve. I was paranoid, convinced that no one but Jimmy cared about me. I even quit writing or calling my parents. It got so bad that if I could have, I would have kept my son with me twenty-four hours a day. There were nights when even with all the drugs, I couldn't sleep. I would beg until Jimmy came and laid down beside me."

Tears were running down her face, and though her words were directed at Dixie and Jake, she looked into her son's eyes. "Poor baby—he held me and rocked me to sleep more times than I can tell you. Howard caught him in my room once, and there is no way I can repeat the things he said." Her voice broke. "He nearly beat Jimmy to death."

Dixie saw Jake wriggle in his seat, and knew he thought the time had come for them to tiptoe quietly away. She understood the sentiment, but did not budge.

Several emotionally charged minutes passed before either Jimmy Baldwin or his mother were able to talk again. Mrs. Baldwin finally got up and went into the kitchen, returning with a coffee tray. Jake helped her pour.

As Jimmy talked to Dixie, he watched his mother move

from one room to another. "She is strong, Sergeant, really strong. Much more so than she thinks."

"I'm sure you're right, Jimmy. Your mother has had a rough time, but she's cut from very different cloth than some of the parents we've run into lately—the parents of some of your friends."

"Thinking about it now, I'm not so sure," Jimmy said. "Gretchen was a crazy kind of girl, you know. Maybe she was wrong about some other things too. I think I told you already—I think that she *picked* us. She really wanted something, something she knew she shouldn't have, and she was trying to make it okay. Can you understand?"

Dixie nodded. "We all try to justify our actions, right or wrong. Maybe that's what Gretchen was doing. Like you say, she was a crazy kind of girl."

"But funny, too, most of the time. A great sense of humor. And prettier than any girl I've ever met. When she decided to accept you for a friend, you felt lucky. All that weird business—it was a big game. I wasn't lying when I told you that either. In the beginning we were making fun. We knew it was all stupid, or we did until it began to get out of hand, until certain things started cropping up. We had a good time. We went to the park a couple of times, the one right downtown, across from the library. We would sit under the trees, making believe they were Sacred Groves, moaning and scaring the drunks that sleep there half to death. It was like being little kids again. We did go to the Winchester Mystery House. We took three tours one weekend. Really got this one old guide pulling his hair out. We went back the next Thursday night. Only thing is, we never made it inside. There was an alarm, and it went off. That time it was us who nearly got scared to death. The security guard almost caught us. Then there was the shrine at the Rosicrucian Museum, off-limits to everyone but members. But, of course, that didn't stop us. We went right over the fence and tried a little astroprojection."

Jimmy ran a hand through his hair. "It was right about that time that things started changing. Tony, and especially Gretchen, began acting like it was for real. Wendy wasn't totally immune, and I have to admit, neither was I. Gretchen almost had us convinced that night at the Egyptian Museum that she really did it, really left her body. She even got mad when we started giggling. She said that she had become the goddess Isis and that she was searching the universe for Osiris. I went home and started thinking about things. I even called Wendy. We began to wonder if maybe Gretchen was taking something. But whether she was or not, she was definitely *after* something.''

"What do you think she was after, Jimmy?''

"I don't think—I *know*. And I'm pretty sure you do too. She took her time, listening to us talk, dropping a comment here or there. Putting ideas into our heads about how special we all were, how different. Tony really ate that up like candy. He didn't need much convincing that he was a cut above the rest of the world. It was Wendy I felt sorry for, because even though I think she was beginning to catch on that it was all some kind of bizarre game, a way of making wrong seem right, she wanted to believe it was all true. Gretchen's *new religion*, her *new race*. Gretchen was fun. She was pretty, and she was smarter than all the rest of us put together. But she also had problems that were making her a little sick. Crazy.''

Dixie, Jake, and Betty Baldwin were all listening intently. Jimmy looked from one face to another.

"Sitting here talking about it now, I know it seems ridiculous, the things we were doing, the things we started talking about, almost planning. But you didn't know Gretchen. She was very, very convincing. She was sneaky in a very clever sort of way. In one way what she was doing wasn't all bad, either, especially not for someone like Wendy. When Gretchen started getting into how certain things were really okay— more than okay, *sacred*—Wendy really listened. I could see how she was feeling, and I think that's when I started smelling the biggest rat of all. From that day on I really *listened* to everything Gretchen said. I could never tell if she was taking drugs, but I knew she sure wasn't right in the head. And on one subject she was downright nuts. More and more often everything we discussed or talked about came back to the same thing. The same rotten thing!''

He looked at his mother and then at Dixie. His face was red. "And she picked *me* for her little club, her new religion, to help start her new race. She picked me because she was sure . . . because . . .''

"Never mind, Jimmy," his mother said to him softly. "Sergeant Struthers knows what you mean. But it doesn't matter anymore. We have only new days now. Lots and lots of bright, shining tomorrows."

As Jimmy walked them outside, Dixie felt a certain grim satisfaction that her assumptions had been correct. There could no longer be any doubt about Gretchen's motivation, her half-hearted pursuit of the occult, exploring the old religions, with all the incestuous overtones such study provided. She was Pete's darling, his 'little goddess,' and she was in love with him—in love with all the intensity, the passionate lust of youth. Without a father—a father she desperately wished to have—she settled on Pete. But for all her intelligence, Gretchen was a very troubled girl. She had gnarled it all into a messy ball of imagination, including in her plot others who could validate her own feelings, her illness, and make it come out right.

With her theory confirmed, Edward Nakamura became Dixie's prime suspect, the only plausible candidate.

"I don't want you to think Gretchen was terrible," Jimmy said. He and the two detectives stood beside the unmarked car. "She's dead now, and it would be wrong for you to think she was a bad person. She was mixed up—we all were. But I don't think any of us were *bad*. We just needed something to hold on to. I think it was something different for all of us. Tony wants to be special, to be famous. Wendy wants to believe that everything in her life is happening because her father loves her so much, and she wants to make that *right* almost as much as Gretchen did. The difference between them was that Wendy was a victim and Gretchen wasn't—but she *wanted* to be."

Jimmy sighed and shook his head. "And you want to know something really strange? We all thought she lived with her father. It wasn't until she died and it came out in the newspapers, that anyone but Tony Castellano knew different. He told me afterward that it was her uncle—the man she wanted, I mean. Her *uncle*."

Dixie nodded, remembering what that uncle had suffered, what he would suffer for a long time because of Gretchen's fixation.

The regret must have shown on her face, because Jimmy

looked closely at her and repeated himself. "Don't think too badly of Gretchen, Sergeant Struthers. She wasn't really a bad person. If she had been bad, I mean really low-down, she would still have been hanging out with that sicko friend of hers. Now *that's* a sick person."

Dixie had already opened the passenger door, but now she stopped, turning back to him. "What friend was that, Jimmy?"

"Oh, just some girl she used to hang out with. We never met her, but we saw her once. She came into the library for some reason, poking around in the W.S. section. She and Gretchen didn't even speak, but she was so geeky-looking that after she left, Gretchen told us about her. You should have seen her, Sergeant. She was in the right section for sure—*weird shit*!"

Jake Spatlin laughed, but only until he got a good look at Dixie's face.

"What was her name, Jimmy, what was the girl's name?"

Jimmy also keyed to the urgency now. He scrubbed one temple, his face a study of concentration. "Wait, let me think for just a minute. It's been a long time. It was a Thursday night, of course, the day we joked about making our new sabbath. The girl came in, all punked out. Gretchen told us they used to be friends, and had been ever since they were little. They even started studying some of the religious stuff together until this . . . this . . . Penny, I think it was, began to really flip out. Gretchen said she wasn't really a punker, either, that she was doing Druid stuff. Killing cats and chickens and stuff. Making spells against people. She even scared Gretchen with her shit. Later I didn't believe a lot of what Gretchen said, though, because she claimed this Penny person— 'Penny the Punker' she called her—was jealous of everything Gretchen had. Gretchen claimed the girl wanted to sleep with her father, and we all know now that Gretchen didn't even live with her dad, that she didn't even have one."

"Get in, Jake, over here." She was already moving around the hood of the car. "I'll drive."

She called her thanks to Jimmy even as she fired the car motor. Jake fastened his seat belt and muttered a prayer as she headed down the steep driveway at breakneck speed. He was to mutter many more as she crossed the Santa Cruz Mountains, taking them back to the city.

Jake silently prayed while Dixie ranted aloud. "It was right under my nose all the time! Damn it, Jake, it was all right there! I even dreamed about a lot of it, night after damn night!"

"About what, Struthers—will you please slow down!"

"Druids! The earliest punkers of all!" she yelled, banging the steering wheel several times with the heel of her hand. "Druids!"

Jake's face washed from a beautiful cocoa color to elephant gray as she whipped their buff-colored Dodge around a lumber rig. "Oh, my ever luvin' stomach . . . you know a few Druids, do you?"

"I know *one*, or someone that at least pretends to be. One who did not like, who in all likelihood *hated*, Gretchen Willis. One who has twinkle-toed in and out of this investigation from the beginning, laughing out her cowl sleeve the whole time, no doubt. Priscilla Smith herself."

"A.k.a. Prissy the Punker, if I remember right. You told us about her in the beginning. But she was only mentioned in—*look out!*—passing. Mostly because she was so—*oh, lordy!* —outlandish." Jake gripped the edge of his seat and closed his eyes, afraid that if he kept them open any longer, he would throw up all over the windshield.

"You've got it, Spatlin. Prissy the Punker. I'm just hoping she'll twinkle past us one more time before she does damage to anyone else!"

Jake clutched harder, every nerve in his body tense, wondering if they would make it back to the city without damage to him.

CHAPTER 34

THE COUPLE STANDING behind the screen door at Prissy's address on Linda Loma Drive were quite elderly. Both were thin, gray, and slightly stooped.

"We don't know where she is, officers. We never know anymore. She should have been home from school an hour ago," the woman told them.

The man had an arm around his wife's shoulders. "What Martha doesn't want to come right out and say is that Priscilla is almost never here. Her clothes are here, and she comes here to change. That's about it. She doesn't really *live* here. Not like other youngsters live with their folks."

"When did you see Priscilla last, Mr. Smith? Have you seen her today?"

"Yes, this morning," his wife answered for him. "George was still asleep when she came in, and I was glad. I hate to hear them argue. Prissy came in and got dressed. She was in a good mood. She even kissed me before she left, and said she would see me this afternoon."

For all its age, Mr. Smith's face did not lack expression. "So you got a kiss, Martha, so what? She probably wants something—money, something. And I don't want you to give her whatever she's after. I mean it, Martha."

The old woman looked miserable, but she rested her head

against her husband's shoulder. "I know, George. I know. Its just that I keep remembering what a beautiful baby she was, how cuddly. And even now, such a talented girl. Such a shame to waste what God has given her. So artistic. So clever with her hands."

"Yes, clever at getting what she wants too. She'll steal. Lie. Cheat. Even from her own folks." Mr. Smith looked at the detectives through the darkness of the screen door. "Maybe you officers should know how it is. Priscilla may be our daughter, and I know Martha can't give over the loving of her, but I can. I did, a long time ago. There is something wrong with Priscilla. I guess it's probably partly our fault. We were so old when she was born. We should have quit trying to have kids when we started getting up in years, but Martha wanted a baby so much. You're going to think I'm a rotten human being, but I've known about how Priscilla is since she was ten years old. A wicked little girl. Mean and selfish. Greedy. And you can take my word or not, she never got any different. Rotten to the core. She hit her mother once. She's stolen from us, lied about us. I don't think she has many friends, and that doesn't surprise me a bit."

"She did have one friend—Gretchen Willis—right?"

"Oh, that poor little girl," Mrs. Smith said. "Poor child!"

"Yes, Sergeant," Mr. Smith affirmed, "they *were* friends, up until around the time Priscilla got arrested for being in a bar with that boyfriend of hers."

"What boyfriend is that, Mr. Smith?"

"He wasn't really a boy, and I don't know who in the hell he was. The only reason I found out about him at all was because Priscilla got picked up in that bar. She had been drinking and taking drugs. I saw the guy one other time, caught him dropping our daughter off down at the corner. Too old to be going out with a young girl, even one like Priscilla. Maybe forty years old. He drove a van, an old rust bucket with hippie junk all over it. I tried to chase Priscilla, keep her from getting back into the van after she saw me. I couldn't, of course, but I sure as hell heard them laughing when they drove away. That was it for me. The last time I ever tried to do anything for her. The only reason I don't throw all her things out is because of Martha. But if she's in trouble again, that's it for both of us."

There was nothing else to be learned from Prissy's aged parents.

The door of the house closed softly as Dixie and Jake walked to the car.

"You up for a Code 5?" she asked her temporary partner.

"I hate stakeouts like poison, Struthers, but I can stand it with someone to talk to."

"That's just it Jake, you won't have anyone, not for a while. I'll come back, but only after I've checked out a couple of things. I need to get back to the department, but first I want to ask Pete a question or two—ones I could kick myself for not asking before. Prissy told us that she and Gretchen had not been friends for a long time, but we only had her word for it. We just never thought to check it out. I need to talk to Pete about that and a few other details. Then I'm going back to the P.A.B, to Records, and pull the file on Prissy. Maybe it will tell us who was with her when she got popped. If I can get a name, we'll have to put a Code 5 on his place too."

"And just how do you plan to do all that, wonder lady, fly?"

"No need. Pete lives less than three blocks from here. After I talk to him, I'll just borrow his truck. If all else fails, I'll call Delaney or hitch with a beat unit. Hey, don't look so glum. I won't be long. Believe me, I want her worse than anyone—except for Pete, that is. He has a right to know what's going on."

Jake sighed. His only compensation was that he now had control of the car. Backing halfway down the block, but staying close enough for a full view of the Smith house, he waved Dixie on her way.

CHAPTER 35

IN SNEAKERS, THE short trek would have been a snap. In two-and-a-half-inch heels, it had been no fun at all. Dixie's feet hurt. She pulled off her shoes as she rang Pete's door bell. When he didn't respond, she rang again, lifting her foot to massage her toes. By the third ring she was frowning. She did not want to wake him, but even if he had no additional insights into the relationship between Prissy and Gretchen, she needed the loan of his truck. She knocked hard on the door and listened for movement inside. There was no sound at all, but warning bells were beginning to go off in the back of her brain.

He was sick, she told herself. Maybe he had gone to the doctor. The pharmacy. Out for a bowl of hot chicken soup. She tried to remember exactly how he had been the night before.

Tired. Disgusted by Edward Nakamura. Too beat to take her up on a dinner invitation.

Then she remembered him hunched over, feeding names into the computer—a list of names they had painstakingly compiled together. She remembered, too, that one brief moment when he had looked at her with blank face and glazed eyes.

Going around the side of the condo, she began looking in

windows. Her frown deepened as she peeked into the first and
saw his bed neatly made. Likewise, the kitchen was immaculate, no coffee cups or other dishes on the counter. Pete might
be neat, but he was also supposedly sick. Sick people made
themselves food, they slept and took aspirin, they did not
play Mr. Clean.

She was at the back, eyes straining to see through a set of
sheer drapes covering the sliding glass door of Pete's living
room, when a voice startled her.

"You looking for something, lady?"

She turned to see a man in Bermuda shorts and a polo shirt
glaring at her. His eyes raked her from head to stockinged
feet. She still held her shoes in one hand.

"Yes, for Peter Willis."

"Well, I don't think he's here." The man folded his arms
across his chest, waiting.

"I'm a friend," Dixie said, knowing that she looked more
like a sneak thief, or a spying, jilted lover. "He's been sick
and I got concerned when he didn't answer the door."

"I live in the other half of the building," the man said,
"and even though I don't know Pete real well, I can't believe
he would appreciate having you peek into his windows. He's
a private kind of a guy. Real quiet. He's also a *cop*." He
made the title sound intimidating.

"Yes, I know—so am I. We work together."

His eyes widened and he looked her up and down again
with obvious reservation. Dixie suddenly wished that she had
selected a somber dark blue business suit for work that morning instead of the white gabardine jumpsuit, lapis jewelry,
and blue silk scarf she had on.

"Sergeant Struthers," she said, introducing herself, pulling
badge and identification from her blue lizard-skin handbag.
"I really am a little worried about Pete, Mister . . ."

"Vern Drye." He stepped closer and gave the badge a
long, hard look. "I saw you creeping around, and I thought—"

"I understand," she interrupted him, her worry increasing
with every minute. "Pete would be glad to know you're
keeping an eye on his property, I'm sure. Do you know what
time he left?"

"Frankly, I thought he must have gone out of town or
something, since he didn't come home last night."

Dixie's pulse began to race. "What makes you think he didn't come home?"

"The automatic garage-door opener. If I'm home, I always know when he comes in or goes out because I hear the door go up and down. To be honest, it's annoying sometimes. Like when he comes in late, which is an awful lot of the time. If I'm sleeping, the damn thing wakes me up."

"And you're absolutely certain he did not come in last night? Maybe he parked at the curb, or in the driveway."

"That guy? With his Bronco? You must be kidding. He treats that thing better than most guys do their wives. I wouldn't be a bit surprised to find out he covers it up and kisses it good night."

"Would you mind if I use your telephone, Mr. Drye? Police business."

She followed him back to the front and then on to the other side of the building. The floor plan of his home was a duplicate of Pete's, but the similarity ended there. Vern Drye's more closely fit the typical image of a working bachelor—mismatched and slightly messy. But she paid little attention to the lack of decor as she dialed the police department. When Doty answered, Dixie asked to speak with Di Franco.

"He's not in," Doty told her. "No one is. I'm just sitting here all by my little lonesome."

Dixie was quiet for a moment, thinking, wondering what Pete had learned that might possibly have sent him off on his own—against her express orders. Then she remembered again, Pete sitting, staring down at the computer monitor, clearing it before she could see what was on the screen.

"You still there, Sergeant Struthers?"

"I'm here. Doty, grab a piece of paper. I need a favor, a big one. It will take time, but it's very important that you do it just as quickly as possible. I'm going to give you a list of names to feed through R.I.S. I know you'll have to switch phones, but I'll wait. I *have* to wait."

"Shoot." Doty's lazy southern drawl disappeared almost completely. She had picked up the urgent vibes loud and clear.

Dixie gave her a list of names, the same ones Pete had run the night before, putting Priscilla Smith's first. Vern Drye was staring at her as she listened to Doty make the phone transfer, tapping one bare foot. She put on her shoes.

Doty repeated, almost verbatim, Pete's rendition of Prissy's single arrest. A minor picked up for being in a bar, under age and under the influence. Whether she had been under the influence of booze, drugs, or both was not noted.

"Thanks, Doty," Dixie said. "Just make a note of the case number and go on."

She could hear the soft click of the keyboard. Doty was fast, and she made no jokes, added no comments as she read each result into Dixie's ear. *Edward Nakamura—no record. Susan Banks—no record. Lillian Jackabcin—no record.* And on it went for the next ten minutes.

"Grady Summers—no record," Doty continued, her voice no less crisp, no less efficient. "Okay, here we go, now we're getting one."

"On whom?"

"Andy Wilson . . . a.k.a. Andrew Williamson, a.k.a. Anthony Wilkes, a.k.a.—oh, my God!"

"Doty?"

After a slight hesitation, the homicide secretary continued, repeating the last name. "Anthony Wilkes, a.k.a. Drew Truman Willis. Born 12/30/48; height six feet, three inches; weight 210 pounds. First arrest, 8/2/65, Civil Disobedience; second arrest, 10/16/67, possession of a deadly weapon, possession of narcotics, statutory rape; third arrest, 4/9/74, armed robbery; fourth arrest—"

"That's enough, Doty." Dixie felt like the skin on her entire body had tightened. Her heart thumped with fear. "Has anyone come in yet?"

"No, sorry. Do you want me to track down the *leuy*?"

"No time. Call dispatch and have them send a black-and-white to 320 Oak Leaf Court. I need a lift to the Winchester Mystery House. Hurry, Doty!"

She hung up and went out to the street, pacing as she waited. Vern Drye followed her, but the expression on her face forestalled chitchat. The black-and-white had no time to show before Jake came roaring around the corner in the Dodge. Dixie jumped in.

"Move it, Jake—take the quickest route to Winchester Boulevard!"

"There is no quick route," he said, pulling away from the curb, causing the tires to squeal. His face was angry and embarrassed. "I lost her, Dixie! She came up behind the car without me seeing her until the last minute. Then she turned and did a rabbit on me! Made like a bunny and split!"

"It doesn't matter, Jake." Dixie's eyes were glued to the road, her heart still hammering against her ribs.

Jake didn't slow any more than necessary to avoid an accident, but he didn't quit talking either. "I'm telling you I blew it, Struthers! That little bitch ran like hell. I saw her as I was turning the car around. She got into that van her dad told us about, but by the time I got there, it was like that junker had vanished into thin air! I circled and switched back, but I lost them, Dix. I'm goddamned sorry, but I blew it! Didn't even get a chance to make the plates!"

"I know who the van belongs to, so like I said, it doesn't matter. It doesn't even matter if they split altogether. Right now, I don't care if they blew the planet. All I care about is Pete, and I think he's in that house!" Her voice caught. "Damn this traffic! Hit it, Spatlin! We're going Code 3!"

She reached under the seat, pulling out the red light, plugging it onto the panel bracket and attaching it to the roof. Jake flipped on the siren and punched the accelerator.

The cars on Capitol Expressway separated in front of them, but not fast enough to suit Dixie. Rush hour traffic had begun, and Jake was forced to weave through, slowing at intersections.

"What in the hell is Pete doing over there?" he asked, keeping his eyes glued to the road. "I told you, he was sick as a dog this morning."

"Did he ask for you by name?"

Jake thought for a minute. "Maybe not. He just called in. Doty picked up the phone, and when she found out who it was, put him right through to me. He just said he was sick. No particular reason for him to use my name."

"Especially not if it was his brother you talked to."

"His *what*!" Jake looked at her and then quickly back at the street again. The driver of a white Continental seemed not to have heard the siren until the last minute. The big car weaved and almost came to a stop as Jake whipped around on the left shoulder.

"You've got it, Spatlin. It was his brother, I'm almost sure. Not a sore throat, not a cold. And I think Pete's long-lost brother and Prissy the Punker's chauffeur are one and the same. Let's just pray that in this case blood is thicker than water."

Terrible pictures were flashing through Dixie's mind, and the heart-plummeting memory of what had happened to Drew's own daughter, his own flesh and blood. It was a picture she did not want to think about.

She saw Pete as the extremely handsome rookie cop, a little older than his academy mates, but young all the same. A young man who had been on her patrol team. Fresh-faced. Courteous. But obviously unhappy about finding himself saddled with a female field supervisor. And then Pete as he had looked when she came charging through the door of the Dunkin' D Doughnut Shop. Laying in his own blood. His leg and arm blown half away. And the thief taking one last aim at his head.

Somehow, from that night on, their careers, their lives, had been irrevocably intertwined. Dixie had saved his life that night, but the debt had been long since repaid. During the Bouchard case he had kept her from being trampled to death by a mad woman on a demonic stallion. To Dixie their fates seemed star-crossed.

Pete had fought for his life once before, a hard fight, and won. The thought of him being killed now, sacrificed to the same evil that had taken Gretchen, turned Dixie inside out. She wished there was indeed magic, a power that could enable her to fly over the infuriating traffic. An inner, all-seeing and powerful eye she could send out to find Pete. To protect him. She strained forward in the seat, wishing for even a touch of extrasensory perception, anything to tell her that her friend would be well, that she would find him, that he would look at her and grin his boyish grin.

CHAPTER 36

THE WINCHESTER MYSTERY HOUSE was closed down for the day. Even Grady Summers was gone. The mansion was locked and quiet, ready for a night's slumber, nestled into its incongruous island of peace. The theater marquee advertised a new horror film, complete with gruesome special effects, *Angel in Black*. The Town and Country Center was quiet, suffering the usual lull between day and evening shoppers.

Jake and Dixie cut light and siren two blocks before they reached their destination.

"Go past and make a U-turn," Dixie said. "We'll use the theater parking lot. That will give us plenty of cover. If Pete's there, rushing in like gangbusters isn't going to do him any good."

"If he's in there, and if he's not already—"

"Don't say it, Spatlin!" Her voice quavered. "Pete's there, and he's very much alive. He *has* to be!"

"Never mind me," Jake apologized with a lame smile. "My mama tells me I was born a pessimist."

He parked deep in a center row of cars, just behind a big four-wheeler which would protect them from being seen by anyone in the mansion.

"You ready?" he asked. He could see that she was shaken, but her face had hardened in a way that almost frightened

him. There was something about her eyes, beautiful but
deadly. He hated to throw any barriers at her, but he knew he
had to warn her. "Unless you call the manager, or the
security man, we're liable to set off the alarm."

Dixie almost laughed, but there was no time to explain. No
time to call the manager. No time for anything at all. "Let it
ring," she said. "Let it ring its bloody head off!"

They got out of the car and started for the mansion, watching as they went for any movement, either in the parking lot
or along the high, clipped hedges. The house, the rambling
structure Sarah Winchester had built, sat silent, white finials
glowing silver gray in a sunset that promised rain. The witch's
cap tower and cupolas looked menacing, brooding in shadow.
Waiting.

The weather had cooled suddenly. Clouds were billowing
over the mountains, sending thin wisps, fingers of fog into
the valley.

Even after all the gruesome reading, Dixie did not believe
in haunts, in ghosts or goblins, or terrors that went bump in
the night. But as she and Jake separated, weaving around the
cars of unsuspecting theater patrons, she wished that there
were spirits—benevolent, ethereal beings—watching over her
friend, protecting Pete from evil.

"Oh, God, please," she whispered. "*Please!*"

As if the wrong deity had heard and given perverse answer,
a van came roaring into the mansion parking area. It was old
and weatherbeaten. A large peace symbol had been sprayed
on the back, garish against flaking yellow paint. But there
were other symbols, too, more artfully done, and Dixie recognized them all, the same patterns that had been carved into
Gretchen's dead flesh.

Dixie ducked down and saw Jake, three cars away, do the
same. They were two rows back from the narrow street that
separated one parking lot from the other. Dixie dropped onto
her stomach, looking between tires to see two sets of feet
emerge from the van, one pair small and black-booted. The
other feet belonged to a man who wore sensible shoes, black
and spit-shined to a nice official gleam.

"*Pssst!*"

Dixie looked over her shoulder to see that Jake had moved

up behind her. He was crouching, peeking over the hood of the Chevette compact she lay beside.

"They're going in," he said. "He's unlocking the damn gate. Who in the hell is he, anyway? How come he's able to—"

"The helpful West Side Security Service Patrol, at your service." Dixie ignored the stare Jake gave her. "Wait until they get in. We'll give them time to take care of the alarm, but not too long. They'll be making a beeline for Pete!"

Two minutes later she and Jake were moving, running for the gate, but they did not have keys, or Pete's previous luck. The padlock had been shoved firmly home.

"Shit!" Jake looked up at the double strand of barbed wire along the top of the Cyclone fencing.

"Hurry!" Dixie said.

"Hurry, my ass!" Jake balked.

"That's what I said, Jake!" Dixie hissed at him. "Hurry your ass, up and over! *Now!*"

She took her gun from her purse and shoved it into the deep front pocket of her jumpsuit. Tossing her purse into a hedge, she started up, clinging to the gate like an ape. Jake stared as, halfway up, she kicked off her shoes.

"Damn!" he mumbled, and then followed her lead. "What I'm gonna do here is rip my ass right off!"

She reached the top and gingerly grabbed the wires, pressing them down and together. Jake was tall, but relatively agile and in good physical condition. Coming up beside her, he added the pressure of his weight and the wires flattened. A barb bit into his palm and he swore.

"Go, little woman," he said. "I'll be right behind you, unless I get hung up. In that case, just go anyway, and I'll play scarecrow."

Dixie got her right foot over the wire and then the left, using a gate post for balance. She paused for only a moment and then jumped, knees flexed, to the cement pathway below.

Jake, holding the sharp, spikey wire, found the maneuver more difficult. He had to grab a post and, holding the wire down with one foot, leap clear quickly. He went fanny over teakettle, doing a graceful *ukimi* as he landed. The momentum of his roll took him into a prickly shrub. He glared at Dixie, but the show of animosity was wasted. She was already on her way to the far side of the house, running, keeping low.

"Try the front," she called over her shoulder.

Jake took the front steps in a single bound and tried the ornate door. It was locked tight.

It took only two or three more minutes for them to reach the main rear entrance, and this time they found the door left slightly, hospitably ajar.

Once inside, Dixie put a finger to her lips and flattened her body against the carriage-house wall. They could hear voices, indecipherable but not too distant, and what sounded like the thump of footfalls on stairs. Prissy and her companion seemed to be arguing.

Dixie bolted through another doorway and into the house proper, pulling her gun as she went, motioning Jake to follow. They moved quickly but with care, stopping every few seconds, trying to hear what was being said. It was impossible to be sure of anything except that the argument continued. The two inch easy risers—the tiny steps Sarah had long ago installed to aid her arthritis—were no help. It was dusky going, and Jake had never been in the house before. He could not see, and he almost tripped several times. Only the frowning disapproval Dixie telepathed over her shoulder kept him from swearing aloud. He barely fit into the narrow stairwell, the Sarah-sized maze that switched back and forth, time after time, using one hundred feet of stairs to ascend a mere nine.

They moved through what in the original old farmhouse had once been a hay loft, and then on, past a small sewing room. A guest bedroom was next, a room never slept in because Sarah Winchester never had guests.

The deeper they moved into the bowels of the house, the harder it became to see. Jake finally pulled a tiny penlight from his inner jacket pocket and mouthed, *voilà*!

The voices stopped, and so did Dixie and Jake, waiting for what seemed an eternity before a series of creaks told them that their quarries were one floor up, almost directly overhead.

Dixie's frustration and fear for Pete mounted with each minute that passed. They had to move very slowly now, attempt to match their steps to those above. At the same time, Dixie searched her mind, trying to recall where they would find the nearest staircase.

"This is one damn scooby-do house," Jake whispered. "That dizzy old broad was on acid for sure!"

They found the stairs, more normal in size this time. The banister was fit with old gaslight fixtures which had long since failed to serve any purpose. Just as they crept to the top, they heard a man yell.

"No!"

Though not spoken nearby, the word was distinct. Another voice sounded, lower, feminine, argumentative and adamant. But still indistinguishable. To the best of Dixie's recollection, they were all on the floor that had once housed Sarah's original bedroom, the one in which she had been trapped for so many frightening hours, calling out her terror, her acquiescence to the spirits' demands.

"Where now?" Jake whispered.

The voices had ceased again. Dixie listened for several seconds and then pointed to the left, making it all too clear that they were separating, splitting forces. Jake to the left. Dixie to the right.

Jake had been experiencing an ever-increasing sense of disquiet since entering the house, a house widely rumored to be haunted. He wanted to shake his head in refusal, but did not dare. He could see Dixie's face, the bitter lines creasing both sides of her normally soft mouth. The determination in her eyes. Besides, Jake told himself, a man had his pride. Dixie was all of five feet. One hundred five pounds, max. If she could go traipsing around in the dark old house, who was he to balk? He stood six feet, two inches tall and weighed in at 190 pounds. He had no intention of looking in the mirror the next morning and seeing an oversized sack of chicken shit.

Jake offered Dixie the tiny light, finally insisting with emphatic hand motions. She finally acquiesced, watching him snake away.

He moved very slowly, for fear he would run into a wall or fall down a flight of stairs, or drop into one of the purported pits of nothingness, forever to remain, until he was nothing but a pile of bleached white bones. He kept straining his eyes and listening, wishing he were somewhere else. Anywhere else. Or, if he had to stumble, that it would be over the living, breathing body of Peter Jacob Willis.

Every now and then an unexpected wall would appear, jump at Jake from nowhere. There was no rhyme or reason to the house, no architectural logic. At times, when there was no window to guide him, no light at all, he would feel his way, reading the richly embossed walls like braille.

In his own mind, though he would not have dared repeat the sentiment to Dixie again, Jake considered Pete long gone. He had seen the crime-scene photos of the Willis girl. If Pete had not returned home, if he had come slinking in here at night and run up against the person who had mangled that little girl, he was a goner. Plain and simple. No scooby-do. *Dead meat*!

Jake cursed as he ran into a velvet barrier rope and almost went down, nearly dropping his gun on the wooden floor. He cursed under his breath. He cursed Sarah Winchester and her crazy house. He cursed the dark . . . the killers he was supposedly stalking . . . *and* Dixie T. Struthers.

Dixie prayed for voices. She slinked, taking long, silent steps through the Hall of Fires. There were no drapes now to close Sarah in, to surround her with soothing, dry warmth. Only empty silver hooks above the arched doorways. A dull glow filtered in from the tiny parlor beyond, painting the colored tile of the grand old fireplaces silver and a dull, muted gold.

She moved on through the Oriental bedrooms and into the solarium, a room where plants once drank in sunshine while Sarah basked in the healing warmth. A glass room, now lighted by only a dark and rapidly waning sunset and the reflected glow of city lights.

Dixie felt exposed. Vulnerable. Still hearing no voices to give her direction, she imagined that she was being watched, that malevolent eyes tracked her, waiting for her to continue on and enter the darkness again. Her heart hammered in her ears and her intestines twisted with fear as she ran on tiptoe for cover. She stopped in the doorway, breathing heavily, afraid that someone would hear her.

But then she thought of Pete, saw him tied up somewhere, possibly unconscious, the perfect victim. Dixie saw Priscilla Smith, too, not as a little girl dressed in high-topped tennis

shoes and oversized sweatshirts, not as a teenager on a fad-
dish binge—but as a savage, an acolyte of the Old Religion.

No, Dixie thought, not even that. No sincere worshipper,
not even an ignorant peasant following the dictates of an
ancient bloodthirsty gods would do the things Gretchen's
killer had done. To Dixie, Priscilla Smith was Hecate, goddess of the underworld, the embodiment of darkness. Not a
human being, but the essence of all evil, emanating all the
noxious vapors of hell. A devil woman clothed in flesh,
walking upright on two legs, preying on humankind—with
Drew Willis as her witting or unwitting high priest, her
consort and lover. Dixie saw the two of them towering over
Pete, chanting obscenities as in her dreams, ready to feed on
his blood.

The vivid waking nightmare dried the perspiration from her
forehead. She stood in the darkness, her fear turning to icy
resolve.

Another few steps took her into a hallway. A tiny beam
from the light Jake had given her told her that she was once
more in an older section of the house, the part damaged by
the devastating earthquake and never used again.

She stopped, hearing whispers.

"No," the man's voice said again. "This has gone too far,
Prissy, way too far. They probably know we're here by now
. . . will you quit popping that shit into your mouth. It's not
candy, you know. They're liable to show up here any minute!"

Dixie cut the light and quit breathing.

"Bullshit, Drew. Who are they? That cop I saw hasn't got
the faintest idea where we are, none of them do, because they
don't know who *you* are. If they did, someone would have
come charging through here today. If he had told them anything, you can bet that little redheaded bitch would be here
sniffing around. She probably has the hots for him too. All
the ladies love Pete. You're just second best, Drew baby."
Prissy laughed an ugly laugh. "You are also the ultimate,
altogether awesomest chicken shit on earth."

Prissy spoke low, but she was not whispering. "You're
paranoid, just like I told you from the beginning. A paranoid
bastard who can't find his dick with both hands."

"If you're so fucking smart, how come that nigger cop

showed up on your doorstep? You're a crazy bitch, Prissy. Crazy!''

"So you keep saying." Prissy laughed again softly. There was a creak on the floor, as if she was walking, and then it suddenly stopped. "But if you say it again, you'll be very sorry, Drew. Very sorry. Now, shut your mouth and let's get this over with. Actually, I'm kind of looking forward to it. Too bad they won't find him for days, weeks maybe. By that time we'll be long gone. We'll have to send for newspapers."

A slap sounded. Prissy spoke again, in an angry, dictatorial voice. "And I've told you already, put that goddamn popgun away! It would be worthless, even if it did work right."

"But someone might—"

"No one's going to do anything, you asshole, not unless you accidently fire that thing and bring the whole world down on us. Now, put it away!"

Dixie was suddenly bathed in light, surrounded as beams danced through the lathing, making crazy patterns on her arms and face. She closed her eyes, not moving, knowing that they were again right beside her, just on the other side of the damaged wall. She once more searched her mind, trying to remember the path she and Herb had taken with Grady Summers. The light swung away, and she sidestepped around a corner. She could see the light dancing up ahead, far back and beyond the routes taken by tourists, an area Grady had shown them with great caution. In many places the floor and walls were open, exposing a nest of wires. It was an area completely unused, even for storage.

The light flashed again and she hung back, knowing they had to be just beyond where she stood, enclosed in the rounded room of an old cupola, long since deserted by all save Sarah's wandering spirits and resident rats.

Pete was in there with them. Dixie knew it. She could feel it in every fiber of her being.

Prissy spoke again, her voice coming back at Dixie through a narrow doorway, an opening as distorted by the earthquake as in Jimmy Baldwin's drawing, low and slanted to one side by the awesome forces of nature.

"Hello, *Uncle* Pete." Prissy crooned.

Dixie heard a grunt, and tears of relief blurred her vision.

Pete was alive. Bound, she had no doubt, and gagged, but alive.

"Don't do it!" There was a note of desperation in the voice of Drew Willis. "He . . . he is . . . that's my brother, you crazy bitch! Just leave him and let's get the hell out of here!"

"*Ohhhh*, your little baby brother." Prissy's voice oozed condescension. "Do you hear that, Petey? He killed his own daughter, but he—"

"I didn't kill her! I didn't even know who in the hell she was until . . . until after you drove off in the van and did it. You *made* me help. It wasn't me who brought her back all . . . I didn't do it, Pete . . . I thought she was just another . . . I didn't . . ." Drew Willis was gulping in air. Stuttering. Crying. "We were just . . ."

"*Fucking!*" Prissy hissed. "You're the one that saw her at school when you were supposed to be looking for *me*. You're the one who picked her up and brought her here. You screwed her. I saw you, remember? Greedy Gretchen, getting just what she always wanted, or almost. She knew who *you* were. She knew all the time. She didn't care. She was Pete's little goddess, and a goddess can do anything, with anyone, just so long as it's *special*. And you made it special for her every time, didn't you, Drew baby? She loved every minute. She even swallowed that stuff you gave her the last time. She loved it. Pete's little goddess loved swallowing that *magical* shit, and then letting you—"

"Shut your crazy mouth! I didn't do it, Pete, you've got to believe me! And I'm not going to let her—*aaaagh!*"

The sickening gurgle was followed by a thump. The reflection of light did one last crazy dance before it dropped and grew still again.

Dixie winced, every nerve in her body jangling, but she forced herself not to run. She was afraid to move, afraid to go banging into the little room. Drew Willis was dead. She knew that beyond any shadow of doubt, but not Pete . . . not Pete . . . not *yet*. The small thumps, the grunts, told her that he was still alive, struggling.

It took every reserve of willpower she possessed to slowly lower herself onto the floor, onto the patchwork of planks and

exposed beams. She went down on her belly and crawled to
the doorway. She looked and sucked in a silent breath.

The flashlight had not been picked up, but the single
glaring shaft of brightness showed Dixie all that was necessary—Drew's body, with blood still spurting from his throat
in a crimson geyser. And Priscilla Smith, hovering over the
indistinct form of a man. A tall blond man who was laying on
his side over open floor beams. A filthy rag had been tied
around his head, forcing his jaws apart. His feet were bound,
and his hands were behind his back. Other ropes bound his
body to the open lathing of one wall, pinioning him at neck
and knees. He was trying to squirm, barely able to move his
feet, thump his ankles against the wood.

Prissy stood above him, her hair sending grotesque spiked
shadows around the room. Her arms were raised high, both
hands gripping a long, bone-handled dagger. The blade plunged.

Dixie screamed and fired. There was no time to take aim,
no time to bead in and slowly squeeze the trigger. She just
jerked and fired.

The blade went wild, tearing into Pete's chest, slashing
downward and then up again. But if the blade went wild, so
did Dixie's aim. The bullet had pierced Prissy's thigh, glanced
off the bone and made a clean exit into the cupola wall. She
shrieked in rage, filling the small room with a demon cry.
She moved like lightning, pulling the gory blade free and
running for the only door. Dixie rolled to one side, but not
soon enough. Pain burst through her head as Prissy kicked,
her tiny booted foot making firm contact with Dixie's
cheekbone.

"*Bitch!*" Prissy was in a panic now, mad with the desire to
flee. But she took time for one last swoop of her deadly
blade.

Dixie rolled again and then felt a searing hot pain shoot
through her upper back. The floor was shaking, the world
around her reverberating as her assailant took flight. She
crawled forward into the room, scooting, using her elbows for
support to get to where Pete was tied. He was silent and still.

Dixie was sobbing as she reached him, no longer aware of
her own pain. As she drew closer, she could see his eyes in
the glare of the flashlight. His eyelids were moving, blinking.

An ever-widening circle of blood soaked through the back

of Dixie's jumpsuit as she came up onto her knees. She put her gun to one side and, using both hands, pulled the gag down and out of Pete's mouth. His face was deathly pale.

"Pete," she wept, not wanting to see the mean gash, the blood. She put a hand against his chest, pushing, willing the flow to stop, knowing it was futile. "Oh, Pete!"

There was no sign of pain on Pete's face, no grimace. He did not groan or attempt to move. Dixie thought she would die as he smiled at her. A slow, sleepy, boyish smile.

"Sorry, Sarge, guess this means I'm back in patrol."

"Shut up, Pete. Please, don't talk."

His eyes left her face, going to the body of his brother. No sympathy, no grief or remorse altered his expression. He was still half smiling as he looked back up at her. He did not seem to notice the tears hitting his face. "She's dead, isn't she, Dix? You killed her?"

"Yes," Dixie lied, giving him the peace he needed. Her voice was a hoarse croak. "She is very, very dead."

She bent closer, feeling his blood soak into her clothing, covering her from shoulders to waist, not caring. Her hair cascaded down around them both, shielding them from the world, veiling out the horror of their surroundings. Their faces were only inches apart.

"Have I ever told you," Pete whispered, "how damn good you smell?"

She brushed her lips across his cheek, and then his mouth, her heart ripping in two as he expelled one last, sighing breath.

She pulled away from him slowly, the dangling tendrils of her hair trailing through their mingled blood. Her face was oozing from the gash in her cheek. Both the front and back of her clothing, which only a short time before had been a soft, ivory white, was now crimson, clinging to her upper torso.

Her face was expressionless as she picked up her gun. She stood, bent again to pick up the flashlight, and left the room, left Pete and his brother lying almost side by side in the darkness of Sarah's house.

It was not until she came back into the main part of the mansion that she heard the noise. Feet running. Thumps and creaks. The air seemed to vibrate with echoes, shouts, not one but many, all coming from different directions. The very walls seemed to breathe with life. But Dixie was neither frightened nor confused. She had the perfect guide. Not one of Sarah's spirits, but a trail of blood.

She moved quickly along, following the bright droplets with beams of light bouncing from elaborate walls and frescoed ceilings to show her the way. The pattern was erratic, going from side to side, up a short flight of stairs, along a hallway and then up to the next floor.

She thought she heard her name being called from somewhere, but she paid no attention. Moving on, walking faster and faster as the spots of blood grew closer together, she saw them eventually turn into an almost steady, unbroken line.

She was on the top floor, walking without stealth, stalking the thing known as Priscilla Smith.

She could see the uppermost room now and knew there was a covered balcony beyond, the highest vantage point in the old house, but one not without an avenue of escape.

Dixie's mind was functioning clearly. Her determination invalidated pain. She felt only an icy, razor-sharp rage. Her memory was crystal clear. She had been here before, listening to the nostalgic voice of Grady Summers. She knew that beyond the last unfurnished room was a turret, and beneath it a balcony, giving an eagle's nest view of the gargantuan house.

Given youth and agility, there was one place, a sizable drop, that would allow Pete's murderess to run along the rooftops and then seek a lower and less dangerous place to jump again, to flee the grounds. But Priscilla was wounded, bleeding a heavier glistening trail with every step.

Dixie's lips pulled back from her teeth in a cold, contemptuous smile as she slipped into the last room and found it empty.

She silently flicked off the flashlight and set it on the floor, freeing one hand, holding her gun upright in the other. There was a sound from outside the door, a groan. To Dixie it was the sound a wounded animal might make. A vicious animal. An animal of prey.

The wide balcony was in shadow, but Priscilla Smith was clearly visible, her white painted face almost blue in the shaft of moonlight that had broken through the clouds. Her eyes circled in thick black pencil. Her hair spiked into a Mohawk of inordinate length. Plastic jewelry did not dangle from her ears or wrists now, nor around her long neck. There was no subterfuge or camouflage about the golden-colored torque or the silver chain. A long silver spiral dangled from one ear, an ankh from the other. Her bracelet was wrought in the shape of a serpent. She was straddling a rail at the far end of the balcony, but seemed unable to pull her injured leg over. At first, struggling, gritting her teeth in pain and frustration, she did not see Dixie standing in the shadows. She still clung to her dagger.

"Hello, Prissy." Dixie greeted her in a monotone.

The girl started, but only slightly. She sat in frozen tableau, moonglow streaming over her features. She stared at Dixie for long, drawn-out seconds with dark, unfathomable eyes.

"Get down, Priscilla, slowly, and drop the knife."

She still did not move, but her face altered dramatically. She began to whimper. "My leg . . . it hurts . . . it hurts bad. . . ."

"Drop the knife."

"You don't know what Gretchen was like . . . she treated me like I didn't exist . . . she thought she was the only—"

"Drop that knife."

"I . . . I can't. If I move, I'll fall. I . . . I'm frightened. Oh, my leg!" There was a pool of blood around her foot. She seemed suddenly very young. An injured child.

Dixie took several steps forward, stopping less than six feet from her. "Get down, Prissy. Pull your leg over the rail and drop the damned knife." There was no change in the tone of her voice. She looked at Priscilla Smith without blinking, the gun in both her hands now, raised, pointed at the teenager's head.

"Don't shoot me!" Prissy whined. "I know what I've done is bad. Sometimes I can hardly think, hardly remember . . . but you can't shoot me again. Help me, please! I can't move my leg!"

"Dixie, don't! Don't do it!"

The voice came from behind her—not a yell, but the surprise of hearing Herb, caused her to half turn.

"*Dixie, look out!*"

Prissy was tumbling toward her, half jumping, half falling, the lethal blade raised high in the air.

Just as Dixie jerked the trigger she clearly heard the feral, bitch snarl, saw the bared teeth, the evil glinting eyes.

A small black hole appeared between Prissy's eyes as her head snapped back. But to Dixie the animal eyes still glowed, still lived. The knife was still raised in clawlike hands. She fired again. Twice.

One bullet lodged in Prissy's lower jaw, the other at the cleft of her throat. Neat round holes, black in the moonlight. She dropped from the rail, hitting the balcony floor with a dull thud. Her body twitched in the afterthroes of death, the nerves in her fingers gripping and ungripping the hilt of her dagger.

Dixie stood staring down at the back of Prissy the Punker's head. She was hardly aware of Herb beside her, and then Jake.

"I called the department," Herb babbled. "Doty told me where—"

"And he comes banging in here with crutches, for chrissake!" Jake said. "Hopping around like a damn stork! Only smart thing he did was bring a flashlight!"

"We finally found the blood, we thought it was . . ." Herb could see her clearly now, the pale face, the eyes gone dull—the clothing, dark and dripping wet. The gash in her cheek. "Oh, my God, it *was* you! Dixie, you're hurt! Dixie!"

When she still did not speak, he shook her, very gently at first, and then a little harder. His hands were immediately soaked with blood. A small sound came from somewhere inside her, a tiny hiccupping groan. She sagged against Herb as Jake looked on.

He enfolded her in his arms and gently lowered her to a sitting position. He spared not a glance for the body lying beside them. The wound in Dixie's back oozed over his arm. His voice shook. "Take the light, Jake. Go call an ambulance. Hurry!"

But there was no need. The siren wail of patrol cars and ambulance warbled in the night air. The house was alive with the sound of running feet. Pat Delaney and Bill Brooks were the first to reach the upper room, with Tony Di Franco right on their heels. Behind them streamed a line of men, all uniformed in midnight blue.

EPILOGUE

SEPTEMBER IN SAN Francisco was at its best. No fog. No clouds. A bright azure sky hung over the sweeping terraced-and-rose-planted grounds surrounding the Marks mansion. Just over two hundred guests were on hand to celebrate the sixtieth birthday of Franklin Marks, Esq., one of the most wealthy and successful corporate attorneys on the West Coast. Built of gray stone, the mansion itself sat at the top of a gently rolling hill in Saint Francis Wood. It wore the soft patina of four generations.

Rose Marks was a small woman, dark and violet-eyed. She supervised her staff without seeming to, drifting gracefully from one guest to another, casting a calm, hawkish eye on all that transpired. The garden party would soon end. She would take a short rest and then begin anew, overseeing preparations for a smaller and more intimate dinner. No one looking at her would have guessed that she was just a bit weary—and worried.

She felt great pride, too, of course. The celebration was an obvious success. More importantly, both of her children were in residence for the weekend. A rare event in and of itself. Just a few moments before, her son Ryan had ambled by, delivering a quick peck to her cheek. For just a moment their eyes had met, reminding her of their long talk the night before.

Rose sighed. Sons were so much different than daughters. Or so it seemed with Ryan and Dixie.

Looking into the near distance, she watched as Dixie stood talking to the friends who had come with her. The four, a slightly somber group, were separated from the main ebb and flow of guests.

Concentrating on her daughter, Rose felt her heart squeeze with both pain and pride.

Dixie, dressed in a three-piece ensemble of sherbert-green organza, was ravishing. No one looking at her could know that she had been released from the hospital only four days before. The color she wore was perfect with her eyes and riotous copper hair. Her figure was superb, and her smile—when it appeared—dazzling.

Rose let her gaze drift away from her daughter. She skipped quickly over Herb and Janice Woodall. A nice couple. Janice was a darling, and Herb acceptable—for a policeman. Rose's main interest, however, rested on the person of Art Cochran. She pursed her lips, concentrating on the rugged features of the crop-dusting pilot who had become Dixie's amour.

He had definite appeal, Rose decided. No doubt on that score. Not the suave, debonaire type, but a man who radiated sensuality through every pore without being really handsome. Art was a man who would be irresistible to a certain type of female.

She smiled, realizing that she had once been exactly that kind of woman herself. She recognized the pure animal magnetism of a man like Art. Jimmy Flannigan, Dixie's own father, had possessed much the same quality. A craving for excitement. A lust for life—a life that in Jimmy's case had been snuffed out all too soon.

As always when thinking of Dixie's father, Rose felt a stab of remorse for the loss of a love so deep, so exhilarating that it could happen only once. She turned away from the sight of Dixie and Art—and from her memories.

Janice looked at the trays they had just set down on the thick white carpet. The remnants of two continental breakfasts consisted of little more than honeydew rinds, well hulled.

"Room service, no less. The maid, or whoever she was, was actually wearing a uniform."

Dixie's lips twisted into a wry smile. "Yeah, ain't it just grand." Her tone was faintly sarcastic. "I hope Herb and Art are enjoying their early morning skeet shoot at Franklin's club."

"I'm sure they are. I think Herb half expected your stepfather to suggest a game of golf or something. He hates golf."

"So does Franklin."

Janice was quiet for several moments, and then she made her pronouncement in a half-shy voice. "Truly, Dixie, I *like* him. To be honest, I'm a little surprised that I do. He's a nice man."

Dixie nodded. "Yes, I suppose he is. Rich as Hades, but nice enough in his own rather stiff and conservative way."

"I can hardly believe my ears, Dix. Here I was, all set to spew forth a lecture on family togetherness, and you blow it all away." Janice was smiling. "I saw you two talking after dinner last night, all tucked into a corner. That must have been one whopping conversation."

"A little heavy, perhaps." Dixie's eyes were suspiciously bright. "I thought I was all grown up until Pete died. You know, Jan, he wanted a family more than anything in the world. People to care for. To love and to love him back. And I've spent years moaning and groaning when all the time I had it all. It makes me feel rotten, but waking up late is better than sleeping forever."

Dixie winced as she bent over to put her coffee cup on one of the trays. Her back was still sore. "Sorry if I sound maudlin. I suppose it's hard for you to understand how I've felt about Franklin."

"Not so hard. You wanted him to be your father, and he couldn't be, no matter how hard he tried. He is a very different sort of man, I would imagine. Certainly he's nothing like Patrick."

"Hardly." Dixie laughed. "But he has been very good to my mother. Ryan loves him. If you get right down to it, he's been pretty damn patient with me too."

Janice took Dixie's hands. "I'm so happy for you—for Ryan and your parents, too, but especially, for you. I'm sure your mother is delighted."

Dixie rolled her eyes and flopped back on a pillow. "Now, *she* is a different clump of petunias altogether. She's never going to give up trying to manipulate me into quitting the force."

Their conversation was interrupted by a loud tap on the door, which almost immediately swung open. Ryan poked his head in. "Sorry to barge in ladies, but if you value your peace of mind, Missy Tulip—" he ducked the pillow Dixie threw at him—"I suggest you get your buns downstairs on the double. Mom has Art cornered in her *parlor*, if you get my drift, and I do believe she's playing the spider to his fly."

"But he's supposed to be with Herb and—"

"I know where he is supposed to be, sis. I'm just telling you where he *is*."

"Oh, hell!" Dixie literally tumbled off the bed. "Lord only knows what she's up to!"

Open-mouthed, Janice watched her dash to the closet and then into the bathroom, slamming the door with a bang.

Ryan laughed. "Never mind her," he said, strolling into the room. He sauntered over, picked up a silver carafe, and filled Dixie's empty cup with fresh coffee. He then perched his nineteen-year-old frame unselfconsciously on the edge of the bed and took a loud sip.

"It's an endless battle between Mom and Dix—a long, long story with a very convoluted plot." His eyes twinkled with mischief. "Shall I fill you in?"

With the exception of those eyes, Ryan looked nothing at all like his half sister. But he had a face and manner that Janice warmed to immediately. She returned his broad, impish smile.

"Please do." She settled herself comfortably into a large feather pillow. All ears.

Dixie felt disheveled and half pasted together as she entered the room Ryan had jokingly referred to as the parlor. Actually, it was a small solarium, a glass-enclosed patio Franklin Marks had added especially for his wife's enjoyment. Of all the places on the estate, it was the one Rose favored most. A place where she could recline in a rattan lounge, read and muse surrounded by lush plants, hothouse flowers, and a humidity that suited her pale complexion.

Rose was no fool. She knew very well how she appeared to anyone fortunate enough to be admitted to her aromatic lair. On the rare occasions when she and Franklin argued, she always managed to have him come to her there. In the solarium, surrounded by nature's forced opulence, she became the innocent, languid, almost southern femme fatale, a facade to which Franklin always succumbed, and to which Dixie was absolutely immune.

"Good morning, Mother." She bent to kiss Rose's proffered cheek, almost wishing she could nip it instead. "Enjoying yourself?"

She could not keep the slightly sarcastic suspicion from her voice, and she shot Art an equally venomous look. "Good morning to you too, bwana."

He grinned at her, leaning back in a large fan chair.

"Art was just telling me more about your case, darling." Rose shuddered. "My, what a grisly business."

A tray containing croissants and melon sat on a tray near Rose's elbow. Dixie helped herself and then settled uncomfortably into another chair. She did not want to talk about her case, could not without reliving the pain and a terrible sense of loss.

"Art was also remarking on how much he likes my little refuge," Rose said with her best feline smile. "It would seem that he and I have more in common than either of us imagined. He likes the tropics too. I was telling him about—"

"Yes, the unpretentious little condo at Wailea Bay, no doubt," Dixie interrupted, guessing at her mother's transparent line of reasoning. "I'm sure Art would *love* to go with you this Christmas, Mother. Maybe he can even find someone to take with him—some nice *non*-police person."

Art flushed, but whether the color change was caused by guilt or embarrassment, Dixie could not tell.

Of the three, only Rose seemed completely unperturbed. She gazed at Dixie thoughtfully, sipping her own drink, a frothy peach-colored elixir, delicious and completely virgin. "Actually, I was thinking of our mutual interests in other areas. I find Art likes plants and flowers almost as much as I do. And then, of course, we both fly—even if I don't go bombing about in an open cockpit."

"I'll be glad to give you a ride that will take your breath away anytime you say the word, Rose." Art smiled at her.

"I'll pass on that, my boy, but Dixie was right, I was going to suggest spending your holidays with us. Maui is delightful in December."

Conspirators. The word popped into Dixie's mind, and for just a moment she hated them both.

"It would be lovely having you all." Rose looked at Dixie. "Franklin, you and Ryan, Herb and Janice. That is, if your precious department can spare two of its best detectives at the same time."

Dixie's eyes widened in surprise. Art looked confused.

"And you, too, Art. Of course, you will have to come with my daughter—who is very much a *police type*. It runs in the family, you know."

Dixie came slowly to her feet. For once she smiled at the innocent expression on her mother's face. "You are a vixen. I don't suppose anyone has ever told you that."

Rose's lower lip quirked wryly. "As a matter of fact, dear, Franklin has often made the same observation. And stop looking at me that way. Surrender is difficult at my age. If you go all mushy, I won't know *what* to do."

The two women looked at each other for several long moments. Finally, Dixie knelt and gathered her mother into a grateful embrace.

Art looked at them, his normally bright eyes a dark, brooding gray. Standing, he turned and walked out of the solarium. Out of Franklin's vast home. Out of Dixie's life.